The Tissue Tr

*To Jacky, my wife.*
*For her love and patience.*

# ACKNOWLEDGEMENTS

I am grateful for assistance and advice received from many quarters including the following:

*The National Criminal Intelligence Service Drugs Division*, Blackfriars, London

*The Secretariat of the International Olympic Committee*, Lausanne, Switzerland

*The Central Criminal Court*, Singapore

*Liz Hoban*, US author (**The Cheech Room**) who recommended The Tissue Trail to Old Line Publishing

*Alison Buckley (nee James)*, whose experiences on the tissue trail lead to the story

*Jo Gunston*, for the location blog and website

*Alison Davis*, for dragging me kicking and screaming into social media and with Jo Gunston, developing the website

*Chris Holifield*, Writersservices, London – for her professional guidance and encouragement

*Lucy Abelson*, UK author (**Murder in a Surrey Tribe**), for her professional guidance

*Drs Stephen and Ione Inman*, for guidance on medical aspects of the torture scene

*Dr Tony Insall*, for guidance on Chinese politics and background

*US Military Command Centre*, Hawaii, for guidance on flying in extreme winds

# the tissue TRAIL

# GARTH GUNSTON

Old Line Publishing
Hampstead ◊ Maryland ◊ United States

Printed in the United States of America

ISBN-13: 9781939928146
ISBN-10: 1939928141

This book is a work of fiction. Any references to real people, events, establishments, organizations, or locales are intended solely to provide a sense of authenticity and are used fictitiously. All other characters, incidents, and dialogue are drawn from the author's imagination and are not to be construed as real.

Cover Design by Kline Productions
Initial Edits and Critique by Jacky Gunston

OLD LINE PUBLISHING

P.O. Box 624
Hampstead, MD 21074
Toll-Free Phone: 1-877-866-8820
Toll-Free Fax: 1-877-778-3756
Email: info@oldlinepublishing.com
Website: www.oldlinepublishing.com

# PREFACE

I've always been a storyteller—right from the young age of eight when I used to tell my younger siblings stories about a character called rubber man, making it up as I went along. And I've always enjoyed messing around with words—from student newspapers, to articles for the Pharmaceutical Journal, then running a medical advertising and communications agency.

When an employee of the medical agency telephoned from Kathmandu after being asked to carry something suspicious to Singapore, my curiosity was aroused and through my contacts in the medical business I talked to the National Criminal Investigation Service Drugs Division. What they told me gave me just enough inside information to make *The Tissue Trail* story possible.

As I had travelled extensively in the Nepal, Himalaya region I had nearly everything I needed. Filling the gaps proved remarkably easy with assistance readily forthcoming from sources as disparate as the Central Criminal Court, Singapore; the US Military Command, Hawaii; and the International Olympic Committee Secretariat in Lausanne. Given my obsession with wild open country the most enjoyable part of the research was chartering aeroplanes and helicopters to reach otherwise remote inaccessible locations in the high Himalaya.

It took me a long time to write because heading up significant businesses didn't leave much spare time. I finally finished in March 2013, and I started to look for a publisher. The trials and tribulations of getting this book published would make a book in itself. For a glimpse of this emotional rollercoaster visit http://wgarthtttribulations.wordpress.com for the story so far. Yet to come is the blockbuster movie and interactive spin-offs such as the History of the Lost Kingdom of Mustang or Meteorological Effects of Monsoon winds in the Kali Gandaki Valley.

And speaking of the blockbuster movie, check the results of the aerial location research at http://thetissuetrailsynopsis.wordpress.com/.

So, after all this how would I describe *The Tissue Trail* in one sentence?

*The Tissue Trail* – a trek between the world's most beautiful mountain and deepest gorge – becomes the backdrop to an explosive global conspiracy.

# CONTENTS

Chapter One - *The Execution* — 11

Chapter Two - *The Arrest* — 15

Chapter Three - *The Problem* — 25

Chapter Four - *The Researcher* — 36

Chapter Five - *The Salt Caravan* — 49

Chapter Six - *The Elegant Woman* — 76

Chapter Seven - *The Pilot* — 96

Chapter Eight - *The Reporter* — 111

Chapter Nine - *The Clinical Assistant* — 118

Chapter Ten - *The Side Effects* — 159

Chapter Eleven - *The Cousins* — 182

Chapter Twelve - *The Trials* — 187

Chapter Thirteen - *The Orchestration* — 215

Chapter Fourteen - *The Prison* — 225

Chapter Fifteen - *The Breakthrough* — 239

Chapter Sixteen - *The Money Trace* — 244

Chapter Seventeen - *The Invitation* — 253

Chapter Eighteen - *The Swiss Bank* — 267

Chapter Nineteen - *The Yak and Yeti* — 284

Chapter Twenty - *The Motive* — 297

Chapter Twenty-One - *The Kidnapping* — 319

Chapter Twenty-Two - *The Reaction* — 344

Chapter Twenty-Three - *The Aftermath* — 370

# CHAPTER ONE
## *The Execution*

*Changi Women's Prison*
*Singapore*
*5th July 2001*

In all normal circumstances, twenty-four-year-old Scot, Catherine Miller, would have been scheduled to hang on Friday, 6th July. Hanging day at Singapore's Changi Women's Prison was always Friday. But the level of protest in Catherine's case, and that of four other young female western backpackers, had reached such extremes that at the last minute and with no public announcement, the Singapore Government had brought forward the executions to six p.m., Thursday the 5th, in an attempt to wrong-foot the mass protest planned for dawn on the Friday.

Catherine had been on death row since the beginning of June after being found guilty of the capital offense of importing heroin into Singapore despite being unaware of having done so. In the time since her trial and sentence, she had lived through the sounds of the hanging procedure and the hours preceding it on four separate occasions.

Each time she had laid on her bunk in the darkness of her cell, awake for most of the night, the heavy silence broken by gentle whimpering or sobbing and occasional agonised cries. Few, if any, of the women slept after two or three in the morning, all waiting for the sound which heralded the start of the hanging ritual: a distant heavy prison door closing with an echoing metallic thud. A few seconds later they would hear the distant footfalls of the approaching execution party gradually become louder, then stop and wait for an electronically controlled door to allow access to death row. There would be a further short silence before the hum of four electric motors opened four cell doors; followed by the sound of muffled voices as the condemned women were told it was time. And it was always "women" plural. Such was the frequency of executions in Singapore, even of women, that the execution chamber was designed to hang four simultaneously, with an elongated drop plate and a line of four black nooses.

Familiarity with the procedure after four weeks did not make it any easier. Little could soften the horror of women being lead or dragged or carried away either screaming with terror, or crying out for mercy, or shouting defiant abuse, or quietly whimpering. Or even making no sound at all. In the chamber, the condemned women would have their wrists bound behind them, felt hoods placed over their heads, the nooses lowered electronically and adjusted to lie round the base of the neck. Then, when the prison clock struck the hour, the elongated drop plate would be released. There would be a resounding crash as the metal plate smashed into the walls of the concrete pit below. The echo would reverberate around the prison's stone walls, then gradually fade as life faded from the four twitching and writhing bodies.

A factor which had helped in Catherine's case was the deep catatonic depression she had descended into since the shock of her arrest and incarceration some three months earlier. It had served to dull her senses and effectively surround her with a protective mental cocoon. But on the next occasion it would be of little help. On the next occasion the execution party would stop at her door.

Two days earlier, in the British tradition, Catherine had been taken down to the chamber to be weighed and measured, and the wire supporting the noose had been electronically adjusted so that the noose could be pressed into the required position, fitting evenly around the base of her neck. Even then she had felt little reaction, just a shiver as the cold black oiled plastic rope touched her warm skin.

On Wednesday, 4th July, her lawyer Philip Lee had made an unexpected visit and her spirits had risen as she knew every effort was still being made to stop her execution, but the look on Lee's face had been enough. He had not come to tell her there was going to be a last minute pardon or granting of clemency or commuting of the sentence. On the contrary, he had to tell her that the time of the execution was being brought forward by twelve hours to six p.m. on Thursday, 5th July.

# The Tissue Trail

Philip had said something else about two other backpackers being hanged with her, but she didn't really take it in. All that mattered to her was that she was to have twelve hours less for the efforts of Lee and the others to stop or delay her execution.

### 5th July 2001, 5:00 p.m.

Lee visited her at five p.m. to say that all efforts had failed and that the execution was to proceed.

### 5th July 2001, 5:40 p.m.

As the minute hand edged past the half hour and started moving upwards, Catherine's protective mental cocoon started to fade. At 5:40 p.m. the dreaded heavy metallic thud of the closing distant door sent a shudder of fear through her emaciated frame. Some fifteen seconds later she heard the approaching footfalls, this time the full execution party. The footfalls stopped and there was a short silence; then a click, and the door of her cell slowly opened. Philip Lee and a priest entered. Behind them she was vaguely aware of various people, some in suits, the government lawyers and prison officials, the others in light brown military style uniform, the prison guards. Philip Lee's eyes were moist as he told her it was time to go. As a defence lawyer, he had attended many such executions and normally remained outwardly unmoved, but he had come to like Catherine Miller; he knew she was innocent in the sense of having had no intent or knowledge of the crime of which she had been found guilty, and it had taken its toll on even his emotional resilience.

A priest stepped forward and intoned some kind of blessing, closing with the words, "may the Lord have mercy on your soul." Catherine managed to question to herself the logic of such a request when she had not committed the crime for which she was about to lose her life. When the priest had finished, he backed away, leaving Catherine to the mercy of two guards who turned her round, pulled her arms behind her and handcuffed her wrists. A fifth man entered whom she remembered from the previous day organizing the fitting of the noose and weighing her. She felt the first faint twinge of fear as she recognized him as the executioner. It was he who led her from her cell.

# The Tissue Trail

She walked a little unsteadily, but did not need assistance beyond the executioner's gentle hold of her elbow. She made no sound. She thought she could hear other people behind her.

The double air-locked doors into the execution chamber opened, and as she entered she drew back from the intense bright, white light of the chamber itself. The sight of the four suspended black nooses finally removed the remaining shreds of her protective depressive blanket; her legs felt weak and unsteady and a wave of nausea enveloped her.

She was manoeuvred into position under a noose at the left hand end of the drop plate, and she heard the quiet whirr of the electric motor as the final fine adjustments were made. She started to struggle, tears rolled down her face. The executioner gently but firmly restrained her, then stood looking into her eyes and lowered the black felt hood over her head. She tried to scream, but nothing happened. The noose was lowered into position, and she felt the executioner's fingers gently press it into position.

She thought she heard a door open and more people enter. She was sure there was movement on the drop plate, she could feel the vibration. Then she remembered Lee saying something about two or three others being executed at the same time. She thought she heard crying, but such awareness as she was capable of was mostly concentrated on her own predicament.

In any event, any other sounds were largely drowned by the heavy felt hood.

There was perfect quietness as the executioner waited for the prison clock to chime at 6:00 p.m. Catherine was close to vomiting and was conscious of wetness running down her legs.

Seconds later, there was a violent crash.

# CHAPTER TWO
## *The Arrest*

*15th April 2001, twelve weeks earlier*

Catherine Miller had been captivated by Nepal from the moment she had landed at the tiny airport of Pokhara in the Annapurna Himalaya. Clouds had hidden the mountains on the 150 mile flight from Kathmandu, but were clearing as the flight came in to land, and as she stepped down onto loose stone; a twin-peaked snow covered mountain emerged as if it were overhead. It towered over the corrugated iron roof of the single storey terminal building.

Catherine was 5'5" slim with short darkish red hair, a short turned up nose and a few freckles. Born and raised in Edinburgh she was happy-go-lucky and enjoyed taking things as they came. Helen, her travelling companion, was a little shorter in height with short brown hair, full figured, and in contrast to Catherine, liked to know exactly where they were and exactly what they were looking at.

"That mountain is called Fishtail," Helen told Catherine and anybody else who wanted to listen, "or Macchu Pucchare in local language...and these are the Himalaya – not the Himalayas – the singular is Himal."

She looked up at Fishtail, "It looks a lot like Matterhorn doesn't it? But it's nearly twice its height...24,000 feet...yet it seems as if we are standing next to it."

Catherine knew the Himalayas were the world's highest mountains, but she had had no concept of the scale. The following morning there was to be another unbelievable demonstration of the height of these magnificent mountains.

# The Tissue Trail

The trekking company had picked them up from the airport and driven them through the bustling centre of Pokhara to the assembly point on the edge of Lake Phewa. There they had been introduced to other members of their trekking group and had picked up ground sheets and sleeping bags. They were accompanied on their trek by a team of Sherpas who carried the tents, tables, chairs, food and water. It had never ceased to amaze Catherine that the trekkers would set off before the Sherpas who would clean-up after breakfast and decamp, and within a couple of hours, these skinny looking Nepalis, often with bare feet, would pass them carrying forty to fifty pound loads.

The first afternoon of the trek, they climbed in warm mist and afternoon cloud through giant rhododendron bushes and blue-purple flowered jacaranda trees making their way up a ridge to their overnight campsite. The following morning the mountains were still hidden, and they had sat huddled in the cold by their tents on the Panchase Ridge sipping mugs of hot tea made by the Sherpas, waiting for the cloud to clear. As they had been told, they were twenty-five miles from the main Annapurna Range and had been expecting to see the peaks of the mountains straight ahead. But as the sun came up, Catherine thought she caught a glimpse of something in the swirling mist – not straight ahead but looking upwards at least forty-five degrees from the horizontal. She couldn't believe it. But seconds later it appeared again in a small break in the cloud, and this time there was no mistaking the peak of a snow covered mountain. Despite the distance, the magnificent southern wall of the Annapurna massif slowly formed in front of them as if it were no more than a few hundred yards away.

For the next five days they had worked their way westward, steadily gaining altitude. Initially, Maccha Pucchare dominated, but Helen kept them informed as they slowly made their way past other peaks in the Annapurna Himal by naming them as they went. Catherine didn't care about the names; she drank in the magnificent kaleidoscope of ice-white snow peaks, near vertical ice walls and ridges sweeping down to the Indian plain.

The highest point and end of the trek had been Poon Hill, a point on the Ghorapani Ridge at 10,000 feet from which they could see the entrance to the world's deepest ravine. The Kali Gandaki Gorge appeared as a giant split in the wall of the Himalaya, the entrance to which they could see some ten miles further to the west sitting between the Annapurna Himal and Dhaulagiri. It was an incredible 20,000 feet deep. Helen had read that the gorge led to a high altitude desert region north of the Annapurnas called Upper Mustang – and to the Tibetan border. She wished that she had had time to go further, and she had promised herself that one day she would come back to Nepal.

In contrast to the grandeur of the gleaming ice-white mountains, the cottages were built of warm ochre-coloured walls of mud and brick with yellowish brown thatched roofs surrounded by the sub-tropical vegetation. The dark-skinned small-boned Nepalis were warm, gentle and friendly. She had never been anywhere before that she had so instantly loved and had been sad to leave. Even though she was only a few weeks into her six-month backpack, she had wanted to take something home and had bought a doll from a Tibetan refugee camp on the edge of Pokhara as a memento. The number of Tibetans in Nepal had been a big surprise. Some had their own shops, but most lived in camps and worked in cottage industries and sold the produce – much of it to tourists.

She didn't remember anything in particular about buying the doll or talking to anybody about it except remarking to Helen that she liked it. The only conversation she remembered was sometime after she had bought the doll, when a Canadian boy a bit older than herself had got into conversation and asked her where she was going when she left Nepal. She had told him they were going to Singapore, unfortunately missing Thailand and Malaysia because they didn't have time.

On April 25th back in Kathmandu, they made their way to Tribhuvan Airport for their flight to Singapore with mixed feelings: sadness for leaving such a beautiful country and excitement heading for a new and totally different place.

It was a typical Kathmandu spring day with a heavy morning mist which shrouded the Royal Nepal Airlines from Kathmandu to Singapore as it nosed its way gingerly through the maze of blue and white taxiway lights and turned left onto the main runway. Catherine leaned back against the seat. She had her eyes shut and a slight smile of satisfaction played on her lips as she thought back to the highlights of the trek. Next to her by the window Helen was not smiling. She still could not see more than half the length of the wing and couldn't believe it when the engines started to run up to full power. She waited hopefully for the pilot to change his mind, but in vain; he released the brakes and the Airbus 310 surged forward and accelerated down the runway. Helen tried to hide the fact that she was anxiously gripping the armrests waiting for an impact. It did not come and her grip slowly relaxed, as first the nose wheel lifted, then the main wheels left the ground. But just as she was about to relax, having worked out that the flight was going to take-off to the west – the airplane tilted steeply to the right, to the north towards the mountains, and the white knuckles reappeared as she gripped the arm rests even more tightly. She turned to Catherine and nervously asked why she thought the flight was turning north towards the mountains in thick fog.

"You're asking me?" Catherine's voice was raised with mock incredulity. "I didn't know which way we were turning, but if you'd like me to worry about it, I'll see what I can do!" She smiled at her friend.

There were two French women seated behind them who they had met on the trek in Nepal, and the four of them had teamed up when it turned out that they too were travelling direct from Nepal to Singapore.

Helen started to relax again as the Airbus maintained the turn with no more shifts in direction or engine pitch. Two minutes after take-off, and with a 180-degree right turn completed, the Airbus broke out of the low level mist into bright cloudless sky. The eastern Himalaya seemed a few yards away, but curiously not as high as they had looked from below in the Annapurnas. Helen checked off the Langtang and Ganesh Himals as they headed east. Then, as the pilot altered course away from the mountains to turn southeast, she saw what she had been looking for – the unmistakable black triangular peak of Everest. One of the owners of a book shop had told her the exposed peak with its steep sides rarely retained any snow and this made it stand out from the rest even more than its extra altitude.

Nepal had retained its magic and majesty to the last moment.

After breakfast of orange juice, coffee and fruit, Catherine had dozed – vaguely aware, thanks to Helen, of the Ganges delta passing below as they crossed Bangladesh and the coast of Burma with its dramatic sand estuary of the Irawaddi and the entrance to Rangoon.

*Staff Viewing Gallery*
*Changi International Airport*
*Singapore*
*25th April 2001, 12:30 p.m.*

A blonde, tanned woman in her late thirties, with the well defined

# The Tissue Trail

muscles of someone who kept herself well conditioned, stood resting her right elbow on her hip and looking in the direction of the incoming flights. She was Stephanie D'Aunay, French Canadian, dressed in the medium-grey uniform of a customs officer, but her lapel badge revealed her true function, "Drug Liaison" – part of the international drug intelligence network. In the midday heat of the equator the sky was a shimmering hazy pale blue, reducing visibility to a few hundred yards. The Kathmandu flight was on time and had reported final approach and as she watched, a black speck in the haze gradually hardened then grew, gradually taking the shape of an airliner. At 12:32 the Royal Nepal Airlines Airbus touched down, slowed as it approached the end of the runway, turned and started to taxi back towards the terminal. Stephanie D'Aunay stubbed out a cigarette, turned and walked back towards the customs section of the arrivals hall.

The landing at Singapore was uneventful, and the four women pulled their rucksacks down from the overhead racks and stood in the aisles waiting with impatient excitement for the two hundred other backpackers and travellers to start moving. At the forward exit they were met by a wall of heat and humidity and in the short walk from the aircraft to the terminal, Catherine felt the back of her shirt turn wet and warm. Once inside the terminal, and a twenty degree drop in temperature, she felt the sweat turn cold. It also appeared that at least two other flights must have disgorged their loads at much the same time.

Despite the frustration of waiting over an hour to reach an immigration desk, Catherine remained cheerful, her natural effusiveness, amusing not just the three friends but other passengers around her. When she finally reached the immigration desk, processing her new EEC Passport had been routine and had taken just a few seconds.

Her only baggage was her rucksack which held her spare shorts, T-shirts, underwear, two bikinis, medical pack, lightweight walking boots, a lightweight anorak, two sweatshirts, and a money and document pack buried at the bottom of the sack with the Tibetan doll.

All four women headed for the customs hall sharing the excitement of arriving at a new and unfamiliar place. They entered the "Nothing to Declare" channel laughing and joking with that slight nervousness which comes from wondering if, however innocent they were, they might be the ones stopped. Most of the jokes related to the embarrassment of customs officers pulling out underwear and bras.

# The Tissue Trail

The customs area was the usual wide corridor with open-legged tables placed end to end. Two customs officers sat just inside the entrance in khaki brown shirts, neatly creased trousers and polished brown belts. They appeared to ignore those passing them. None of the women saw one of them stand up and give a signal to the two officers who sat at the exit.

As they approached the exit, one of the two officers rose and stepped in front of the laughing group. Without hesitation he asked Catherine to stand to one side. She was surprised, but not particularly concerned. Presumably they stopped a certain number at random, and she was not carrying anything which could cause any concern. She called to Helen, who was also looking worried, "don't worry, I'll be with you in a minute."

She expected the officer to place her rucksack on the table in front of him, and she frowned when instead he asked her to step into an office behind him. In the office two more customs officers sat behind a table, one of Malay extraction, the other Chinese. As she came in, a blonde-haired, athletically built woman, smartly dressed, rose and moved away from the table. The officer who had brought her in took over the seat vacated by the woman and placed the rucksack on the table.

Catherine now felt uncertain, apprehensive and alone. Why had they brought her into the office? Why couldn't they have simply examined the rucksack outside on the tables in the customs channel as she had seen in so many airports before? The officer had started to untie the neck of the rucksack but stopped, pushed it back towards her and motioned to Catherine to empty it herself.

She released the clasps and opened the neck of the rucksack, then pulled out the anorak and sweatshirts, followed by the medical kit and her dirty clothes. As she pulled out each item she looked nervously at the customs officer – waiting for him to pick up something and examine it. He sat with his arms folded shaking his head inviting her to continue. The rest of the items followed until two remained – her money/document case and the doll.

The palms of her hands were sweating and she felt sick. Something was not right. The officer picked up the doll, turned it over and unbuttoned the covering Tibetan dress. He opened the dress and laid it on the table exposing a small polythene slip cellophane-taped to the stomach of the doll. It contained something white. Catherine put her hand over her mouth. She did not understand, but she was terrified.

# The Tissue Trail

The blonde woman stepped forward and signalled to the officer who proceeded to cut off the corner of the slip. The woman picked up the slip and tipped a few grains of the crystalline powder onto the palm of her hand and gently dipped the tip of her little finger into it to taste.

She said something in a language Catherine did not recognize – except for one word – "heroin." Catherine's stomach turned and she vomited into the corner. Two policewomen came to her side to steady her. The officer who had stopped her picked up the telephone.

The blonde woman stepped in front of her.

"Catherine Miller you are being detained on suspicion of bringing a Class A substance into Singapore."

Catherine screamed at her, "Why? Why? – I didn't bring it – I didn't even know it was there."

The woman was unmoved and continued the formalities of the arrest. Catherine did not hear her, she felt disoriented and lightheaded. She could not believe what was happening. The woman still spoke, "...you will be taken to an arrest centre where you will be visited by your embassy representatives and a lawyer tomorrow morning."

The woman looked at her without sympathy and shook her head. "Why do you kids do it?"

The two small but heavily built policewomen handcuffed her with her hands behind her back and guided her toward the door of the office. Catherine felt panic and nausea engulf her. Outside the office door crowds were moving past, but stopped to look at the distraught woman. She remembered seeing the drawn faces of her three friends – then blackness as she collapsed unconscious with the shock.

When she came round she was vaguely aware of strong arms lifting her and of being carried back into the office and being lowered onto a chair. The blonde woman impatiently thanked the man who had carried her in, but asked him to leave the restricted area.

"We will look after her now."

Catherine heard the man say, "Half an hour ago this woman was the life and soul of the party – hardly looked like somebody worried about being caught with this sort of stuff."

She turned to try to see him, but through the tears she could only discern a man of medium height who was strong enough to lift her easily and had an English accent. The blonde woman thanked him sarcastically for his opinion and repeated her instruction to him to leave the restricted area. Catherine did not remember much of the journey from the airport to the arrest centre, nor being led to a cell where, at least, she was on her own.

### 26th April 2001

The next morning she was offered breakfast, and she managed a little fruit and tea. At 10:00 a.m. she was taken to a meeting area where she was introduced to Philip Lee, a lawyer of Chinese extraction, short, slim and smartly dressed, and a man in his early thirties with an upper crust English accent who introduced himself as David something "from the British Consulate."

"We will be doing what we can to help you."

After a formal introduction and expressions of regret that they had to meet in such circumstances, the three sat at a table while Lee made notes, Catherine trembling, her hands clasped tightly together. Lee appeared to be going through the questions with routine detachment, but was watching her closely.

"Where did you fly from to Singapore?"

"Kathmandu," she replied quietly.

"How long were you in Nepal?"

"Just under two weeks."

"What were you doing?"

"We spent two days looking round Kathmandu—the rest of the time trekking."

"Where were you trekking?"

"In the Annapurna Region, west of Kathmandu."

"Where did you buy the doll – on the trek or in Kathmandu?"

"I bought it in a shop in a refugee camp on the edge of Pokhara."

"Refugee camp? What sort of refugees?"

"Tibetan. There are quite a lot of them in the Pokhara area."

"Where exactly is Pokhara?"

"It's the airport town for the Annapurnas – where you fly to from Kathmandu."

"You say you bought the doll?"

"Yes."

"Can you describe what happened?"

"What do you mean?" she asked.

"Describe what happened before you bought it – and anybody you spoke to before you bought it or when you were buying it."

"There is not much to tell. We had gone around the refugee camp watching them go through the whole process from carding the raw wool, spinning and dying the yarn, right through to weaving the cloth – then making carpets, jackets – and dolls…"

Lee noticed getting her to talk reduced some of the tension.

"Then we went to the shop where you could buy the things they were making – I wanted to buy something for my sister, so I bought a doll."

"Did you talk to anybody about buying it?"

"Only Helen, Abbie and Marie, the women I was travelling with."

"Nobody else?"

She thought about it briefly, but there was nobody else.

"So you spoke to nobody about buying the doll nor anyone who wanted to meet you after you arrived in Singapore?"

Catherine paused for a few seconds then shook her head. "Nobody at all."

David Johnson from the embassy asked for details of her next of kin. She frowned and asked him why he wanted to know. "Surely I am not staying here, now you know I had nothing to do with it?"

Johnson looked at Lee for help. Philip Lee knew she was in a fragile condition, but had no choice but to tell her that bringing a Class A drug into Singapore was an offense whether or not she knew she was carrying it. Her eyes filled and her trembling hands reached out involuntarily across the table. "Are you really saying I've got to stay here?" She looked from one to the other. "How long for?"

Lee told her she would be detained until her commitment hearing, and if it was found that there was a case to answer she would have to await trial. "I'm afraid you will be here for a few days." He watched the fear and despair in her face and couldn't correct himself. She was led away to her cell by two female prison warders, her shoulders heaved as she sobbed uncontrollably. Lee looked after her without moving. David Johnson asked Lee what was troubling him. Lee told him that he had seen more than his fair share of heroin carriers, but this one didn't make sense.

"She clearly doesn't have any idea where the heroin came from, which means she didn't knowingly pick it up from anybody – and she bought the doll quite normally which means that nobody gave the doll to her without her knowing. There are two ways traffickers load their mules and that takes out both of them."

"Mules?" David asked.

"Carriers – people who carry the substance for the traffickers," said Lee. "Traffickers never carry the drug themselves. They always use somebody else – often in twos and threes – with one of the traffickers on the same flight to make sure none of their mules go astray. The traffickers use a variety of passports and buy their tickets at different travel agents so there is no connection to the mules. But whatever happens and however they do it there has to be some sort of contact, some arrangement to meet after going through customs even if the carrier has no idea what is going on. In this case, there is no sign of any contact at all."

# CHAPTER THREE
## *The Problem*

*Edinburgh, Scotland*
*25th April 2001*

At four o'clock in the afternoon, in the comfortable north Edinburgh suburb of Comely Bank, the telephone rang. Elspeth Miller was relaxing, enjoying the sun of a warm spring afternoon and drinking a cup of Earl Grey tea. She picked up the receiver:

"Hello, Elspeth Miller," she said, still looking over the magazine.

"Mrs Miller, I am calling from the Foreign and Commonwealth Office in London, my name is Courtney."

She frowned and sat upright, pushing the magazine to one side.

"Yes, Mr Courtney?" she said immediately.

"May I first confirm that you have a daughter named Catherine Marie Miller?"

"Yes, I do," she said with rising apprehension.

"I am afraid Mrs Miller, I have some disturbing news. Catherine has been arrested on suspicion of importing a Class A substance into Singapore."

Elspeth Miller's stomach turned over. She had two virtually simultaneous reactions, the first was that the last thing Catherine would knowingly do was to do something blatantly illegal. The second, that her daughter was in serious trouble. Unable to keep a tremor out of her voice she said, "What does a Class A substance mean, Mr Courtney?"

"It means a serious drug such as cocaine or...," he hesitated, "...heroin."

Just hearing the word "heroin" produced a kaleidoscope of press, TV and film images all with connotations of despair, violence and death. Elspeth Miller shuddered. "Mr. Courtney, firstly, Catherine would not knowingly do anything like this so please tell me what happened."

"We have very little detail Mrs Miller. All we have is a preliminary report from our Consulate in Singapore. But it appears that a doll she had bought in Nepal was found to have a small packet of heroin hidden in its clothing."

"Where is Catherine now?" she asked almost in a state of panic.

"She is being held at the Narcotics Remand Centre in Singapore."

"And what happens now?"

"She will be held until committal proceedings when the court will decide whether to send the case to trial."

She remained silent.

Courtney went on, "Mrs Miller if at all possible, and bearing in mind Catherine is in custody, would it be possible for you and your husband to visit your daughter in Singapore and talk through the situation with her lawyer?"

Thirty-six hours later Catherine Miller's parents flew into Singapore where the British Consulate had arranged for David Johnson to meet them with a car at Changi Airport. The car drove along the manicured modern four-lane highway to the Narcotics Remand Centre close to the centre of the town where Philip Lee, Catherine's defence lawyer, waited for them. They were dreading what he had to tell them.

The Millers were what Philip Lee would have expected of a typical British professional middle-class middle-aged couple. Ian Miller, slightly overweight, receding grey hair, wore a pale grey suit which showed signs of a long flight, a pale, blue shirt and dark tie, and well polished black shoes. Elspeth Miller wore a navy pleated skirt and white blouse, low heeled brogue shoes, and carried a light jacket and handbag. Her hair was greying and professionally cut. But if they matched his expectations in dress they were far from it in demeanour. Both showed clear signs of the shock and stress of a situation so completely foreign to their normally quiet suburban existence. Elspeth Miller was red-eyed with heavy bags under her eyes. Ian Miller looked pale, strained and thin lipped.

After the tense and tentative introductions, Lee asked to have a few words with them before they saw Catherine. He sat, fingers interlaced on his knee, leaning forward towards them and spoke deliberately and slowly.

# The Tissue Trail

"Firstly," he said, "I am sorry to have to meet you in these circumstances. Unfortunately, with Singapore's rigid stance on matters affecting Class A drugs, such circumstances are all too common. I have to warn you before you see your daughter that despite the relatively short time she has been in custody her condition has already deteriorated – she is showing signs of weight loss and signs of lack of sleep. She is having difficulty understanding what has happened and because she knew nothing about the presence of the heroin she does not understand why she is not being released. This is part of the problem. In Singapore it is an offense to carry heroin into the country whether or not you are aware you are carrying it."

He paused to allow the point to register. Ian Miller gently squeezed his wife's arm.

"The most you can do today is appear calm and sympathetic. If at all possible please try not to appear distressed. I will tell you more when you have seen her.

"One more thing I need to prepare you for," he added, "you will only be able to speak to Catherine through a metal grill."

The Millers were taken into the "detainee" interview room and seated in front of the screen. Lee sat alongside them. A door opened on the detainee side of the screen, a uniformed guard entered followed by Catherine. Her hands were tied in front of her, her head bowed, and it was only when she sat down that she realized her parents were already there. Her face lit up when she saw them, and she tried to reach out to her mother. To see her daughter tied and led like an animal and her large eyes dull and frightened was very difficult for Elspeth Miller to cope with, but she held herself together.

Catherine started to repeat over and over again that she did not do it. She had no idea how the heroin got into the doll and nobody had talked to her about it. Her father told her nobody doubted what she was saying.

"So when can I get out?" she asked.

Lee intervened, "There are certain aspects of the law we have to deal with here first," he told her. "We are doing all we can, but everything takes time."

"So when?" she persisted looking from one to the other clearly at the point of breaking down.

"It will take some time," repeated Lee uncomfortably. "In Singapore the legal system is very hard on any offense or suspected offense involving a Class A drug. I can only ask you to try to be patient."

"But I didn't have anything to do with it, I didn't know it was there!" She raised her hands and brought them down heavily onto the table in front of her and laid her head on them sobbing. A guard sitting behind her stood, started to come forward, then pulled back.

Elspeth Miller tried to reach her daughter, but couldn't and she stood and turned away to hide her distress.

Ian Miller, fighting to hide the tremble in his voice, told her they would work with Philip Lee and the Foreign Office to do all they could, quickly, to resolve her situation. The guards came forward, her time was up.

Elspeth Miller turned back to her daughter as she was led away, looking backwards with tears streaming down her face.

Philip Lee sighed as he led Mr and Mrs Miller out of the interview room and to an anteroom close by. He was not looking forward to the next few minutes.

He remained silent for a few moments looking down at the table, deciding the best way he could think to convey that even after what they had just gone through, there was more and worse to come.

"I am afraid I have not been able to tell Catherine the full extent of the difficulties she faces. As you have seen for yourself she is already in a weakened condition mentally." The Millers were looking puzzled and apprehensive.

"I need to explain the legal position carefully, as I told you earlier, simply carrying heroin into Singapore is an offense. It does not matter whether or not the carrier knows he or she was carrying or how the drug came to be in their possession. Catherine was clearly oblivious to the fact she was carrying the drug. But in the eyes of the law she has committed an offense and," he paused, "there is no defence. In most legal cases the law specifies available defences, for example in a case of murder, if it can be proved there was no prior intent or that the death was the result of the accused acting in self-defence then these are acceptable defences. In Singapore there is no defence to carrying a Class A drug. The carrier is automatically guilty."

Ian Miller intervened, his voice low but angry, "So what was all that talk about 'doing all we can'?"

"I did say Singapore was very hard on any drug offense – and we will do all we can – but I need to explain how difficult that is going to be. And I am afraid there is worse to come," Lee paused, trying to ease the way forward as gently as he could.

"Unless there is something extraordinary and unprecedented about this case, Catherine will be found guilty."

"Even though she knew nothing about it?" Ian Miller's voice rose. He was finding it increasingly difficult to control his mounting anger.

"That is the law and whatever we do, we have to work within it."

Miller looked exasperated and turned his head sideways to expel a hiss of air between his teeth.

Lee paused for several seconds, "It is also the law that above a certain level the death penalty is mandatory." This time he moved on quickly. "That is to say the judge has no discretion. Above fifteen grams of pure substance he has to impose the death penalty."

Ian Miller's look of exasperation disappeared, "And how much was Catherine carrying?"

Lee paused, "It has to be confirmed, but the initial measurement was 16.2 grams."

Elspeth Miller, who had looked to be in such a state of shock as to be incapable of taking in what Lee was saying, broke down. Her husband put his arm around her shoulders and tried to comfort her. But there was little he could do. She became hysterical, shouting, almost screaming, at "The insanity of such a law!" Lee picked up the telephone and said something in a local language. A few seconds later the door opened and a woman in a nurse's uniform entered.

"I am afraid this sort of situation is all too common here," said Lee. "If you and your wife agree I think it would be better if your wife is given a mild sedative." Ian Miller agreed and held his wife gently as the nurse pushed up her short sleeve and injected the muscle at the top of the arm. The effect was almost immediate and as she became calm Ian Miller cradled his wife's head into his shoulder.

"Is there anything else?" Miller asked.

"I have to prepare you for the worst and at the moment it could not be any worse. The only legal hope is that the State would grant a pardon or at least clemency. But I have to tell you that in Singapore no person convicted of a Class A drug offense has ever been pardoned or clemency granted."

Miller looked straight into Lee's eyes and spoke calmly, but said each word as if he were spitting bullets. "So you are saying that even though Catherine did not have the slightest idea she was carrying, she will be condemned to death and has no chance of clemency?"

Lee looked back at Miller without saying anything – then nodded.

"So there is no hope whatsoever?" Miller said.

"We will be trying everything we can. There is bound to be a media uproar and diplomatic protest from the UK Government and other governments including the US as there have been two American women arrested a couple of days before Catherine. But again I have to tell you that there have been such protests before without any effect. What is needed is some unprecedented explanation which would enable the Administration to break its policy of zero tolerance without creating a precedent – but I cannot even conceive what such an explanation could be."

Ian Miller was only half listening, "I think I need to get my wife back to the hotel."

Lee led them to the entrance hall and went to the reception desk to call a taxi. On his return he told Ian Miller there were a couple of press photographers outside.

"There is nothing unusual about this," he said. "If there was nothing important going on elsewhere in the city the Remand Centre is as good a place as any for the possibility of a bit of a human interest story." Lee realized that had been a bit insensitive and put his hand on Ian Miller's arm.

He advised the Millers not to answer any questions, in fact to say nothing at all. When the taxi arrived, Lee lent Mrs Miller his jacket to cover her head. The photographers and a press reporter gathered around them as Lee hustled them across the walkway to the taxi. Lee stumbled and dropped his jacket, revealing Mrs Miller's tear-stained white face. The reporter tried to get Mrs Miller to say what was wrong.

As Lee replaced the coat, Ian Miller tried to push the reporter away saying angrily, "You work in a country where you knowingly execute innocent people, and you ask her what is the matter!"

The reporter turned to Philip Lee for an explanation.

"You will have to wait for the committal proceedings!" Lee said, pushing Mrs Miller gently into the car.

"Was she carrying more than fifteen grams?" persisted the reporter, picking up on Ian Miller's reference to execution.

# The Tissue Trail

"I cannot add anything more at this stage," Lee held the taxi door as Ian Miller got into the taxi behind his wife.

He gave Miller his card. "If you will let me have your contact details, I will keep in close touch."

Ian Miller was too preoccupied to reply.

## 9th May 2001

Ten days later, Catherine Miller appeared before the Magistrates at New Bridge Road Court for her committal hearing. She was led into the courtroom – her wrists handcuffed and seated in the defendants' position to the right of the Bench. The Bench comprised three men – two of Malay origin and one Chinese. There were three men in the press section including the reporter who had been outside the Remand Centre ten days earlier and a handful of people in the public area. Catherine's parents were in court despite Lee's entreaties that they should not attend.

At two p.m. the court was brought to order and the Chairman of the Bench asked the prosecution to read out the charge. Prosecuting Counsel rose and obliged:

"The defendant is Catherine Marie Miller of Edinburgh, Scotland. She is accused of entering Singapore on April 25th carrying heroin in contravention of Singapore Import of Class A drug regulations. The facts of the case are clear and the state asks the court to send the case to trial, and that the defendant be remanded in custody."

The chairman asked Philip Lee if he wanted to make any opening remarks. Lee said that he did, "It is unfortunately not a rare occurrence for visitors to Singapore to be found carrying Class A substances despite the severe penalties for such offenses. However, there are unusual circumstances relating to this case, which will lead me to request some latitude in certain areas of questioning."

The chairman replied, "Mr Lee this is a not a complicated matter. We are simply deciding if the defendant was carrying a Class A substance and if so to send her for trial. But I note your submission, and we will take a view at each point when you wish to seek -- latitude."

The hearing initially followed normal procedure with the arresting customs officer called to give evidence that Catherine Miller was the person arrested and to give time, date and place of the arrest. He also confirmed that the doll shown in evidence was the doll in which the heroin had been found in a polythene slip hidden under its outer clothing.

The prosecution then called a chemist from the Public Analyst Department and asked him to state the results of his analysis of the substance found in the slip. He told the court he had found the substance to be an unusually pure white crystalline powder, which was almost 100% pure diamorphine hydrochloride. The prosecutor asked him to confirm that that was the active ingredient in heroin, which he did. The prosecuting counsel then asked what quantity had been found.

The analyst turned to look at Catherine Miller and said speaking slowly for absolute clarity, "sixteen point two grams equivalent of diamorphine hydrochloride."

There was an immediate buzz of conversation around the court and the three pressmen rose as one and hurriedly made their way out. Christine Miller's parents lowered their heads, Mrs Miller unable to hide the rise and fall of her shoulders as she sobbed silently. The Chairman turned and spoke to each of the other magistrates on either side of him and then asked Philip Lee if he wished to question the witness. Philip Lee indicated that he did and that this was an area where he requested some latitude.

"Let us see how far you wish to go, Mr Lee."

Lee turned his attention to the witness.

"Why do you say the heroin is unusually pure?"

"Because heroin from the normal large scale producing areas such as Thailand or Afghanistan is normally transported in a crude form, more like a soft, brown sugar."

"And this was...?" prompted the lawyer.

"Almost pure white powder."

"What do you deduce from that?"

The Chairman intervened, "I know you are looking for some latitude Mr Lee, but is this relevant? The court simply needs to be satisfied that the defendant was carrying heroin and the amount of active ingredient. It is of no consequence to the court in what physical form it was carried."

"In view of the serious implications of the amount of heroin carried in such a small physical sample, the defence wishes to have placed on record all expert testimony when the opportunity arises."

"You will have that opportunity at trial, Mr Lee."

"I will complete this matter with two more questions, Sir."

# The Tissue Trail

"Two more questions, Mr Lee."

Lee turned back to the analyst, "I was asking what you deduce from the pure form in which the heroin was presented?"

"Well firstly, that it is not from any of the established mainstream sources unless it has been heavily refined, in fact it looks like the sort of production you would expect to see from a laboratory – certainly from a very small scale production."

"Anything else?" Lee asked.

The analyst hesitated, "Only that if there was access to heroin as pure as this, then the doll could have carried ten times as much heroin without being any more obvious. Why did the traffickers only secrete sixteen grams?"

Lee addressed the bench, "I have no more questions. Thank you, Sir."

The court considered routine submissions regarding custody, but the chairman cut the process short. "This is a Class A drug case. The defendant will remain in custody."

~~~~~~~~~~

Over the succeeding days and weeks, unable to take in the fact that she was still incarcerated even though she knew nothing of how the heroin came to be in her possession, Catherine's mental state steadily deteriorated and she remembered very little of what happened after the committal proceedings. She remembered something of the trial and the judge putting on the soft black hat to pronounce the death sentence. She remembered something about one of the witnesses being killed in a road accident. After the trial, she remembered Lee visiting her every two or three days – trying to encourage her by describing the media outcry and the increasingly high level diplomatic efforts to persuade the Singapore authorities to relent. She remembered that although she was the third or fourth to be arrested, the ones arrested before her were not British and had taken longer to process with the result that she became the first in line for execution.

~~~~~~~~~~

Philip Lee had seen enough of the effects of heroin to understand and support Singapore's hard line on Class A drug offenses, and he had become hardened to the distress of those who had fallen foul of the rigid penal code. But in Catherine Miller's case, he had been sure from his first meeting with her the morning after her arrest that she had no idea she was carrying heroin and the fact that she clearly had no arrangement to meet any third party after entering Singapore troubled him. The case did not make sense and yet under the law there was no way she could escape the hangman's noose. The Singapore authorities were not only totally committed to the zero tolerance, but enjoyed a certain satisfaction, even pride, in never having given in to media and diplomatic pressure when foreign nationals became involved. Indeed, the greater the press and media outcry in such cases the more determined Singapore became in its resolve to hold the line. He knew that her only possible hope of escape was to find some aspect of the case which was so extreme and extraordinary that even Singapore's hard -bitten administration would be forced to relent.

Even in his wildest dreams it was hard to imagine what such an extreme scenario could be.

~~~~~~~~~~

Lee tried everything to find an explanation for the "nonsensical trafficking" but nothing of assistance emerged despite the combined efforts of the drug enforcement agencies, drug liaison services and the criminal intelligence teams in both Nepal and Singapore, and of countries of origin of the arrested women. Then, at the end of the first week in June there was a development. At first it did not seem to amount to much, but at least it was something unusual that had happened in the same area of Nepal. One of Philip Lee's young trainee lawyers, Baahir Ramahn, in his mid-twenties, had been out with friends the previous evening and had run into an English woman of similar age who was in Singapore working on a clinical trial with Professor Aw Swee Lim, a psychiatrist at Singapore Medical School. The Professor was known to Lee because members of his department were often called to assist with defendants and prisoners who were suffering mentally under the strain of incarceration and legal process – particularly those in capital cases.

The woman worked for a medical research firm, but the reason Baahir Ramahn mentioned meeting her to Philip Lee was that her boss, a man called Edward Thurston, had diverted to Pokhara on his way from London to do some photography on the Nepal Tibet border, and when he returned to Pokhara he was questioned for three hours by Nepali security. They did not believe the reasons he gave for being in the area and would not tell him why he was being questioned.

"So he either did something or saw something on the border with Tibet which concerned Nepal security?"

"So it seems," said Baahir.

"I think we had better find out a bit more about this Mr Thurston," said Lee.

# CHAPTER FOUR
## *The Researcher*

Edward Thurston was thirty-six years old and owned and ran his own medical research company. He was in Singapore to do some clinical trial work with Professor Aw – a world expert in a field which would help Thurston with a project for which he had been commissioned by a major pharmaceutical company, Imperial Pharmaceuticals. He had first met the professor a year earlier at a conference of psychiatrists in Johannesburg.

Thurston had graduated as a pharmacologist which he usually had to explain was the study of the effect of drugs and chemicals on human and animal tissue, and had spent the first ten years of his career in the research and development divisions of two major pharmaceutical companies working on clinical trial designs.

He had been good at the work, but he found the emphasis on proving conformity and safety to be frustrating as his natural flair was finding the very opposite: small, unexpected variations in the clinical performance of chemically similar medicines. As a result, in 1996 he had taken the brave, some had said foolhardy, decision to set up his own business to try to exploit his ability to "spot the difference." In researching the market for his alleged talents he had concluded that the opportunity lay, not with pre-registration medicines still in development, but arguably those which had already been introduced to the market and had failed commercially. He was fully aware that for every blockbuster drug like Valium or Viagra there were hundreds of medicines on the market – all of which had cost millions of dollars in development and yet sales had come nowhere near covering development costs, never mind producing a worthwhile return. He liked to preach that critics who attacked the industry for making obscene profits from sick people never took account of the huge cost of on-going and rarely productive research and development.

Starting with smaller projects, he had been successful from the outset. As his reputation had grown, he had moved on to more and bigger challenges and by the end of 2000 his team of researchers had grown to double figures.

### February 2001

In February 2001, Thurston's agency had been approached by Imperial Pharmaceuticals to present its credentials with a view to being invited to try to rescue an antidepressant – brand name Surmil, which they had introduced two years earlier. Not only had Surmil failed dismally, but its meagre sales were already declining. The reason for the failure was well described by an American doctor working in a UK general practice, "It is so sedative it has them falling over on the sidewalks. For a depressed patient who probably hasn't slept too well, the last thing they want is to take something which knocks them out during the day."

Thurston knew his agency was good enough to take on the project. It had as good a chance as anybody of finding a solution to the poor sales figures, probably better than most, but because of his and the agency's relative youth, he thought they would be lucky to get any further. But at the end of February he was delighted when he was told they had been short-listed. Each of the selected agencies now had to produce a more detailed proposal to Imperial Pharmaceuticals, on the basis of which a final selection of agency would be made.

There were two stages in their search for a solution. The first was going over the development history of the drug prior to registration, then interviewing doctors and patients in everyday general practice to explore reactions to the medicine in the rough and tumble of real life.

Only one thing of interest came out of the pre-registration history and that was a small study which showed that Surmil did not suppress dream sleep whereas other medicines in the category did. Thurston wasn't sure how significant this might be, but made a mental note. On its own he couldn't see it being what they were looking for.

# The Tissue Trail

The agency's real breakthrough came at the interview stage. It was one of the recent recruits who "had hit the golden button." Jaci Linthorpe was twenty-four years old and a pharmacist who had worked in hospital pharmacy for two years after graduation before looking for something a bit more exciting. She was strikingly attractive with genuine long blonde hair and large green eyes, but she made no attempt to exploit it. In fact, she tried to play it down – she "wanted people to react to her for what she could do, not what she looked like."

At birth she had been lumbered with the name Jacintha, but this had been quickly whittled down to Jaci. She had had a conventional childhood attending the local grammar school, collecting the normal quota of examination passes and gone on to the London University School of Pharmacy where she had graduated with a first. Her value to the agency was the combination of her natural and intuitive intelligence which together with her played down attractiveness enabled her, albeit unwittingly, to get under the guard of the most hardened of professionals of either sex – not to mention patients from all walks of life.

Thurston, with Imperial's help had selected a number of general practitioners who had prescribed Surmil and patients who had taken it. He had then divided them into groups which he, Jaci, and two other members of the team interviewed. The reaction was almost universal. The drug was too sedative to be tolerated by active patients during the day and as a result in almost all cases, the practitioner had had to switch the patient to something else. On the last day only three interviews remained and it was looking hopeless. Two of the final three interviewees were doctors – one of whom was on Jaci's list. After an hour, the interview had not produced anything and Dr Jackson was starting to become restless, wanting to get back to his practice duties. Jaci was tidying up her notes and starting to thank the doctor for his time when he just came out with it:

"It's a pity we have to stop using Surmil– nearly all of the patients on it say they sleep better."

Jaci stopped in her tracks thinking quickly, "sleep better, in what way? Getting to sleep more easily or sleeping longer?"

"Both," Dr Jackson had replied. "The sedative effect puts them to sleep and for whatever reason, early morning waking is reduced."

"Which must mean they feel better in the mornings?" she added.

"Oh yes," he replied, "at least until the daytime sedative effect takes over."

"And that 'feeling better' happens before the antidepressant effect begins to show?"

"Yes," he replied, "The effect on improving sleep is almost immediate, certainly within two or three days – the antidepressant effect doesn't begin to show for at least ten days as you presumably know."

Jaci had come back to the office with eyes shining. She knew she was onto something. Thurston listened and, had she been fat and ugly, he would probably have given her a full-blown bear hug. But as most of the males in the agency spent quite a lot of creative time working out ways of spending time with her, he felt constrained in the interests of professionalism to avoid being over demonstrative. And also in the interests of professionalism, he avoided showing his own excitement when he summarized to the others in the agency team who had gathered to hear just what Jaci had come up with.

"Normally the best we can hope for in our line of business is to exploit some small subsector of a disease area and produce some increase in sales – but this is different. Seventy percent of depressed patients in general practice suffer some form of sleep disturbance. So if we get this right, instead of going for a minor market segment, in the case of Surmil we can have an impact on the whole therapeutic area." He paused for the magnitude of what he was saying to sink in, then added, "There is of course one minor obstacle. We have to persuade Imperial to alter the dosage regime to concentrate all or most of the daily dose at night."

Jaci managed to interrupt Thurston's animated flow to say that there was something else. They all turned to listen.

"Dr Jackson and two of his partners had actually tried moving the midday dose to the evening."

They waited expectantly.

"It had worked like a dream," she smiled at her own pun. "Better sleep, better mood in the morning, and reduced or even eliminated day time sedation."

This time Thurston forgot professional detachment, forgot that she was not fat and ugly, walked over to her and lifted her off the ground and swung her around in an unrestrained bear hug. But this moment of delighted achievement was just the start of the process. They would now have to persuade Imperial to fund clinical trials to confirm the effect in larger numbers as well as persuade the registration authorities to allow trial with a non-registered dosage, and to check that changes in blood concentration patterns did not result in unexpected side effects or any significant change in the underlying antidepressant effect. If they achieved all this, they finally had to persuade the regulatory authorities to accept a permanent radical change to the dose regime relatively quickly after initial registration. There was one man who stood out as the ideal candidate for this work; the psychiatrist Thurston had met in Cape Town a year earlier, Professor Aw Swee Lim from the Singapore Medical School. His speciality was the study of secondary effects of psychiatric medicines and in particular effects on sleep, a field in which he was a recognized world leader. The professor's potential importance to Thurston and therefore to Imperial was that if he could be persuaded to do the secondary effect work on Surmil it would go a long way to persuading the regulatory authorities to accept a change of dosage.

### 23rd March 2001

Thurston knew it would not be easy to persuade Professor Aw to participate. As a leader in his field, the professor was normally asked to work on major new medicines still in development, not products which had been on the market for two years and were already commercial failures.

Difficult propositions were, in Thurston's experience, better dealt with in writing rather than on the telephone where one wrong word can cause a wrong impression which is then difficult to erase. So he e-mailed a carefully worded letter outlining the "unusual proposition" of inviting Professor Aw to become involved in converting a commercially failed medicine into a therapeutic class leader. He emphasized that they already had anecdotal evidence of the positive effect of the night-time dose. There was one factor which Thurston held in reserve.

### 30th March 2001

Seven days later there had been no reply and Thurston telephoned Aw's secretary to check that the professor had received the letter. She told Thurston that the professor had received the letter, and that he seemed quite interested but that he had a very busy schedule over the next few months. Thurston sensed a "polite brush off" and decided to play his reserve card.

"There is one factor which I did not mention in my letter which I would appreciate it if you would be so kind as to pass on to Professor Aw."

"Yes, Mr Thurston, and what is that?"

"That Surmil does not suppress REM sleep."

There was a silence followed by a muffled conversation at the other end. After about fifteen seconds, Aw's secretary returned.

"Mr Thurston, Professor Aw is in his office and would like to have a word with you if you can spare a few seconds."

"Of course, I would be delighted."

There was the click on the line as he was switched through.

"Good morning, Mr Thurston, nice to hear from you, I see you have an interesting problem with Imperial's antidepressant."

"Yes, we do professor." Thurston did not need to restate the case, the fact that Aw had taken the call was a strong enough buying signal.

"How good is your anecdotal evidence?"

"The numbers are small, but where family practitioners have tried concentrating the dose at night they have been pleased with the results and by talking to the local pharmacies we've checked that the number of prescriptions for Surmil, which had been declining, have started to increase. Not only that, but GPs who have not previously used it have started to prescribe. We have identified five areas in different parts of the UK where this is happening."

"Interesting, now tell me what you have just told my secretary about the effect of Surmil on dream sleep."

"We have been working through the development history with Imperial and this was an isolated bit of work but conclusive. They compared the effect of Surmil with two other drugs in the same class and whereas there was marked rapid eye movement sleep suppression with the competitors, there was none with Surmil."

There was a long silence.

"Are these findings published, Mr Thurston?"

Thurston confirmed that they were and gave Aw the reference.

"If I can confirm what you say Mr Thurston, I would be very happy to take this further. I will get back to you in the next few days."

Thurston put down the telephone and punched the air.

Professor Aw would know only too well that most, if not all of the medicines in this class, suppressed dream sleep which later in the night would rebound causing vivid dreams and often nightmares. The effect was to wake the patient early, which was one of the main symptoms that antidepressant therapy was intended to reduce.

The time spent on the development history had been far from wasted.

Professor Aw was true to his word, but it only took two days for him to renew contact. "This is a very interesting project Mr Thurston, in which we would very much like to be involved. What exactly do you have in mind?"

Thurston briefly outlined his clinical trial design.

Aw paused then said, "If you can spare the time Mr Thurston, I would appreciate it if you would come out to Singapore to go into this in detail."

"I don't think I will have any difficulty finding the time Professor!" They agreed to meet for three or four days on a date to be finalized. Thurston punched the air again.

Aw's parting shot left Thurston punching even more air.

"Assuming we can confirm your findings to date Mr Thurston, if Imperial decides not to go with this it need not be the end of our conversation. The drug is available on the open market, and we would like to look at your proposals anyway."

The gods, it seemed, were not just smiling, they were laughing their heads off.

~~~~~~~~~~

By the end of the first week of April the proposal for Imperial was virtually ready. Only the details of the Singapore trial were needed to complete it. The deadline for the final proposal was not until 30th April, so with the thirteen members of the agency fully occupied with other work, Thurston calculated he could afford to spend a few days on one of his "wild country" photographic diversions on his way to see Aw Swee Lim.

Looking at a map just to see what lay between his starting point and final destination, created the same moment of creative adrenaline for Thurston as a painter contemplating an empty canvas. In this case, his flight from London would pass over the eastern Med, the Middle East, the Indian sub continent, Indo China and Malaysia. There were many points where he could find a reason to stop but as a mountain man, the Himalaya were an irresistible magnet even though he had visited Nepal twice before. He did not have the time for a long trek, so whatever he came up with had to be something he could do using local flights and transport. He remembered seeing a *National Geographic* magazine article about a medieval, square-walled city called Lo Manthang in Mustang – a small "lost kingdom" close to the Tibetan border in western Nepal. Although part of Nepal politically and geographically, Lo Manthang was situated on the Tibetan plateau at an altitude of 13,000 feet, only a few hundred feet lower than the Matterhorn. To reach it from the Nepal side it was necessary to fly through the world's deepest ravine, the Kali Gandaki Gorge, which split the western Himalayan wall between the 26,000 feet himals of Annapurna and Dhaulagiri. This was Thurston's meat and drink, particularly as the airplane used could only fly at 14,000 feet and this meant the mountains would tower 12,000 feet above it as it flew through the gorge.

And this was not all. He had been fascinated by an article, also in the *National Geographic*, describing the high altitude yak caravans brought salt into Nepal from Tibet, which historically had been routed to a place called Jumla to the west of Lo Manthang. But part of the traffic was now being brought to the old city. If he could reach Lo Manthang and photograph an incoming caravan this would be remarkable. There were no roads into Mustang, the only access was by foot with a minimum trek of ten days from Jomsom, the nearest airstrip. In the rain shadow of the Annapurnas, Mustang was a desert yet only fifty miles to the south, on the other side of the gorge the country was subtropical. Even if he didn't make it to Lo Manthang, getting through the gorge would be a great experience and colourful photographic opportunity. How he could get to Lo Manthang he had no idea, but from many years of trying such things in different parts of the world, he knew you could only solve this kind of problem on the spot.

From every standpoint it was an attractive and challenging trip, and he decided to give it a go. On 20th April he left on the overnight flight from Heathrow to Kathmandu, then flew to Pokhara, the airport town and trekking centre for the Annapurnas. It was the third time he had been to Nepal in recent years, but the 150-mile wall of the Himalaya rising over 25,000 feet from the Indian plain had lost none of its magic. It was disappointing that the Fishtail mountain which towered over Pokhara Airport was hidden in afternoon cloud, but he was happy to save his luck for the next two or three days.

# The Tissue Trail

*15th April 2001*

At first light the following morning, he took the first flight of the day to Jomsom, an administration centre and small airport situated just through the 20,000 feet deep Kali Gandaki Gorge. The nineteen-seater Otter took off in clear skies and headed northwest, rapidly becoming a barely perceptible speck climbing slowly against the 24,000 feet snow covered wall of the Annapurna himal. He installed himself immediately behind the cockpit, which was divided from the passenger cabin by a loosely hanging curtain, which for the short forty minute flight the crew hadn't bothered to close. Twenty minutes after working its way westward, and at its operational ceiling of 14,000 feet – still 10,000 feet below the towering white ridges and cornices of the Annapurnas, a giant chasm opened up ahead and to the right into which the Otter slowly turned. The weather was brilliantly clear and calm, so it was a surprise when above the roar of the engines and the animated chatter of the travellers the captain's voice came onto the intercom:

"We have just received a weather report and it is not good. The wind in the gorge has started early. We will try to get through, but be prepared for some turbulence – and I am not talking about the sort of minor vibrations they call turbulence on a 747. Please fasten your seatbelts – tightly."

Thurston knew that the Kali Gandaki was subject to violent winds as the hot air from the Indian plains forced its way through the four mile deep ravine and out onto the cold Tibetan plateau, but as one of the world's most noted optimists, he had not expected it to happen when he was trying to get through. When the wind did start it was usually in the morning sometimes persisting for two or three hours but sometimes for four or five days, isolating trekkers who were trapped on the wrong side of the gorge for as long as it lasted – unless they fancied a seven day trek back to Pokhara.

Thurston did not tighten his belt immediately, preferring the freedom to move into position to photograph the peaks on both sides as they headed into the gorge. When the first wave of turbulence hit them there were gasps from many of the passengers and Thurston was lifted cleanly from his seat. When he came down, he tightened his seat belt. The next fifteen minutes were the roughest he had spent in any form of transport even though as a private pilot he had enjoyed some pretty rough amateur aerobatics of his own making. He wondered how the wings remained attached to the fuselage. It was as if the aircraft was flying into violent spirals of air being shaken first in a horizontal circular motion followed either by a sickening drop or being thrown upwards like a cork on rough water.

Initially the passengers tried to remain stoical; all keen to get through the gorge to Jomsom and to continue their trek from there. But as the violence of the turbulence grew so did the level of distress; mothers tried to comfort crying children, husbands tried to comfort wives, white-faced teenagers gripped their seats and looked either wide eyed dead ahead – or at each other. It was when a particularly violent surge seemed to throw the airplane onto its side that several people screamed. The stewardess seated at the back reached up, pulled down the telephone and spoke to the pilot. A few seconds later the Otter started to turn. Thurston estimated they were one third of the way through the gorge. Ten minutes later they were flying back towards Pokhara in calm weather. Even so, Thurston could hear good use being made of the airline's sick bags.

"I'm sorry," said the pilot over the intercom, "I know you are very keen to reach Jomsom, but the wind is too strong." Thurston did not hear anybody argue.

Back on the ground at Pokhara the flight crew helped the most badly affected passengers. Thurston offered to help and his help was welcomed. When the last of them had been ushered back to the terminal, Thurston asked Captain Chaudrai if he could have a word about the flight. The captain asked him what was on his mind.

"Could the Otter have got through?" asked Thurston.

"Oh, yes," the captain smiled, "These things are built for whatever the mountains can throw at them. We would give in long before the Otter."

"Do you train to fly in those conditions?"

"Yes, when we can. If we can't we have to make do with the simulator."

"Would you be interested in having a go through the gorge as a training flight?"

The Captain still looked puzzled. The young first officer looked excited.

Thurston came to the point. "I haven't got time to wait for the wind to drop. I have less than seventy-two hours in Nepal, and I don't get many chances to get into this part of the world. If I can charter the Otter with a crew I'll try and take her through the gorge. If that isn't possible it is a wasted trip."

# The Tissue Trail

The young first officer caught the captain's eye and said something in his own language. Chaudrai replied shaking his head – but Thurston thought he saw a hint of a smile.

Chaudrai turned to Thurston, "I don't know if you can persuade the station manager to allow this – but Jethwa here is just out of flying school and to use an English expression would 'give his eye teeth' to have a go. I suppose if it is a training flight it is not too much of a risk even if I am coming up to retirement. I assume you realize it costs $1,500 per hour to charter?" said Chaudrai.

"I don't get into this sort of situation very often," Thurston explained, "and I've already spent far more than that getting here."

It was clear from the exchanged looks that the two pilots had difficulty understanding that someone could spend more in an hour for fun than they would earn in a week.

The small terminal was crammed with waiting passengers —with the Kali Gandaki closed and Kathmandu typically fog bound, nothing was moving out of Pokhara. It did not take long for word to get around that somebody was talking about taking an Otter through the Kali Gandaki when it was closed to normal commercial traffic – and paying $3,000 an hour (the price later reached $10,000) for the privilege. As Chaudrai tried to introduce Thurston to the station manager in the check-in area they found themselves surrounded by a sea of interested faces – both trekkers and locals.

The station manager invited them into his office to get away from the crowd and after finally managing to introduce Thurston, Chaudrai told him that Thurston would like to charter the Otter as a training flight to get through to Jomsom.

The station manager's eyebrows lifted as he turned to address Thurston, "Why are you so keen to get to Jomsom?" he asked.

"I'm not, it's the gorge I want to see and as much of the Tibetan plain to the north of Jomsom as possible – and my time's limited."

"You realize what conditions will be like?"

"We have just been into the teeth of it. I can cope with that."

The station manager turned to the two pilots, "And you two are happy to go?"

Chaudrai managed a slight grin, "One of us more than the other – but yes we would do it."

The manager picked up the telephone. "I will have to speak to Kathmandu."

# The Tissue Trail

As he waited for the line to connect, Thurston said, "As it's a training flight, how about doing it for $750 per hour." The station manager did not appear to hear him. Even so, Thurston did a quick mental calculation. Assuming the flight would be tax deductible as a photographic exercise – he would submit anything good to *National Geographic* or anybody else who would pay for it – that would take forty percent off the $750, the flight would cost him $400 instead of $1,500. He liked that – so would his accountant. And, why not? Thurston was a businessman whose natural mentality was to make the most of every dollar.

An animated conversation followed in the local language, but with the manager making notes he presumed that the conversation was not entirely negative. The manager made a final note and put the phone down.

"We almost made it Mr Thurston, but at this time of morning they cannot make the necessary insurance arrangements. If you were ever to come this way again they suggest that you let us know in advance."

Thurston immediately switched to, "how to get round this little local difficulty" mode. "Suppose we wait until the offices in Kathmandu open?" suggested Thurston.

"It would not help," the station manager said. "By then the fog will have cleared in Kathmandu and we will need all of the aircraft to clear the passenger backlog."

Thurston suggested one or two more ideas such as taking off and flying around the mouth of the gorge, ready to dash through if they got clearance, when the offices opened at 9:00 a.m. But his various suggestions fell on stony ground and he finally had to admit that for once he had failed to crack the problem. For someone who preached that, "There were no such things as problems, only opportunities" it had become, to use another of his favourite phrases, "an insurmountable opportunity."

He finally thanked them for trying and asked how soon he could expect to get a flight back to Kathmandu.

"The fog is clearing in the Kathmandu valley," the station manager told him. "We should be moving the first flights out within half an hour."

A telephone on the desk rang and the station manager excused himself. Thurston shook hands with the two pilots again.

"Pity," said Jethwa smiling. "Perhaps another time."

Thurston left the desk and worked his way through the crowded terminal to the coffee stall. He took his drink outside into the hot sun and took photographs of the twin peaked Fishtail and studied the peaks of the Annapurnas that rose behind it.

As he left the building he looked back to the desk and saw the station manager in animated conversation with a middle-aged, suited Nepali in heavy black-rimmed glasses and pointing at Thurston. Thurston wondered what that was about.

## 16th April 2001

Thurston had carried on to Singapore without further incident where he had worked with Professor Aw to develop the Surmil trial protocol. The professor even started to identify patients he intended to admit to the trial as and when Imperial signed the contract. "Or even if they don't," he had added with a smile. "Off the record, I've tried Surmil on one or two depressed patients who were experiencing particular sleep difficulties." He looked at Thurston, "The results were encouraging." The word "encouraging" in clinical trial parlance could be roughly translated as a rave review.

After three days in Singapore, Thurston returned to the UK where he put one final twist into the Imperial proposal. Encouraged by the reaction of Aw Swee Lim together with the evidence of increased prescriptions in local pockets in the UK, he decided to introduce what he melodramatically termed the "killer option." Instead of the normal substantial fee they charged for trial work, he would offer Imperial a much-reduced fee in return for a small percentage of any increase in sales. This would reduce the risk of a substantial outlay with little return if he failed and would only require them to pay if the outlay was covered by an increase in income.

By the end of April, the trial design in Singapore was complete and the first thirty patients selected. Technically, Professor Aw was ready to start; the contract with Imperial was a standard document with a schedule setting out the details of Thurston's particular proposals. He had already signed the agency copy and agreed the terms with Professor Aw for his work. Everything was ready to go the moment they received confirmation from Imperial, and Thurston had decided to have another go at getting to and photographing the walled city of Lo Manthang. This time he had forewarned Royal Nepal Airlines that he might wish to charter an Otter for a training flight if commercial flying was suspended and asked them to have the paperwork in place.

# CHAPTER FIVE
## *The Salt Caravan*

*Baker Street, London*
*Edward Thurston's Office*
*19th April 2001, 6:24 p.m.*

The atmosphere had become quiet and tense. An hour earlier, the agency team had been laughing and joking, confident that the phone call they were waiting for would arrive by the promised 6:30 p.m. The office clock now showed 6:24 p.m. They had gathered to wait for the call with morale high and Thurston was quietly delighted that all fourteen members of the staff had stayed on after hours to wait for the call even though only four of them had worked directly on the project.

As the clock moved on and the call didn't come, Thurston was conscious of the uncertain glances in his direction. They all knew how much this one meant to him. Firstly, it would put the agency into the top three after only four years in existence – a remarkable achievement in a highly conservative area. Secondly, the logic of their proposal was unbreakable and unless there were unexpected side effects the company would benefit by millions of dollars. If they had not won the contract with Imperial there was something wrong.

One of the wits suggested that if they didn't get it Thurston ought to put one of his favourite sayings into practice: "If at first you don't succeed, go and find something you're good at." This was a digest of Thurston's fabled optimism on the one hand and equally fabled impatience on the other. Another of his common quotes in a similar vein was: "You only live once, make the most of it."

# The Tissue Trail

But the look on his face at that moment would have raised yet another Thurston mantra, "Don't come to me with problems, just solutions – then I know you've thought it through." And in the small print you would find the real guts of the message: *"it also means you waste less of my valuable time."*

There was another reason why winning this contract was important to him. On his way back from the conference in Johannesburg where he had first met Professor Aw almost a year earlier, he had stayed an extra night to try to reach Victoria Falls the following day. He had been told it wasn't possible to do a return trip to Victoria Falls in a single day. But after doing his own checking he had decided that it was. He had taken the first flight to Victoria Falls Airport, then the twenty-five minute shuttle to Victoria Falls Hotel and then run the last third of a mile to the Zambezi Gorge. He had literally watched and photographed the falls for fifteen minutes and had come back soaked to the skin from the spray. But it was fifteen minutes that he would not have missed. Unfortunately Emily, the woman he had been with for eight years and with whom he expected to spend the rest of his life, was not so impressed. Although she understood and accepted that building his fledgling business necessarily required more than a nine to five commitment and her irregular hours as a hospital consultant didn't help, she had not been happy with him taking the extra day at the end of a long trip particularly as it was a Saturday, which they both normally regarded as their "gold dust time." Rather than sit at home she had decided to go and see her parents for the weekend and had died in a car crash on the way.

The agency team knew that her death had hit him hard. The perceived wisdom was that he needed to succeed with the Imperial project even if it would only go a very small way towards exorcising the blame he attached to himself for her death.

And now it began to look as if it was not going to happen.

For his part, as the clock moved on, his concern was not so much for himself, but for the effect on members of his young team. Thurston had been around long enough to know that human ego could override the most compelling of logical argument even when accepting the obvious would make millions for the company. Imperial's research director's name even sounded egotistical – Dr Vilnius Villiumy. Villiumy's overt resentment of Thurston's "young upstarts" could well lead him to put whatever obstacles he could devise in the way of him winning the contract. But the others in the agency, Jaci in particular, had not yet experienced such perversity, and he was concerned that her flowering talent could be damaged if not crushed by the ego-driven stupidity of someone like Villiumy. He looked in her direction and found her gazing steadily at him. She looked mildly uncomfortable as he caught her gaze, but she did not look away. He looked up to the clock to break the moment. It was 6:28 p.m.

Nicola, the office manager, had been trying to get Thurston onto his feet for the last half hour before his flight to Kathmandu left at 8:30 p.m. with a check-in time of 6:00 p.m., i.e., about now!

Nicola finally got him to his feet and edged him towards the office door even though the telephone had still not rung. When he reached the office door he glanced back at the team with a mixture of emotions; an angry disbelief that Imperial would not go with their proposition whatever the ego pressures, a feeling of having let the team down and yet still some satisfaction that they had all waited for either the pleasure or the pain. He shook his head slowly, looking around the faces most of which were looking for clues as to what he was thinking.

At 6:37 p.m. Nicola pressed the elevator call button, half a minute later the doors opened and she pushed him into it. He managed a smile.

As the doors closed he thought he heard the ringing tone of a telephone. He tried to stop the elevator door with his foot, but it was too late and of course it stopped at nearly every one of the six floors. It seemed an eternity before he stepped out onto the ground floor foyer, then made his way to the exit door and crossed the pavement to his waiting car. He didn't need to look back; he could hear the shouts and whoops of jubilation. When he did look back, most of the fourteen were hanging out of the windows waving and shouting. And something close to twenty-eight thumbs were pointing to the heavens.

Thurston jumped into the back seat conscious of his mobile vibrating in his breast pocket. Nicola confirmed that the telephone call had been from Imperial and that they had been awarded the contract. The delay had been Villiumy persuading the board to appoint a second agency – the other, a longstanding conservative set up "to give some stability to the research." Thurston didn't care; he knew their idea was a winner. But Villiumy had succeeded in lining up one of his long-standing cronies to pick up the pieces if Thurston made a mistake. For the money they were going to make on this one, he thought he might just cope with a little extra pressure.

# The Tissue Trail

The traffic was cooperative and Thurston was entering the terminal at 7:45 p.m. – a respectable forty-five minutes before take-off – particularly as having won the contract, he had phoned ahead and treated himself to first class.

At 8:15 p.m. he was sitting back comfortably aboard the Royal Nepal Airline's Airbus sipping a glass of champagne and feeling mostly pleased with life. The contract was a major win and there was plenty of other agency work for those not involved with Imperial. His team was in good shape, and he was looking forward to the long weekend in Nepal. Since Emily's death he had become adept at finding diversions of various sorts to avoid being alone on weekends, which were always the times when he missed her most. It was the thought of how much she would have enjoyed sharing this moment which accounted for him being only "mostly" pleased with life.

He removed the memory by turning to the more pleasant prospect of the next three or four days. It was beginning to look as if it would be a good idea to charter the Otter even if the weather was good. He did not have the time for the ten-day round trip to the old city of Lo Manthang and there were no roads, so flying over it was the only option. As for the possibility of catching sight of one of the high altitude salt carrying yak caravans which had recently started using Lo Manthang as opposed to the traditional route via Jumla to the west, again, over-flying was, realistically, his only option.

But even if his normal good luck held and there was a caravan coming in, aerial shots, even with a powerful lens, would give the impression of a line of ants stretched out across the landscape. Not very helpful, and certainly not very saleable.

As he sipped the champagne, his mind drifted back to the contract and his first meeting with Imperial's Director of Research – Vilnius Villiumy. It had been a good example of the frosty reaction of development department personnel to Thurston being called in. The problem was, that the need for Thurston's services normally occurred when management of a company, usually at board level and usually in desperation, invited researchers like Thurston to have a look at the situation over the heads of their own research and development department. Implicit in that invitation was that R&D had failed.

The opening salvo from Vilnius Villiumy was typical. He had kept Thurston's team and his own staff waiting for nearly quarter of an hour beyond the appointed time, then he had swept into the meeting room, made some inside joke to his people as he sat down, then launched straight into his attack:

"So you think your bunch of amateurs can turn round the fortunes of Surmil do you, Mr Thurston?"

It wasn't the first time that Thurston had faced this sort of question, and he hoped that one day he would have the opportunity to say what he really wanted to, which was something along the lines of: "My bunch of amateurs have succeeded eleven times out of twelve in similar cases, so why do you think your particular little catastrophe is any different?"

Instead he had trotted out the familiar diplomatic code he had developed of necessity for these situations. "I think our techniques have a fair chance of finding a solution if there is one." Thurston held Villiumy's glare. Tall with receding swept-back grey hair and well cut dark, blue pin-striped suit, Villiumy had placed his hands on the table, finger tips touching and was looking over his half-rimmed glasses at Edward Thurston at least twenty years his junior. With nothing in the Imperial drug research pipeline close to market, the commercial performance of Surmil was critical. The company's share price was already on the slide, and unless they did something about Surmil, it would continue to slide. As was normal in such cases the board, over the head of Villiumy and against his vote, had called in a number of research agencies to present their credentials and then asked a short list of three to make detailed presentations as to how they would plan to rescue the problem drug.

Villiumy had no choice but to cooperate with Thurston, but he wasn't obliged to make it easy, and he didn't.

"If there is a significant difference between Surmil and other medicines of the same type," Villiumy maintained his attack, "would you not expect that one of the most respected research and development teams in the industry would have found it in ten years of research?"

Again Thurston wanted to say, "The solution is so obvious I would have expected a team of brain dead donkeys to have found it in ten days never mind ten years," but he restrained himself and trotted out his diplomatically correct and tested retort, "It is easier for us to look for differences in the rough and tumble of day-to-day family medicine than in clinical trials designed to prove conformity."

The exchanges continued with Thurston holding his well practiced ground until Villiumy finally let it go, "As you say Mr Thurston, the company has asked you to do a job so I will leave you to establish with my team what you require to...," he hesitated, "to come up with your rescue plan." He got up brusquely and left the room.

The last of the contract related conversations Edward recalled before he fell asleep was an exchange he had had with Jaci. She had asked him, if they won the contract, if she could go with him to Singapore to set up the trial – "since it was my interview which found the idea the pitch is based on." She had smiled, a smile which normally got her what she wanted even if she was not aware of it. But he had declined. "Your time will come," he had told her.

There were two reasons why he had refused; the first that although she was twenty-four, her attempts to play down her looks left her looking eighteen and this would not go down well with senior university professors when he was trying to portray his fledgling agency as a serious player in a world where fifty-five was young. Secondly, he did not want to be seen to be over familiar with any particular member of staff, particularly an attractive female member of staff. Disappearing to the other side of the world with Jaci would not have been in the best interests of developing even better morale between members of his emerging team. He pictured the jubilation of the team hanging out of the office windows and twenty-eight thumbs pointing to the heavens, and smiled.

After a final sip of the champagne, he pushed his seat and headrest back and closed his eyes. His last thought before he slept was of Emily's laughing smile at the airport just before he went through the departure gate for the Johannesburg flight almost exactly a year ago and the sad smile which had replaced it when he looked back at her for what turned out to be the last time.

### 20th April 2001

He missed dinner and didn't wake until breakfast was being served two and a half hours out of Kathmandu. A folded copy of yesterday's *Kathmandu Post* lay on a breakfast tray. Presumably it had been there last night, but he had been too pre-occupied to notice. When he had finished eating he picked up the paper and casually skimmed through it not expecting to find anything of particular interest. He was wrong. On the second page a three-column inch article was headed:

# The Tissue Trail

## *NEW EMERGENCY AIRSTRIP NEARS COMPLETION*

*A new airstrip is nearing completion close to the Mustang capital Lo Manthang. Mustang has recently been opened after years of closure to the outside world. There are no roads and access to the Kingdom. It is limited to a restricted number of visitors prepared to do the ten-day round trip trek to the capital Lo Manthang from the nearest airstrip each paying a visa fee of $75. The tight restriction on numbers is partly due to the need to protect scarce resources in the desert rain shadow of the Annapurnas. Visitors are required to carry all cooking and heating fuel for the ten-day trek and each group must be accompanied by a security officer. The landing strip is being built largely for emergency purposes as the survival of any seriously ill or injured tourists is seriously jeopardized by both the 13,000 feet altitude and the five-day return trek to the nearest airstrip at Jomsom. Work on the Lo Manthang strip is scheduled to be completed in the early spring.*

The article read like a filler – something that could have been printed almost anytime and was used just to fill a few spare column inches. But they had chosen to print it now, so clearly the gods were still smiling on Thurston. This could somehow be the answer to his getting close enough to the yak caravan to take meaningful photographs – although precisely how still needed to be worked out.

He was just about to close the paper when he noted a small item at the bottom of the front page:

## *SECOND NEPAL TREKKER ARRESTED IN SINGAPORE*

*Twenty-two-year-old Californian, Karen Leopold was taken into custody at Changi Airport in Singapore this morning after customs officials found white powder believed to be a Class A substance hidden in an artefact she had bought in Nepal as a memento of her trip. Miss Leopold will be kept in custody at least until the substance has been identified. This is the second arrest of a young woman in almost identical circumstances in two days.*

# The Tissue Trail

*The first, also American, Maria Gonzales from Miami was arrested on April 17th also on arriving at Changi Airport from Nepal after trekking in the Annapurna Region. American consular staff are said to be in touch with their nationals.*

He finished folding the newspaper and didn't think much about the article except that somewhere in the recesses of his memory he thought he recalled that the Singapore authorities were particularly severe in Class A drug cases.

~~~~~~~~~~~

Within two hours of landing at the international terminal at Kathmandu's Tribhuvan Airport, Thurston had cleared customs and was waiting for the next internal flight out to Pokhara. Flights from Kathmandu to Pokhara left three or four times an hour at peak times. Passengers to mountain centres fell broadly into two groups; the majority were young trekkers wearing boots, socks, shorts and anoraks. The minority group were older and well-heeled and clearly not expecting to do anything much more strenuous than looking up at the mountains from comfortable hotels. Thurston wasn't sure that he fit into either category.

Just before lunch his flight to Pokhara took off and he looked down at the white dome of the Swyambunath Temple disappearing under the starboard wing as the flight climbed out of the Kathmandu basin and headed west.

He took a taxi from Pokhara airport to the Fishtail Lodge, which looked over Lake Phewa. This hotel was famous for the reflections of the white mountains in the Lake's smooth surface.

### *21st April 2001*

At 5:30 a.m. the next morning the airport was still dark and the well-heeled were thin on the ground. All of the shadowy figures talking quietly in the early hours were young trekkers. Thurston checked into the desk to register his presence and that he was ready to take the charter as soon as they were. It was the same station manager he had dealt with on his previous trip.

# The Tissue Trail

"You are persistent, Mr Thurston."

"Yes," Thurston smiled, "So I'm told but it wasn't wind that stopped us last time, just the paperwork."

The manager's eyes shifted to look over Thurston's shoulder to somebody behind him.

Thurston turned to see two Nepalis in airline uniforms grinning from ear to ear. Choudrai and Jethwa from his first flight. The three men greeted each other like old friends.

"You two again?"

"When we heard about this charter we put in for it," said Choudrai, "having come so close last time."

"Well what's the forecast for today?" asked Thurston.

"It's calm now," said the manager, "but the forecast is not good. They are talking about strong winds by 11:00 hours."

The pilots – including Thurston, studiously avoided showing too much concern.

"But in any case," the manager smiled, "we have classified the flight as a training flight, so that normal wind limits can be exceeded."

"Does that mean you are charging me at the training rate?" Thurston asked with a half smile.

"As it happens, yes," the manager replied. "I think Mr Thurston, you must have caught somebody's imagination."

As they gathered their bags the manager told them there was one other thing – that all travellers entering Mustang had to be accompanied by a security officer.

Thurston frowned. "Nothing to worry about," said the manager, "purely routine, all land treks are accompanied in the same way."

He introduced Inspector Pandeha Nepali in police uniform. He was a quiet man who didn't speak much English and seemed a little overawed by the assignment. The party of four made their way to a twin Otter parked some way from the normal aircraft standing, waiting for their Jomsom and Kathmandu services. Many of the passengers waiting for normal commercial flights stood watching the second Otter. As Thurston and the other three boarded the Otter, the wind was rising.

Chaudrai looked concerned. "If it's blowing down here it's going to be difficult in the gorge!"

"Well let's get on with it before it gets worse," replied Thurston.

# The Tissue Trail

By the time they started the engines and carried out pre-flight checks it had deteriorated. By the time the Otter had taxied into position and started the take-off run, the wind was sufficient to be moving it laterally, even on the ground.

Extra fuel had been taken on to try to replace the ballast normally provided by nineteen passengers, but it did not come close to compensating. Twenty minutes later as they entered the gorge, the sensations of being rotated horizontally and thrown upwards or downwards were noticeably more violent than they had experienced during the previous attempt. The wings seemed, to Thurston, to bend like a long bladed wood saw. He tried to keep an eye on the flight instruments to check speed and altitude, but the vibrations were so violent the dials were a blur.

The pitching, rolling Otter fought its way through the aerial maelstrom, inching its way toward the northern end of the gorge and to the widening plateau ahead of them. Thurston was concerned that Jethwa, who had started the flight high with excitement, was now looking pale and apprehensive.

Finally, the brief moments of calm became slightly longer and the violent upward spiralling and sickening drops became slightly less catastrophic. The flat roofed administration buildings at Jomsom passed slowly beneath them and they were through the worst. But listening on the spare headset, which Jethwa had handed to him on take-off, Thurston could hear air traffic control telling them that the wind conditions were rapidly deteriorating and that until the wind dropped, landing at Jomsom would not be possible. They were stuck in the air. The crew hadn't seen it at this level for two years. Even Chaudrai, who must have seen everything, looked shaken.

Thurston's natural instinct was to see the positive in any situation, but this was "a bit tricky." The air traffic controller was telling them they could not turn back to land at Jomsom, and they were surrounded by peaks twice the altitude of the Otter's operational limit.

Thurston spoke into the mouthpiece of his headset, "Since we can't land or go back, why don't we use the flying time to have a look at Mustang while we wait for the wind to abate?"

It was Chaudrai who responded first, "I think in view of our predicament we had better stay close to the mouth of the gorge so that if there is a temporary respite we can make a dash for Jomsom."

Thurston could not fault this argument, but he was not ready to give up. He was over the Mustang plain eighty miles from the Tibetan border in an area that had only been seen by a handful of Westerners. Lo Manthang, the square walled medieval city which had changed little in 500 years was also a few minutes away and was now one of two places where a Westerner could hope to see one of the high altitude salt caravans.

"Isn't there a new emergency airstrip outside Lo Manthang?" He asked Jethwa to pass him the chart, but Jethwa had beaten him to it and was checking.

"I have already thought of the airstrip," said Choudrai. "Firstly, it is not commissioned and secondly, it is for emergencies only."

Thurston and Jethwa exchanged glances and neither spoke waiting for the point to dawn on Choudrai.

"OK," Chaudrai said finally, "This is a bit of an emergency – but if the strip is still not commissioned, we would not be insured if we make a mess of the landing."

Thurston spoke quietly, "true, but perhaps the insurers wouldn't be too overjoyed if we flew around until we ran out of fuel either!"

Chaudrai was no longer in the mood for flippancy. "It is alright for you Mr Thurston, you are not nine months away from your pension – if you need a pension."

Thurston sat back and considered the position then spoke into the mouthpiece again, "Look the wind is not going to drop in the next two hours – it never does before eleven a.m. If we go back we tear the wings off, and we can't land at Jomsom, so we have two hours when all we can do is fly."

Chaudrai thought about it. Jethwa looked at him hopefully. Finally Chaudrai said he would agree to fly north for half an hour.

Thurston threw a mental high-five, he knew that was long enough to reach Lo Manthang. He saw the now recovered Jethwa squeeze his fist in delight.

With the sun still low in the eastern sky the deep black fissures and the orange, yellow and purple desert colours were a photographers' dream. So were the fortified villages which perched on the promontories between the fissures. To the north, the white topped ridges, which denoted the Tibetan border, looked only a couple of miles away. Two white, perfectly symmetrical cones which looked like 2,000 feet sand tips each with a ruined fortification at its peak, loomed ahead.

# The Tissue Trail

At 9:50 a.m., just three miles in front of them, lay the perfectly square walled city of Lo Manthang. Streaming towards it was a black line of what looked like ants – coming in from the north. Thurston pointed towards it.

"Yak caravan," said Chaudrai, "bringing salt in from Tibet. You are very lucky to see that. It's very rare."

Thurston was more than prepared to believe he was lucky, but he was already wondering how to make sure that they landed on the emergency airstrip.

He need not have worried. Air traffic control told them that the gusts in the gorge were now consistently over 100 miles per hour and strengthening. Chaudrai told them he was considering using the Lo Manthang strip. The controller said he would relay that to Royal Nepal Head office.

Ten minutes later he came back, "I am told to tell you the answer is 'pilot's discretion.'"

Chaudrai's silence was enough to indicate his concern. Roughly translated in this situation this phrase meant, "your decision, your responsibility."

Chaudrai flew three slow, nose up, powered passes into wind, on each occasion looking for any signs of obstruction or that the landing strip was not complete. There did not seem to be any detritus or works or incomplete surface sections and on the fourth run he came in for the landing. The wind was fifteen degrees off the nose, but for the Otter it was no problem. Chaudrai landed with full flap and nose up in a slow powered descent. The landing was good and he came to rest in just over 200 yards. They had noticed the yaks and the local cattle running aimlessly in panic, unused to the noise of aircraft. The reaction of the city dwellers of Lo Manthang was different. They flooded out of the town in curiosity. Chaudrai spoke a bit of Tibetan and was able to make himself understood. He explained what had happened to an older man who showed some sign of being in authority. They would try to take-off later in the day. If the weather was still poor they might have to stay overnight and try again the following day. Thurston asked about the caravan. He was told that the yak caravan would camp outside the city – they would be arriving throughout the day.

Thurston spent the morning in the old city mostly built with their roofs at ground level and lowered walkways to escape the wind. He was fascinated by the old buildings though not as fascinated as the people were with him. With his modern outdoor gear he must have looked as if he came from another planet – assuming the concept of another planet was something they were familiar with. After a light midday meal of lentil and rice with two of the elders together with Chaudrai and Jethwa, Thurston wandered out of the city gate to watch the incoming yaks. Chaudrai, Jethwa, and the security officer, Pandeh watched with him.

"Why are you so interested?" Pandeh asked.

"It's just something that is unchanged over the last 1,000 years – and isn't going to be around much longer."

By four o'clock nearly half of the train had arrived, perhaps fifty yaks and the semi-nomadic Dolpo Pa were setting up camp. The leader was Harka Tensing – a surprisingly young man in his early forties with a wide grin, a deeply etched leather skinned face, slanted Tibetan eyes and a loosely wrapped grey turban which lay round his head rather than on top of it. Chaudrai did his best to translate, but although the Dolpo Pa spoke a form of Tibetan, it was a heavy dialect and Chaudrai found it hard going.

Thurston asked if Tensing would mind him taking photographs. Tensing did not understand so Thurston showed him the moving picture on the side of his video camera. First he showed the surrounding view of the mountains and the city. Then he pictured Chaudrai and Jethwa to familiarize them with the idea of seeing images of people. He knew that showing them pictures of themselves would be a bit of a shock.

He pointed the camera at Tensing and reversed the screen so that it too was facing forward. Tensing looked at the image on the screen, initially without comprehension, then slow recognition led to a smile – then an excited laugh followed by pointing at the image of himself he had only seen before in mountain streams.

Tensing invited them to join him in a drink of chang, a sort of alcoholic yogurt made from yak's milk. Most of what the Dolpo Pa used to survive came from their yaks – milk, meat, hides for shelter and hair for clothing. The chang tasted pretty foul, but improved as the alcohol anaesthetised the palate and the mood rose.

So did the ability to translate as the alcohol removed inhibition and Chaudrai became more used to the dialect. Thurston kept the camera running. He didn't want to miss a thing. Tensing told them that the route into Mustang was new. The caravans used to go down to Jumla, which was several days to the west and not so far south. He told them that the new route was not popular because it added three weeks to a trek which already took them away from their homes for five months of the year. But when the previous leader had tried to argue against the new route he had died suddenly. Nobody knew how. But nobody had argued after that.

Thurston asked Chaudrai to ask Tensing who the argument had been with.

Tensing appeared surprised at the question and had some difficulty getting Jethwa to understand the answer. Finally Jethwa turned to Thurston and told him that the problem was with the local Chinese administrator. He explained that the Chinese ran Tibet even in remote areas such as Lake Drabye where the caravan started and regulated the level of export of commodities such as salt, which had been the mainstay of the caravan for centuries. In recent years the salt export quotas had declined to a level where the viability of the yak caravans and the way of life of the semi-nomadic Dolpo Pa who operated them, had been threatened. The reason for the change of route was the addition of a new cargo – a vinegary liquid used in the manufacture of palm oil. The Nepalis had set up a new palm oil plant on the other side of the gorge. The Chinese had agreed to supply the raw material from Tibet using the caravan.

"Could they not find a more convenient way of sourcing the stuff?" asked Thurston. "Seems a bit extreme bringing it over the Himalayas."

It was Chaudrai who answered. "They could," he said, "but the Annapurna Conservation Area Project – a government sponsored operation – was keen to preserve the old ways of life, partly for the sake of the Dolpo Pa, and partly in the interests of developing tourism. They had just opened up Mustang and the opportunity to bring one of the old caravans into the area and help to preserve it at the same time was good business on both fronts."

Thurston remained puzzled, "Why would anybody want to kill the old leader if all we're talking about is vinegar and palm oil?"

Chaudrai wondered how to ask the question and took his time. When Tensing replied it was still inconclusive. "He was not sure that the previous leader had been killed as there was no sign of any injury. As to why the Chinese – if it was the Chinese – were so keen to have the new commodity brought into Mustang, he had no idea."

Thurston asked if he could examine the liquid they were talking about. Tensing seemed amused but good-naturedly spoke to one of his men who moved off into the darkness towards the loads which had been removed from the yaks for the night.

# The Tissue Trail

He returned with a one litre white plastic container which seemed incongruous amongst the salt sacks or phadsees which had served as containers for centuries.

Thurston examined the container but it was of little assistance as the text looked like Chinese. He asked if Tensing had any objection to him opening it. Tensing shrugged, it was not sealed in any way – just a screw cap. Thurston opened it and looked at the liquid. It was colourless and as Tensing had described there was a pungent vinegary smell. Inspector Pandeh joined in the inspection.

In the middle of the evening Thurston started to get an irritating cough and the start of a headache. Both got progressively worse and Thurston recognized the symptoms of acute mountain sickness. He had come from 2000 feet at Pokhara to 13,000 feet in less than a day and he was clearly not acclimatized. He knew that mountain sickness, otherwise known as altitude oedema, was a serious condition that could kill in twenty-four hours. The cause was a build up of retained fluid in the brain and the lungs. The build up in the brain caused an increasingly painful headache followed by coma and death. It is almost like the head blowing up.

A build up in the lungs caused an increasingly intractable cough leading to the production of white froth at the mouth – which turned pink as the condition deteriorated and coughing started to produce blood from the pulmonary mucosa. In the end, as one colourful medical writer had put it, "you drown in your own blood and sputum!" The normal solution was to lose altitude as rapidly as possible. In most situations this was not a problem – just walk back down the mountain. However that was not an option when camping outside Lo Manthang on a 13,000 foot plateau with a three-day trek from the nearest point where the plateau began to descend.

The Otter would have been an option if the Kali Gandaki Gorge had been open for business, but in its present condition the only alternative it offered was to stay put and wait for his head to blow up or to drown in his own sputum or have the Otter's wings torn off and be smashed to a pulp in the bottom of the gorge. Stupidly, he had not brought the drug which might have been some use in achieving some relief – acetazolamide. It was a classic element of the mountain sickness syndrome that its victims were often the young or the fit who thought that it could not happen to them.

Thurston did have a slightly better excuse – that being stranded at 13,000 feet outside the ancient walls of a medieval Himalayan city, drinking alcoholic yogurt with a bunch of Tibetan nomads surrounded by several hundred high altitude, malodorous, long haired yaks – had not actually been in his day plan.

He told Chaudrai and Jethwa what was happening and that he would turn in and be ready hopefully for an early departure at first light the following morning. Meanwhile, Tensing had despatched one of his men into the darkness who had returned with a small leather bottle of a sweet and sour black liquid, which Tensing explained was a medicine of herbal origin and might help.

Help it certainly did, if not quite in the way intended. He lay on a yak hide in a tent supplied by Tensing and within ten minutes was floating some feet above the ground and drifting off into a deep hallucinogenic sleep.

### *22nd April 2001*

When he woke, the sky was just beginning to lighten. His head still ached, but whether it was AMS or a hangover he wasn't sure. Most of the camp was on the move, but there was no sign of Jethwa or Chaudrai or Inspector Pandeh. Thurston was coughing, but no worse than the previous evening. It would still be good medicine to lose altitude as quickly as possible.

They were preparing the Otter for take-off when a small party appeared from the gates of the city carrying what looked like a small bed or stretcher. They were carrying a sick child, a girl of about eleven. By sign language and Jethwa's bit of Tibetan, they explained that the girl had difficulty breathing and was getting worse. She was now so weak that unless something was done they did not think she would survive. Would they take her to a doctor through the gorge? Chaudrai looked at Thurston, "It's your charter – it's your decision. There is no aviation reason why we should not take her out."

Thurston had looked at the girl and although not a medic he could see was in poor condition with some sort of infection, which was way beyond tribal remedies. Inspector Pandeh watched, but did not interfere.

"The only problem," he said, "is that the violence of the gorge and the extra altitude we need to take-off from here might do her more harm than good. On the other hand if she stays here," he shrugged, "she stands virtually no chance. We'll take her."

He collapsed into a fit of coughing – the violence of the resulting movement caused havoc to his headache. When the attack had passed he smiled thinly at Chaudrai and told him they had better get him out in the not too distant future.

Fifteen minutes later, with an amazed audience of Tibetan faces – both the city dwellers of Lo Manthang and the Dolpo Pa yak herders, the twin Otter started up and taxied slowly back to the downwind end of the strip then turned 180 degrees into the wind to do its final take-off checks. Chaudrai checked with the control tower at Jomsom who told him the wind was still pretty strong, but not as bad as the previous day.

The yaks – not the easiest of beasts to control at the best of times – had taken fright at the sound of the engine noise and were running in all directions. Tensing looked remarkably unconcerned. Presumably he took the view that there was nowhere for the yaks to go and that they would be back. Or perhaps Tensing and his men, who had never seen an airplane before, were so enthralled at the prospect of watching them take-off that they would just worry about the yaks later.

The airstrip seemed impossibly short, but they checked the manual and had paced out the length of it the previous day. It was tight, but sufficient. With brakes on, Chaudrai ran the Otter up to full power then released. Driving into the strong wind they were clear of the runway with fifty yards still to run.

The Otter made a shallow climb, initially to 500 feet above the ground, partly to avoid any further adverse altitude effect on either Thurston or the girl and partly because the altitude of the plateau at 13,000 feet was close to the official operating ceiling of the non-pressurized Otter. It was fifteen minutes before the plateau started to descend and Choudrai could start a gradual descent into the Kali Gandaki Gorge.

The flight through the gorge was not as bad as their flight north into Mustang, but this time they were all in far worse physical condition. Thurston in particular was in poor shape, passing in and out of consciousness. Jethwa tried to turn back occasionally from the cockpit to comfort the young girl who was strapped into the seat just behind him, but in the gorge his full attention was needed trying to help Choudrai keep the Otter stable. The violent upward kick when they hit an upward spiral of wind followed by an immediate and sickening drop back into an air pocket threatened to leave the Otter in an attitude from which a stall could not be prevented. If that happened in these conditions, normal stall recovery would be difficult. They had to keep the Otter as straight and level as possible.

But with the wind coming from the south straight at them it was slower progress than it had been going north. Chaudrai and Jethwa were becoming physically weak trying to hold the column steady. If they did not get through it soon they would not be able to fight the movement. The exit did not seem to be any closer. The two pilots tried not to look at each other – neither wanting to admit to the other they were in trouble. But Thurston had been improving slowly as the Otter had fought its way south gradually losing altitude. He forced himself into the cockpit doorway against the motion of the airplane and jammed himself into position. He reached forward grabbing both port and starboard control columns just below the cross tees, and the Otter slowly fought its way out over the Indian Plain.

The Mustang girl was looking at Thurston through narrow Tibetan eyes – still frightened, but now calm. Thurston reached out and touched her forehead. "Don't worry, not all flying is quite as rough as that!" He hoped the tone of his voice communicated something of what he was trying to say.

Choudrai and Jethwa brought the Otter in to land at Pokhara in warm early morning sun. The news had soon got round that there was an Otter fighting its way through the gorge in wing ripping winds carrying a dying mountain girl and a substantial crowd had turned out to see if they would make it. There had been a cheer when the distant black speck had appeared in the northwest against the grey slopes of the lower levels of the Annapurnas.

The pilots had been cheered again when they appeared somewhat shakily from the cockpit. But the press had reserved their attention for the western businessman who had paid a fortune, so it was said, to fly through the gorge and who was now trying to bring a dying girl back through it in suicidal conditions. There was also a rumour that Thurston was in trouble with Nepali security for landing in a restricted area without clearance.

The girl was carried from the Otter by airport staff. Thurston insisted on staying on his feet, but needed considerable assistance. The press insisted on taking shots of the two together. Both were then taken to the newly opened International Clinic despite Thurston's protests that he was recovering quickly.

Thurston thanked Choudrai and Jethwa for their incredible effort. Choudrai looked subdued. Thurston told him to let him know if he needed any help. It was Thurston's charter and Choudrai had had official approval to make the flight through the gorge. It was not his fault that conditions had deteriorated further. Choudrai smiled weakly and said that he would bear Thurston's offer in mind. Thurston had one last question which was to ask how he could find the palm oil plant Tensing had referred to. Choudrai told him to contact the Annapurna Conservation Area Project Office – the slight trim figure then went off to the Royal Nepal Office accompanied by two airline executives.

Inspector Pandeh was talking to two other security officers who had appeared from the terminal, and gesturing at intervals towards Thurston.

The attendants from the International Clinic had finally persuaded him to sit in a wheelchair to be taken to the taxi, which they had organized to transport him to the clinic - the girl had already been taken. But before he was transferred to the car he was told by the two Nepali security police, who had been talking to Pandeh, that he would be required to speak to them before leaving Pokhara and, despite his protests, his passport was confiscated. Thurston asked to use a telephone to contact the British Consulate in Pokhara. He was told it would be easier from the clinic. He insisted on noting the identification details of the two security officers.

Thurston was then taken to the International Clinic on the shores of Lake Phewa – followed by the local press – and was in bed being cared for by Nepali nurses before ten a.m. It had already been a long day.

## 23rd April 2001

Thurston continued to recover steadily, as was normal with such cases on return to normal altitude. By lunchtime, he was out of bed and moving about freely and arguing about how quickly he could see the security police and leave Pokhara. He was told he would be seen the following morning. The doctor asked him to stay at the hospital overnight for final observation, but he was free to move about during the afternoon. He did not ask whether that meant within the grounds of the clinic – he would argue about that later. Right now he had half a day to kill and he might as well try to find the palm oil plant. He started by casually asking the medical staff if they knew anything about a new palm oil plant which the caravan operators had told him they were supplying. He was lucky. One of the nurses knew where it was – about four miles from Pokhara outside a village called Naudhara.

# The Tissue Trail

His next action was to telephone the British Consulate to report that he had had his passport confiscated by Nepali security. The consulate knew of his case – apparently it was all over the local newspapers, *"British Businessman Rescues Dying Mountain Girl"* – the article also reported his difficulties with the security services.

He told one of the nurses he was going for a walk omitting to say how far, but within minutes he was enjoying the warmth of the midday sun amongst the crowds of trekkers and other tourists who were milling about in the mini "trekkers riviera" alongside Lake Phewa. It was a colourful area of bars and cafes and stalls selling everything from anoraks, sweaters, shorts, boots, rucksacks ropes and ice axes to local tourist goods, carpets, dolls, books and postcards. He found a three-wheeled taxi and haggled with the driver over the return fare to Naudhara, finishing at a third of the initial asking price.

The taxi left the tourist area and made its way initially through the main part of the town which centred on a wide street with every conceivable form of produce piled in front of open fronted workshops from wooden planks for building, fruit stalls with melons and oranges, bicycle parts, pots and pans and meat hanging in the open to the pleasure of the local insect population. Behind the bustling scene the distinctive shape of Fishtail towered over the town in a haze of midday warmth. Behind Fishtail the main massif of the Annapurnas was just visible.

He headed northwest towards Sarankot, a high point on the end of a ridge reached by trekkers after a stiff forty-minute climb and popular as an early morning viewing point. The ridge ran away from Sarankot to the west. Three miles along the ridge, the village of Naudhara stretched in a double row of wooden dwellings either side of the dust track, which led out to the popular trekking trails up to Ghorapani and to the Kali Gandaki Gorge. The nurse had told him the palm oil plant was at the far end of the village a little way off the ridge to the north – on the trail to a village called Damphus. It was hidden in a secluded area of trees.

As the taxi driver dropped him at the end of the village of Naudhara, he noticed a Nepali sitting astride a motor scooter some two hundred yards behind them apparently not going anywhere and looking as if he had just stopped.

He had to walk about 400 yards before he found the Damphus trail and set off down it towards a band of trees some 200 feet below. The plant was not difficult to find lying behind a newly constructed fence with an open gate and a sign announcing that the plant had been constructed under the auspices of the Annapurna Conservation Area Project and funded by the Canadian Overseas Aid programme. There were three men working at the plant which consisted of a single story corrugated iron roofed building in which the manufacturing process took place, plus a selection of small outbuildings each marked with the name of materials and chemicals used in the process. These included the locally grown raw palm kernels from which the oil was extracted.

One of the operators came over to him, a Tibetan looking man in his early forties in a rough blue shirt and long "skirt" which had once been white, wrapped around his waist. His feet were bare. He asked if he could help. Thurston said he was here out of curiosity having run into the caravan in Mustang which was bringing in one of the intermediates. The Tibetan, unusually, was not of particularly friendly disposition and told him visitors were not encouraged as it distracted the workforce. The other two men "in the workforce," also Tibetan in appearance, did not seem particularly distracted, but he did not think getting into an argument was likely to help.

Thurston shrugged and said he had seen most of what there was to see, but there was one favour the man could do for him on his way out – and that was to show him the containers which the caravan brought in. The man saw no harm in this and led Thurston over to a low hut and opened the door. He picked up one of the white one litre plastic containers and showed it to Thurston who took it from him and examined it. It was the same as he had seen outside Lo Manthang with the same Chinese looking script. Inside the shed, Thurston wondered if a couple of 100 rupee notes would sweeten the man's disposition. It seemed to do the trick – not surprisingly, as 200 rupees may only have been three pounds or about five dollars, in Nepali it was the equivalent of $20 or $30.

Thurston asked what the liquid was and the Tibetan replied that he did not know the name in English, but it was used in many processes. Thurston asked if all of the delivery was used in manufacturing palm oil or if it could be used for anything else. The operator hesitated, then told him that as far as he knew it was all used to make palm oil except a small part of it was taken from time to time to be tested.

"Tested?" Thurston queried.

"Tested for quality," the Tibetan told him.

"Who does the testing?" Thurston asked, still examining the container.

"It is tested at the pharmacy at the International Clinic," the Nepali answered, showing increasing signs of discomfort at Thurston's inquisitiveness. That discomfort increased further when a more senior man appeared and immediately remonstrated with him, clearly indicating his unhappiness with Thurston's presence.

Thurston took the hint and thanked the man who had helped him and headed for the gate. The senior man followed and made a point of closing and locking the gate behind him.

Thurston had satisfied his natural curiosity and seen the end result of Tensing's high altitude salt caravan. Now he had to get back to the clinic and explain how he had not understood that "allowed out for a walk" meant a casual saunter around the immediate vicinity of the building. Then he could turn his attention to Nepali security.

He climbed back to the ridge road and back to the waiting taxi. He stood by the door pretending to be looking for something in his pocket, but in fact was looking around for the motorcyclist who had stopped behind him when he arrived. There was no sign of the motorcyclist, but the taxi had only been underway for thirty seconds before Thurston saw him in the wing mirror. Initially, the motorcyclist stayed well back, but as they got closer to Pokhara and the traffic built up he got closer. When they reached the clinic there was no sign of him.

He was greeted by the expected questions as to where he had been for his short walk and by "an invitation" from Nepali security to be at the Central Police Office at 11:00 a.m. the following morning.

Thurston asked if he could see the girl from Lo Manthang and also the pharmacy. The girl had an operation to remove excess fluid from her lungs that afternoon and was coming round from the anaesthetic. He stayed with her for a few minutes but she was barely conscious and, not surprisingly, showed little sign of recognition. He was told she should now make a full recovery, but would have died without intervention. He asked how she would get back to Lo Manthang. The doctor told him they would fly her back to Jomsom and she would be taken back by mule from there.

He asked a nurse to take him to the pharmacy which she did, but found the door shut. She knocked and a Nepali in a white coat came to the door and partially opened it. She spoke to him and turned back to indicate she had Thurston with her. There certainly seemed to be a problem and the second worker, more Tibetan-looking, came to the door and opened it a few degrees further. The nurse again indicated Thurston, but the Tibetan shook his head and the door was closed.

In the few seconds that the door had been open, he had seen the expected small room with the usual shelves of medicines and a dispensing and liquid preparation area. When it had been opened a few degrees further he had caught a glimpse of the Tibetan taking a few drops of liquid from one of the commodity containers carried by the caravan.

"I'm sorry," the nurse smiled. "They were in the middle of a difficult operation and did not want to be interrupted."

"No problem," Thurston said. "I saw what I came to see."

Back at his bedroom the staff had brought him a local newspaper, and as he waited for his evening meal he skimmed through it and stopped at an article headed:

### THIRD POKHARA TREKKER ARRESTED IN SINGAPORE

*Following close on the heels of the arrest of two American women earlier in the week, a third woman, this time French, 24 year-old Francoise Dumas, was arrested at Singapore's Changi Airport carrying an illegal substance. She too had been trekking on the Jomsom trail, a popular trek for travellers with limited time. With three almost identical arrests in such a short space of time the authorities in Pokhara are showing concern as all three went straight on to Singapore changing at Kathmandu, but without leaving the airport – suggesting that the illegal substance was picked up in the Pokhara area.*

Again Thurston didn't think much more of the item except to think that suddenly Pokhara was becoming a place to avoid.

### Pokhara Police and Security Office
### 24th April 2001

The following morning Thurston paid his bill and left and took a taxi to the Police and Security office.

The interview room had seen better days with green gloss finish paint,

71

where there was any paint – the rest was broken plaster and in some areas bare brick. A collection of seats included a high backed chair which twenty years ago might have been described as "executive," it had at one time been padded. In addition there were three wooden chairs of varied design and origin all of which had seen long service.

Three men were standing when he entered. Two were in uniform and one in a western style suit. The older of the two policemen, Thurston estimated him to be in his fifties, asked Thurston to sit. The younger policeman, sporting a light moustache and thin-rimmed glasses and looking more like a lawyer, spent the entire meeting taking notes.

The man in civilian clothes, also in his fifties, was heavily set with black heavy framed glasses and black, well-greased hair swept straight back. There was a touch of grey at the temples. Thurston knew he had seen him before and it took a few seconds to recall the man who had been conversing with the station manager after his first abortive attempt to charter an Otter from Pokhara. To Thurston's surprise it was the man in civilian clothes who took the executive chair and took charge of the meeting. He introduced the two uniformed men as security police, although Thurston didn't catch their names, and himself as Major Jha. His "British educated" voice and bearing gave the impression of a man of experience and competence.

"Thank you for your time Mr Thurston, we won't keep you any longer than necessary. I am head of the Annapurna Conservation Area Project, a government organization which, put simply, was set up to balance management and conservation of natural resources in the Annapurna and Mustang area and the impact of tourism. The reason for this meeting is, shall we say, curiosity about someone wanting to spend a small fortune to fly in what most people would consider to be near suicidal conditions to get into Mustang which, as you know, is a restricted area."

Thurston was aware that Mustang had been a "lost kingdom" for centuries and lying to the north of the Himalayan chain, although politically part of Nepal, it was geographically and ethnically part of the Tibetan Plateau and ethnically part of Tibet. He had heard that Mustang's closure in recent years had been in some way tied into Tibetan resistance to China's "occupation" and even that there had been some CIA involvement. But he had never seen anything of substance to support that.

"So we would appreciate it if you would tell us what your interest is in this area?"

# The Tissue Trail

Thurston responded openly enough, he had nothing to hide.

"I am primarily a businessman, but my other main interest is photographing dramatic landscapes. I sell my best photographs to people like *National Geographic* when I can, but as I run my own business, chances to get into a remote country these days are pretty limited. I am actually on my way to Singapore and diverted to Nepal for four days to try to find some way of reaching Mustang."

"Mustang is an arid plateau," said Jha. "Stopping off to take photographs of the Himalaya I understand, but why anybody would want to pay $1500 an hour to photograph a featureless desert isn't quite so obvious!"

"You understate the attractions of Mustang, Major Jha. First you have to fly through the world's deepest chasm – the Kali Gandaki – with the peaks of the Annapurnas and Dhaulagiri towering above you. Then up onto the edge of the Tibetan Plateau and possibly catch a glimpse of the square walled medieval city of Lo Manthang..."

"But you were on a flight to Jomsom – that only takes you through to the far end of the gorge not far enough to have any chance of seeing Lo Manthang."

"Not on the commercial flight," agreed Thurston. "I had no idea how I would get beyond Jomsom, but I had heard it was possible to charter an Otter, someone I know had done just that two or three years ago. That seemed to be one way of flying further north and getting closer to Lo Manthang."

"Had you checked with the airline that you were covered to enter Mustang?"

Thurston was now becoming curious himself at the level of detail in the questioning.

"No," he replied slowly. "As I wasn't expecting to land it didn't arise."

Jha switched his line of questioning. "How did you hear of the Kali Gandaki Gorge and Lo Manthang? Not exactly Sunday supplement material." Jha confirmed again his familiarity with things British.

"No, it isn't," replied Thurston. "But it is *National Geographic* material. I've come across it several times. The first time must have been six or seven years ago, but this is the first time I've been in the area since then with a few days to spare."

Jha again switched, "When you managed to get through the gorge and the weather then started to deteriorate further why did you fly up to the border with Tibet instead of the safer option of staying closer to Jomsom?"

Thurston answered that the new airstrip outside Lo Manthang was the safer option.

"Even though it was not officially commissioned?" persisted Jha. "How could the crew be sure they could land on it?"

"Which would you have chosen – a nearly finished runway – or risking winds which could tear your wings off?"

His interrogator did not answer the question.

"Mr Thurston, you tried to do this fairly recently," he checked an entry in a beige file.

"Yes," replied Thurston.

"So this sight-seeing must be pretty important to you?"

"I think I have told you why I have tried to get into this area – and I don't usually give up easily."

The line of questioning changed again.

"You met the operators of the Dolpo caravan?"

Thurston affirmed.

"What did you discuss?"

"They talked about the new route and complained about its extra length."

"Anything else?"

"They mentioned the reduction in salt quotas and the introduction of the new commodity."

"Did they tell you what it was?"

"They showed it to me – a clear liquid in litre bottles – smelled of vinegar."

Again the questioning changed tack.

"Why did you go to the palm oil plant yesterday, Mr Thurston?"

So he had been followed. In some ways he supposed that was a relief that he had been followed by official security.

"I did not have much to do and I was interested to see the end point of Tensing's efforts. Just curiosity."

"So, in summary, you spend $1,500 an hour to fly through the Kali Gandaki Gorge in wind conditions that were so bad that commercial flying had been suspended. Then you make an unauthorized, in fact illegal, landing in Mustang. Finally you take the trouble to locate the destination of a common chemical intermediate. What are you looking for, Mr Thurston? And why does it matter so much?"

Thurston sighed and looked at him, "I've explained all that." He was finding it difficult to hide his growing irritation. Why couldn't they simply give him a telling off for the unauthorized landing or even give him a fine and have done with it?

"Do you mind telling me what this is all about?" he asked.

"We will ask the questions, Mr Thurston." The heavy-set Nepali leaned forward and picked up the file from the table.

For some time Jha said nothing as he scanned the contents of the file before finally extracting his passport. "Mr Thurston, we are not satisfied that you are telling us everything," he flicked through the pages of the passport then detached the visa. "I am returning your passport with your visa endorsed to limit your stay until seventy-two hours from now. In the meantime, please report to a police station or security office each day you remain here and have your visa stamped at each reporting point. Failure to do so will result in a further fine and difficulty in obtaining a visa to visit Nepal in future."

Thurston asked them to stamp his visa for today as he would be leaving Nepal the following morning. He was being deported and they weren't going to tell him why.

He took the first flight back to Kathmandu and spent the evening at his hotel, the quaintly named Yak and Yeti, checking over his video records. And wondering what exactly the problem was in Mustang.

Whatever it was it was not over yet. He knew he was being followed as he travelled back to Kathmandu and to the airport the following morning and whoever it was made little or no attempt to make himself other than pretty obvious.

# CHAPTER SIX
## *The Elegant Woman*

*25th April 2001*

The following morning Thurston took a cab to Tribhuvan International Airport early to make sure he had time to register with the security police. The same Nepali in a dark brown kaftan and pale loosely bound head turban jumped into the next taxi and followed him into the airport.

The security officer took his details with no comment then stamped his passport and returned it to him. Thurston made his way to the check-in desk and checked in. His shadow was still entirely obvious. At customs, the officer checked his name on a screen then looked though his passport and countersigned the daily reporting order for a second time and added a stamp. Thurston then headed for the first class lounge.

Half an hour before the flight was called the door to the lounge door opened and an exquisitely elegant woman in an expensively cut, navy blue suit entered. Few male heads did not turn to glance at her. She checked in at the desk where she seemed to be known. The lounge was busy and she picked her way to a seat a short distance from Thurston, sat down crossing her long legs, placed her business case alongside her and opened up a newspaper. She looked over the front page and looked directly at Thurston catching him looking at her directly. Before he had even had time to start to think about how to react, she had returned her attention to the newspaper.

A short time later a member of the Royal Nepal Airlines staff came in, came over to her, bent down and spoke to her quietly. She stood up to follow the steward, but stopped and looked back at Thurston and turned the front of her newspaper towards him. "Nice move!" she said, "You saved her life."

She smiled and turned to follow the steward out of the lounge with a movement no businesswoman, if that is what she was, had any right to employ.

Shortly after, the flight was called and Thurston made his way and was ushered to his seat. The elegant woman had already been seated and was sipping sparkling water. It was clear the seat next to her was "unavailable" and a "large gentleman," who did not look like a regular first class traveller, was seated on the aisle seat in the row behind her.

On arrival at Singapore, she received the same royal treatment. She was led to the exit before the rest of the first class passengers and was then whisked away in an electric courtesy vehicle. On the way out of the cabin Thurston smiled at the hostess and asked who the illustrious guest was. She smiled back, but told him they were not allowed to divulge such information. Thurston found this somewhere between frustrating and irritating. He wanted to know who she was, why she was so exclusively treated and why she seemingly made a point of indicating she recognized him from the photograph on the front of the newspaper. Now, it appeared, he would never know. In fact he wondered later – she had spent such a short time in the first-class lounge, why had she come into the lounge at all?

Thurston joined the immigration line, but there was no sign of the woman – her fast track treatment was obviously continuing. As he waited, he read the copy of yesterday's *Straits Times* until his attention was drawn to a disturbance ahead of him. At first he thought it was an argument, but the noise turned out to be laughter rather than anger and seemed to centre on four female backpackers and one in particular, a tall attractive red-head whose antics were amusing the crowd around her. Whatever they were up to, the fun and games continued until they were called to the desk a minute or two ahead of him.

Thurston finally reached the desk himself. He did not normally have any trouble with his passport. It was well stamped, not so much because of his business travel, but because of his diversions and excursions to out of the way destinations. However, this time the immigration officer took more of an interest.

"You are travelling to Singapore from London, but you go via Kathmandu?"

Thurston was beginning to wish he had stayed at home and read a book.

# The Tissue Trail

"Yes, I had a few days to spare and Kathmandu is pretty much on the way – and no extra cost."

"You have two security office stamps. Why is that?"

"I was forced to make an emergency landing and the place where the aircraft landed was restricted, and I didn't have official permission to be there."

"Wait a minute please," the officer said, and picked up the telephone.

A more senior officer appeared and went through the same questions again before asking why Thurston was in Singapore.

"I am working on a clinical trial with Dr Aw Swee Lim at the Singapore medical school."

"How long are you here for?"

"I expect to be here for about two weeks, it depends how quickly we can get through the workload."

This seemed to satisfy them. Aw Swee Lim was obviously well known and in any event Thurston's story could easily be checked.

"Where are you staying?" asked the senior officer.

"Raffles," said Thurston.

His passport was handed back to him and he moved on to baggage reclaim. Thurston picked up his bags and started to walk through customs. At the far end of the hall he saw three of the four women who had been amusing other passengers in the immigration queue, but not the red-head. As he neared them, the red-head appeared from a side office, ushered by two female police officers. She was ashen faced, tears streamed down her already tear stained face, arms behind her as if she had been handcuffed. Her three friends now also in tears were trying to shout to her to ask what had happened, but they were being pushed out of the way by another officer who had come to the scene. As Thurston drew alongside the red-head, she collapsed and virtually fell into his arms. He caught her and lifted her, resting her head on his shoulder, then carried her back into the office from which he had just seen her emerge followed by the two policewomen.

Two Malay officers and a blonde western woman were seated. A polythene slip containing a white powder and a short bladed knife lay on the table. It did not need rocket science to work out what had happened. As he lowered her into a chair he said, "There is no way this woman knew she was carrying. She was the life and soul of the party."

The blonde woman cut him short coldly, "Thank you for your opinion, but you are in a restricted area. Please leave immediately." He noticed she spoke with a North American accent and that she was wearing a lapel badge. He made a point of reading it.

"Stephanie D'Aunay – Drug Liaison."

Just inside the exit to the arrivals hall the red-head's three friends were still waiting in a distressed state. Still in tears they stopped him and asked if he could tell them what was happening. He tried to soften what he had to tell them by saying that it seemed unlikely to him that someone who was in such high spirits could possibly have been worried about being caught with anything illegal, but something had been found hidden in a doll.

The three women protested, all talking at the same time. She had bought that doll in a refugee shop, how could anything have been hidden in that? Thurston said he couldn't answer that, but his advice was that their friend was going to be taken into custody and they should continue with their arrangements and contact the British Consulate tomorrow. By then they should have been informed of the intentions of the authorities.

While the women stood bemused and tearfully wondered what to do, two customs officers had approached Thurston and were now standing in front of him.

"Mr Thurston, we would like you to return to the customs area to answer one or two more questions."

He wondered if they could do this, but he was still technically in the customs area, and he didn't fancy leaving the airport with the Singapore police on his tail. He was escorted back to an office where the blonde Stephanie D'Aunay was sitting alone looking down at an A4 sheet of paper, which it seemed she had just been given.

She looked up. "Sit down, Mr Thurston." He obliged, slowly, noting again her North American accent.

"Your passport?" she held out her open hand.

She carefully studied every page of his passport making it clear she had no intention of hurrying and somehow communicated she enjoyed her position of control.

There was not a lot he could do, and she knew it.

Finally, she looked up.

"What do you do, Mr Thurston?"

"I carry out research projects for pharmaceutical companies."

"Don't they have research facilities of their own?"

"Yes, but there are areas they don't cover."

She let that point go, "So, you are an expert on drugs?"

"Noting your line of business," he made a point of looking at her lapel badge, "I would put that as 'medicines.'" His attempt to lighten the proceedings fell on stony ground.

She turned to his passport, "Your passport shows unusual travel patterns, Mr Thurston."

"Oh? How?" he asked.

"You visit places for one or two days that most people wouldn't contemplate for less than one or two weeks," she listed a variety of places, from Tokyo to San Francisco and Malta to Zimbabwe. He told her that most of them were visits to medical conferences which were key parts of his job. Medical conferences usually lasted for three or four days, he told her, but he would only stay for sessions which related specifically to his interests.

"Does that apply to your one day in Zimbabwe?"

"That was a bit different. I had a twelve hour holdover between flights in Johannesburg and managed to get a quick return flight and grab a few minutes at Victoria Falls."

"A few minutes?" her tone was challenging.

"What would you do with twelve hours at Jan Smutz Airport – get slowly smashed or take the chance of seeing one of the world's most dramatic natural sights even if only for a few minutes?" he countered.

She had moved on from Zimbabwe in his passport and had her fingers marking two pages.

"Perhaps you would tell me about two trips you made in the same year to the Afghan/Pakistan and the Thai/Laos borders?"

Thurston immediately recognized the link she would see between the two.

"I know they are both heroin growing areas," he said, "which for obvious reasons would interest you – but in my case both were photographic trips. I was in northern Thailand photographing the Hill Tribes and in Pakistan photographing the North West Frontier."

The next question took a different tack, "When did you first meet Catherine Miller?"

"Who? Sorry?"

She looked at him waiting for an answer. He didn't add anything.

"Mr Thurston, I don't think you realize the seriousness of your position."

He looked at her with genuine lack of understanding.

"Do you know what a mule is, Mr Thurston – apart from the obvious?"

"Not in this context, no I don't," he said.

"When traffickers move drugs by air there are normally three or more carriers or mules on the same flight. One of the traffickers travels on the same flight to keep an eye on the mules," she waited for this to sink in, "and on arrival, to make sure the mules do not run into trouble...or go astray."

"So, Catherine Miller is the backpacker I just carried into your office?"

"So may I repeat my question. When did you first meet her?"

"I repeat my answer. I have never heard of Catherine Miller never mind met her until a few minutes ago. The first time I saw her was in the queue for immigration – as I mentioned when I brought her into your office she was in high spirits and amusing other passengers around her."

"And you are telling me that is the first time you have ever seen her?"

"Yes, that is what I am telling you."

"Despite the fact you have just arrived on the same flight from Kathmandu to Singapore – and were on the same flight as Miller from Pokhara to Kathmandu?" She waited again. "And in the same week as three other arrests of young women coming in from the same area of Nepal carrying an illegal substance which looks to be from the same source."

This time Thurston frowned.

"And it was Pokhara where she bought the item that contained the substance." Again a pause.

"I was not aware of any of that, but I repeat I have never met Catherine Miller before."

Stephanie D'Aunay made notes on the paper in front of her and then looked up.

"How long are you staying in Singapore, Mr Thurston and what are you doing here?"

"I'm here for about two weeks working with Professor Aw Swee Lim at..."

"I know who Professor Aw is," she cut him off. "You realize there is enough here for me to detain you, Mr Thurston?"

Thurston's reaction was a mixture of annoyance and apprehension. He had not previously been on the wrong side of the law beyond a couple of speeding tickets.

"But if you are working with Professor Aw that might help."

She got up and walked into the next-door office where, a few seconds later, he could hear her on the phone. The conversation was relatively brief, and she returned in less than a minute.

"We will need to be able to contact you, Mr Thurston."

So he wasn't going to be detained. "I'm staying at Raffles where you can leave messages, and you can reach me anytime via Professor Aw."

"Heroin trafficking is treated seriously here, Mr Thurston. If you stay here any length of time you will find out just how seriously." She picked up her notes, placed them in her briefcase and rose to her feet. "Alright, Mr Thurston. You are free to go." Again she communicated her enjoyment of dismissing him. It crossed his mind that he would like to cross swords with her on more equal terms.

He cleared the customs area and walked to the taxi rank deep in thought. He could see why his movements between Pokhara and Singapore were arousing interest in view of the heroin arrests. But he couldn't understand why his excursion into Mustang had caused such a reaction. The "stay at home and read a book" thought crossed his mind again. But the image he found difficult to shake as he took a taxi to his hotel was of the sobbing, disbelieving distress of Catherine Miller.

Thurston checked into his hotel and telephoned Aw Swee Lim to confirm that he had arrived. Aw suggested that he would come by the hotel on his way home around eight p.m. to welcome Thurston to Singapore and asked Thurston if he would be ready to start work the following morning. Thurston appreciated Aw's offer to come and meet him on his own time, but declined the suggestion. After the day he had had an early night was top on his agenda. He sat down and took a beer from the mini bar and turned the television to the local English news channel. Catherine Miller's arrest was the third item. After the factual report that this was the fourth arrest of young women coming into Singapore from the same area of Nepal, the reporter asked a police spokesman what the police were making of four similar arrests in such a short span of time.

His response was guarded, "We are not sure if they are connected yet or even if the women were carrying the same substance."

"But they all came from Pokhara and had all been trekking the same trail," the reporter persisted.

"We are aware of that, but it is too soon to draw conclusions."

It was clear the interviewer was not going to get anywhere and switched back to the studio with the parting shot, "Given Singapore's record in Class A drug cases, it is unlikely that this is the last that will be heard of the Catherine Miller case, not to mention the other three."

## 26th April 2001

The next morning, Thurston took a cab to the University Hospital and to Aw's office. There Aw introduced him to members of the team he had assembled to work on the trial. There was genuine enthusiasm for the project and appreciation for Thurston's agency's achievement in finding a novel way forward with Imperial's drug when the "legions of researchers" at Imperial had failed. The rest of the day was spent going over the trial protocols and finalizing reporting procedures.

By close of day, the exertions of recent days were catching up with him, and he told Aw he would go back to the hotel and have a quiet evening.

## 26th April 2001, evening

Back at the hotel, there were three messages for Thurston, two were from his office, but the third was different. It was a letter in an elegant and expensive envelope with an embossed logo in blue and gold on the reverse – "The Royal Bank of Canada."

"It was delivered by hand at lunchtime," the receptionist told him, "with a request to ensure that it was handed to you as soon as you came back to the hotel."

*Canada seems to be getting into everything at the moment*, he thought. He carefully opened the letter. It was typewritten.

> *National Bank of Canada*
> *Singapore*
> *26th April 2001*
>
> *Dear Mr Thurston,*
>
> *You do not know me although you might recognize me! I work for the above referenced bank and I am involved in my government's administration of the substantial aid program*

*which Canada provides to Nepal and includes initiatives under the auspices of the Annapurna Area Conservation Project. One of these could be prejudiced by the potential impact of the current spate of heroin arrests of young women, all of whom have been trekking in the Annapurna area. I am aware of your recent involvement in matters relating to this part of Nepal, and I believe I might be able to throw some light on some of the questions which must have been troubling you. Equally, your experiences and observations might well be of assistance to us in responding to the effects of the heroin trafficking. I am in Singapore for three days, and if your diary allows, I would like to meet, perhaps over an early evening drink. Might I suggest 7:00 p.m. in the Raffles Courtyard this evening or the same time tomorrow? If you are happy to meet, please contact me on my cell phone number at the foot of this letter or leave a message with Raffles reception.*

*Yours sincerely,*
*L. C. Chase*

He folded the letter thoughtfully, wondering how a bank had become aware of his involvement so quickly – and why.

Thurston checked his watch. It was five p.m. He decided to telephone the cell phone number at the bottom of the page and try for tonight. An early drink and early night suited him down to the ground.

There was no reply, so he left a voice message. Three minutes later there was a text message confirming receipt of his voicemail and confirming meeting in the courtyard bar at seven p.m.

Thurston freshened up and changed into a lightweight jacket and open neck shirt.

A few minutes before seven p.m., he made his way down to the courtyard bar. He picked up a *Straits Times* from reception on the way through. He took a seat at a table for two and started to read the lead article. Only then did it occur to him that they had not agreed any means of recognizing each other. He need not have worried.

The lead article in the *Times* was about the arrest of the fourth young backpacker, Catherine Miller, and the anticipated diplomatic outcry, which would follow the reaction to committal proceedings when it became clear that all of the arrested women were carrying more than fifteen grams of pure heroin, which triggered an automatic death penalty. He had his head down reading the article when he was aware of a stir as if something was happening – or someone of note had entered.

He was right. Few heads did not turn to look at the tall slim strikingly attractive, smartly dressed Caucasian woman who had entered from the other side of the courtyard. She had rich, shining dark hair pinned up above a slender neck, a sheer black business suit fitted her slender curves exquisitely. Highly polished black high heels and a ruby and diamond brooch at her throat completed the remarkable picture.

Even more remarkable was the fact that he had seen her before. It was the pampered woman who had come into the first class lounge at Kathmandu Airport – and left just as quickly. And who had seemingly made a point of letting him know she had recognized him from the front page of the newspaper. She walked or perhaps more accurately, glided towards him – but showed no sign of recognition. Perhaps he had been wrong that she had been checking him out over her newspaper in Kathmandu. She continued past him or so he thought, until a voice which could only be hers and from just behind him asked, "Mr Thurston, I presume?" He looked up in surprise, checking involuntarily that there was no one else close by she could have been talking to. He was not unused to attractive female company but what he had presumed to be near royalty was a couple of ranks above his normal station.

"L. C. Chase," she smiled. "A bit presumptuous of me to assume you would recognize me – my name is Lauren."

He felt as if he was being picked up by an extraordinarily refined and beautiful woman.

A hovering waiter held her chair as Thurston rose to greet her.

"What would you like to drink?" he asked.

"A sling?" she suggested. "But not from a tourist tank, I prefer the real thing."

Thurston nodded to the waiter, "Make that two."

The waiter departed.

"I'm Edward Thurston," he volunteered as she took her seat. "Nice to meet you."

"Yes, I know who you are," she smiled.

"And which particular dynasty do you hail from?" he asked.

"Oh, you mean the airport stuff? Oh, it's just charm and I suppose I'm not bad looking," she laughed.

"That isn't normally enough to get that sort of treatment – not to mention the heavyweight covering your rear – sorry, let me reword that– sitting behind you."

"OK," she conceded, "you're right. I've got two parts to my magic wand. Being attached to the Canadian Overseas Aid program, I get treated like a minister by my government when I'm travelling and when I arrive I'm seen as a source of financial assistance. So people have to be extra nice to me!" More seriously she said, "Nepal in particular is a major beneficiary of Canadian aid."

Despite all the references to Canada he registered her North American accent for the first time. It was barely noticeable. She took an elegant sip from the sling. "So, I've told you how I get spoiled, what about you – it sounds as if life doesn't treat you quite so generously."

"Well actually that's not the case, in fact very much the opposite. What the fates managed to dish up in Mustang was pretty damned good."

He told her about the Mustang trip, chartering the Otter as the only way of getting a glimpse of the old city of Lo Manthang, then being forced to land and running into an incoming salt caravan.

"The odds of that happening just when I happened to be there must have been pretty astronomical."

"The dying girl must have had similar thoughts," Lauren grinned. "She's on her way out and a Brit turns up with the first airplane to land at Lo Manthang!"

He didn't comment, but wondered how she could have been aware of such detail.

"Yes, I suppose that was a bit of a break for her."

"So what went wrong?"

"I don't know," he replied. "I could understand being rapped over the knuckles for landing in Mustang without authorization, but not a three hour interrogation, then to be fined and virtually deported by the Internal Security Service."

"Anything else?"

"Well I don't know if it is connected, but I was given a pretty rough ride by the immigration and customs people here – one of them was a compatriot of yours: Stephanie D'Aunay."

Again she smiled, "Oh don't mind Steph, she's just come through a very nasty divorce – men are not exactly on the top on her list at the moment, unless she has the upper hand."

"You know her, too?"

"Yes. She is head of Canada's Drug Liaison team. She liaises with the drug intelligence services of other nations so that everybody can benefit from shared intelligence. She's part of the Canadian presence out here and we pretty much all know each other."

"Well she is certainly not the friendliest woman I've ever met. I even carried a woman who had fainted back into her office and she ungraciously kicked me out."

"Fainted?"

"She had just been arrested."

Lauren looked at him, "Why don't we eat if you are not doing anything? As I told you in the note I might even be able to throw some light on some of this!"

His quiet evening and early night was seemingly on its way out, but he didn't find the prospect too devastating.

He asked the hovering waiter for both food and wine menus. She suggested they split the bill and make the most of it. They agreed that she would order the white wine and he could do the red. She chose a Montrachet so he matched it with a Musigny.

"Nice," she said. "Two of the greatest and only twenty kilometres apart!"

She knew her way around.

"Now before I do some guessing about what might be behind your recent grilling, why don't you tell me what you do and what you are doing out here."

He did a quick mental count -- she was the fifth person in forty-eight hours to show a keen interest in his movements and what he was doing in Nepal and Singapore. This one was by far the most enjoyable. He described the Imperial project which had brought him to Singapore as a perfect example of what his company did. He described how Jaci had come across the answer by getting a family doctor to talk openly about his experiences with the drug.

"Is she good?" asked Lauren.

"A natural," replied Thurston. "Attractive, intelligent, three years out of college, but she tries to play down her looks and looks half her age – she wants to be recognized for what she is capable of not what she looks like – maybe a touch of pinky politics."

"Are you married?" she smiled. He paused – the first grey moment in their exchanges.

"I lost a long-term partner last year – died in a car crash."

"Sorry," said Lauren.

"Are you married?" he asked, switching away from the subject of Emily.

"No," she smiled. "I'm having too good a time to settle down."

"Isn't that sort of remark supposed to be a man thing?"

"Possibly," she said. "It must be something to do with my pinky politics."

The easy conversation continued over an excellent Caesar salad with pacific prawns which worked well with the Montrachet, followed by Tournedos Rossini which worked well with the Musigny. "I like to fit the food to the wine," Thurston had quipped as he savoured the Musigny. Neither wanted a sweet and as he slowly put down his glass she said, "Somebody's just given me a rather decent old Armagnac. Would you like to try it?"

"You keep pinching my lines."

"Well, just put it down to a bit more pinky politics. It can come in quite useful."

For the moment her theories regarding his recently acquired pariah status had assumed a lower priority. So had the guilt he should have felt while still mourning Emily– but this evening was taking on the feeling that he had stepped out of his previous life.

Her room, or rather suite of rooms, lived up to her "royal" billing. Everything about this woman was top drawer. She threw off her high-heeled shoes and asked him to open the Armangac and pour two glasses while she slipped into something a little less like she was going to a board meeting.

Lauren was one of those rare people who knew what she wanted and just collected it as she went along without a second thought – and she did it without the slightest risk of offense. Tonight it just suited her to be with him. He would worry about what lay behind it some other time.

The Armagnac was very, very good.

And so was she.

### 27th April 2001

It was a long night, but she was up and showering bright and early.

They ordered room service. Over orange juice, coffee and fruit she told him what she thought might be behind his various interrogations.

"I know a bit about this because one of the projects we – the Canadians – are providing funding for is the Annapurna Conservation Area Project."

"You mentioned that in your note. One of my interrogators in Pokhara was from ACAP."

"Do you remember his name?"

"Yes, unusual name – Jha."

She looked thoughtful but didn't take it any further.

"So how do you know Mr Jha – or was it a military title?"

"Major," she said. "He is pretty much in charge of ACAP which is why I know him. ACAP," she continued, "is a state sponsored operation set up to encourage tourism in the Annapurna region, but at the same time balance the effect of income from tourism against the impact on limited resources. For instance, anybody going into Mustang which as you now know is virtually a desert, has to pay a $75 fee and take all fuel requirements with them for the whole trip."

"But that's a ten-day trek in and out," he said.

"Unless you charter a nineteen seater airplane," she retorted.

"Don't you start!"

"One of the activities we have been funding is trying to keep the Himalayan salt caravans going."

He couldn't help casting an eye over the expensive silk suit, expensive sheer tights, Louis Vuitton high heeled shoes and $500 hairstyling and wondered how this apparition could be connected with one of the most basic human life forms in one of the remotest parts of the world and a nomadic tribe whose way of life had not changed for a thousand years.

"Why are you doing that?"

"Tibetan salt export quotas have been declining as the Chinese administration channels more of it back for 'internal' consumption." She emphasised the word *internal*, "and the caravans were finding it increasingly difficult to survive. ACAP suggested finding an alternative to salt to try to keep the caravans going partly as a means of preserving an ancient heritage and partly as a tourist attraction for the future."

"So that's why there was an ACAP representative at my inquisition."

"I assume so," she said. "Anyway, the new commodity is used in the manufacture of palm oil, hence the palm oil plant in Pokhara."

"I saw the containers," said Thurston. "But in a script I couldn't read."

She took a sip of orange juice. "Acetic anhydride," she said quietly.

He stopped in mid-chew – then swallowed.

"...Vinegary smell, colourless liquid – why didn't I think of that?... an acetylating agent."

She nodded slowly and waited.

"Used in a wide variety of chemical manufacturers."

She still waited.

"Including diamorphine hydrochloride?" he said.

"Yes," she said, "diamorphine hydrochloride – pure heroin."

He finished the piece of orange, taking in what she had just said.

"Which is why you are suddenly the target of everybody's curiosity – or suspicion if you prefer?"

"So you think somebody is diverting part of the shipment from the palm oil production and brewing up heroin?"

"Very early days – only five arrests, although they have all the hallmarks of the start of a new ring – and no sign of the production source. But what has got people thinking along these lines earlier than they might otherwise have done, is that just after the backpacker arrests started in Singapore and just after the intermediate started being brought in through the barely heard of Kingdom of Mustang, an expert on drugs charters a nineteen seater aircraft for his own personal use and takes it through the Kali Gandaki Gorge in suicidal winds, manages to land on a barely completed landing strip and makes contact with the caravan bringing in the all important chemical intermediate. His story is that he has gone to all this trouble to photograph the city of Lo Manthang and a few yaks. Then he visits the palm oil plant and if that wasn't enough, he flies from Pokhara to Kathmandu on the same flight as one of the women caught carrying and then on the same flight to Singapore where he is so close to her in customs that he catches her when she faints after her arrest."

Thurston looked at her without expression, then slowly held out his wrists in handcuff position.

"Interesting thought," she smiled, uncrossing then re-crossing her legs. "Pity I'm flying back to Toronto."

"Agreed," he said. "Pity!"

The conversation paused while they disposed of a little more coffee. Then Lauren returned to the theme.

"Did you get any idea of what Jha and his men were concerned about?"

"They weren't very forthcoming, although I did ask them. But Jha seemed particularly interested when I told him Captain Chaudrai managed to have a conversation with the herders – and that I took some video footage of it."

This time Lauren paused to consider what he had just said and slowly detached another segment of a satsuma she was dissecting.

"That conversation included reference to the previous leader dying in suspicious circumstances and the resistance to the new longer route collapsing."

"Did they say who they suspected?"

"Not in so many words, but when we asked who was organizing the new route they simply pointed out that all local administration decisions of that sort were taken by the Chinese."

She thought for a moment, "Pity we haven't got more time. I would have quite liked to have seen the video – assuming you've still got it."

"Still in the camera – not used it since."

"Is there anything else?"

He considered the question. "No, I don't think so," he paused, "except the officer on immigration duty picked up on my recent visits to Afghanistan and northern Thailand, both ..."

"Heroin producing areas," she cut in. "Yes, Steph mentioned that."

She paused, elegantly sliding another small slice of satsuma between her lips – even eating an orange she managed to radiate sensuality.

"Have you given any thought as to where the traffickers might be producing the heroin?" she asked, bringing him back to the subject in hand.

He thought about it. "No, I haven't. I suppose – my main preoccupation has been wondering quite whatever it is I've done or seen or heard which has made me the target of curiosity. For instance, how do you know so much about my activities?"

"Mostly from Steph D'Aunay at immigration, but I also got a report on Jha's interrogation."

Thurston looked surprised.

"I told you Jha is head of ACAP and I provide the funding, so anything significant he lets me know. Steph is part of the Canadian 'mafia' if you like and in a case like this where she knows we are worried about the effect of these arrests on our intended good works, she makes sure I'm up to speed with anything new which might be relevant. This is not a good position for my government —trying to help the Nepalis. Then somebody starts using what we're doing to start a pretty deadly drug ring."

After the last sip of coffee he stood up. "So, you've spoken to her since she had a go at me the day before yesterday?"

"Yes, and once she told me you had been questioned by the Nepali security in Pokhara I got on to them. It seemed you were our first lead to what might be going on."

"So, when I arrived you were already on the lookout for me. And there was I thinking it was pure animal magnetism."

"A bit of both," she said. "I was looking for you after reading about you. So I checked you out at Tribhuvan Airport..."

"So, you came into the first class lounge just to check me out. I wondered why you had bothered for just two minutes."

"...But if it's just information I want, I can normally manage that without resorting to a good Armagnac and a night on the tiles."

"I'll try to take that as a compliment," he said, looking at her. "So have you decided what I'm up to? Am I part of the drug ring or part of drug intelligence trying to find out what is happening?"

"Or are you just an overindulged businessman who doesn't mind spending a small fortune to get into remote areas to take a few photographs?"

"Always a possibility... " he said.

As they dressed, he asked her what she or they were doing to try to figure it out.

"We're getting close to Internal Security in Nepal and people like Steph D'Aunay in the Drug Liaison service. Most countries participate in drug liaison in an attempt to collate drug intelligence. Seventy to eighty percent of arrests are down to prior intelligence."

"And how are you getting on?"

She paused, "Not very well. The Nepalis cannot find any sign of the production source, nor can we find any trace of how the acetic anhydride is being diverted."

Edward was thoughtful.

"And until you find out where it is being produced you presumably don't have much chance of finding out who is behind it?"

"It certainly would be a lot easier if we could," she replied. "We are interested in the possible Tibetan connection. All five women bought the items in which the heroin was secreted in Tibetan artefacts and from Tibetan-run shops in Pokhara itself, or in Tibetan refugee camps."

Again she waited for the point to register, "then of course the intermediate is being shipped in from Tibet."

"But why would the Tibetans get involved?" asked Thurston.

"If you knew how much the Tibetans detest the Chinese you wouldn't ask that. There is almost nothing they wouldn't do to raise funds to support their resistance."

"Even if it means the execution of young women?"

"I must admit, even with their level of hate that does seem to be taking things a bit far."

After a moment's reflection he asked, "What will you do next?"

"Let's talk about that on the way out," she said. "I'm running out of time."

They were both heading for the same part of town and shared a taxi. Once ensconced in the rear seat she continued.

"One of the things we will be doing is checking for new cash movements."

"Cash movements?" he repeated, frowning.

"In a drug ring even though the traffickers try to disguise it, a new movement of acetic anhydride is almost always matched by new cash movement to or through the delivery point for the intermediate."

"So the drug intelligence people are screening this sort of thing routinely, looking for matching movements?" He shook his head in amazement, then asked, "Have you found anything?"

"Yes," she replied looking directly at him, "small so far and not enough to be significant. But some new movement of cash," she paused, "into Lhasa."

Thurston whistled, "So acetic anhydride coming out of Tibet and cash going back in – the classic signs of a new drug ring."

The taxi stopped on Orchard Street. She got out first.

"If you are ever in Toronto give me a ring." She gave him her card as she eased her way out of the taxi, brushing her lips against his neck. "And by the way, one of us is being followed. And I'm pretty sure it isn't me." She looked back to a pale fawn Honda Civic, which had stopped fifty yards behind them.

"It's followed us from Raffles – I kept seeing it in the rear view."

"I think I must have been leading a very sheltered life," he half smiled.

Then Lauren Chase disappeared from his life as quickly as she had entered it.

***Drug Intelligence Division***
***National Criminal Intelligence Service***
***Upper Ground, Blackfriars, London***
***26th April 2001, 8:00 a.m.***

Head of Drug Division of the British National Criminal Intelligence Service, Jonathan Warrender, had heard the report of Catherine Miller's arrest on the 11:00 p.m. BBC news summary the previous evening. At 8:00 a.m. the following morning he looked through the overnight messages to see if anything of interest had come in. His long time assistant, Barbara Murdoch, was ahead of him and was already studying a report. She held it out to him.

"Stephanie D'Aunay sent this in. She was on duty at the airport when Miller came in. The woman was carrying a small amount – about twenty grams equivalent of diamorphine. She says it is not from any of the mainstream sources: looks like some new local small-scale production. Catherine Miller brought it in from Nepal hidden in the clothing of an ethnic doll."

"Ethnic?" Warrender queried. "What sort of ethnic?"

"Tibetan. She doesn't go into any detail – just that Miller bought it in Pokhara in the Annapurnas."

Warrender read over the report. "Twenty grams?" repeated Warrender thoughtfully, "What's the capital punishment level?"

"Fifteen grams," Barbara reminded him.

Warrender sucked in air through narrowed lips. "Not a nice situation," Warrender said. "No legal defence, mandatory hanging and no history of clemency. What do we know about Miller?"

"Nothing yet," Barbara Murdoch almost smiled at his presumption that at eight in the morning there would be anybody around to ask for a background report. "Ask me again in a couple of hours."

She turned to leave the office, but turned back. "On the second page she asks us to run a check on a chap called Edward Thurston."

Warrender frowned, "Didn't security in Pokhara turn in a report on him a couple of weeks ago, the English chap who wanted to spend a fortune trying to get into Mustang?"

"Yes," replied Barbara. "And now he's turned up again, arriving in Singapore on the same flight as Miller."

Warrender sucked in air for a second time. "Then we'd better have a look at Mr Thurston hadn't we? Let me know how you get on."

# CHAPTER SEVEN
## *The Pilot*

*Kathmandu Airport*
*Royal Nepal Airlines Office*
*29th April 2001*

Captain Chaudrai sat outside an office on the top floor of Royal Nepal Airlines head offices at Kathmandu Airport tense and apprehensive. He had been called "to review the Mustang charter flight" and was seriously concerned. The radio exchanges during the flight had made it clear that the decision to fly in those conditions was his responsibility as captain of the flight and he had compounded any wrongdoing by landing on a non-commissioned and therefore uninsured runway. As to what would have happened if the mountain girl had died, he tried to shut from his mind. With only months to go to his retirement, the prospect of losing his job and the implications of that to his pension could not have come at a worse time. If he lost his pension he would be close to destitution.

The door opened and a secretary called him in. Inside there were three men sitting at a table facing him, a bit like a court martial. A single chair was placed in front of and facing them.

"Sit down, Captain." It was an instruction rather than an invitation from the man in airline uniform sitting in the centre of the triumvirate. To his right was a man of medium height and solid build with heavy black rimmed glasses, to his left a younger slimmer man with light rimmed glasses who looked like a lawyer.

"Captain, we have asked you to meet us to review the events of 25th and 26th April. The proceedings at this stage are exploratory. Depending on what we hear this morning a decision will be made on whether further formal proceedings will be put in train. I am Sarwan Patel representing the airline assisted by Mr Swirindinath," – he indicated the lawyer to his left, "and Major Jha of the Annapurna Conservation Area Project. The major is interested in your contact with the salt caravan when you landed at Lo Manthang. To start the proceedings can you please describe the sequence of events as you saw them?"

Chaudrai described how a passenger who had been turned back on a previous flight to Jomsom had arranged to charter the Otter with its crew to make sure he could get through the gorge even if the wind was bad.

"And on the day, the wind was bad?"

"Too bad for normal commercial flying, but acceptable for training purposes – which is what had been arranged. There was no danger to the aircraft; it was built to withstand worse turbulence than the gorge. In addition it seemed a good opportunity to give First Officer Shah some experience of serious weather."

He went on to describe the very rough flight through the gorge and if he had to do it again he would take on a full fuel load as ballast. The questioning to this point seemed to be routine and not particularly challenging, but so far he had done everything by the book. That was about to change.

"But when you got through the gorge you were advised not to land at Jomsom as the weather had deteriorated still further. Please tell us what happened then?"

"My natural inclination was to orbit – that is fly in circles – close to the northern end of the gorge so that we would be in a position to take advantage of any drop in the wind to get back. But the charterer, Mr Thurston, was keen to fly further so that he could catch a glimpse of Lo Manthang. He argued that once the wind had started to funnel up from the Indian plain through the gorge to the Mustang Plateau it was almost unheard of for it to reduce significantly in the first few hours, so if we were stuck on the wrong side of the gorge we might as well use the flying time to get the most out of it."

"So what persuaded you to do what Mr Thurston wanted against your better judgement?"

"Mr Thurston knew about the new landing strip at Lo Manthang, he even knew it was not commissioned, but he argued that if the wind remained at that strength for several hours we would not have enough fuel to remain in the air and get back through the gorge to Pokhara. He suggested that it would make sense to examine the new strip and assess its serviceability as a further escape option. That made good sense to me."

"Did it surprise you that Mr Thurston knew so much about flying conditions in the gorge and about the new landing strip at Lo Manthang?" asked the man in the heavy rimmed glasses.

"In some ways it did, in others perhaps not."

"Can you explain that?"

"He was obviously a determined and persistent man who knew how to get what he wanted – presumably why he seems to be successful in business. If he was really so determined to see the gorge and the city of Lo Manthang and, as he put it 'in his dream world' to see the salt caravan, it would be entirely in character that he'd have done his homework in some detail."

The Chairman took up the questioning again and asked him to explain his decision to land on the new strip.

"Jomsom tower reported that the wind was even worse and the forecast was for even further deterioration. I did three low-level fly pasts over the new strip and satisfied myself that it was clear and a better option than remaining in the air and running out of fuel."

"Even if you were not insured?"

"As Mr Thurston put it, the insurance company would be far happier with an intact airplane on an uninsured landing strip than a number of pieces of an insured airplane scattered over a mountainside!"

The chairman just about succeeded in suppressing a smile. Major Jha did not seem to be amused.

"So you landed on the strip?"

"Yes."

"Even though at 13,000 feet you were at the limit of the service altitude of the aircraft?"

"That is more a question of oxygen supply. It was handling perfectly in the thinner air. It was one of the parameters I checked. As for oxygen level, as you know there is a twenty percent margin of error as with most safety factors. We could have flown up to 15,000 feet."

"But not be insured?"

"In those weather conditions every decision was beyond normal limits."

"Alright Captain, I may want to ask you more later, but Major Jha has some questions he would like to ask on other matters."

Major Jha took over the questioning, "Captain, you made contact with the incoming salt caravan?"

"Yes, Major, we landed as the caravan was arriving. Mr Thurston would have been pleased just to have seen Lo Manthang. The caravan was beyond his expectations."

"Do you believe that?"

Chaudrai was puzzled. "Yes, I have no reason not to, he seemed genuinely delighted."

"You managed to converse with the Dolpo Pa?"

Chaudrai frowned. "Yes, a bit difficult to start with, but it got easier as I got more used to the dialect."

"Can you tell me as much as you can remember about the conversation?" Jha asked.

Chaudrai recalled all he could, including Thurston's interest in the new chemical and the caravan leader Tensing showing him the container.

"Did Thurston ask about the chemical first?"

"No, I don't think so. No," his memory cleared. "It came up when Mr Thurston asked why the new route had started coming further east to Lo Manthang instead of the old route to Jumla."

"And that was when they mentioned the chemical for the first time?"

"Yes, and once it was mentioned he asked what it was and what it was used for and they showed him the containers."

"And he photographed them?"

Chaudrai hesitated then said, "most of the time during the conversation he was using his video camera."

This seemed to stop Jha.

"Thurston videotaped your conversation with the Dolpo Pa?"

"Yes."

Jha drew in a breath, "I'm sorry to ask you Captain, but can you go back over the conversation again and try to remember everything that was said?"

This questioning was becoming more intensive than the flying part of the enquiry.

Chaudrai did as he was asked.

Jha stopped him at the point where Thurston queried the reason for the new route.

"Was there any discussion about the new route other than the matter of the bringing in the new chemical?"

Chaudrai paused, trying to remember. "Yes, there was. Tensing said they were not happy with the new route – because it added several more weeks to the journey, five I think he said, and the old Jumla route already took five months of the year."

"What was the reaction to their unhappiness?"

"Tensing wasn't specific, but he did say that resistance faded when the previous leader died."

"Died?" queried Jha, "Just died?"

"I think they said died in mysterious circumstances, no obvious sign of the cause."

"So they didn't say killed or murdered?"

"Not in so many words, but the fact that the death was mysterious and resistance fell away after that, left it sounding as if they thought the death was not an accident."

"Anything else?" asked Jha.

"Thurston asked who was pressing them to adopt the new route?"

Again Jha paused and adjusted his sitting position. "And?"

"I remember Tensing looking surprised at the question."

"And what was the answer?"

"Tensing replied that decisions on routes and loads and export quotas were made by the local administration in the Lake Drabye area – that is the salt lake which is the source of the salt," explained Chaudrai. "Then Tensing added, spitting out the words, that administration in Tibet these days means the Chinese."

Jha spoke behind his hand to Patel then turned back to Captain Chaudrai.

"Thank you for your assistance, Captain Chaudrai. I have no more questions – ah, except one – who else heard your conversation with Tensing – your first officer I presume? And Thurston, of course? Anyone else?"

Again Chaudrai thought carefully. "There was one other person who heard it and could have understood what we were talking about – the security officer who came with us on the flight, Sergeant Pandeh."

"Thank you," said Jha, making notes.

The rest of the questioning was routine covering the return flight and its control problems and the rescue of the girl from Lo Manthang. In fact, the rest of the questioning was, if anything, hurried and Jha was visibly restless and anxious to leave.

Patel finally closed the meeting. "Thank you for attending this hearing, Captain Chaudrai. If you will be good enough to return at two p.m. I will let you know what further action, if any, we will be recommending to the board. By the way, if you incurred any expenses attending today please let my secretary know."

Chaudrai thanked the chairman, stood up and walked to the door.

He had two opposing thoughts as he left. One was that the chairman's parting comments and tone of voice seemed to indicate that there would be no serious repercussions over the flight aspects of the meeting. The second was that the real concern seemed to be over the conversation with the Dolpo Pa. And why would the airline be interested in that? In fact why was a representative of ACAP at the meeting at all?

His next concern was to try to contact Thurston. He thought he would appreciate being put in the picture with regard to the interest the enquiry had shown in his contact with the Dolpo Pa and in his use of a video camera in particular. He remembered that Thurston had given him his business card with his London office details and his cell phone number. Thurston had told him he was going on to Singapore after Nepal and had told him the name of his hotel, but he could not remember it. He found the business card in his wallet; it also showed Thurston's e-mail address. E-mail was probably the best route as someone like Thurston probably checked pretty regularly and in any case, from what Chaudrai had heard, using a cell phone for international calls would cost him a week's salary. He found a workstation in the pilots' office and checked in to his private e-mail. Thurston had two e-mail addresses, one with his own name and the other a general enquiry listing for the agency.

He sent the following message to both addresses at 10:47 April 29th:

*Good morning Mr Thurston,*

*I thought you would like to know that I have just been questioned by the Airline about the Lo Manthang flight. It seems to me that they believe I acted reasonably in all the circumstances, but another man was very interested in our conversation with the Dolpo Pa, particularly when I mentioned that you had videotaped parts of it. I hope you are enjoying the rest of your trip. If you wish to contact me please do so on my private e-mail or on my cell phone or home number which are listed below.*

He sent the message twice to each address as he had been advised to do by his brother who ran his own business in Kathmandu, "E-mail is not a one hundred percent reliable medium so anything important send at least twice."

~~~~~~~~~~

Thurston received the e-mail from Chaudrai shortly after it was sent and immediately telephoned him on his cell phone. After exchanging pleasantries, Thurston asked Chaudrai to describe the "other, non-airline, man."

He only had to say heavy dark rimmed glasses before Thurston asked, "Was his name Jha?"

"Yes, how did you know?"

"He was the principal interrogator at my 'hearing' in Pokhara."

For the third time that morning, Chaudrai went over the Dolpo Pa conversation.

"So they were interested in the fact that I used my video camera?"

"Yes, does any of that make any sense to you? Why does it matter whether it was an ordinary camera or a video?"

"I think, my friend, that there was something in that conversation that somebody did not want to get out and if that's true then the video camera does one thing the still camera does not do – apart from taking moving pictures, and that is it records the conversation."

"Do you have any idea what it was in the conversation that mattered?"

"Well I don't know for sure, but it sounds as if they are concerned about the death of the previous leader coming out and that it was the Chinese who were insisting on the new route. But on the other hand it is no secret that the Chinese cooperated with ACAP to set up the new route and the transport of the new chemical."

"So, what will you do?"

"I'm not sure Captain, but I'm grateful to you for taking the trouble to let me know. I'll return the compliment and let you know what develops."

# The Tissue Trail

Despite his denial, Thurston was pretty sure what was causing the problem. It was one thing for the Chinese cooperation with ACAP to be public knowledge; it was quite another for the Chinese to be seen to be so insistent on adoption of the new route that they were prepared to eliminate the previous leader.

And that in itself raised a whole raft of further questions. What could be so significant in the actions of a remote nomadic Himalayan tribe that any resistance by them would be forcefully squashed? What were the Chinese up to in an area that was not so much a backwater, but barely part of the planet and if they were concerned enough to prevent knowledge of the death of the previous leader becoming public, how much at risk were those who had heard that conversation – Captain Chaudrai, First Officer Shah, the security officer Inspector Pandeh – and the owner of the video camera?

## 27th April 2001

Thurston's first action following the telephone call was to take his video camera to a photographic shop close to the hotel. He asked them to make six copies of the videotape, no editing, just straight copies, but to one copy he added a sequence of himself explaining the footage and why he had made the copies. This was to prove an inspired move. He then sent un-edited copies by registered post to his solicitors, accountants and bank in London. The original he put back into the camera and put the camera back into the holder. The copy with the added section he copied onto his laptop on the basis that if he lost that he might as well leave the planet.

~~~~~~~~~~

Thurston spent most of the day with Aw Swee Lim working through trial details and meeting members of the team. In the evening he telephoned his office taking advantage of the time difference. He also tried a couple of times to contact Chaudrai, but without success. There were no surprises at the office except that Jaci reminded him that she had booked two weeks off. "I suppose you had forgotten?" she said lightly.

"Sorry, yes," he replied. "There has been a fair bit going on."

She told him she could cancel the break if she was needed on the Imperial project in the next two or three weeks, but if not, it would be a good time to take it.

"I would have thought things were too exciting for you to want to take time off at the moment," he teased her gently, although he realized he felt unreasonable resentment when staff wanted to take time off. After all, he owned the business, so paying people for unproductive time was like paying them out of his own pocket.

"It would be exciting in Singapore," she said, still smarting over his refusal to take her. "That's where the action is."

He deflected the Singapore jibe and said, "Actually, I do remember you talking about going to Nepal? Whereabouts?"

"To a place called Ghorapani," she told him. "A ten-day round trip trek to the west of Pokhara."

He stopped dead at her mention of Pokhara.

"I take it you've seen the press reports of arrests in Singapore of women carrying heroin from Nepal?" he asked. "In fact, not just Nepal, but the Pokhara area."

"No, I haven't," she replied. "There hasn't been anything about it over here."

"Well, if you do go, be careful." He spoke to her as if he were her father.

She took this advice as a bit of an insult. "Don't you think I've got the sense not to carry anything dodgy through customs?" she said indignantly.

"I'm sure you do," he replied. "But according to press reports here, none of these women had the faintest clue they were carrying – it's one of the things puzzling the police."

"OK, Edward I'll be careful." Her tone was that of the teenager humouring a parent, but as an after-thought she added, "Did you say all five were women?"

~~~~~~~~~~

When his call had first gone through, Nicola had mentioned that his accountant wanted to have a word, so he quickly telephoned Henry who had looked after his affairs for several years. Edward asked him what was on his mind.

"Have you been doing anything on the business side you haven't been telling me about?"

"You can't be serious," Thurston told him.

# The Tissue Trail

"Well, the tax boys have launched a bit of a blitz, coming at you from all directions, personal, company and VAT. They've even asked for travel records, all out-of-pocket expenses, the works, even telephone and mobile phone records. They want to go over the last five years with a fine tooth comb."

Thurston frowned and thought for a minute before saying, "Henry, as long as you have dealt with everything according to the book at your end they can investigate until the cows come home. Yes, we've made a bit of money, but everything has been dealt with as straight as a die."

In fact, since starting the agency, his income levels had increased steadily for the first two years, but had been in seven figures in both of the last two years.

"I know that and you know that," said Henry. "But I would be interested to know why now? They have had the most recent accounts for nearly a year."

"I'd be interested to know why now, too," Thurston agreed.

"I suppose," Thurston mused, "the last two years income would have raised a few eyebrows. What do you think the business is worth, Henry?"

"You're not thinking of retiring are you, Edward?"

"No chance, Henry, I'm only just starting to enjoy life."

"Well, back of envelope and don't hold me to it, but the fact that you have negotiated those deals based on sales increases rather than a fee means you've got a steadily increasing, on-going revenue stream and that's what the pension boys like. That could give you ten to fifteen times earnings; I suppose you could be looking at five to seven million."

Thurston whistled, "I suppose that would make the Revenue's eyes water!"

"And it wouldn't matter if you dropped dead," Henry continued his line of thought, "it's all contractual revenue."

"Nice to know you're concerned for my welfare, Henry."

"Perfect client," said Henry smiling down at the phone. "Loaded; and all I've got to worry about if you hand in your dinner pail is a bit of inheritance tax. Still, it's a bit of a puzzle; I'll keep you posted." Then as an after-thought he added, "Any reason why they should hone in on your trips to Afghanistan and northern Thailand?"

Thurston did not say anything to Henry, but the Revenue had homed in on the two areas which had interested Stephanie D'Aunay – the opium poppy growing areas of North West Pakistan and the Thai Laos border. That struck him as odd. Why would the Revenue have an interest in any particular area of travel? Surely their interest should only be in collecting their pound of tax flesh wherever it came from. Was it genuinely just a tax enquiry? Perhaps he was becoming paranoid. Whatever the answer to that, they had uncovered another string to the prosecution's bow he thought – in addition to the accumulated dossier of circumstantial evidence tying him to drugs in general and the new drug ring in particular, his net worth had suddenly gone into orbit.

Clearly he had stumbled across something that was of concern to a lot of people and whatever it was, he was clearly under suspicion himself.

### 30th April 2001

Thurston tried Chaudrai's cell phone again, but there was still no reply. On the first two or three occasions he was diverted to voicemail and he left messages. After that he got an immediate cut-off indicating the phone was switched off or the battery was dead. Either way, Chaudrai had gone off air and Thurston was concerned.

When he got back to the hotel everything seemed normal and when he checked his video case the camera was still in place. But there was something wrong, he always laid the carry strap over the cylinder of the camera, but it was now lying under it. He picked up the camera and examined it. There was nothing to see externally, but when he turned it on and set the controls to replay, it was blank. It hadn't taken long for the leak from Chaudrai's interview to reach the operators and for the operators to take action. It was a good job Thurston had acted so quickly.

He wondered if there was any point in reporting it to the hotel management, but he thought it unlikely they would be particularly concerned. There was no physical damage and no sign of a break in and he could not prove that he had not accidentally wiped the tape clean himself. And as he had not used the camera since he left Nepal he could not be sure when the intrusion had been.

The more serious issue arose from the fact that there was no sign of a break in. It meant that someone on the hotel staff with access to the computerized card entry system must have been involved. So whatever was going on and whoever was concerned about its exposure, they had the ability to organize a sophisticated break-in beyond the borders of Nepal.

And that was way beyond the capability of a few renegade Tibetan refugees, never mind a remote tribe of nomads.

He finally persuaded himself not to report it to the hotel until he could find out what he was up against, it would be "good medicine" not to make himself any more conspicuous than was absolutely necessary.

He tried Chaudrai again with no success and this time decided to phone the airline. Raffles' receptionist located the number of Royal Nepal Airlines head office in Kathmandu and dialed the number. A female voice answered in a sub- continent accent. Thurston explained that he was trying to contact Captain Chaudrai with whom he had flown recently and he was having difficulty contacting him. The voice asked who was enquiring; Thurston gave his name.

"Please wait Mr Thurston, I will try to connect you to someone who can help."

It seemed a long time before a male voice came on to the line.

"Mr Thurston, I gather you are trying to contact Captain Chaudrai?"

"Yes, I've been trying his mobile for three days without success."

"What is your connection with Captain Chaudrai?" The question and the way it was asked immediately raised Thurston's already elevated concern.

"Captain Chaudrai was the pilot who flew my charter which landed at Lo Manthang and brought out the sick girl."

"And do you mind telling me why you want to speak to him?"

"Not at all. We've both been asked quite a lot of questions since the Mustang charter and until the last two or three days we've been keeping in touch. But you are giving me the impression that there is something amiss."

There was a pause at the other end.

"Captain Chaudrai was found dead at his home the day before yesterday."

This time Thurston paused. "How did he die?"

"We won't know until the post-mortem report."

"But was it ..."

"I'm afraid I can't tell you anymore Mr Thurston, I'm sorry." The line went dead.

Thurston slowly put the phone down.

The tone of the reply from the airline and the need for a post-mortem suggested Chaudrai's death was not regarded as routine. This meant a second death connected to the salt caravan coming into Mustang. Added to that, some sophisticated operators had removed the contents of a video camera that had photographed the same caravan. All this seemed to mean that the Tissue Trail traffickers were prepared to kill to protect their operation; and that they knew where Thurston was and could reach him without difficulty. On top of that, drug enforcement, as evidenced by Stephanie D'Aunay's interrogation, also regarded him with a level of suspicion which had almost seen him taken into custody. So he was in the uncomfortable position of being regarded as "the probable bad guy" from both sides of the fence. Not a great position to be in. He was vulnerable to any action either the law enforcement agencies or the traffickers decided to take, and at the moment no one except himself, knew what was going on.

He decided to confide in Aw Swee Lim whom he respected and trusted and would have enough of an academic background and political awareness to take it on board. Neither of them normally bothered to break for lunch – both would grab something they could eat while they kept working. But Thurston told Aw he had something he would like to discuss and invited him out for lunch the following day.

### 1st May 2001

At lunch the next day Aw listened carefully. At the end, Thurston apologized for bringing him into the "risk ring."

Aw smiled.

"It is a bit of a dilemma for you isn't it? You need to keep someone informed of your discoveries – but that immediately puts whomever you select in the firing line."

Aw agreed to act as Thurston's confidant.

"I know a lot of the movers in Singapore. The time might come when I will need to get involved. This looks as if it could cause problems for us politically."

On his way back to the hotel that evening, Thurston thought he kept seeing a pale fawn Honda in the wing mirrors —the same make and colour as Lauren said she had spotted. It drove slowly past as he alighted from his taxi at Raffles. And just as he reached the door, he saw a Malaysian woman, in a distinctive green wrap around, get out of another small vehicle that stopped on the main road. He had also seen that garment earlier that morning. Was he being followed by two people – or was he just being over-paranoid?

# The Tissue Trail

At the hotel he sat in the courtyard bar with a beer and read over the evening papers.

~~~~~~~~~~

They were full of reports of the latest Tissue Trail developments led by the reports of a fifth arrest of a young woman bringing heroin into Singapore from Nepal. Birgit Heller was German born in Dusseldorf. The case was *identical* to the other four – the woman had no knowledge that she was carrying, no contact or conversation with anybody when buying the artefact in which the heroin was hidden or about collecting it once she had entered Singapore.

In italics below the report was an editor's note:

*Heroin cases dubbed "Tissue Trail girls"*

*All five of the young women recently arrested carrying heroin into Changi Airport had trekked a trail in Nepal known locally as the "Tissue Trail" because of its heavy use and difficulty in burying tissues and other waste when the ground is frozen hard in the early mornings. One of the two Americans arrested earlier had mentioned the nickname and the press corps immediately adopted it.*

*Ed.*

It was also clear that the level of heroin the Americans were carrying had been leaked. The *Straits Times* featured the headlines from other papers:

## HEROIN BACKPACKERS FACE EXECUTION
## WOMEN TRAFFICKERS HEAD FOR SINGAPORE HANGING
## TISSUE TRAIL TRAFFICKERS "OVER DEATH LIMIT"

Reports centred on the fact that analysis of the heroin carried by both women confirmed they were carrying in excess of fifteen grams of the active ingredient diamorphine hydrochloride. At this level, the death sentence is required. The *Straits Times* report was typical:

## *HEROIN WOMEN TRAFFICKERS EXCEED EXECUTION LIMIT*

*The committal proceedings of two backpackers caught carrying heroin into Singapore in April this year were held at the Central Court today. Maria Gonzales (18) an American from Miami, Florida and Karen Leopold (20) from Los Angeles, California were both sent for trial after confirmation that the substance found secreted in items they were carrying from Nepal was heroin. It is understood that in both cases the amount carried was in excess of 15 grams equivalent of diamorphine hydrochloride at which level the death penalty is mandatory. Philip Lee, whose firm is defending both women, is said to be following up a number of unusual aspects of these cases. However, in a statement he acknowledged that with Singapore's zero tolerance of Class A drug offenses, he faces an uphill task in preventing the law taking its course.*

# CHAPTER EIGHT
## *The Reporter*

**28th April 2001**

Edward Thurston's work had brought him through Nepal and to Singapore and had resulted in him starting the process of uncovering an explanation for the "nonsensical Tissue Trail trafficking."

Twenty-five hundred miles to the northwest, a second major player in the drama was about to become involved.

*CNN*
*Far Eastern Region Office*
*New Delhi*
*28th April 2001*

Just before lunch, Barry Schultz called his Far Eastern anchorman, Victor Najinski, into his office.

"What do you make of these heroin cases in Singapore?"

"Not sure," said Najinski. "No history of serious drug activity in Nepal since the hippie days. All the women were arrested coming into Singapore and nowhere else. No obvious connection between Nepal and Singapore and all women were carrying small amounts, but enough to require the death penalty. Very odd."

"My feelings exactly," said Schultz, "and given that they are all western women you can bet your bottom dollar that there's going to be a media storm. I think we should have someone out there. And someone who knows what he's doing."

# The Tissue Trail

"When do you want me to leave?"

"You could just make the 1600 and be there tonight," Barry laughed. "But seriously, I don't think we should hang about."

Najinski caught the 1600 the following day and was on the case in Singapore the morning after that. His first telephone call was to Philip Lee asking if the lawyer could spare him a few minutes to fill him in on the Tissue Trail cases.

Lee would normally have steered clear of the press at this relatively early stage of the process, but in this case he needed as much help as he could get and the resources of an international media giant might just uncover something he and the local drug liaison services might miss. He agreed to meet Najinski.

The two men met initially at Lee's offices later that afternoon and continued into the evening "over a couple of beers" where Najinski told an interesting story.

~~~~~~~~~~

Najinski would not have been in Singapore for the Miller case or even been based in Delhi if it had not been for a broadcast he had made eight years earlier in July 1993. At that time he was a senior reporter with BBC television based in London and was in Monaco covering the International Olympic Committee vote for the city to host the first Games of the 21st Century, the Millennium Olympic Games. One of the audience of millions around the world watching the announcement of the result either live or on news reports was Barry Schultz, CNN Regional Manager, Far East. He had been looking for a charismatic anchorman for the Far Eastern desk for some time and had been watching Najinski. Two inches of wiry grey hair added to his six foot slightly round–shouldered, but broad frame and large lensed pink rimmed glasses and a luxuriant pepper and salt walrus moustache, completed his standout appearance. Najinski had been born and brought up in New Zealand before moving to the UK in his late teens and this had left him with enough of an antipodean accent to give him what Schultz called a "mid-ocean" accent. That was almost the final tick in Schultz's list of boxes.

Najinski was also a good television news reporter. Schultz only needed one more top performance to clinch it and he was about to get it.

In the final seconds before the host city result was announced, Najinski stood facing the camera and spoke into the microphone summarizing the position. It was an account he told Lee that he never tired of relating. In fact, it had become a classic in the industry and part of Najinski's resume was a transcript of his report. It read as follows:

> *The Members of the Olympic Committee have now completed three rounds of voting and two of the original six contenders remain – Beijing and Sydney. The last city to be eliminated was Manchester with 11 votes and these have now been re-distributed to give the final vote. Beijing, who have been in the lead from the first round, have gone into the final round leading with 41 votes to Sydney's 36, needing only 4 of the final 11 votes to secure the accolade of hosting the Millennium Olympic Games. The Chinese are trying not to show it, but they are clearly expecting to win and are equally clearly delighted at the prospect. In contrast, the Australians look downcast. They obviously think they have too much to do to close the gap.*

The cameras turned to show the president of the International Olympic Committee entering the hall from the committee room, climbing onto the platform and taking his position in the centre of the executive members as chairman of the meeting. He studied the sheet of paper on the table before him, rising to make the final announcement. The tension became palpable as he stretched out the proceedings by acknowledging the time effort and expense of the six candidate cities over the previous two years, preparing their highly professional proposals and referring to the particularly pleasing points of each in turn. With the atmosphere electric, he finally came to the result.

"And now it is my privilege to announce the decision of the International Olympic Committee and to declare which of these two great cities will host the Millennium Olympic Games." He looked out over his glasses and, squeezing every last scintilla of tension, slowly raised his gaze to the back of the hall. "The votes cast in the final round for the venue for the Millennium Olympic Games are as follows: First Beijing..."

As the words "first Beijing" were translated, the camera turned to the Chinese delegation.

They had instantly broken into delirious celebration, a group of three standing, jumping and hugging each other; two more were punching the air in the aisle. One was just standing with her hands on the back of a chair, head bowed, shoulders heaving. Most of the rest of the delegates in their immediate vicinity gathered round to congratulate them.

It was fully thirty seconds before the slow realization that the president was still standing.

Laughter and tears of joy were replaced initially by uncertainty and then as they retook their seats uncertainty was replaced by apprehension. The president completed his pronouncement – "first for Beijing... the number of votes cast...was forty-three." The camera showed a close-up of the slow dawning of horror on the face of the female Chinese delegate who had been standing with her hands on the back of the chair in front, her mind refusing to register that forty-three was not enough. The president intoned her worst fears, "The number of votes cast for Sydney was forty-five."

Nine of the eleven votes redistributed from Manchester had gone to Sydney.

Najinski's team filmed the Chinese woman as she collapsed into inconsolable sobbing. The group that had been hugging sat frozen-faced looking unseeingly at the stage. The two air punchers stood with hands on the back of the chairs in front of them heads bowed.

No one seemed to be taking any notice of the celebrating Australians.

As the meeting broke up and delegates and committee members streamed out of the hall, Najinski's team caught one of the Chinese delegation leaving the auditorium and asked him for his reaction. In English the Chinese spoke into the proffered microphone fighting back the tears, "That was not a vote for Sydney – it was a vote against the Chinese."

The result of the IOC vote was to have far reaching effects. For some, it would be years before those effects became apparent, for Victor Najinski it was to be little more than twelve hours. The following morning he was still in his hotel room when the telephone rang.

"Good morning, Mr Najinski. You do not know me, but if you will give me ten seconds of your time I think you will be interested in what I have to say. I am calling on behalf of a television news network that is looking for someone to anchor its Far Eastern News Service – do you happen to know anyone who could be interested?" Najinski recognized the "indirect" approach of the head-hunter.

He had studied English at university and then gone into journalism working initially on Fleet Street before moving into television. After thirty years he had been thinking more in terms of having had a good inning and giving it three more years before hanging up his typewriter and enjoying a well earned retirement. But there was nothing to lose in having a beer with the man on the telephone. Sheila, Najinski's wife, not only agreed that there was nothing to lose, but rapidly came to the conclusion that there was a great deal to gain; in particular, a tax free salary three times his net London pay and of even greater significance was the effect of doubling his pension. Spending his last three years in Delhi may not have been what Najinski had in mind, but Sheila's enthusiasm persuaded him to follow up the inquiry.

Barry Schultz had virtually made up his mind before meeting Najinski, and when Schultz offered him the job Najinski had accepted. He handed in his notice to the BBC working out a reasonable length of time to tidy things up and to hand over his contacts to his successor.

Schultz was happy enough with this, but asked Najinski if he would do what he could in the immediate aftermath of the IOC vote to check on Chinese reaction to losing the Millennium Games. Schultz's people were telling him they had taken it badly.

Victor Najinski and his wife Sheila moved to New Delhi in November 1993. They immediately fitted into the international and expatriate community and enjoyed the posting from the first days. Schultz spent the first morning welcoming Najinski aboard, showing him around and introducing him to other members of the team. Over lunch he asked Najinski what he had picked up from Beijing.

Najinski confirmed that the Chinese had indeed taken the loss of the vote badly. They had seen the accolade of hosting the first Games of the 21st Century as a right and proper acknowledgement of their presumption that they would become *the* super power of the 21st Century. Some hardliners had argued that a decision of such political significance should not have been left to an open or democratic vote. To lose to "insignificant Sydney" was an unnecessary and intolerable loss of face.

In the days following the vote, heads had rolled at all levels of the Chinese Sports Federation and even in government. In the following weeks, battle lines had been drawn between those who favoured abandoning the Olympic movement altogether as a "western celebration" and those who argued that China should take their rightful place as world leaders in sport as well as other spheres. The argument was won, comfortably enough, by the pro-Olympic lobby, but the fact that it had even gone to a vote was a clear indication of the seriousness of China's reaction. And what no one in Beijing seemed to doubt was that the main reason for their failure at Monaco was western rejection of Chinese treatment of political dissent in general, and in Tibet in particular. In fact, what the Millennium Games rejection brought home to Beijing was just how potentially damaging issues such as human rights and freedom of expression could be to their cause. Serious and "unacceptable" loss of face was one thing, but if the effect on western thinking was as graphic as that indicated by the last round of voting then the potential damage in wider political and economic spheres could only be imagined. Nine of the eleven recycled Manchester votes had gone to Sydney. So the problem was clear. But given that Beijing would not remotely contemplate changing its attitude, policies or practices, the solution was not clear.

One respected political analyst known for accurately reflecting Beijing's thinking wrote:

> The loss of the Millennium Games to Sydney, initially just a blow to Chinese pride, has proved to have a more deep rooted significance. China is a "sub-continent" with a massively disparate population of 1.5 billion, Muslims to the west, Hindus to the south, Mongols to the north and the main body of ethnic Chinese in the centre and to the east. With such a conglomerate of populations and beliefs and traditions preserving law and order and a structured society and still observe the West's vague concepts of democracy, human rights and unspecified aspirations to freedom is not a realistic proposition. One only has to remember the effect of dismantling the political structures of the Balkans and the USSR in the interests of democracy and independence. Order and organization was replaced by chaos, mass killing and universal corruption. China is not going to abandon the good order of the last fifty years simply to acquiesce to Western ideals. Rather it will be a matter of educating the West to recognize political realities.

Najinski's report continued. This analysis is believed to have been material to the derivation of Chinese policy in response to the Millennium Games loss. Reaction could have been contained simply by managing reaction to the loss of face and then by making sure that the next time they applied they would be better prepared, their lobbying better organized and they would drop the damaging assumption that their political power and influence would carry the day. But recognition of the deeper implications led to a more profound shift of ground. Beijing decided to change its posture from defending its position on maintaining good order to justifying it and one of the means of doing this would be by demonstrating the result if policies and political strategy designed to preserve good order is abandoned.

Reacting to the loss of the Millennium Games and the perceived role played by Tibet and their fellow travellers was seen as an opportunity to implement this change although at the time there was no clear plan as to how this might be done. But the resulting brief was to seek to "level the playing field with those who had caused their humiliation in 1993," but with the wider political agenda to seek to strike a blow against western human rights prejudices in general.

For the same reason, Najinski's sources had told him, part of the brief was to ensure that whatever scheme emerged as far as Tibet was concerned it must implicate Tibet as a nation – not just a few renegade extremists.

The final step in Beijing's thinking was that given the wider agenda the next application to host an Olympic Games would be overseen at government level and not by the "amateurs" of the Olympic administration within the Sports Federation. The Beijing Olympic Venue Committee still served as a convenient and politically acceptable front, but with its expanded agenda it would be dealt with at the highest levels and chaired by a ranking minister. Najinski had thought it significant that the Minister had an intelligence background.

Schultz told Najinski he wanted him to adopt the Chinese Millennium Games reaction as a special project within his Far Eastern desk responsibilities. His first job was to produce a full written report of what he had just related.

Over the ensuing months the Tibet issue and Beijing's reaction to losing the Millennium Games started to fade into the background, at least on the surface. And when Beijing did not contest the 2004 Games venue, the whole issue dropped off the media radar altogether. The Chinese continued their policy, not only of subsuming Tibet, but encouraging migration of ethnic Chinese into Tibet and improving access with a modern road system. They were also starting to work on a rail link to Lhasa.

The only other development of significance was that Victor and Sheila Najinski so enjoyed the ex-patriot life in Delhi that in 1996, he readily accepted an open-ended extension to his contract. That decision resulted in Najinski still working for CNN in 2001.

# CHAPTER NINE
## *The Clinical Assistant*

*Drug Intelligence Division*
*National Criminal Intelligence Service*
*Upper Ground, Blackfriars, London*
*1st May 2001*

Jonathan Warrender had asked his assistant, Barbara Murdoch, to update him on the enquiries into Edward Thurston's activities.

"It is a strange picture," she told him. "He is a pharmacologist, an expert on the actions of chemicals on body tissues and works in pharmaceutical research, looking at the effect of drugs if you like. His income has risen rapidly in the last five years and particularly in the last two."

"To what?" Warrender asked.

"Last year," she checked her file, "his company netted 1.2 million, Sterling."

Warrender raised his eyebrows, "And?"

"It all seems legitimate. His taxes are up-to-date although his accountants have done a good job with pension contributions and dividends from his limited company."

"Go on."

"But what got Stephanie excited in Singapore is that in addition to his rapidly rising income he's been in both the Pakistan and Thai opium growing areas in the last two years – although claiming both to be photographic expeditions."

"So what's her reading now?"

"She thinks that if it was just his income and his involvement in drugs and the opium area, visits could just about be coincidence, but it's his exploits in Mustang she can't figure. His twin Otter flew through suicidal conditions then managed to land close to Lo Manthang and made contact with the caravan bringing in acetic anhydride."

Warrender whistled.

"And he visited the palm oil plant near Pokhara which is using the stuff."

"I'm surprised she hasn't brought him in! What are they waiting for?"

"Well, his clinical trial business and semi-professional photographic work is either a very good cover or he's genuine. Whichever it is they are keeping him under observation, so if he is involved they're hoping he might lead them to something or somebody which could help."

"OK, keep me posted. The Minister is turning the heat up and we need some answers."

"So are the Americans. They're pretty unimpressed with the lack of progress by the Nepalis leaving their nationals unprotected."

"So what are they going to do about it?"

"Not sure. So far just a rumour that they are not likely to leave things as they are for much longer."

### Kathmandu, Nepal
### 5th May 2001

Jaci who was "between boyfriends" travelled to Kathmandu alone, but had arranged to meet up with Jane Anthony, a woman she had known from home in North Yorkshire and who was on an around the world back pack tour. The idea was to spend ten days together in Nepal, then Jaci would return to the UK and Jane would carry on to Thailand. It was the first visit to the sub-continent for both, and Kathmandu was not at all the small religiously atmospheric town she had seen in travel magazines. The photographs she had seen were of Hindu temples and palaces; streets of open fronted shops selling wares that were made in workshops in the rear. The impression she had formed was of a small town from another time and another world. What she actually found was a city of three million, teeming with chaotic traffic and wall-to-wall with people. From what she had seen on film and television she could have been in Bombay or Calcutta. The two women decided "to do" the key tourist sites in Kathmandu, but both could not wait to get into the mountains and decided to travel to Pokhara on their second day.

Jane had not heard anything about the Tissue Trail heroin arrests and to see the press coverage in Kathmandu and then Pokhara was a bit of a shock. Jaci told her that her boss had warned her to be careful, particularly as none of the women arrested so far had had any idea they were carrying. He was in Singapore and it had been in the press there. Not surprisingly in Thamel, the trekker bar district of Kathmandu, the talk was of little else. The word was that in all cases heroin had been found hidden in tourist items such as dolls, shoes or jackets which the women had bought as mementos or presents. It seemed the safest thing to do was to avoid buying any such items in or around Pokhara.

If the publicity surrounding the heroin arrests had not been a surprise to Jaci, an old copy of the *Kathmandu Post* was. There on the front page was a photograph of Edward Thurston. The headline read:

### FLYING BUSINESSMAN SAVES DYING MOUNTAIN GIRL

He hadn't mentioned this. She showed it to Jane.

"This is my boss," she said with a mixture of uncertainty and a strange sort of pride. Those within earshot gathered around trying to read the article over Jaci's and Jane's shoulders.

Jaci had just finished the short article when one of the crowd leaned forward and pushed another copy of the *Post* from two days later onto the table in front of them.

"If that's your boss then you'd better read this one as well. He could be in a spot of bother."

The headline in the *Kathmandu Post* two days later was:

### MOUNTAIN GIRL RESCUE
### HERO QUIZZED BY SECURITY POLICE

*British businessman Edward Thurston, who two days ago saved a dying girl by flying her through the Kali Gandaki Gorge, has been interviewed at length by security police. His chartered Otter made a forced landing on a newly constructed runway outside Lo Manthang when strong winds made the gorge impassable. The Security Police are believed to have become interested when it transpired that the runway, although physically complete, is not yet commissioned and that Mr Thurston did not have clearance to enter Mustang.*

"So what's your boss up to?" asked Jane looking into her friend's puzzled face.

"I have absolutely no idea," Jaci said. "The first article makes him look like a hero, but the second implies that he's up to something. But why would the security police be interested in whether or not the runway was commissioned?"

"Good question," said Jane.

Jaci looked at her watch. It was eleven p.m. and too late to telephone him in Singapore, but she would try in the morning.

### 6th May 2001

The following day she got up at five a.m. – she was awake with jet lag anyway – and managed to use a credit card street phone in Thamel and called Edward at what she estimated would be about eight a.m. local time. It hadn't been difficult to get the number for Raffles, which in turn had not been a difficult name to remember.

"Good morning, Edward," she said cheerfully, pleased that she had timed it to catch him in his room.

There was a moment's hesitation before he exclaimed, "Jaci? Where the hell are you calling from? Is something wrong?"

"You tell me, I'm calling from a pay phone in Kathmandu and I'm doing it at great expense because I spent most of last night reading about you in the local press."

"Yes, sorry – all that hero stuff – just happened to be in the right place at the wrong time."

"It's not the hero stuff I'm bothered about, Edward. It's your run-in with security. The papers make it look as if they think you're up to something."

"Jeez, don't you start – this is the sixth inquisition I've had on the subject in a week!"

"Why, what's going on?"

"It's a long story."

"Well, I'm paying."

"OK, but don't worry. I haven't gone rogue overnight."

"But why are the security people interested in you?"

"Because I landed in Mustang without permission. Just a technicality."

"And they questioned you for hours because of a technicality?"

"Again it's a long story and to be honest, I'm not totally quite sure what they were after. But I'm in Singapore now and getting on with the job. Nice of you to be concerned about me!"

She hadn't meant it to come over like that, so she tried to put it right.

"I'm sure you can look after yourself, Edward, that's not why I rang. I just thought, after your warning to me to be careful, I had better check, after your little chat with security, to see if there is anything else I should know."

"No, not really," he hesitated realizing there was something else, and he wanted to tell her without overdoing it. "Actually there is something. The heroin the arrested women have been carrying is almost pure which under Singapore law means they are carrying a small amount physically just a few grams, but at street dilution it would be several kilograms..."

"Which means?"

"Which means if found guilty they would be subject to a...," he hesitated, "...a severe penalty."

"Are you telling me they could be hanged?"

"Not *could* Jaci, if they are carrying over fifteen grams they will hang and there has never ever been any relaxation of the penalty. So just don't buy anything in the Pokhara area – and I mean anything."

The tone of his voice stopped her. "Alright, Edward. I won't."

She started to replace the handset, then added, "How is the trial work going?"

There was a moment hesitation before he answered. "Routine so far. The first few patients have been entered, but it's too early to see anything significant."

"OK," she still sounded uncertain.

"Oh, one more thing," Edward said, "just in case you run into any problems while you're out there perhaps it would be a good idea if you have my mobile number."

She wrote it down frowning. Giving her his mobile number was out of character. He must be seriously concerned.

# The Tissue Trail

~~~~~~~~~~

After having breakfast in a street café, Jaci and Jane shared a taxi to the airport and four hours after Jaci's call to Singapore, they were on a flight to Pokhara.

Their reaction to the towering Fishtail Mountain was the same as all travellers who see it for the first time – sheer disbelief at the 24,000 feet double snow peak towering over them as soon as they left the airplane. But Pokhara, like Kathmandu, was far bigger and more commercial than the picturesque village the old postcard shots showed on the shores of Lake Phewa. The centre of it was a wide-open "commercial boulevard" with a loosely defined lane of traffic on either side. Each trade was identified by a pile of the commodity tradesmen were working with, whether wood or bicycle parts or vegetables or pots and pans. There were no kerbstones or other means of marking where roads ended and pedestrian or working areas began, nor obvious demarcation of where one activity started and the next one finished.

The trekkers "domain" was situated on the north shore of Lake Phewa —a mile long lake renowned for its reflections of Fishtail and the Annapurna Range. There were rows of tea shops, cheap restaurants, cafes, bars, book and map shops, and shops selling trekking and mountaineering gear — colourful rucksacks, tents, sleeping bags, boots, paraffin stoves and anoraks. The travel and trekking shops themselves together created a throbbing riverside trekkers riviera. This was the vibrant atmosphere they had been looking forward to. They located the trekking company they had booked with and were taken by minibus to the open distribution area further down the lake where they collected their ground sheets and sleeping bags. As they did, so the Nepali manager told them there was one other thing they might be interested in. A travel magazine was offering $50 US for trekkers in this area to take notes of what they did and to take photographs to record what they had seen or whom they had met. A camera was provided, which they would return to him with their notes at the end of the trek. If for any reason they could not get back to him, the bookshop at the Soaltee Oberoi Hotel in Kathmandu was an alternative drop-off. The notes and photographs would be used in a series of articles about trekking in the Annapurnas.

Jaci and Jane could not see any harm in this proposition and the $50 would come in useful.

"How many people are doing this?" Jaci asked curiously.

"Twelve to begin with," the manager replied. "You two are the first. They will see how it goes with the first twelve and ask for more if needed."

The camera was not a make Jaci recognized. It's body was yellow plastic and waterproof with a neck strap so they could carry it "at the ready."

There were ten in the trekking group that gathered for the briefing by the trek leader – a typical small-boned, clean-featured, fit-looking Nepali in his late thirties. He told them that the first two days of the trek would be through sub- tropical vegetation with blue and purple flowered giant rhododendron bushes and red flowered bougainvillea. In the warm, humid conditions it would be normal to wear boots and shorts. The only downside was that the long wet warm grass was an ideal habitat for leeches, although not so ideal that the small pale brown "suctorial annelids" would not prefer switching to the nice warm flesh of human legs. There was a general communal shuddering at the prospect. The leader then went on to say that to the north, there would be frequent views of the majestic towering, gleaming white Annapurnas through gaps in the vegetation. On the third and fourth days they would climb above the tree line and into colder conditions with early morning frosts and hard ground.

On the last morning of the outward leg they would get up before first light and climb another 1,000 feet to the viewing point at Jha Hill to watch the sun light up the mountains at dawn. Their stopping points were not fixed, but they were advised to aim for eight to ten miles a day bearing in mind that they should only increase their altitude by around 1,000 to 1,500 feet a day. But the trail involved crossing deep river gullies each of which could mean climbing down 1,000 to 1,500 feet then climbing back to their original altitude. So, walking ten miles per day would be more than enough. They had opted to stay at teashops and fixed camps to keep the cost down rather than the more "luxurious" Sherpa assisted moving camps.

They had a couple of hours to spare over lunchtime and Jane had noticed a large tent in army camouflage amongst the trekking company stalls sporting the sign "ACAP Exhibition."

"I think this is something to do with conservation," said Jane, "let's have a look."

Jane was right. ACAP stood for the Annapurna Conservation Area Project. Leaflets, photographs, diagrams and graphs were spread along the table describing the various activities, which in summary were to balance encouragement of tourism with conservation of resources, even including birth control policy. "Looking at the crowds of people here and even more in Kathmandu I can see why," said Jaci, "but I'm still a bit surprised they are that advanced."

Jane was even more surprised to see two, fit European-looking men in their twenties behind the table at the far end engrossed in conversation with a Nepali in his mid-fifties wearing dark heavy rimmed glasses.

"What are they up to?" wondered Jane.

They worked their way along the table picking up different pieces of information until they could see a section in front of the men with the heading "Canadian Aid in Nepal."

"That explains it," said Jane, picking up a folder and flipping through it with Jaci looking over her shoulder. "Well I didn't know that," she said, reading it, "Canada is the largest single provider of overseas aid to Nepal."

The two younger men, who Jaci presumed to be Canadians, were wearing simple name badges – one Pierre, the other Jacques. The more senior Nepali's more imposing name badge proclaimed, "Major Jha – ACAP." Unusually, certainly for Jaci, the three men were so engrossed in their conversation that they did not react to the presence of the two women. But there was nothing in particular they wanted to ask. They had enough information to give them a good idea of what ACAP did. However, on the way out, Jane did notice something new and picked up three leaflets referring to "The Lost Kingdom of Mustang" and its old walled capital of Lo Manthang – and that the only way to reach it was through the world's deepest valley the Kali Gandaki Gorge.

"Are we going anywhere near there?" asked Jaci.

Jane looked quickly through the leaflets and stopped. "We don't get very near it, but according to this we will be able to see the entrance from Poon Hill."

In the early afternoon the group set off to cover a few miles and to get out of Pokhara. Jaci and Jane walked with the two Swedish women who were also carrying the disposable yellow cameras and also involved in the magazine initiative. They took photographs of each other and made notes about the trek. They had been asked not to take photographs of the mountains – there were more than enough of those from other sources.

# The Tissue Trail

## 7th May 2001

On the second morning an American, Steve Foster, a bit older than the women in their mid-twenties walked with them for twenty to thirty minutes but then moved on ahead. Jane, in particular, fancied his easy moving rangy build and was pleased when they found him alone at lunchtime just starting to eat at a roadside café. They asked if he minded if they joined him and he pointed to two empty chairs, "Help yourselves."

Both ordered the usual lentil soup and local bread and talked inconsequentially about the morning walk until Jane asked, "Isn't it unusual to trek on your own?"

"Yes, I suppose it is," he smiled.

"So why are you?" she put her chin on her upturned hand and looked up at him.

"I'm not really trekking," he said. "I'm heading for Annapurna base camp for an attempt on Annapurna Two. The Annapurna himal," he explained, "consists of a number of peaks Annapurna One, Two, Three and Four, then Hiunchuli." He pointed out the peaks, "and a number of others." Jane already knew this but didn't interrupt him.

"Where are the other climbers?" Jane asked.

"A couple of days behind," he said, "but I'm interested to see Poon Hill which is a bit off the normal base camp route. So I left early. They're going direct."

On the second night two new males caught up with them – the two Canadian's they had seen talking to Major Jha at the ACAP exhibition. They arrived at the teahouse after sunset and as the rest of the "tea shop" guests were already eating they ate by themselves. It was a repeating process, new people joining the group some of whom they ran into again at lunchtime or in the evening or the next day, some they never saw again.

## 8th May 2001

On the morning of the third day the Canadian boys joined them at breakfast chatting easily. They introduced themselves as Pierre and Jacques – both French Canadians. Steve Foster was also around, but was with another group.

# The Tissue Trail

The Canadians were intrigued by Jaci's and Jane's cameras and the notes they were taking – and the fact they were getting paid for it. Pierre asked if he could look at Jane's camera. She handed it over and he looked at it briefly, seemingly trying to see the make and model. Jacques asked what sort of notes they were making and was curious about what they had been asked to do. Pierre was more persistent and asked Jaci if he could see what she had written. She said she was happy to answer his questions, but preferred not to let anybody see what she had written, at least not in its rough, unedited form.

Jane laughed and started writing, "I'm just making a couple of notes about very nosy Canadians." Both laughed, but Jaci thought she detected some tension beneath the humour.

### 9th May 2001

On the fourth day and the last on the outward leg, the Canadians were around at breakfast time, but were paying more attention to the Swedish camera-carrying women. Steve Foster was nowhere to be seen at breakfast, but a couple of hours after they had set off he caught up with them.

"Looks as if the Canadians fancy you two," he laughed.

"I don't think they fancy either of us," Jaci said. "They are more interested in the cameras."

Just before their planned midday stop Jane stopped to look at some rare plant. This did not interest Jaci who found herself walking alone with Steve Foster. Being thrown together suddenly left them talking a little self-consciously about the excellent weather and the brilliant views until Steve asked Jaci how she was getting on with the "suctorial annelids"—breaking the ice with a warm moment of laughter.

A few moments silence followed until Jaci said, "I'm a bit puzzled."

"Oh?"

"Well you could move at twice our speed, but you just amble along at our sort of pace."

"There's no particular reason, I'm just taking it easy," he smiled.

"Perhaps," she replied, "but moving at half pace all the time would drive me crazy."

"Is it that obvious?" he asked. "Or are you just unusually observant."

"It's what I'm paid for," Jaci said. "As a medical researcher I need to be observant."

"Wow! Bit of brain then?"

"Not sure about brain. I suppose most people are quite good at something! I'm quite good at being nosey."

"So I've started to notice." Steve half smiled, but then looked thoughtful himself, remembering something.

Jaci tilted her head to one side, "What's the matter?"

"Medical research did you say?" he asked.

"Yes, why?"

"I'd never heard the term medical research, now it comes up twice in a few days – a guy who's been in the news getting everybody excited in Mustang. Now you!"

"This 'guy' you're talking about – you mean the one who rescued the dying girl?"

"Yeah, him." He looked at her.

"I work for him," she said.

"You do?" Steve was incredulous. "Does he often try to commit suicide just to take photographs?"

Jaci looked surprised, "What do you mean?"

"His flight into Mustang. He chartered an airplane as a training flight because the wind was too bad for normal commercial flying, then it got worse and they couldn't get back to their take-off point, so they had to land on an unfinished runway!"

"I didn't know any of that," she said. "But he did tell me he had been questioned for three hours because of it."

Steve paused.

"I assume you know about the Tissue Trail women being arrested in Singapore?"

"Yes."

"And that the trail they are referring to is this one?"

Jaci stopped in her tracks, "No, I didn't. I knew the arrested women had bought the items where the heroin was hidden near Pokhara, but not that this was the Tissue Trail."

"Well it certainly is," said Steve. "Up to yesterday there have been five, all on this part of the Poon Hill trek."

Jaci frowned, still not moving. "So that's why Edward was so bothered?"

"Edward?"

"My boss."

"What did he say?"

"He told me to be careful – and not to buy anything in the Pokhara area."

"Good advice from everything I've heard."

They had stopped near a roadside shop and café and decided to stay for lunch.

"Where is your boss now?" he asked as they sat down.

"Singapore," Jaci replied. "Doing some clinical trial work."

"Singapore? So, he's just been in the area where the women are picking up the substance and now he's in the place where they are getting themselves arrested? He'll be getting himself into another serious interview."

Jaci looked concerned. "If the security people think like you then they must think he's somehow involved with these Tissue Trail arrests?"

"That's pretty much the bottom line." He looked away as if he had said something he regretted and hoped she hadn't noticed – but he was out of luck.

"How do you know all this? It wasn't in the papers."

He hesitated, "My father is seconded to the Metropolitan police and out here helping set up some new computer system, so I get to hear some of the inside story."

"So what have they decided? My boss is a drug runner?"

"They don't know. They're still working on it."

"Well I think I know him pretty well, and I also know he is earning a fortune with his day job so I reckon they're way off the mark. He wouldn't get involved in anything like that in a million years."

"OK, I'll tell the old man," Steve said smiling. "He can pass it on."

Both were silent for a time, then Steve asked an unexpected question. "What do you make of Pierre and Jacques?"

Jaci shrugged, "They seem nice enough."

Steve shook his head, "I mean their interest in your cameras?"

"I don't know. I should think they are a bit fed up that they didn't get the chance to earn a few dollars themselves."

"Doing the magazine job?"

"Yes," she said. Jaci thought for a minute. "But apart from their interest in the cameras there is another thing."

"What's that?"

"I'm not completely sure, but I think they are both avoiding being photographed."

Steve frowned.

"Why are you so interested?" she asked.

"Like you – just nosey."

Jaci looked at him. "There's more to this than you're letting on, isn't there?"

He returned her look. "No," he said evenly, "as I said, just curious."

When they started the final outward afternoon session, Pierre and some of the others appeared and joined them as they moved off. It was a big group and soon broke up into twos and threes. They were now above the tree line and looking up at the massive gleaming snow walls and ridges sweeping down from Annapurna himal. Ahead they could see a ridge, which formed a shoulder on the skyline ahead of them. It was the Ghorapani Ridge; another four hours walking and they would reach their furthest point.

Jaci updated Jane on what Steve had been telling her. Jane asked Jaci what she made of it and what she thought her boss was up to.

"I really don't think he's involved in anything he shouldn't be. His problem is he always thinks he can get to do what he wants even when any normal person would think it impossible, so what he does can look unusual or even, I suppose, suspicious."

"What sort of thing do you mean?"

"He was told in Johannesburg last year he couldn't get to Victoria Falls and back in the ten hours between his incoming and outgoing flights. But he disagreed, bought a return ticket and did it – even if he only saw the falls for ten minutes."

"Was it worth it?"

"He said so. The way he saw it, if he never got to see the falls again, that ten minutes would be priceless. But anybody seeing him do that would have wondered what on earth he was up to."

"Any more stories like that?"

"Oh, yes! He had four hours one afternoon on the north coast of Mallorca and wanted to see a mountain called Formentor. He tried to find a local to take him in a boat, but on a Sunday afternoon there were no boat owners around. But he found a Sunday school outing of a hundred kids on a pleasure cruiser going to Formentor for a picnic. He offered to pay, but they were so amazed they took him for nothing – Edward and a hundred kids."

"See what you mean."

"So chartering a plane as a training flight fits the bill – even if it's dangerous," Jaci mused. "He once chartered a plane to get to the active volcano on Montserrat and it erupted in front of him. Most people would have turned away, but he kept going to try to get the best possible video shots."

"So what he did in Mustang was, for him, pretty routine?"

"Yep, pretty much."

"Meanwhile there's another problem."

"Oh?"

"Steve is curious about the Canadians."

"Well aren't you? They seem to be obsessed with the cameras."

"And if I'm right they're avoiding being photographed themselves."

"We can soon put that to the test."

"And Steve's story about his father being in the police doesn't ring true, nor him being a mountaineer."

"So what's going on, Sherlock?"

"Don't know, but if Steve is not quite what he says he is and the Canadians are acting strangely, I'm just beginning to wonder if this magazine camera exercise is quite what we were told it is."

Jane looked worried. "And if it isn't, what do you think it is?"

"We were told not to bother taking photographs of the mountains, but to concentrate on who we met and talked to. And we're on the Tissue Trail where all five of the arrested women trekked!"

"What?"

"That's what Steve just told me."

"We're on a trek which all five of the arrested women used and they are all going to hang?"

"That's about the size of it."

"Holy cow, so you think this magazine thing is a spying mission?"

Jaci raised her hands palms upwards. "Well at least a fishing expedition."

Jane thought for a minute, "Are you saying Pierre and Jacques are linked to whatever it is?"

"I just don't know. But I'm getting pretty uncomfortable about it."

During the course of the afternoon, Jaci and Jane tried to get the Canadians into several photographs including a "last day group" but both came up with every excuse in the book.

After the third attempt Jaci said, "Not much doubt about it now is there?"

"No," Jane replied, "I just wish we knew why."

On the final hour long climb to Ghorapani the Canadians split up. It didn't occur to Jaci until later that this on its own was worth comment; but of more interest was that both became involved in animated conversations, Jacques with the Swedish camera women and Pierre, not just animated but, it seemed to Jaci, in a conversation with Steve that could have been strained.

Just after four p.m. they arrived at the village of Ghorapani with its pale ochre and white walled thatched houses and the high peaks hidden in afternoon cloud. Jaci and Jane selected a tea shop, walked in and stowed their backpacks in the small dormitory.

Half an hour later they made their way downstairs to the eating area. Jaci was a few yards ahead and as she made her way across the small courtyard to get a drink, Steve intercepted her indicating he wanted a quiet word. He clearly wanted to avoid being overheard and took her into the shadows.

"The Swedish women think somebody has been trying to get at their notes, even their cameras. They're pretty sure their rucksacks were given the once over last night."

"Right." Both Jaci's voice and expression indicated that she wasn't sure why he was telling her.

He paused, "OK, I'm going to have to level with you. As you've guessed I've not been telling you the whole deal; this magazine exercise is a long shot attempt to look for something or somebody which might give a lead to the Tissue Trail traffickers. It is important that your notes and camera are protected, so don't let the Canadians, or anybody else, get near them. Just hang on to them and get them back to Pokhara."

Jacques and Pierre, now together again, appeared a few yards away. Steve stopped dead and changed the subject. Jaci lifted the camera and took a shot of Steve pointing away from the Canadians, but as she lowered it she pretended to fumble and as she turned, "accidentally" pressed the take button with the camera pointing roughly in the direction of the Canadians. She was fairly sure that neither suspected what she had done.

The evening meal was set round a large table with the atmosphere somewhat subdued. Jacques appeared a few minutes later, but Pierre was half an hour after the others. After the meal of meat soup, bread and lentils, Jaci said she was getting a headache and was going to get an early night. Steve wondered if it was the first sign of mountain sickness even though 10,000 feet is a bit on the low side. As Jaci got up, Jane told her she wouldn't be far behind. In the dormitory Jaci checked her rucksack and was sure it had been disturbed – but she had kept her camera and notes in her money bag which she kept strapped around her waist.

"That does it," she told Jane when she came up a few minutes later. "When the others go up to Poon Hill tomorrow morning I'm going to pretend to be worse and when they've gone I'm going to head back to Pokhara."

"OK," said Jane. "I'll stay and look after you, then we'll go together."

### *10th May 2001*

The next morning, Jaci announced over a large weak re-hydrating orange juice that she was feeling worse and that she was going to stay put and try and shake off her headache. Pierre said he would stay with her, but Jaci thanked him and told him she would be fine with her friend Jane. Jaci and Jane both had everything packed and as soon as the Canadians were out of sight on the Poon Hill climb, they left the tea-shop and took the trail east back towards Pokhara. Steve realized what they were doing and, as he brushed past Jaci on the way out to join the Poon Hill climbers, he wished them good luck and added, "If they start to come after you I'll shadow them."

"Thanks," said Jaci. "By the way, were you having a punch up with Jacques and Pierre yesterday afternoon?"

Steve frowned. "Yes, you could say that, they were having a go at me along the same lines as you've been – what am I really doing here?"

"And?"

"I told them the same as I told you, making for Annapurna base camp – and what business was it of theirs anyway."

"Looked unpleasant."

"It wasn't particularly amusing."

The weather was crystal clear and the Annapurna peaks were sharp edged shining white against the azure sky. And if they had not had other things on their minds they might even have noticed. They had a three to four hour start on anybody, doing the Jha Hill climb before setting off on the return trek. It might not be enough if fit young males were determined to catch them, but both women were in good shape and the return trek was mostly downhill. Jane reckoned if they kept going they could get back by lunchtime on the third day. They were not quite sure what they would do when they reached Pokhara, but they had time to think about it.

They kept going until darkness started to fall and managed to reach a village which they estimated was just under half of the way back. They bought some bread, cheese, fruit and tomatoes, avoiding bars and anywhere where trekkers collected and ate their supplies in a small outbuilding on the Pokhara side of the settlement. They stayed in the same place to sleep, or at least tried.

### 11th May 2001

The weather stayed fine and they made good time eating the last of their rations and setting off as the first glimmer of sunlight touched the tops of the Annapurnas. Within half an hour there were a number of other trekkers making their way in both directions. They stopped to buy more basic supplies and kept going over lunchtime. As darkness fell at the end of the second day they were three quarters of the way back, and there was no sign of Jacques or Pierre. Before eating they found an outbuilding on a small farm and asked the owner if they could sleep there. He looked uncertain, but a ten rupee note did the trick.

### 12th May 2001

On the third day, three hours after setting off at first light, they were four miles from Pokhara, walking along the Naudhara Ridge to the road head. A further fifteen minutes and half a mile ahead they could see the four -by-four that would take them the last three miles into Pokhara. They looked nervously backwards. There were two or three trekkers behind, but none of them looked remotely like either of the Canadians.

The bus did not work to a timetable, but waited until it was full before setting off. The previous bus had just left and the two women were the first on the next departure and started to wait nervously for additional trekkers to fill the bus. Twenty minutes later it had not moved and only three more passengers had joined the eight seater. They could see the last half mile of the ridge road and watched anxiously. Jane was the first to see what looked like a male figure taking shape at the end of the straight. Within half a minute the green and yellow colours Jacques had been wearing came into focus. He was moving quickly. Jaci told the driver she was running short of time to catch a flight and showed him a $10 dollar bill. He may not have been sure of its worth, but he could see it was significant enough to stifle any debate and he started the engine and moved off. The Canadian had closed to within 400 yards and was waving frantically, but $10 was more than enough to induce a remarkable loss of awareness on the part of the driver.

"This is not amusing," Jane said.

"No it isn't," said Jaci.

"So what do we do now? It's not going to take him long to find a way into town – we've got fifteen minutes on him, maximum."

"Which rules out going directly to the airport. No way we could check-in and catch a flight before he caught up with us."

Jaci looked at her companion. "If we can get lost for twelve hours they will be pretty sure we've got out of Pokhara. So I think our best chance is to catch a bus which is just on the point of leaving in a direction he wouldn't expect."

"Do you have any idea what bus we will need? We'll only have a few seconds."

"Go south," said Jaci, "towards Chitwan and the Indian border. There should be plenty of buses heading in that direction. It's the only other main route out of the place."

"Did you say the Indian border?" asked Jane. "I'm not sure I'd want to come back to Pokhara. I think I'd prefer to carry onto Delhi and fly out of there. I've got one of those around the world tickets which I can use from anywhere as long as I keep going east."

"That would be good thinking for you," said Jaci. "But I've got a fixed inclusive return from Kathmandu. If I go from anywhere else I'd have to pay a new full fare!"

"Well if you're happy to take the risk?" Jane left the question hanging.

"Let's get out of Pokhara first, then we can talk about it again."

The Nissan dropped them alongside the busy bus station and Jaci gave the driver the $10 bill as they climbed out of the bus. He reacted with a broad smile. She just hoped he would know what to do to cash it without being swindled; but right now she had to focus her attention on escaping the attentions of Pierre and Jacques.

There were about a dozen buses in the station, some loading, ready to leave, others unloading after inward trips, in all cases passengers inside, luggage on the roof. Jaci asked one of the bus company employees where the next bus heading in the Chitwan direction was leaving from. He pointed to two buses, which he told them were due to leave together in about five minutes. She asked him where the Kathmandu buses were, as almost certainly Jacques would search those first. He pointed to the other side of the station.

The first Chitwan bus still had a few seats at the back and they worked their way towards them. It was chaos, with passengers packing themselves, their parcels and boxes into the available seats; the mixture of smells of not particularly well washed humanity and of stale curry was colourful. They would not be able to bribe the driver of a scheduled bus service so they would have to sit and sweat it out. They could see the traffic approaching from the Naudhara Ridge direction and watched nervously for the next four-by-four from the road head. They worked their way as deeply into their seats as possible, with rucksacks on their laps hiding themselves from view.

Ten minutes later the Chitwan bus was full and people were boarding the second bus. Their driver had appeared and was fussing around the front of the vehicle making last minute preparations to leave.

"It's amazing how long it takes people like drivers to do absolutely nothing when you're late or anxious to get going," said Jane, trying to squeeze even further down into the seat.

Their respective heart rates rose sharply when the next four-by-four appeared round the corner about three hundred yards away, making its way through the melee of traffic and pulled up where theirs had stopped. The first to alight was one of the Canadians, but it wasn't Jacques, it was Pierre.

"Jacques must have gone to the airport," said Jaci.

Pierre immediately ran to the nearest member of the bus station staff where he clearly asked for directions and then headed straight for the Kathmandu stand. There were three Kathmandu buses lined up, two already heavily loaded and the third just starting to take on passengers.

Pierre worked his way round the first bus peering into the crowded interior. Their own driver was now on board and in the driving seat, but still talking to somebody outside the bus.

"Come on, come on," Jaci whispered urgently under her breath.

Pierre started on the second Kathmandu bus. "What will he do next?" Jane had her fingers tightly interlocked.

"I suppose he'll just start checking the rest, but there are another eight or nine buses. So unless he thinks of doing the long distance ones first we should be out of here if this bloody driver ever gets going!"

Just as Pierre gave up on the second bus their driver started the motor. Seconds later, he was pushing his way into the pedestrians, bicycles, tempo taxis and small cars and flat back trucks which filled the roadway. As the bus pulled away from the station the two women maintained their low profile positions for a full five minutes before finally easing themselves up out of their seats and celebrating with sighs and low key high fives.

"But it's not over yet," said Jaci. "They could still guess that this is the most likely way to get out of Pokhara if we were not heading for Kathmandu."

Jane was silent for a moment looking thoughtful then said, "Why are two Canadians interested in something that's happening in Nepal?"

"No idea. Not the faintest clue!" said Jaci.

Both sat quietly for a time watching the crowds and the slowly thinning traffic as the bus nosed its way south and into increasingly lush vegetation.

"What are we going to do with our cameras?" said Jane.

"I've been thinking about that," said Jaci. "My first thought is to dump them and avoid any risk of them helping the Canadians or anybody else to trace us."

"But Steve was pretty keen for us to get them back to the trekking organizers."

"But he wasn't being chased by a couple of psycho Canadians was he? – but you're right. Even if the postmark tells them which way we went it will be several days later and it'll be too late to be any use to anybody."

"So what, at the first opportunity we parcel them up and post them back to the trek organizers?"

"And include our addresses for them to send the checks. I reckon we've more than earned the money?"

"Might as well. But what are you thinking about your way out?" Jaci said.

"The same as we talked about before," said Jane. "Carry on to Delhi and fly on from there. What about you?"

Jaci thought for a moment, "We've got a lunch stop at Kurintar in a couple of hours. I'll try and give Edward a ring. He'll have one or two ideas, he normally does."

"You quite like him don't you?"

Jaci smiled, "I wouldn't kick him out of bed."

She tried to phone at the Kurintar stop but could not reach him either on his mobile or at Raffles. But by the time she got back to Jane she had decided what she was going to do. "That bus," she pointed across the road, "leaves for Pokhara in ten minutes. It gets back about four o'clock and I'll go straight to the airport and get a flight to Kathmandu tonight."

Jane frowned, "You're sure that's a good idea?"

"No. It's probably a very silly idea. But ..."

Jane now looked crestfallen. "So it's good-bye now?"

"'Fraid so."

"And you're sure you are prepared to take the risk?"

"Yes. If the worst comes to the worst and they find me and turn nasty I'll just have to give them the camera."

"And what if they ask where I am?"

"I'll tell them you're spending a few days in Chitwan looking for tigers."

The two women looked at each other then hugged. Jaci got up and carried her rucksack forward and stepped down from the bus.

Both waved, both trying to hide their glistening eyes.

### 11th May 2001, 4:10 p.m.

The return bus arrived in Pokhara ten minutes later than scheduled, but with an hour and a half daylight left which was Jaci's main concern. She let most of the other passengers alight first so that she could have a good look around. There was no sign of either Pierre or Jacques or for that matter Steve, which would have been a nice twist. So she got off the bus and jumped into one of the three wheeled tempo taxis' because its deep black canvas hood with no windows made it easier for her to remain hidden from view. And it was cheaper. She told the driver she wanted to go to the airport then sat back scanning the traffic and the milling pedestrians. As the tempo moved away from the bus station she caught sight of the screen of one of the public televisions mounted on a telephone line support with the usual crowd of mainly younger people looking up at it – but she forgot she was supposed to be sitting back out of sight and shot forward when she thought she saw Steve's face on the screen.

She thought about asking the driver to go back, but decided she would have time to find a television at the airport – hopefully with more opportunity to hide in the crowds.

At the airport she paid the driver and checked around her before dashing into the terminal and heading for cover between two large potted plants. She could not see anybody to be worried about, nor could she see a public television, but she did see a newspaper left on a seat a few yards from her cover. She needed to move further into the terminal and after checking again she moved quickly past the seat, grabbed the newspaper and carried on into a crowd of travellers making their way towards a departure area where a flight had been called. She came to a ladies' toilet and nipped through the door as two women came out. She shut the door of the closet, put down her rucksack and lifted the newspaper to look at the front page; Steve's full head and shoulder shot was on the front page. It was alongside the headline:

### TREKKER MURDERED ON POON HILL

*A 27-year-old trekker was found dead with stab wounds near the top of Poon Hill a popular viewing point near the village of Ghorapani on the Pokhara Jomsom trail, on Sunday. The man has been identified as Stephen Foster, an American who it is reported to have been trekking on his own. He was found in a roadside hut at lunchtime on 10th May. Pokhara police believe that he had been killed earlier that day. There is no immediately obvious motive and police have started to interview trekkers who were on Poon Hill that day. They are said to be anxiously tracing four women; two Swedish, two British, all of whom are reported to have been taking photographs for a travel magazine. So far, our reporter understands, the police have found no trace of any of the four.*

Jaci felt sick and her stomach tightened with fear and uncertainty. Steve was dead, murdered. It had to be the Canadians and now she was being sought by the police. And on top of that the Swedish women had disappeared. There was no way they could have reached Pokhara ahead of

Jacques and Pierre because they had all climbed Poon Hill together. It was clear that she had had a much more serious near miss than she had realized when Pierre didn't find her at the bus station. It was hard to believe that it was only that morning. She was not sure what to do and her mind was spinning with questions. Should she contact the police or jump on the first flight out of Pokhara? Did they know her name? They would if they had checked at the trekking centre. And if they had, surely she would be stopped when her passport was examined at check-in or passport control. There was one person she would like to go over the options with – Edward Thurston. He might be a bit of a pain and some people thought he was a bit too sure of himself, but there was one thing he was never short of and that was advice.

She tucked the newspaper into the top flap of her rucksack, opened the closet door and peered out, then moved, keeping close to the walls as she had seen them do in spy films. She eventually reached a point where she could see without being seen. She had her long blonde hair, a sure fire giveaway, piled up under a baseball cap and wore her large rimmed dark glasses. She was looking for a credit card phone and found one where she could hide her head and shoulders in the sound hood and stay out of sight of the crowded floor of the terminal. It was four p.m. in Nepal which would be about 6:30 p.m. in Singapore. She made a call via the operator to Raffles Hotel and asked to speak to Edward Thurston. Almost immediately a male voice came onto the line.

"Edward Thurston," said the voice.

"Edward, I need to talk to you." This statement of the blatantly obvious and her quiet voice had the desired effect. There was a brief silence at the other end before he said, "Go on."

She told him the story of the last five days – since her last call, in fact. She told him that the trail she had trekked was the one they were calling the Tissue Trail where all five arrested heroin women had also trekked; she described the camera initiative, the antics of the Canadians, the strained conversation with Steve Foster and animated conversations with the Swedish women. Then Jacques and Pierre chasing back to Pokhara and almost catching the two of them. She told him about Steve, including him seeming to know more about Thurston's activities than he could have picked up from newspapers. Then an hour ago, seeing the reports of the murder of Steve Foster and the police were looking for both her and Jane and the two Swedish women. She concluded by saying she wasn't sure whether to go to the police or get out of Nepal.

For a few seconds Edward was quiet then started asking rapid fire questions.

"Where are you now?"

"Pokhara Airport."

"Can you see the Kathmandu departure gate?"

"Yes."

"Any sign of the Canadians or police?"

"No."

"Are people going through?"

"Yes, but not many. By the looks of it most of the passengers on this flight have already gone through."

"Right, this is what I think you should do. When you think they are about to close the flight, move quickly to it, acting flustered, dropping your passport and ticket, that sort of thing. With a bit of luck they'll wave you through without too much checking. Where are your camera and notes?"

"At the bottom of my rucksack."

"If you can, before you get to the baggage x-ray try to get the camera to the top – it will look odd, a tourist with a camera buried in her baggage."

"OK, I'll do it while we're talking."

"If the police or intelligence people are looking for you and have a tight check-in place there is nothing much we can do. Give them your camera and notes, tell them you are concerned about the Canadians who you saw having a row with Foster and who chased you back to Pokhara and say you are worried about getting out of Nepal safely and – you don't want to be left alone."

"Wow, is that all?" she half laughed down the phone. "I'd better get going."

"Wait for it," he stopped her. "Pokhara is not the biggest danger now. The Canadians know you arrived in Pokhara this morning so they will assume you must have got out of the place somehow. So they'll be concentrating on Kathmandu, because unless you go south to India they know you will have to fly out of Nepal that way. So when you get to Kathmandu go to the tourist desk and ask for an expensive hotel – something like the Yak and Yeti or the Soaltee Oberoi. As soon as you arrive at the hotel tell them you have to unexpectedly go to a business meeting and you need some decent clothes. Then get yourself a business class ticket or first class if business is full to Singapore."

"Singapore?" she almost shouted. "Why?"

"First, because it is unlikely they will think of looking for you heading in that direction. In fact, if they are as sophisticated as it is beginning to look, they will have checked your flight details and know you are booked to go back to London. But there's another reason. Some unexpected side effects are appearing with Surmil and we can't figure out why."

She managed a smile, "I told you, you wouldn't manage without me."

"We'll talk about that later – I assume your mobile is dead?"

"Yes, not too many places to charge it in this sort of country, oh, and how am I going to pay for all this?"

"I've already arranged for your credit card account to be in funds. But if you manage to blow that, phone me and I'll give them my credit card details. And try to get your phone charged and keep me in the picture."

"OK, I'd better go, it looks as if they're about to close the flight."

She hung up and half ran, half walked, to the check-in desk, pulling her passport and ticket out of her money belt as she went. She didn't have to pretend to be flustered, she *was* flustered and dropped the passport and ticket quite naturally.

"Can I get on this flight?" she asked breathlessly.

"You'll have to hurry miss, but you should just make it if you've no hold baggage to check-in."

The attendant looked briefly at the passport to check the name against the ticket and gave her a boarding card. Jaci looked around nervously. She saw two Indian-looking businessmen staring at her, but that was not unusual. There was no sign of the Canadians or any curious police.

She boarded the flight nervously looking around for anybody she knew or anybody she didn't know showing any interest in her. She saw neither.

Her late check-in left her seated at the rear, which meant she could see anything and anybody on the twenty seater and she could remain largely out of sight. Nothing happened and two hours later, in near darkness, she had left the flight and entered the domestic terminal of Tribhuvan Airport, Kathmandu. There had been no passport check as the flight had been internal and again she edged her way towards the exit staying away from open areas. In the exit concourse she saw what she was looking for, a kiosk advertising tourist information and accommodation. There were five or six people waiting and she stood behind a display of maps and books waiting until the number reduced.

She didn't want to be exposed at the end of the line any longer than absolutely necessary.

She had decided to take a taxi to one of the top hotels and if there were no rooms available she could make more enquiries from there. The woman at the kiosk suggested a hotel called the Yak and Yeti which sounded just right. Jaci made her way outside into the darkness and into the crowds either leaving or arriving or as seemed common at airports not actually going anywhere. She felt more comfortable surrounded by people and out of the light. She looked around to see how the taxi system worked and decided there wasn't a system, just a melee of vehicles —mostly of the hooded tempo variety. She was just trying to decide what to do when she saw a traditional European type of upright four to six seater vehicle with a Yak and Yeti Hotel logo on the door. It had just offloaded four expensively dressed passengers, one of whom was paying the driver, the others calling porters to take their baggage. She looked down at herself: dusty walking boots, rolled down grey woollen socks, legs stained with sweat, mud and dust, grimy grey shorts and an even more grimy, once white T-shirt. And instead of Gucci cases she had a battered dusty rucksack. This was going to be a bit of a problem but there was no other way, she would have to brazen it out. She pushed between the alighting passengers and jumped into the back seat. The driver was still sorting out the change for the incoming group's fare and didn't initially notice her. This gave her a few seconds to find two $10 bills one of which she kept in her hand and pushed the other into her pocket in case one didn't do the trick.

Finally the Nepali driver finished with the previous group and looked round at her. He couldn't see her clearly in the darkness but the rucksack, shorts and boots were clearly not the attire of the normal clientele of the Yak and Yeti.

"This is going to the Yak and Yeti, Miss."

"I know, that is where I want to go."

"Are you sure, Miss?"

"Yes, I'm sure and I'm in a hurry if you don't mind." She held up the $10 note.

"OK Miss, but I will need to wait to see if there are any more travellers wanting to use this shuttle."

"If I share with other people I assume I won't pay if this is the hotel shuttle?" she said, still holding the $10 note in her hand.

He looked around quickly to make sure there weren't going to be any angry Yak and Yeti guests complaining about the shuttle leaving the airport with five empty seats. When satisfied, he started up the engine and moved off. It was about a ten minute ride through the heavy traffic near the airport then down the Durbar Marg to the famous hotel.

The taxi drove into the hotel approach and parked some way from the normal drop off point. The driver explained this was because he wasn't supposed to accept money for the trip and didn't want to be seen. She handed over the $10 bill, making a mental note that if she ever did run into Jacques or Pierre again she would ask them to reimburse the taxi driver bribes. They were costing her a fortune!

She walked into the reception area, conscious of heads turning with surprise to see this apparition from another world, but she carried on up to the surprisingly empty check-in desk. There were three staff on duty, two men and one woman. She selected the younger of the two men and stood in front of him.

"I'm sorry to arrive like this, but I've had to break off from a trekking holiday to attend a business meeting."

Despite her smile he still managed to produce a classic nose in the air, *"What dung heap have you just crawled out of"* look followed by, "Do you have a reservation, madam?"

She was ready for this. "No, but my managing director told me to take any room available including the bridle suite if necessary" – she turned up the smile a couple of notches – "and, if necessary, to use his black credit card."

The eyebrows rose dutifully.

"I see, madam, let me see what we can do."

"And I will also need to buy a smart business suit; do you have somewhere I can buy that sort of thing?" She would have enjoyed playing the Julia Roberts role in *Pretty Woman* when she tried to buy expensive clothes in Rodeo Drive, if the situation had been a little less serious.

He looked up and started to say, "Yes, we do madam but it is very exp..."

Jaci cut him off. "If I can afford the bridal suite I don't think a few smart clothes would be too much of a problem. But of course I would have to be a resident."

The conversation had now attracted the manager who was standing behind her check-in position. It had also attracted the attention of the travellers standing in the queues which had now formed on either side of her. It was becoming quite a show, the very opposite of the "keeping a low profile" she had intended.

The manager reached forward and pointed to something on the computer screen. "I'm sure Miss Linthorpe would be happy with that." The check-in man half turned with surprise to his boss who leaned closer to him and whispered something into his ear which Jaci guessed was along the lines of *"just do it and quickly and get this woman away from here."* The manager asked Jaci to give him her passport and credit card and then asked, "Will you be eating with us tonight, madam?" which again she roughly translated as: *"If you are eating in the restaurant we might need to do something about your clothes now."* She smiled, "No I don't think so. I am very tired so I'll just get something from room service – but I would like to buy my clothes tonight as I want to leave as early as possible in the morning."

The manager glanced at his watch. "I'll ask them to wait for you," he said, picking up the internal phone.

The listening crowd were making noises of approval, but Jaci kept faced forward to avoid drawing any more attention to herself. But at least neither the manager nor the check-in man had connected her passport details with her appearance on the front page of the *Kathmandu Post*. So far, so good.

"There is one more thing," she told the manager, who had now effectively taken over. "In fact two more things, I would like to have my hair done, and I need to book a flight to Singapore."

"I think we can help you with both, madam. What time do you want to fly?"

"As early as possible tomorrow."

The manager pointed to the travel desk on the other side of the reception area. "I think there is a flight at eleven a.m." He handed her a room key, passport and credit card.

"If you don't mind, madam, would you please go to buy your clothes first, they are waiting to close...and we have arranged your hair appointment for 7:30 p.m., that is in about an hour and a half."

She thanked him and turned back through the now substantial crowd waiting to check-in.

The travel desk confirmed that there was a flight at eleven a.m. and that there were business class and first class seats available. She hesitated, but decided to settle for business.

# The Tissue Trail

The manager personally took her to the small but elegant shopping area and to the expensively appointed women's fashion shop. A trim Nepali man in his early forties had already selected three suits which to her eye all looked gorgeous. Two were pale grey, one dark blue. The dark blue suit was a shiny mohair material and the one she immediately hoped would be the best fit. All three were over $1,000!

"I like them," she told the two men. "Give me fifteen minutes to shower then I'll try them and perhaps you can find a blouse or shirt and shoes to go with the navy."

The manager seemed pleased at the prospect of a good sale this late in the day and was more than happy to wait for her.

Her room, if you can call a three room palatial suite a room, continued her brief escape into luxurious unreality. No wonder the check-in man had been surprised. She threw her rucksack onto the bed and threw herself into a comfortable low chair, stretching out with her arms above her and her head back. She had made it – so far. But then she remembered the photograph of Steve and the fear and uncertainty returned. The main obstacle was still to go to the airport in the morning. She stayed in the chair for a few moments then hauled herself to her feet, turned on the shower and removed the clothes she had worn for nearly three days and hosed herself down, including her hair, in the hot needles of the shower for a full five minutes.

After drying herself in the luxury towel she put on some clean underwear, a clean T-shirt and jeans and made her way down to the emporium. With her hair washed straight and the mud and dust removed she was barely recognizable and the shop manager looked at her twice before responding with, "Ah, Miss Linthorpe."

He had laid out the mohair suit with what looked like a silk shirt in pale blue, dark blue choker with simulated ruby motif, pale tights and navy blue, soft leather, medium heeled shoes together with an elegant navy blue handbag. He ushered her to the changing room.

She carefully put on the shirt and the rest of the outfit, hoping against hope that it would fit.

It did, and even with her hair hanging straight and damp she had to admit she looked good.

The manager looked her up and down as she came out of the cubicle. "I don't need to say anything, do I?" he said with a polite smile.

"No," Jaci replied. "I don't think you do."

"Do you want to take everything?"

"Yes, I do," she said. "In fact, I'd like to wear it now." It would be nice to have people in the hotel looking at her because she looked smart.

She paid with her credit card, remembering Edward had said he had funded it to make sure she would not be embarrassed. She wondered how he had done that.

She had half an hour before her hair appointment, which she needed to update Edward with the good news that she was still alive and the bad news that she was costing him a fortune.

Back in her room, she picked up the phone.

"I want to make a call to Singapore please," she said. "Mr Edward Thurston at Raffles Hotel."

The time would be around 8:30 a.m. in Singapore, perhaps a bit late to catch him in the hotel, but she could at least leave a message. The call was put through and to her surprise Edward answered.

"I was getting a bit concerned about you," he said. "Where are you now?"

"I'm at the Yak and Yeti," she replied, "burning a big hole in your expense account. I hope that isn't too much of a problem."

"I am not interested in money at the moment," he said a little impatiently. "Tell me what's happening – is there any sign of the Canadians or anybody else taking an interest in you?"

She outlined what had happened since the earlier call.

"So they didn't pick up on your details when you checked in?"

"No, but checking in attracted quite a lot of attention. People around me seemed to be interested in my conversation with the hotel receptionists."

There was a pause.

"Is there a flight to Singapore tonight?" he asked.

"I don't know," she replied, "I didn't ask. Why?"

"You are too exposed. Anybody on reception or the travel desk could recognize your details and tip off the police. We've got to get you out of there. If there isn't a flight to Singapore check if there is anything to Kuala Lumpur or Bangkok or Calcutta, anywhere with an onward connection to Singapore."

"But I'm exhausted," she sighed, "and I've not stayed in a suite before."

"Which do you prefer," he asked, still sounding cold and detached, "staying alive or a comfortable night?"

"What's the matter Edward?" she asked puzzled.

"The matter is that the murder of this chap Steve is the third death connected to this business that I know about, including the pilot who flew me into Mustang. Now you are being chased by the Canadians and the two Swedish women are missing. This is not a game. Whatever is behind all this, it is serious."

"OK," she said. "I'll get onto the travel desk and see what they can do."

"At least with a business class ticket you will be able to re-route it."

"I thought you weren't interested in money at the moment."

"Sorry," he said, "Freudian slip!" His voice softened for the first time.

"OK, Edward, I'll see what I can do," she sighed. The interlude of luxurious unreality had not lasted very long. There was a pause then he said, "If you can go tonight just leave the hotel as you are, as if you are just going out to meet somebody for the evening. Don't make it look as if you are checking out," and he added, "leave the rucksack."

"But you told me to…"

"That was before Stephen Foster was stabbed to death." He deliberately spelled it out.

The travel desk suggested taking a flight to Kuala Lumpur at 2330 getting in at 0500 in the morning with an onward connection at 0630 arriving in Singapore at 0800. She could use a Club Lounge to rest between flights. She asked them to make the booking.

She used the hairdryer in the room and piled her long hair up on top of her head, which together with her large framed dark glasses, produced a young woman who was totally unrecognisable from the dust and mud covered urchin who had entered the hotel two hours earlier.

She transferred her money and documents to her new handbag, together with selected essential toiletries, put her rucksack in the wardrobe and walked out. At the entrance she asked for a taxi to take her to the Soaltee Oberoi. Just as she stepped into the taxi two police cars drove quickly into the forecourt, doors opening as the car came to a halt. Four uniformed men walked quickly into the hotel. She fleetingly wondered if she should follow them. It went against everything she had been brought up to believe, to run from the police when she had done nothing wrong, but Edward had made it clear that the police were not the problem and getting out of Nepal was all that mattered. With the police so close she now wanted to get to the airport where she would feel safer. She was about to tell the taxi driver she had changed her mind and to take her to the airport, but decided that changing taxis at the Soaltee would draw less attention to herself. Assuming she managed to switch to another taxi fairly quickly, it would reduce the chance of anybody noticing her.

There was one other problem. Suppose, despite her rucksack still being in the room, they decided to check with the travel desk. They would find she had switched to an earlier flight and that she must have gone to the airport. If they were on time they could alert the airline and ask the airport security to hold her until they arrived. The taxi was now drawing into the impressive modern Soaltee hotel concourse. She tried to remain as cool as she hoped she looked and had the presence of mind to have taken enough in local currency from her purse to pay the taxi without needing change. She gave it to him as she alighted. An attendant opened one of the large glass doors to welcome her in, but she pretended to check her phone then turned to him and said, "Change of plan. I need to meet somebody at the airport."

Within seconds another taxi had pulled up and she was climbing into it. She didn't think anybody had noticed her particularly, except the doorman who had called the second taxi, but he hadn't seemed particularly surprised.

On her way to the airport she decided on her plan of action. She would buy a ticket to a destination other than Kuala Lumpur, but would not trade in the Kuala Lumpur ticket. If the police did discover that she had bought a ticket to Kuala Lumpur they would be left waiting for her to turn up at the check-in and not realize, until the last minute, that she wasn't going to show. And then they wouldn't have a clue where she had gone and wouldn't know where to start looking. For a brief moment she felt quite pleased at how she was taking to this cloak-and-dagger stuff, but as the taxi took the turning into the airport, the fear of what would happen if she were intercepted welled-up and her stomach tightened.

Inside the international terminal and from behind a heavily fronded potted plant which was taller than she was, she checked the departure boards for flights leaving in the next ninety minutes. Apart from the flight to Kuala Lumpur there was one to Dhaka which she did not recognize, one to Doha which she knew was in the Middle East and one to Hong Kong. It almost didn't matter. She looked down the boards again – "where on earth is Dhaka?" she wondered; then noticed that the airline was Bangladesh Airways so it must be what she would call Dacca which was directly on a line from Kathmandu to Kuala Lumpur and Singapore. She would go to Dacca.

# The Tissue Trail

It was only a two-hour flight, but this was a night where she had already decided that sleep was going to be in short supply.

She went to the check-in desk for the Dhaka flight and asked where she could buy a business class ticket. One of the airline women ushered her to a desk a few yards away where she was told she could buy a ticket, but they did not have business class, she would have to go first class. She didn't care anymore. As the ticket was being processed she checked to see where the Kuala Lumpur flight was boarding and saw it two gates away – rather closer than she had hoped. There were two or three staff at the desk starting to open up the flight, but no sign of any passengers.

After checking in for the Dhaka flight, constantly looking around her for any sight of the Canadians or police, she was ushered to the lounge where there were four other people. They were all men and all business types dotted around the comfortable-looking well-appointed facility. All four heads looked up as she was ushered in. The receptionist followed her to a seat close to the door and she accepted the offer of a drink and asked for a mango juice. It was forty-five minutes before boarding and there was now nothing she could do but wait. She asked the woman at the reception desk to let her know when it was time to board. The woman smiled and said she would, but that unless she particularly wanted to board early, the first class passengers were normally left to the end in the comfort of the lounge to avoid any unnecessary queuing.

As Jaci walked across the lounge she caught a glimpse of a stunning-looking woman wearing a navy blue suit. She turned to look, only to realize there was a long mirror. Outwardly she allowed herself a small smile while inside she felt more like a giggling schoolgirl.

Twenty minutes after the appointed time for boarding, the friendly woman at the desk called for passengers travelling to Dhaka. Two of the men rose. With taut, nervous tension again rising in her stomach, she rose just behind them thinking it might help if she appeared to be with them – or one of them. She walked alongside the second man and he looked at her with surprise.

"Sorry," she smiled. "Just not used to first class."

"You surprise me," he said looking appreciatively at her.

She turned away to look at the Kuala Lumpur gate. There were now two uniformed security men at the gate. Standing, talking to them was Jacques. The knot in her stomach tightened to the point where she felt sick. He was facing away from her until one of the uniforms said something and he turned one hundred and eighty degrees and looked straight at her. Instinctively she turned away and back to "her" businessman, heart in mouth. She was just twenty yards from the Canadian and only five yards from the first class check-in desk. It would take her perhaps thirty seconds to have her ticket examined. She steeled herself not to turn back and give him another chance to recognize her and prayed there would not be a tap on her shoulder or a North American voice calling her name. Her businessman let her go first, in fact they both did, and she presented her passport and ticket to the crew at the desk. As the check was made she gave way and looked back apprehensively over her shoulder. A group of passengers obscured the Kuala Lumpur desk, but a gap appeared and she could see that Jacques had not moved but was still looking around him. When she turned back, her passport and boarding pass stub were being held out to her. She wanted to ask if there was a lounge at Dhaka where she could stay until her connection but she decided that could wait and, taking her travel documents from the attendant, she moved towards the corridor leading to the plane.

Two minutes later she had been guided to the forward entrance and shown to what she could only describe as a throne – a huge, wide, comfortable seat, which seemed to envelope her as she sank with relief into the green and yellow colours. The two businessmen were close behind her but although the man she had walked with smiled, she was relieved when he made no attempt to sit next to her.

The hostess asked if she would like a glass of champagne. She briefly considered whether she should concentrate on keeping a clear head, but after the day she had it didn't take more than half a second to decide that she had earned the drink.

It was only six minutes before the flight pushed back, but it seemed more like six hours during which time the police could still have halted the flight. As she sipped the champagne and relaxed for the first time in three days she wished that the flight could have been a real long haul giving her time for another glass, a decent meal and a few hours sleep. Instead she might be able to snatch an hour and a half before she had to leave the plane at Dhaka. She was offered newspapers but declined and, as they taxied towards the take-off runway, she put her head back and shut her eyes thinking the next few hours at least should be relatively stress free as long as the police in Kathmandu did not find out where she had gone. And even then what could they do? She felt a warm wave of sleep roll over her and was only vaguely aware of the acceleration of the plane on its take-off run.

Back in the terminal Pierre had joined Jacques at the Kuala Lumpur gate. As passengers for the flight started to gather, the Canadians separated and moved into positions from which they could observe without being seen. But an hour and a half later there was no sign of Jacintha Linthorpe.

### 12th May 2001

At about the same time the Canadians were deciding, she had managed somehow to get out of Kathmandu. Jaci was being woken from a deep slumber, "Sorry madam, we are about to land in Dhaka."

She told the flight attendant she would like to book an onward ticket to Singapore without going through customs and was escorted to a desk in the transit area where she bought the ticket before proceeding to the first class lounge.

She had managed three, perhaps four, hours sleep in the lounge before being called for the Singapore flight. She still found herself looking around nervously, but there were no further alarms. Her new outfit was standing up well to the pounding she was giving it in the first few hours in her possession; there was not a crease anywhere and it still hung beautifully. If it still looked as good when she got to Singapore, Edward Thurston would be pleased with his investment – at which point she put her hand to her mouth —"oh shit!" she murmured to herself, she had forgotten to contact him as she had promised. There were plenty of excuses but now it seemed that as she was safe for the time being she had better get a message to him, partly she thought, because she had promised to and partly because there was just a chance he might try and meet her. She asked the flight attendant for a telephone and put a call through to Raffles and asked for Mr Edward Thurston. It would be pretty early, but why shouldn't he suffer a bit? She had a pretty disturbed night, in fact she hadn't had a good night's sleep for nearly two weeks.

"Hello," the voice said. "Who is this?" It was fairly clear that she had woken him; she smiled.

"Edward, it's Jaci."

His voice immediately became clear. "Jaci, I've been waiting for you to call all night."

*Typical*, she thought, *worrying more about his uncertainty than her safety.*

"I've been a bit busy," she said.

"Are you OK?"

"Yes," she paused, "So far."

"Where are you?"

"I'm on a flight from Dhaka to Singapore."

"Dhaka? Why Dhaka?"

"If you remember, you told me to change my flight to try and lose the Canadians and at least Dhaka is on the way to Singapore. I might have been on my way to Hong Kong."

She recounted what had happened since her last call and that he had been right about the hotel staff checking her travel details, and that Jacques had been waiting with the police at the Kuala Lumpur check-in.

"OK," he said, "we're going to have quite a bit to talk about when you get here."

"One small detail," Jaci said. "Where do I go when I get there?"

"Good point," he said. "What is your flight number?"

She read the number from her boarding card.

"Did it leave on time?"

She told him it had.

"Well I'd better come and meet you then, hadn't I?" She could sense the smile. But even so she said, "Don't put yourself out Edward, I'll just take a taxi to Raffles."

"Jaci, you'll do no such thing. I don't know what's going on with this Tissue Trail business, but until we work it out I'm not letting you out of my sight. They may not know how you've managed to give them the slip, but they know you're heading for Singapore!"

Thurston arrived at the airport at about the same time as the flight was due to land.

He stood opposite to the exit from the arrivals hall wondering if he might have time for a coffee. He decided against it. Four minutes later the automatic doors swung open and three business looking types came through, two men from the sub-continent and a smart expensively dressed Caucasian woman who seemed to be with them. The doors closed and he assumed they were from a private flight and paid little attention to them. But when the doors remained closed and with nothing else to take his attention he turned back to see what the three of them were doing. The two men were talking to drivers who had come to collect them. The woman had stopped, fifteen yards from him, put down her large but elegant briefcase and was looking at her watch. She wasn't just smart and well dressed. She was strikingly good looking, large eyes, full mouth, hair elegantly gathered on top of her head, her dark well-cut suit accentuated her female curves. She wore light make-up; a woman who knew she didn't need more than the minimum – and she was looking straight at him and, he thought, smiling. He frowned as she started to walk towards him.

"Mr Thurston, I presume?" she raised her hand towards him palm down, still smiling.

For a few seconds he stood unmoving, looking disbelievingly at her, then shook his head and smiled. He pushed her raised hand to one side and with his hand firmly on the small of her back pulled her towards him in a relieved, welcoming, hug.

"I didn't recognize you," he said relaxing his hold. "What happened to the old one?"

"She's still around," her eyes were laughing, "but some well-off sugar daddy has spent a small fortune on my makeover."

"Not so much of the daddy," he said as he picked up her briefcase.

"Wow, I am having an effect on you aren't I?"

"Don't worry, it'll pass, it's not every day you come through so many near death experiences. Let's find a cab and you can tell me all about it."

~~~~~~~~~~

The *Straits Times* had a photograph of Catherine Miller on the front page and he bought a copy as they walked past the stand. There was no queue for taxis and they climbed into the first one in the rank. As she sank into the seat he turned to look at her again. "For somebody who must be absolutely knackered," he smiled, "you really look quite good."

"Thank you kind sir," she bowed her head in mock deference. "And you look suntanned," she replied. "Been swanning around and having a good time?"

"Played a bit of tennis on weekends but not much swanning around," he said, "we've got a few problems which have been keeping me busy."

"What sort of problems?"

"Side effects, and just the sort of side effects we don't need."

"How frequent?"

"Four in every ten."

They were driving smoothly into the city along a dual carriageway with palm trees on the central reservation and neat and tidy beds of flowers and shrubs around their bases.

He described the side effects: agitation, heavy dreaming and broken sleep particularly in the later part of the night and that he and Professor Aw had worked through the preregistration trials looking for any history of anything similar in the past. They had found nothing.

"The side effects we are seeing," he continued, "are exactly what we would expect Surmil to eliminate, and you can imagine Villiumy's delight." As he finished the sentence he felt a weight against his shoulder. While he had been telling Jaci the details of the bad news, her three weeks of broken sleep and the tension of the last forty-eight hours had caught up with her and she had fallen asleep, her head leaning against him. Her hair smelled clean and fresh and she was wearing a perfume, which like everything else about her was understated. The moment reminded Thurston of Emily and he realized that the activity and tension of the last few weeks had, for the first time since her death, pushed her memory a little bit into the background.

He kept still, only moving his weight slightly into each bend to try to keep her head steady. Her head had fallen onto his shoulder.

At Raffles he woke her gently, her eyelids lifting slowly and unwillingly followed, equally slowly and unwillingly by her head. Both said sorry simultaneously, he for waking her, she for leaning on him, causing an exchange of smiles. He told her to stay where she was for a moment while he walked around the taxi to her door and helped her out.

"So I'm staying here am I?" she said, looking around at the imposing entrance. "I thought you would have fixed me up with somewhere in the docks."

"Don't get too excited. Staff quarters only."

"As long as there's a bed I don't mind if it's in the meat cupboard," she said yawning, looking for the first time like the eighteen-year-old looking woman he was used to.

"I'm going to take you to your room," he said. "That is to the door of your room," he corrected himself and turning to the check-in desk said,

"Until Miss Linthorpe has rested please make sure she is not disturbed. If anybody tries to contact her either on the telephone or asks to see her could you please refer them to me, this is my cell phone number and you know my room number." He gave the receptionist his card. They moved away from the check-in desk.

"Are you still worried even though I'm in Singapore?" she asked.

He wasn't going to tell her that he had a video camera wiped clean and that he was almost certainly being followed; he simply told her until they were surer of what was going on, he was going to be extra careful. And in any case, he wanted her to have a good eight hours sleep before giving her anymore to think about.

At the door of her room, she put her hand on Thurston's arm and looked at him. "Thank you for coming to meet me."

"Not a problem," he looked at her, "it was quite an interesting experience. Call me when you wake up." He waited as she started to walk into the room, still impressed with the transformation the purchases he had funded had made. He then realized he had to do something else and stopped her.

"We'll need to get you some ordinary clothes – if you tell me what to order I'll get somebody to fix you up while you're asleep."

She was too tired to put up even a token argument, "Two pairs of jeans size twelve and two medium sized cotton tops. Just tell them I've got blonde hair," she said, "they'll fix the colours. And there's one more thing, I had to leave my rucksack and old clothes at the Yak and Yeti so I've only got one lot of underwear," she smiled. "And I'm wearing it," she yawned.

"You'd better write down those sizes for me," he said. He opened his briefcase and gave her a sheet of paper and a biro. She scribbled some numbers, which he checked for legibility. "OK, Miss Linthorpe," he made a slight mock bow and grinned. "Have a good sleep."

"Don't worry. I'll sleep for a week."

In his room he checked for messages. There was one from Aw Swee Lim reporting another case of severe agitation and sleep disturbance and that Villiumy, who had come out from the UK to check on progress, had asked to see him at ten a.m. Thurston ordered a coffee in his room and he drank it casting his eye over the newspaper he had bought at the airport. In the centre of the front page was an item headed:

# The Tissue Trail

## *"TISSUE TRAIL" BACKPACKERS DIE IN POKHARA.*

*Two women backpackers were found dead in Pokhara to the west of Kathmandu on Wednesday. Their bodies were found by workers, hidden beneath sacks of raw wool in a Tibetan refugee camp. Causes of death have not been confirmed but police are satisfied that the women were murdered and are not denying reports that the bodies are those of the two Swedish women they have been looking for following the stabbing of the American, Stephen Foster, who was known to have been on the same Poon Hill trail known locally as the "Tissue Trail," which has been in the news recently in connection with the arrests in Singapore of backpackers carrying heroin hidden in items bought in the same Pokhara area. Police will not say if they suspect any connection.*

Thurston frowned. If the two women were the Swedish camera women Jaci had mentioned, then it must be assumed that their cameras had been intercepted. Jaci had left hers at the Yak and Yeti. Jane, Jaci's friend, presumably still had hers, but should have been in India or more likely the next stop on her trip, somewhere near Bangkok. Whether the Canadians or whoever was behind them, could trace her, was an open question. For the moment, that left only one known camera, which had been in use on the Tissue Trail, Jaci's, and that was still in Kathmandu. Or was it?

He picked up his phone and asked reception to connect him to the Yak and Yeti Hotel. Two minutes later he was asking the manager, a Mr Nardu, to see if Miss Linthorpe had left her rucksack in her room and if she had, he would like to make arrangements to have it returned to her. Thurston also asked him to check if there was a camera in the bag.

The manager was starting to answer the query when Thurston heard somebody ask to speak to him. He could hear the voices, but not what was being said. The interruption took about thirty seconds before the manager turned his attention back to Thurston. "I'm sorry sir, but that was information which affects what I was telling you. My colleague has just told me that shortly after Miss Linthorpe left the hotel last night we were visited by the police who were keen to see her. At that time we did not know she had left the hotel for good. We thought she had just gone out for the evening, which is what we told the police. They too enquired about the rucksack in connection, they said, with the death of a trekker called Stephen Foster. My colleague asked them to return in the morning when Miss Linthorpe could deal with their enquiries herself. But they returned at midnight with evidence that Miss Linthorpe had changed her flight plans and had left Nepal. As it was a murder enquiry they insisted we handed over the rucksack."

"Mr Nardu, can you or your colleague tell me if there were any civilians with the police?"

Nardu spoke to his assistant and put him on the line. "Mr Thurston, there was one civilian. He was from the Annapurna Conservation Area Project."

"So there were no non-Nepalis – foreigners?" Thurston asked.

"No, sir."

Jaci was delighted to receive an e-mail from Jane confirming she was having a good time heading east through Indonesia – a highlight had been the orangutan sanctuary – the only sad note was her camera had been stolen. In fact, it had been stolen the evening she had arrived in India after the two of them split up.

"They must have caught up with you pretty quickly then," said Jaci.

"S'pose so," said Jane.

"Anyway you're safe, that's the main thing. But I wonder why they were so bothered about the cameras?"

"Well you are where all the action is, if you find out, let me know."

# CHAPTER TEN
## *The Side Effects*

*14th May 2001*

Thurston was not looking forward to the meeting with Villiumy. The clinical trial was going just the way the slighted doctor would have wanted it to happen; nearly fifty percent of the patients were experiencing side effects. Thurston's brash, overconfident and, the most heinous crime of all, young agency was falling flat on its face. But he had little choice.

He told the check-in desk he would be out for the morning at the university. If Miss Linthorpe awoke and asked for him, to tell her he would be back at lunch time and to call him on his mobile if she needed to speak to him before that. Then he took a taxi and prepared to take his medicine. He grimaced at the pun. What he could not understand was why there had been no sign of side effects in the patients who had taken the night-time dose of Surmil in the UK. They were seeing an incidence of nearly one in two in Singapore.

Aw and Thurston met at nine thirty to go over the latest side effects report. It was the same as the others. The patient had gone off to sleep easily and enjoyed a good night's sleep until around five a.m., then suffered vivid dreams and awoke feeling agitated and unable to go back to sleep. The agitation continued into the day before fading away. The next night the pattern was the same. The patient had asked to be taken off Surmil.

Villiumy arrived at precisely ten o'clock; the three men sat down in Professor Aw's office and over tea exchanged pleasantries about the weather and Villiumy's uneventful flight from the UK. Villiumy had met Professor Aw on his previous visit to sign contracts on behalf of Imperial. The interaction had been purely professional and the conversation went forward as if there hadn't been a break.

"I gather you have been seeing side effects with Surmil, Professor?"

"Yes, we have Doctor."

"A high incidence?"

"Over forty percent."

"Can we go through the reports, please?"

The next two hours were spent painstakingly going over the reports. Villiumy showed no emotion, just read each report quietly and without comment. If he was enjoying Thurston's discomfort he showed no sign of it. Thurston said very little; there was not very much he could say.

As he slowly closed the last file he removed his glasses and folded them in front of him.

"Do we have any explanation?" Villiumy asked quietly.

"No," Aw said. "We are working through the literature and checking pre -clinical lab work, but so far we have not come up with anything."

"Do you have any comment, Mr Thurston?"

He thought for a few moments. "We do not have an explanation. In fact, we have more questions to answer. For example, why have we not seen these complications before? Several GPs have tried this dose informally in the UK without a problem. What is different here?"

"And?"

"If we find that difference we might find the answer."

"At this level of incidence, Mr Thurston, the cause hardly matters. The drug is clearly not viable with this dosage regime."

"I think it premature to draw that conclusion."

"Do you, Mr Thurston?" Villiumy said dismissively and turned back to Professor Aw.

"If we abort the trial before it is complete I assume you will not feel obliged to publish."

Aw considered the question then said, "There would not be much point in publishing unless we could find the cause. Simply publishing a report of the side effects would not achieve very much."

"I agree," said Villiumy.

"But we would have to make a formal report to your company."

"Of course."

"And what you do with that report would only be a matter for you."

Villiumy fully understood what Aw was implying; Imperial would be obliged to inform the registration authorities. That could lead to restrictions being placed prescribing the medicine or, at worst, its total withdrawal.

"I think that my recommendation to the board will be to abort immediately and set up our own internal enquiry."

Thurston and Aw exchanged fleeting glances. Both interpreted Villiumy's statement as a formula for burying the side effect questions or at least to delay any intervention by the registration authorities indefinitely.

"When do you intend to put this to the board?" asked Thurston.

"Why do you ask?" Villiumy's tone was again that of schoolmaster to dim student.

"I would like to know how long we have, to find an explanation." He looked evenly at Imperial's head of research.

Villiumy laughed, showing his enjoyment of the situation for the first time. "Mr Thurston, I have never met such an irrational optimist. You have forty-five percent of patients exhibiting exactly the symptoms you are trying to eliminate by using Surmil in this way and you think you can correct the situation? From any scientific perspective, at this level of incidence, it doesn't matter what the cause is. It is not viable." There was a pause. Villiumy realized he had lost his "professional cool" and immediately regretted it. Looking back later, Thurston thought if there was a moment when Villiumy's attitude towards him changed, it was within that outburst. But having calmed himself, he continued.

"As to timing I think, having gone over the reports with you and Professor Aw this morning, I will speak to the COO later today. He may well feel that the situation is so clear cut that he will agree to abort without a board meeting."

"Even though, if we can find a solution, Surmil sales could make a significant impact on your share price."

"And if you don't, the sale of Surmil could collapse altogether." Villiumy shifted in his seat. "Gentlemen," he looked from one to the other, "do either of you believe there is a realistic chance of finding a cause or explanation which could be eliminated or reversed?"

Professor Aw spoke first. "We have spent the last ten days going over the history without finding anything helpful. We are running out of options..."

Villiumy started to gather his papers. "But," Aw continued, "there is one channel which might still produce an answer. We have organized to interview eighteen of the twenty patients who have suffered side effects."

"I'm surprised you haven't tried that already," Villiumy replied testily.

"This is an outpatient trial, Dr Villiumy," said Aw. "Trial patients are monitored for four days as inpatients checking blood levels and rapid eye movement patterns, but then monitored as outpatients. We can only get back to those who have withdrawn through their family doctors."

"How long will it take to complete these interviews?" Villiumy asked, adding, "you are interviewing over the weekend?" – seemingly impressed that Aw and his staff would work outside normal hours.

"Yes," said Thurston. "Eight on Saturday, six on Sunday, and the last four on Monday. Most of them are working people and the weekend is the best time to bring them in. If you could delay your call to head office until late on Monday you would lose very little time with the time shift between here and London."

"That is not unreasonable," said Villiumy. This was the first time Thurston could remember him agreeing with him on anything. "I'm seeing friends in Kuala Lumpur over the weekend, so as you suggest, Thurston, I can let the MD know first thing on Monday morning, his time."

The slight softening of Villiumy's antagonism had been fleeting, perhaps even imaginary.

~~~~~~~~~~

Thurston let Jaci sleep until after lunch, but then called her room. It was a good twenty seconds before the telephone was answered and then by an extremely sleep laden voice.

"Sorry to wake you, Jaci, but if you sleep any longer you won't get to sleep tonight – and there's another reason. Villiumy wants to pull the plug on the trial. We've got until closing time on Monday to come up with an explanation for the side effects – and we need all available resources if we're going to stand a chance."

"He can't stop the trial!" all trace of sleep had gone. "It worked perfectly in the UK. Why is he so determined to kill it?"

"With side effects serious enough for patients to want to come off treatment in over forty percent of cases, he does have a point."

"But why didn't we get these effects in England?"

"That is what we have to find out."

He told her he wanted her to come to the university. Allowing for a coffee and a quick bite to eat, he told her she should be with him in about an hour. He could take her over the paperwork and then she could sit in on the interviews organized for the weekend.

Jaci muttered something under her breath.

"Pardon, didn't quite catch that?"

"Nothing Edward, I'll be there as soon as I can."

He was pretty sure the words she had muttered were "slave driver."

She made it just on the hour – but looked much the same as he was used to seeing her in London – like an unspoiled eighteen-year-old playing down her looks in jeans and an open neck short-sleeved cotton top. But maybe there was a difference – there was something older and wiser about her – she had gone through a lot in the last week.

Thurston gave her an overview of the reports then left her to go over them in detail on her own time. He went in to see her from time to time to see how she was getting on. She worked steadily and methodically in her usual way, but by five p.m. she had not found anything significant.

"How are you doing?" Thurston asked. "Can you do a bit more?"

"If you can organize me another strong black coffee, I think I can get through the rest in an hour or an hour and a half."

At 6:15 p.m. she had finished and looked white with exhaustion.

"I haven't found very much," she said. "Just one report that's a bit different." She handed a sheet from the report file to Thurston. He looked over it.

"Patient number twenty-five, age forty-two, male, Malaysian, suffered agitation and vivid dreams which woke him between 5:30 a.m. and 6:00 a.m. But because the five or six hours sleep he enjoyed up to that time was such an improvement on his normal virtually sleepless nights he opted to continue with Surmil. The agitation and colourful dreaming gradually subsided and by the tenth day he was sleeping a full seven or eight hours and feeling fully rested."

"Doesn't help much does it?" asked Thurston. "Very few patients will put up with it for that long!"

"It's a glimmer!" she said. "Let's hope the interviews add to it."

Even as an unrestrained optimist, Thurston could not see how they would find a solution which could reverse such a cataclysmic incidence of side effects. It was not a bit of a reduction they were looking for, it was a dramatic transformation.

"OK. Let's get you back to the hotel and try and get you a good solid sleep," he said, picking up the files.

"That's the best idea I've heard all day!"

### Singapore
### 15th May 2001, evening

Thurston called a cab and took Jaci back to the hotel. She declined the suggestion of a quick bite to eat. "Thank you, Edward but there's only one thing I want to do now."

She reached up and gave him a quick kiss on the cheek. "Might as well make the most of a bit of informality," she smiled.

He watched the woman in jeans disappear towards the elevator and thought back to the elegant sophisticated woman who had appeared at the airport that morning and remembered her once saying something to the effect that she played down her looks because she wanted people to judge her on what she could do, not what she looked like. *What,* he wondered, *would make a woman who could look like that try to hide it?*

He felt a pang of guilt. "Sorry Emily, but don't worry, she's not in your class."

In her room, Jaci had put her handbag down on the bed then laid down slowly alongside it and fell asleep – fully clothed.

### 16th May 2001

Thurston telephoned Jaci's room at 7:30 a.m. There were a few seconds before it was answered. "Sorry, in the shower," she said brightly.

"You seem to have recovered a bit," he said.

"Amazing what thirteen hours sleep does for you. And are you taking me to breakfast Edward? I haven't eaten for seventeen hours."

"I suppose I need you in top form, so I'll be in the breakfast room in five minutes. Join me when you're ready."

Jaci arrived in her jeans looking fresh and bright. Her first reaction was delight with the breakfast room. The décor was very much in the old colonial style of plain off-white walls with elegant framed photographs and paintings. The dark wood, colonial style chairs were palm backed and the square teak tables were from the 1930s. Waiters in crisp white short jackets hurried between tables and the kitchen. Breakfast was laid out on tables against the wall like an old English country house.

Looking around, her smile slowly disappeared. "Am I a bit underdressed for this, Edward?"

"Fifteen years ago you would have been politely turned away, but since the hotel was modernized in the 1990s so has its attitudes to dress. In any event those designer jeans and cotton shirt look pretty presentable!"

"Thank you kind sir."

"The classic dish is a mild chicken curry, but you might find that a bit much on your first morning in the east."

"I think I'll stick to the old colonial for today. I'll get a bit more adventurous when I've survived a couple of days!" her smile was back.

"That aspiration will rather depend on whether or not we solve the big mystery," he said. "If we don't, we will both be shacked up in the dockside inn for the down and outs you were expecting when you arrived."

The remark spoiled the atmosphere. Both looked down at their menus.

~~~~~~~~~~

In the cab on the way to the University Hospital, Jaci said she had managed to give a little thought to the big mystery. "There is something strange here isn't there?" she said. "Even in a really bad case there might be fifteen to twenty percent of unexpected effects – and even then there would be a spread from marginal to serious – but in this case the incidence is forty -four percent and no gradation. It's either there or it isn't. Whatever it is, we are going to kick ourselves when we find it."

"You seem pretty sure we will," Edward said.

"What's this," she grinned, "a role reversal. *I'm* normally the pessimist!"

At the university they met up with Professor Aw and agreed that he and Edward would lead each interview alternately and Jaci would listen in and intervene if she came up with something. Professor Aw asked her to make sure she did not intervene if either he or Thurston were in a linked sequence of questions. Inwardly irritated at the suggestion that she would not be sensitive to such a situation, she managed to restrain her need to protest, but she was pretty sure that Professor Aw picked up her stiffened body language.

# The Tissue Trail

They steadily worked their way through the first batch of side effect patients and by half past two in the afternoon and after a short break for a lunch snack, they had finished the Saturday group. There was nothing new. All of the questioned patients had encountered vivid dreams and sometimes nightmares, which had woken them and left them feeling anxious and agitated.

On the way back to the hotel Thurston had taken her to Orchard Road looking for some everyday clothes to fill the gap between "super model and street urchin" as Thurston put it. "Thanks for the super model bit," she had replied. She selected three different outfits and kept on a charcoal grey open necked shift. The colour highlighted her blonde hair as had her business suit at the airport and, although she had selected it to be not too close fitting in the equatorial temperatures, it hung down nicely – just hinting at her slender curves.

*She would make a potato sack look good,* he thought. "Quite nice," he said. She gently bowed her head in mock appreciation.

To take their minds off the depressing day, he suggested that he show her a bit of the town. He took her for an early supper in the Chinese open-air market and then to Singapore's night zoo where they were carried around in silent rubber wheeled electric carts. The animals, including big cats, were much more animated than during the day and seemed to be remarkably close to them with no apparent protective fencing or anything else between the punters and their potential predators. The zoo designers had, instead, placed deep ditches at the perimeter of the pens hidden from sight by thick vegetation.

"So you can be eyeball to eyeball with a big cat and be perfectly safe," as Thurston put it.

Back at the hotel, Thurston asked her if she wanted a nightcap.

"Sounds like a good idea," she smiled.

In normal circumstances, being with a seriously attractive woman in seriously exotic surroundings would have been a pretty fair situation, but professional considerations left him feeling awkward. So he avoided taking her to the Courtyard Bar, which would have been open to the balmy tropical evening air and a star filled night sky. Instead he took her to the slightly less romantic Long Bar with its two storey old Malaysian plantation design and décor. It was pretty busy with a buzz of conversation and occasional laughter. He guided her to a corner table. She did not make the situation any easier by ensuring occasional contact, just enough to be noticed but not quite enough to be sure it wasn't an accident. What had happened to the innocent "street urchin" he knew in London?

He ordered two Singapore slings. "You've got to have at least one!" he said.

He wondered how to steer the conversation —to avoid spoiling the evening with business, but also to keep things from getting too friendly. While he was thinking about it she said, "Edward, you're finding this a bit difficult aren't you?"

"What do you mean?"

"A place like this," she looked around. "We get on well," she paused, "but I work for you... and it's still not that long since ..." she knew she didn't need to finish the sentence.

"Pretty perceptive, lady," he said looking at her.

She let the moment pass then leaned towards him with what he could only describe as a mischievous grin and put her hand on his arm. "If we crack the problem with Surmil I think I have an idea to solve your professional..." she paused, looking for the right word, "...hesitation."

He looked at her with his head slightly on one side, as if he was wondering what she was talking about.

### The Breakfast Room
### 17th May 2001, breakfast time

Jaci appeared wearing one of her new outfits, well-cut white denims with a navy blue blouse and a dark choker. She had her hair piled up. He pretended not to notice.

"No compliments this morning, Edward?" she asked with a light smile.

"Mustn't over do it," he said. "At least I recognize you."

After ordering he said, "Two days ago you were running for your life from two maniacal Canadians, but now you would think it had never happened."

"Well, I'm not in Nepal anymore," she said. "In fact, it feels as if I'm on another planet."

"I'm not sure that being on another planet would help," he said. "Whoever is behind this Tissue Trail business seems to have a long reach."

"You think they might still try and get to me here?"

"Assuming there is a tie up between what's happening in Nepal and the women being arrested here, then it must be a possibility." He brought her up-to-date with the newspaper reports of the two Scandinavian women who were found dead. "Until we can find out what is going on, we will have to be careful."

"Have you told anybody else what's going on?" she asked.

"Professor Aw."

"So if anything happens to you I should tell him?"

"Yes, I suppose that would be your only option."

~~~~~~~~~~

The Sunday batch of side effect patients followed the same routine and with the same results – rejection of Surmil by all six patients.

~~~~~~~~~~

Aw was concerned that Jaci would be left on her own when he invited Thurston to dinner to meet his wife. He told Thurston that some of the younger members of his staff often went out as a group on a Sunday evening and, as Thurston was going to be tied up, perhaps Jaci would like to join them. Thurston looked thoughtful, but decided that as long as she was careful and made sure she was never left on her own she would be alright. He told Jaci what the professor had suggested and she agreed it was a good idea —although he thought he detected a degree of reticence.

At lunchtime, Aw Swee Lim invited three of the group to join them so that Jaci could meet them and would not feel like a total stranger. Two were Malay, one male and one female, and the third a Chinese-origin male. All were in their late twenties or early thirties. They were good company and all seemed to be taken with Jaci.

At the end of the afternoon, Jaci thanked Professor Aw for his consideration and left with Thurston to return to the hotel. Two of the group of friends would meet her in the hotel reception at seven p.m.

On the way back in the cab, Thurston said the Surmil situation looked pretty hopeless.

"I know," she replied, "but I feel certain that we are missing something glaringly obvious."

"I agree with you. I just wish we could find it. The problem is we only have one more day."

# The Tissue Trail

## 17th May 2001

On the way to the university for the last batch of interviews, Jaci and Thurston exchanged notes on their evenings. He had enjoyed meeting Aw and his wife in their delightful home, she had enjoyed being with a mixed group, some from the university, some from other professional firms – including "one boy who works for the firm defending one of the Tissue Trail women."

"What did he have to say?"

"He was interested in the fact that I work for a firm that solves problems which the research departments of large pharmaceutical firms have been unable to solve for themselves."

"Nicely put."

"He said that his firm could do with something like that themselves at the moment."

Neither of them thought very much about the remark at the time.

Jaci noticed Thurston glanced at the wing mirrors of the taxi and asked him why.

"Just making sure we're not being followed," he said, making a joke of it but he had noticed the same, now familiar, pale brown Honda not far behind, three or four times.

~~~~~~~~~~

At the university, Aw had introduced a variation to the interviewing pattern in a final attempt to solve the side effect problem, and that was to interview three patients who had found Surmil to be satisfactory interspersed between the problem subjects.

In the morning session they interviewed five of the seven scheduled for the day. There was nothing new from the problem group, but the eulogies offered by the satisfied patients who were sleeping soundly after weeks and months of deprivation only served to add to the frustration. There was one more patient before lunch and the last one at three p.m. in the afternoon.

At about ten-to-one the last interview was concluded with no new developments. Aw thanked the female Malay patient for her time. She picked up her handbag. Jaci and Thurston despondently collected their papers together. One of Aw's assistants came in to tell him he had an important phone call and also to show Mrs Osman the way out. Aw excused himself and said goodbye to her and left the room. Jaci had nearly reached the door of the interview room when she stopped.

"Mrs Osman, may I ask you one more question?"

Jaci had asked the same question several times, but as it had not produced anything interesting she had dropped it.

"Have you ever experienced anything like these effects before?" Mrs Osman stopped and thought about the question then said, "Yes, Miss Linthorpe, when I was on the previous treatment and forgot to take the tablets when I went away for a few days. I got the same dreams and woke up feeling very, how do you say – on edge."

"And were you on this same treatment before switching to the new medicine we asked you to take in this trial?"

"Yes. I was."

"Were you on any other medication?"

"No."

"So, to be totally clear, when you stopped taking the old medicine in this trial, the effects were the same as when you forgot to take the tablets with you on your trip?"

Jaci looked at Thurston, her eyes shining. "What do you think Edward?"

"Yes," he returned her smile. "Mrs Osman, on your trip when you forgot the tablets, did the waking and anxiety get worse or better...or stay the same?"

Mrs Osman thought for a few moments, then said, "I seem to remember it was much the same for the first two or three nights, but after that the dreaming and agitation gradually got better."

"Thank you. One final question. When you switched to the trial drug with Dr Aw, had you been taking the full normal dose of the previous treatment right up to the day you switched?"

"Yes, I think so," said Mrs Osman.

"Thank you. You have been a great help."

For a few moments, after she had disappeared and the door had shut gently behind her, neither Edward nor Jaci moved.

Then Thurston said, "We mustn't get too excited, that's only one report..." but he couldn't contain himself and, for the second time in two months, he involuntarily picked Jacintha Linthorpe up as if she were a rag doll and swung her around emitting in the process something akin to a full blooded war cry. They had done it. The side effects were not caused by Surmil, but were the withdrawal effects of the previous treatment. He was in mid-swing and mid-war cry when Professor Aw returned and was standing in the doorway with something between a smile and a question mark on his face.

"I was aware of a bit of chemistry between you two, but it must have gone further than I thought, or..." he broke into a full smile, "...or do I take it I've missed something?"

Thurston, mildly embarrassed, lowered Jaci to the floor and tried to restore some semblance of decorum. Jaci did not seem at all embarrassed and did not make any great effort to pull away. "Jaci, I think it would be a nice touch for you to tell the professor the good news."

She repeated the last interchange with Mrs Osman —word-for-word. The professor listened carefully shaking his head. "What idiots," he said finally. "I will never live this down. It's so obvious."

"I told Edward we would feel stupid when we found it," said Jaci, "but we have one last patient, let's make sure it applies to him."

"And assuming it does," said Aw, "we will need to check the records of the other twenty problem patients to confirm they were on the same or similar treatment. Then we'll need to work out how to deal with patients who are on medications with withdrawal effects and add an additional phase to the trial to show that we can manage the switch to Surmil without causing rejection."

### 18th May 2001

"One thing still puzzles me," said Jaci. "Why did the family doctors in the UK not see the same thing?"

"I've been giving some thought to that," said Thurston. "Firstly, the doses we are using here in hospital patients are higher than you would see in general practice and are therefore more likely to cause withdrawal effects if the patient is susceptible and secondly, the medicine which is causing such marked withdrawal effects is only at clinical trial stage in the UK and is not available in UK general practice."

Mischievously, Aw asked who was going to break the good news to Vilnius Villiumy. Thurston grinned, "I think first we had better see the last patient then check the other files. But that's a problem I'll enjoy wrestling with."

They adjourned for a quick bite to eat. "We'll think of something a bit more celebratory to do later," said Thurston, finding it hard to remove the smile.

After lunch they interviewed the last problem patient. He had been on the same medication as Mrs Osman and had suffered the same effects. The rest of the afternoon was spent going over the records of the rest of the dropout patients. The conclusion was confirmed. It was agreed that it would now take some time to work out the details of management of treatments, which were known to have adverse effects on withdrawal. Would they need a wash out period with no Surmil or any other drug until the effects subsided, or would a phased withdrawal matched by a slow build-up of Surmil work? There would have to be a period of trial and error to work out the best approach. In the meantime, Aw thought that the results in patients not at risk were so outstanding he saw no reason why he should not produce an interim publication of the results in such cases, with a reserved conclusion for the patients for whom transfer management would be necessary.

They discussed Villiumy and agreed that they should organize a telephone conference call with all three present.

At 4:00 p.m. the call was put through.

"Villiumy," the distinctive baritone at the other end.

"Aw Swee Lim here," replied Aw. "I have with me Edward Thurston and Miss Jacintha Linthorpe."

"Good afternoon lady and gentlemen," said Villiumy formally, "I assume, if you are calling me, that you have now completed your interviews?"

"Yes we have," said Professor Aw, his voice communicated his satisfaction with the position. There was a pause before Villiumy continued.

"If I might say so," said Villiumy, "you sound quite pleased."

"I think that is a fair summary," said Aw, enjoying the moment. There was a further pause at Villiumy's end and Aw thought he detected a delayed exhalation of breath, almost a sigh, then Villiumy astonished them.

"One small thing before you tell me what you have found," said Villiumy. "Just something that came to me in the bath over the weekend. Have you considered the possibility of withdrawal effects of the previous medication?"

~~~~~~~~~~~

When Villiumy had gone, Aw asked them what they made of that.

"Not sure," said Thurston. "What do you think?"

"I think he was going to let the side effects kill the trial then claim the credit for finding the solution himself, take the work back inside, and continue with your night-time dose concept —again taking the credit himself."

Thurston shook his head, "Middle name – Machiavelli, perhaps?"

### *19th May 2001*

Thurston suggested that they have a celebratory drink at the end of the office day and asked Aw if he would be happy to invite the two researchers who had been involved in administering the trial.

The five of them met at a small café overlooking Robertson's Quay. The three Malays did not drink alcohol so Thurston and Jaci joined them in drinking fruit juice. It was a satisfying if not euphoric get together —they had carried out a professional exercise to exacting standards and solved a problem which the trial had not been designed to solve. Surmil had done all they could have expected of it – it was going to be a big time winner. A lot of the conversation revolved around wondering how long Villiumy had suspected the withdrawal symptoms were the cause of the problem without letting on. The quiet celebration broke up and the five said their good-byes outside the café. The three Malays left leaving Thurston and Jaci looking at each other.

"Not quite what we'd call a celebration was it?" he asked.

"Not exactly."

"Well, let's do something about it. What do you fancy, getting dolled up or going native?"

"I'm starving, let's go native."

"OK, I'll take you to the flea market, we can eat on the hoof."

"Fine with me. I've hardly seen anything of old Singapore."

He called a motor rickshaw and took her to the Sungei Road and the oldest flea market in the city. "You are taking me shopping again?" she laughed.

"Don't get too excited, it's not exactly Bond Street."

# The Tissue Trail

It certainly wasn't Bond Street. As they approached the market they could see the bright overhead lighting overtop of them and as they got closer they could hear the noise of what sounded almost like a fairground with the music and chatter and bustle of the crowds and the colour and smells of the stalls and open shop fronts.

It was pretty hectic, and Jaci soon found herself being pushed and jostled by the crowds.

"Let's get a drink," he said, "and I think you'd better take my arm. I don't want you wandering off or being snatched."

"Snatched?" she queried, more than happy to let him link her arm through his.

"Yep, most of the stuff here is stolen or smuggled – and you would be quite a good catch if you got lost around here," he smiled.

He pushed his way to a drink stall and bought two small glasses of something sweet and alcoholic and a couple of bottles of a local beer. He downed the liqueur in one and she followed suit, immediately coughing with the impact on her throat.

"What are you trying to do to me?"

"Making up for lost time." Keeping a straight face, "But we had better get you something to eat before we drink much more."

He raised his beer bottle and took a mouthful and noticed, two or three stalls back the way they had come, a Malay, in his mid-thirties, in a long white shift and loosely wrapped light brown turban. He couldn't be sure, but he looked familiar.

Thurston knew there was one area of the market which was pretty much restricted to cooked food and headed for a corner where he could see steam rising into the night sky. There were a dozen stalls each with a variety of steaming pans and bubbling cauldrons. Most were selling the local laksa soup. It was more or less a meal in itself, Chinese noodles chopped into easily managed pieces, served in a spicy sauce and topped with cockles, bean sprouts and fried fish cakes. It was served in yellow bowls with a chicken motif and a flat porcelain Chinese spoon.

"This is what I had in mind," she said, leaning against the stall, resting her soup bowl on the counter and taking a swig of the local beer. "Real local atmosphere."

He turned to look at her, "What happened to that up-market woman I ran into at the airport?"

174

# The Tissue Trail

"A mirage," she said. "Not real."

They finished the soup and set off to explore the bric-a-brac stalls. She placed her arm back in its guide position.

"I think I should buy you a thank you present," he said.

"Oh?"

"From the company that is – not personal."

"What's the difference? You are the company."

"Just keeping things professional." He kept a straight face.

"And if it's business," she said. "You can put it on expenses?" She cocked her head on one side with a gently accusing smile.

"I don't think I can see anything here that I'd bother to put on expenses."

"You mean this thank you to me for making you several millions, you are going to buy here?"

"It might be more than one present," he said reaching out and picking up a pair of plastic vividly coloured crocodile earrings. "Try these," he laughed, clipping one onto each of her ears with its teeth, leaving the tail dangling.

The stallholder held up a hand mirror joining in the fun. "Great," she said, "but they'd look better on you." She reached up to clip one of the offending animals on his right ear. He paid for them and they walked off, each wearing one of the adornments. He bought two more beers.

There was a disturbance a few feet behind them and Thurston looked back. The Malay man in a fawn turban, he had seen before, was bending over holding his forearm obviously in pain and a Malay woman was moving away, it seemed, into the crowd. Thurston was pretty sure he had seen her before too —the green surround wrapped around her waist was familiar. The Malay man reached down to the ground and picked something up and slid it into his clothing. Thurston couldn't see what it was. He too disappeared into the crowd.

"What's all that about?" Jaci asked.

"Not sure!" said Thurston. "Don't let's worry about it. Nothing to do with us."

The evening continued, the search for joke presents provided a focus for examining the bric-a-brac which surrounded them. Thurston thought that he hadn't laughed so much since before Emily died. And he could not have been unaware of the frequency of "accidental" contact. There was going to be a problem.

# The Tissue Trail

Jaci stopped at a stall selling first aid and medical items and bought a blood pressure measuring kit – and a stopwatch.

"What on earth are they for?"

"I'll tell you later."

He gave her a puzzled look.

They kept the "local" feeling going with a rickshaw drive back to the hotel. On the equator, it was a warm balmy night.

"That was a lovely evening," she said, linking her arm back into his.

The rickshaw pulled into the hotel entrance and with exaggerated courtesy he helped her to alight. As he did so the Malay with the light brown turban stepped out of a rickshaw and walked away back into the crowd. He must have been following them. This was concerning in itself, but although Thurston was not exactly experienced in such matters it seemed to him that the Malay was almost making sure he had been noticed. He did not say anything to Jaci. There was no point in spoiling the evening for her.

At the hotel it was still only half past ten and the place was still teeming with people arriving or going out for a late meal or just standing talking or waiting for companions. They stood enjoying the atmosphere, neither it seemed wanted the evening to end.

*So now comes the problem,* he thought. With any other woman as much fun and as attractive and who had made her feelings perfectly clear, he could have let events take their natural course. And if he did let things take their natural course tonight what then? She was certainly going to be there for several more days and perhaps longer. He knew he could still rely on Emily's relatively recent death as an excuse not to let things go any further and he knew she would respect that but...

"What are you thinking about?" she broke into his train of thought.

"You," he admitted frankly.

She paused. Neither said anything for some time. Then she shifted a little nervously in her seat and said, "Suppose I came up with something to get around the problem?"

He looked at her with a puzzled frown. "It would have to be pretty good," he said, a little ungraciously.

"It is," she said. "In fact it's brilliant. Not just for one night but quite a few nights – and still entirely professional..."

He laughed out loud – "What – a kind of 'Pretty Woman' scenario?"

"No," she frowned at the thought. "Not that kind of professional – I'm talking about our sort of professional. Adding a bit to the trial."

"Go on."

"We've looked at the sleep effects of the night-time dose of Surmil, its ability to maintain daytime alertness, but suppose it had an adverse effect on sexual performance?"

"Go on," he said with a faint smile.

"So to keep it totally professional we carry out an assessment as part of the trial."

He laughed, "With me as the test animal?"

"Naturally."

He paused. It was a pretty good way around the problem, but he felt uncomfortable with Jaci in control of such a conversation and needed to buy a bit more time.

"Do you just happen to have some Surmil with you?"

"As it happens I do but at this stage we don't need it. We just need half a dozen control runs to see how you perform normally."

"You are unreal."

"No," she said. "This time I'm no mirage."

"Anyway we can't," he said, still smiling. He was still wondering how to react, but enjoyed the crazy conversation.

"Why not?"

"There is nothing about sex performance tests in Aw's protocol."

"Already thought of that," she pulled away from him. "Not needed – this is an anecdotal assessment – and assuming we do not find any adverse effects we do not need to worry about it. Only if we find any problems would we need to add a formal assessment to the protocol. I suggest we design a specific protocol for say twelve tests so there is a definite start and a definite finish."

"You have thought of everything."

"Yes," she said lifting the small bag from the market, which contained the stop watch and blood pressure kit.

"You can't be serious!"

"Just keeping it professional ... or scientific if you like?" she grinned.

He was *gobsmacked*. He looked at her in disbelief, slowly shaking his head.

"Is that a 'no'?" she looked up at him plaintively.

"No, it's not a 'no'," he said with a sort of sigh. "It's a crazy idea, but it's ingenious."

"And?"

His response was to pull her to her feet, then guide her to the concierge's desk. "If we order the champagne now it will be pretty much there by the time we get to the room."

She really had put some time into thinking this through. Even to the extent that she hadn't mentioned Emily. She must have worked out that her mini trial idea would have an even chance of getting around Thurston's problems in that area, too.

"I think after all the drink in the market and now champagne we had better think of tonight as a dummy run," she said lightly.

"Let's just see," he smiled.

"I see, bragging again!"

~~~~~~~~~~

In the room he opened the champagne, poured two glasses and put one in her hand.

"A good day," he said, raising his glass, "professionally of course."

"Let's hope the night will be as good," she said, then after a pause added, sipping the champagne, "I think I need this. The effect of that stuff you gave me in the market seems to have worn off and I'm a bit nervous."

"Thank goodness for that," he said. "I was beginning to wonder what had happened to the quiet sensible woman I remember from the Baker Street office."

### 20th May 2001

At a late breakfast the next morning they went over the entries Jaci had made in her report sheet.

"How am I doing?" he said, finding it hard to keep a straight face.

"Well I still don't know what you're like normally, but considering you were tanked up with that stuff at the market plus a couple of beers and half a bottle of champagne, I'd say not bad," she said seriously. But she couldn't hold it, and they both collapsed into helpless laughter.

When they had recovered, Thurston told her he needed to make some phone calls for half an hour and suggested she take a cab and go on to the hospital ahead of him.

Thurston went back to his room to make his calls. She went back to her room to clean her teeth and to collect her briefcase, then went downstairs to grab a taxi.

His calls took less time than he had expected and he was out of the hotel less than fifteen minutes after Jaci.

As soon as his taxi started moving he could see smoke from some kind of incident a short distance ahead. It was a bad traffic accident; a heavy goods vehicle had smashed into a taxi and virtually crushed it. The smoking wreckage was surrounded by police cars, ambulances, paramedics, and the fire service. Thurston's stomach turned and he asked the driver to stop. He asked one of the policemen if there had been a woman in the taxi. "Too early to sure, sir – but if there was anybody in the back..." he turned his palms upwards.

Thurston got back into the taxi and asked the driver to get to the hospital as soon as he could. At the hospital, he told the driver to keep the change and ran to Aw's office. To his initial immense relief he saw Jaci — obviously alive —but she was being comforted by one of Aw's female assistants. She was in tears.

He sat on the other side of her putting his arm around her. She was shaking, seemingly with shock, and unable to speak. Professor Aw came over and gently drew him away.

"She says a man pushed her out of the way when she was about to get into her taxi at Raffles and jumped in ahead of her. It was this taxi which was hit by the truck."

Thurston felt beads of sweat break out on his forehead. He had left Jaci alone for fifteen minutes and they had tried to eliminate her.

Aw asked Jaci if she would like to lie down. She nodded and the nurse helped her to her feet. "I'll take her to a quiet room," the nurse said looking back at Aw.

"Just take your time," Thurston called after her.

~~~~~~~~~~

During the morning he dropped in to see her every half hour or so but she had been sedated and was sleeping, recovering not just from the shock of the taxi incident, but the stress and exertions from the previous ten days.

At lunchtime Jaci was sitting up taking sips from a cup of soup. Her face was still white.

He sat beside her, and she leaned against him.

"It was awful seeing the taxi I should have been in be crushed. I can't get rid of the image."

He put the soup bowl down and gave her a long protecting hug.

To his surprise after a few seconds she lifted her head and reached out for the soup.

"I've been lying here just wondering about where this laboratory scale heroin production could be?"

"I see. I thought you were pretty much unconscious."

"Just thinking to keep my mind off the taxi," she said.

"Well, are you getting anywhere?"

"Possibly," she said. "Check me out."

"OK."

"It has to be in or near Pokhara because that's where the intermediate was taken and that's where the women bought the artefacts in which the heroin was hidden."

Thurston nodded.

"It can't be between Pokhara and the old city – what did you call it?"

"Lo Manthang."

"Because there is nowhere with the laboratory facilities."

"Correct, there are three or four tiny hamlets and none of them could possibly have housed any lab processing."

Jaci continued, "In theory some of the intermediate could have been taken on to Kathmandu or another town in Nepal, but there would be no point if the heroin was being given to the women in Pokhara."

Thurston listened and watched her thinking. "So the manufacture must be in or close to Pokhara?"

"Can't argue with that."

"So where would you find lab facilities in Pokhara?"

"Any ideas welcome," he said.

"Did the guy you met at the palm oil plant mention anything, anywhere which could carry out lab scale work?" Thurston thought about it. "Nothing comes to mind," he said eventually.

"It should," said Jaci. "Didn't you ask him if all the acetic anhydride was used at the palm oil plant?"

"You're enjoying this aren't you? Yes I did."

"Not as much as you are going to enjoy the next question."

"Which is?"

"Well, what did he say?"

Again Thurston considered the question. For a few seconds nothing, then a slow realization. "The hospital pharmacy!"

He put his head in his hands half wondering why he hadn't thought of it himself and half wondering if there could be any doubt.

"Well?" asked Jaci, her pale face tilted to one side.

"Pretty good bet," he said. "Why would you worry about quality control for a process as crude as this? How did I fall for that?"

"I'm feeling a bit better now, if a bit fragile," Jaci said. "If somebody doesn't mind bringing a few files I'll be able to do a bit more work —it'll keep my mind occupied."

For an hour and a half they worked on modifying the trial protocol for patients who were currently taking medicines that had a record of adverse reactions on withdrawal.

Thurston was aware of Jaci occasionally shivering as she recalled the crushed taxi.

At five o'clock she had enough, but she had more than made her contribution for the day.

# CHAPTER ELEVEN
## *The Cousins*

*Drug Intelligence Division*
*National Criminal Intelligence Service*
*Upper Ground, Blackfriars, London*
*21st May 2001, 7:55 a.m., BST*

Barbara Murdoch was at her desk early. She read through for a third time the two overnight reports – one from Singapore, the other from Kathmandu, before picking them up and walking to Jonathan Warrender's office.

"Quick off the mark, Barbara?" Warrender looked up from papers on his desk.

"Yes, some developments in the Catherine Miller case I thought you would want to see, both Kathmandu and Singapore. They are summaries of events over the last week or so."

The Kathmandu report was in three sections, the first a straight news report of the death by stabbing of a twenty-seven-year-old American, Stephen Foster, who had been trekking on the Pokhara Ghorapani trail "otherwise known as the Tissue Trail." The same piece also reported that the police were trying to trace two Swedish and two English women who had volunteered to report any unusual incidents in this area for a magazine article.

The second was a press clip from the *Kathmandu Post* the following day, reporting the discovery of the bodies of two Swedish backpackers in a Tibetan refugee camp on the edge of Pokhara. Both had been trekking the same trail and, it is believed, at the same time as Foster. Cause of death was

# The Tissue Trail

not yet known, but drug overdose is suspected. Police are not denying that the bodies are the two Swedish women they have been looking for since the death of the American Steve Foster.

The third was also a press clip from the *Kathmandu Post* reporting the funeral of a Royal Nepal Airlines pilot, Captain L. D. Chaudrai, who had died in mysterious circumstances at his home two weeks earlier. The post-mortem showed that he had died of an overdose of a popular sleeping pill. Captain Chaudrai had flown with Royal Nepal for nearly thirty years and was due to retire in September. He had been in the news recently as the pilot who had flown through violent winds in the Kali Gandaki Gorge and almost certainly saved the life of an eleven-year-old girl from the remote city of Lo Manthang. Police enquiries into the death are continuing.

"Looks as if whoever's behind this Tissue Trail business will do anything to stop people getting anywhere near it," said Warrender. "And if anybody does they are eliminated."

Barbara handed him the second file. "This is from Singapore and pretty much supports that line of thinking."

There was a short covering note from the Director of Security and Intelligence in Singapore:

*Dear Warrender,*

*The enclosed report is being sent to you at the risk of some embarrassment to ourselves and despite the fact that its conclusions have not yet been fully verified. Its circulation is restricted to the appropriate drug intelligence agencies of those countries whose nationals who have been arrested in the recent so called "Tissue Trail" arrests. Our intention, given the serious consequences of the almost certain guilty verdicts, is to give defence teams the benefit of our emerging suspicions that this drug ring is not the low-level opportunistic operation originally suspected.*

*Choi Shing Kwok*

Warrender read the report carefully. It was an internal report addressed to:

# The Tissue Trail

*Director*
*Security and Intelligence Division*
*Ministry of Interior and Defence*
*Republic of Singapore*

It was signed by a second secretary from the External Intelligence Department and read:

*CONFIDENTIAL*
*Internal Advisory Only*
*22nd April 2001*

*The body of Drug Enforcement Agency officer Stephen Foster was found yesterday near the village of Ghorapani in the Annapurna Region of Nepal. Death was caused by stab wounds to the chest and abdomen.*

*Ghorapani is located on the trekking trail from Pokhara to Jomsom widely referred to in recent news reports as "The Tissue Trail." All five of the backpackers recently arrested in Singapore for importing heroin had bought the items in which heroin was hidden in this area.*

*Foster was on duty as part of an initiative by the DEA to try to establish how the Tissue Trail heroin is being acquired by the backpackers who, even customs officials in Singapore admit privately, had no idea they were carrying. He had been briefed to monitor four backpackers who had volunteered, ostensibly as part of an exercise to collect material for a travel magazine article, to photograph and make notes about events and people they met while trekking The Tissue Trail. Nepali Security are trying to locate the four backpackers who were involved in the magazine camera exercise but so far without success. Two were Swedish, two British.*

*The DEA had initiated this exercise following lack of progress by local agencies in identifying the operators of a drug ring which had already been the cause of the arrest of American citizens.*

*Serious issues are raised by Foster's death. Assuming he was murdered by the Tissue Trail drug ring and since he was not involved in the magazine exercise, it must be concluded that his brief was known to the ring operators in advance. And since knowledge of the exercise was restricted to senior officers in the DEA and no external agencies were notified, I have to conclude that US intelligence has been penetrated at a senior level.*

*If this is the case, then there must be a real possibility that what until now has been thought to be a low-level local drug ring must now be viewed as a more sophisticated operation. Certainly the operation, as it is now emerging, is beyond the capability of a small Tibetan cell raising funds for resistance to Chinese occupation which until now, has been this agency's favoured explanation.*

*Yours etc.*

Warrender drew in air through pursed lips. "That's serious, the cousins don't release anything as self- incriminating as this without good cause."

"But what are they hinting at if it isn't a low-level local ring?" Barbara asked.

"No idea," said Warrender. "But then I wasn't aware that their Tibetan theory was as well developed as he implies either."

"Well, the heroin was found in artefacts bought in Tibetan shops or refugee camps. But they must have had more to go on than that."

Warrender looked over the report again. "What's this?" he referred to a second sheet, unheaded and with a list of four names.

"A list of the four women who were part of the magazine exercise," Barbara explained. "The two British women are shown as Jane Anthony, a graphic designer, and Jacintha Linthorpe," Barbara paused, " a medical researcher."

Warrender looked up, eyebrows raised.

"We are already checking her out."

"In the meantime, we had better get this to Philip Lee. He needs something out of the ordinary and this should give him something to think about."

Just after 10:30 a.m., Barbara came back to Warrender's office.

"We've been onto HMRC and Jacintha Linthorpe is indeed a medical researcher."

"And?"

"She works for a research agency in London."

"And?"

"The company is owned by Edward Thurston."

Warrender looked thoughtful, stroking his chin. But Barbara hadn't finished.

"Her last recorded passport check was yesterday morning when she arrived in Singapore on a flight from Dhaka."

"Dhaka?" Warrender repeated. "Curiouser and curiouser."

"And Jane Anthony's last check was on the Indian border in Chitwan. It almost sounds as if they were on the run and split up."

Warrender thought for a moment. "If Foster, Thurston's pilot and the two Swedish women have been taken out, then Thurston and the two British women must also be at risk. I think we had better find a way of having a word with Edward Thurston in his own best interests. Assuming that is, he is not connected to this in some other way."

"Well he's not been doing anything suspicious; just getting on with a clinical trial. We've been keeping an eye on him. There is one curiosity though – we are not the only ones keeping an eye on him."

### 21st May 2001, later that morning at 11:00 a.m.

Barbara knocked on Warrender's door for the third time that morning. "Come."

"Another development – our people in Singapore are pretty certain they foiled an attempt on Thurston or Jacintha Linthorpe last night. They were in the open market – it was pretty crowded – and a Malay a few feet behind them drew a knife and was getting into a position to use it when our local 'James Bond' – in fact, a Mrs Bond – chopped his arm."

"Well I suppose this is precisely why we've had him under surveillance, and what we have been expecting, but I think we had better make sure he knows what's going on. He almost certainly doesn't know how close people are getting to him. Let's talk to Philip Lee."

# CHAPTER TWELVE
## *The Trials*

### *23rd May 2001*

Jaci was still feeling shaky after the taxi incident, but she had insisted that she preferred engaging her brain and be with people than holed up in the hotel. Thurston hadn't argued and, indeed, in the cab on the way to the hospital he had engaged her brain discussing their ideas for altering the clinical trial design to deal with patients switching from treatments which caused problems on withdrawal.

But even in her fragile state, she could tell Thurston's mind was not one hundred percent on the trial.

"Penny for them?" she asked.

He paused, "...with the excitement of the clinical trial and being hidden away in the university we've been kept pretty much insulated from the real world... apart from the odd little taxi incident."

She sat back in her seat and sighed, "Yes, this has been ..." she sought for the words, "an absorbing period."

"So absorbing," said Thurston, picking up the newspaper he had bought at the hotel, and showed her the front page, "that I'd lost sight of Catherine Miller's trial."

Jaci looked at the headline and shuddered:

### *FIRST TISSUE TRAIL TRIAL LOOMS*

"It's in two days time. Any idea how long it will last?" Jaci asked.

"Just guessing – it's a pretty open and shut case – so two or three days max."

# The Tissue Trail

## *Changi Women's Prison*
## *24th May 2001*

The day before the trial, Philip Lee visited Catherine Miller for a final briefing.

She was brought to the interview room looking grey and her skin lined with the loss of weight. She sat down slowly like an old woman and lifted her dull eyes slowly to meet his.

"I suppose it's a silly question to ask how you are?" He tried not to be too sombre.

"Yes, it is," she said quietly with almost a hint of a smile.

For what must have been the tenth time he went over what would happen in court and the sequence of events in a matter of fact voice trying to calm her as much as he could.

He then asked her to go over the sequence of events before and after her purchase of the doll for what must have been the hundredth time. Again nothing new emerged until, as they were nearly finished, she looked up at the ceiling. "There is one little thing."

He stopped and looked at her, "Go on."

"When I was stopped at the airport they seemed to make a point of stopping me in particular."

"Go on."

"There was a continuous stream of people ahead of us and they didn't stop any of them. There were three of us – and they seemed to make a point of stopping our group and then selecting me."

"You're sure?"

"Well, yes. It was as if someone behind us had signaled, because two of the security people appeared from a door at the end of the corridor, let two or three other groups go, waited for our group then stopped us, then picked me!"

"Interesting," said Lee. "If there was prior intelligence that could be significant."

"Why?" she showed a trace of animation for the first time.

"It is quite common for carriers to be picked up on the basis of prior intelligence, but since we have no idea who is behind it, any suggestion of prior intelligence would be a step forward."

"Good," she said quietly, but sank back into her seat.

The conversation continued for another fifteen minutes then Lee sighed. "I am afraid I have to go, Catherine. I will see you tomorrow."

She managed to say, "Good luck," as he rose to leave.

"You too," he said, placing a hand on her arm.

## Central Criminal Court Singapore
## 25th May 2001, 3:00 p.m.

A delay in the previous case had resulted in a late start, but the bench of three judges decided to make a start despite the late hour.

Catherine's trial was the first of the "Tissue Trail" cases to come to court despite the fact that she was the fourth to be arrested. It was not uncommon for proceedings involving a British citizen in an ex-British territory to still use British legal processes to move more quickly than cases involving defendants from non-British territories.

The press box and public galleries were packed. Media speculation that the Tissue Trail women had no idea they were carrying, yet faced the death penalty, had aroused public interest from the outset and with protests from the press, governments, and diplomats from some part of the world steadily increasing, the case had remained high in public awareness.

People could just about understand that the women had the substance planted on them without their knowledge, but nobody could understand why there had been no arrangement for the imported drug to be picked up.

Lee sat at the defence table watching the familiar proceedings and exchanged the occasional word with Defence Counsel.

There was a stir as a door at the side of the court was opened. Two court officials and two police women entered, then turned back to usher in Catherine Miller. The crowd fell silent as she appeared slowly and shuffled forward towards the dock. The silence broke into an animated buzz of conversation as she climbed the two steps stumbling slightly, then turned to face the court to reveal her haunting appearance.

A second door opened and the clerk of the Court called "All rise" as the three judges entered and took their seats on the bench in front of the Coats of Arms of the Republic of Singapore. Without further introduction the lead Judge nodded to the clerk who rose to initiate proceedings; he announced the case of the Republic of Singapore versus Catherine Marie Miller.

The prosecution opened the proceedings with a short statement of the charge, "That on 25th April 2001 the accused entered Singapore carrying an illegal substance in contravention of Singapore's Import of Class A Drug regulations.

"We shall present evidence that the substance was diamorphine hydrochloride – or heroin and that the amount of active ingredient was 16.2 grams. We shall ask the Court to impose the maximum penalty proscribed by the Singapore Penal Code." There was a murmur of reaction from the public gallery.

Prosecuting Counsel took his seat.

The clerk looked up at Catherine and asked her religion. She whispered inaudibly to the court in general and the clerk placed a Bible in front of her and she was sworn in. The judge twice asked her to speak up.

Prosecuting Counsel rose.

"Are you Catherine Marie Miller of Edinburgh Scotland born 3rd March 1981?"

"Yes," she said quietly.

"You have heard the charge against you that you entered Singapore carrying an illegal substance, namely heroin, on 25th April of this year?"

"Yes."

"Do you plead guilty or not guilty?"

She looked across towards Lee.

"Not guilty," she answered quietly.

There was a stir of reaction around the court as there had been some speculation that she would plead guilty and ask for clemency.

The judge asked Prosecuting Counsel if he was ready to proceed and he affirmed.

"Please call your first witness."

The first witness was a chemist called Patel from the public analyst office who confirmed the opening statement that the substance had been analysed and found to be diamorphine hydrochloride and confirmed the amount – 16.2 grams.

"Are you absolutely sure of the amount?" asked the judge.

"Yes, sir. The calculation was checked several times and by three different technicians. We have submitted full signed records of all tests to the court."

"You are aware of the significance of the question, Mr Patel, and of the answer you have just given?"

"Yes, sir."

The judge turned to the defence bench, "Do you wish to question this witness?"

"We do your honour," said Mr Mahmood Yousop, Defending Counsel.

"Mr Patel, apart from the measurement of active ingredient, did you make any other observations regarding the substance?"

"In what respect?" Patel asked.

"It's quality, consistency, purity?"

"Objection, leading," the prosecution intervened.

"Objection noted, but I will allow the question."

The chemist hesitated, "The substance was unusually pure."

"Please explain."

"Production of heroin is normally a crude process resulting in a heavy sugar-like consistency. This sample was a fine crystalline powder typical of small-scale production. The sort of quality we would expect from a laboratory."

"And what significance do you attach to that?"

The chemist thought for a few moments then said, "Only the same point as was made at committal – that with this purity far more substance could have been secreted in the doll with no more risk of detection. Why go to all the trouble to set up drug trafficking for a fraction of the amount which could have been carried?"

"I am not sure where this line of questioning is going," said the judge. "Do you have any other questions of the witness, Mr Yousop?"

"No, Sir."

"In which case will the prosecution call its next witness?"

The public gallery broke into murmured conversation as the clerk called a Mr Ranjani, the customs officer who had stopped and searched Catherine Miller at the airport.

He took the oath and Prosecuting Counsel approached the witness stand.

"Mr Ranjani, you were on duty as a customs officer on the morning of 25th April at Changi International Airport?"

"Yes, sir."

"And on the morning of the 25th April part of your duty was to stop and search passengers arriving in Singapore from international flights?"

"Yes."

"Do you see in court any passenger you stopped that morning?"

"Yes, I do."

"Can you please identify that person?"

Ranjani pointed to Catherine Miller.

"For the record Mr Ranjani is pointing to Catherine Miller, the defendant."

"And you searched her baggage?"

"Yes, sir."

"Please tell the court what you found."

"I found a small polythene packet hidden underneath the dress of a soft doll, in fact cello taped to the lower body of the doll."

"And you arrested her on suspicion of importing an illegal substance?"

"Yes, sir."

"No more questions of this witness your honour."

"Do you wish to question the witness, Mr Yousop?"

"Yes, your honour."

"Please proceed."

"When you arrested the defendant, how did she react?"

"She appeared surprised."

"Just surprised, Mr Ranjani? Wasn't her reaction a little more than just surprised?"

"I suppose it was."

"Then please tell the court, in your own words, just how much more than 'surprised' Catherine Miller was."

"She was shocked."

"In what way did she exhibit this 'shock'?"

"She was nervous when we searched her rucksack – and when we found the polythene slip she appeared..." Ranjani paused, "horrified!"

"Go on, Mr Ranjani."

"In fact when we tasted it and suspected heroin she vomited and fainted."

"So to confirm, Mr Ranjani, she was not just surprised but shocked and horrified."

Mr Ranjani hesitated then agreed.

"But you were not surprised were you, Mr Ranjani?"

Ranjani frowned. "I don't understand – what do you mean?"

"I am suggesting you were not surprised that the defendant was carrying an illegal substance."

"I, err... I had no opinion. It was a purely random search."

"A random search," repeated Yousop. "Is it not true that one of your colleagues signaled to you as the defendant entered the customs channel?"

Ranjani paused and shifted in his seat. "No, I don't think so – why would he?" Ranjani was clearly discomfited by this unexpected line of questioning.

"Is it not true that when Catherine Miller and her two friends approached your position you reacted to this signal by intercepting them?"

"I did not say there was a signal – I do not remember stopping them... It was just random. I have explained that." Mr Ranjani didn't know where this was coming from and therefore didn't know what Yousop was looking for.

"And having stopped the three of them did you ask any questions before you indicated you wanted to speak to Catherine Miller?"

"I don't remember. There was nothing special about this."

"So you say, Mr Ranjani, but let us examine your claim a little further. Having randomly selected the defendant you took her straight into an office away from the open area?"

"I... I suppose so."

"So you stopped the defendant as soon as she entered the customs area without even checking who she was or asking any other questions? You didn't make any preliminary checks or search her bag in the open customs area, but took her straight into a side office?"

"Yes but ..."

"Is it not true, Mr Ranjani, that a high proportion of drug trafficking interceptions are a result of prior intelligence?"

Mr Ranjani hesitated, "We do receive prior intelligence."

"As many as eighty percent of cases, or four out of five cases, are the result of prior intelligence?"

"I don't know the exact percentage."

"Was the defendant stopped as a result of prior intelligence?"

Slight hesitation then, "No. In this case there was no prior intelligence."

"Let us examine that claim a little further." Yousop raised his thumbs beneath the lapels of his black robe.

Prosecuting Counsel intervened, "I think I have been very patient your honour, but is this line of questioning relevant – all the court needs to establish is that the defendant brought heroin into Singapore."

"I have some sympathy with your objection," said the lead judge, "but I will allow the defence some further latitude to explore the prior intelligence issue. Please continue, Mr Yousop."

Yousop thanked the judge and returned his attention to Mr Ranjani. The court stirred —for what had been expected to be an uneventful and routine hearing, the process was turning out to be anything but.

"Let us look at what happened next."

Ranjani again shifted uncomfortably in his seat.

"The defendant was carrying two bags – a handbag and a rucksack! Which did you select to search first?"

"I don't remember..."

"You don't remember. Is it not true that you didn't examine the handbag at all, but went straight for the rucksack? Again, without asking any questions."

The judge coughed and tapped his watch.

Yousop turned back to the witness Ranjani. "Let me ask that question again, why did you immediately select the rucksack for examination rather than the handbag?"

"I am not aware that I did."

"And why, having selected the rucksack, did you immediately empty its contents onto the table in front of you and, without hesitation, select the doll that had been at the bottom of the bag?"

"Again, I am not aware that I did."

"And having selected the doll you immediately exposed the lower abdomen of the doll and found the polythene slip."

"It was not like that."

The prosecution counsel rose. "Your honour I think this has gone far enough."

"I have one more summary question your honour."

"One final question, Mr Yousop."

"Mr Ranjani, summarizing the position we have reached, you selected the defendant without questioning her, you took her straight into a private side room without any examination of her bags, you immediately selected one of two bags she was carrying without questioning her, you emptied that bag and selected a doll which had been buried at the bottom of it —hidden under a variety of other items without questioning her and then immediately exposed the lower body of the doll where you found a polythene slip containing a white powder cello taped to the fabric of the doll.

"I suggest it is beyond any possible doubt that this sequence of events could only have occurred if you had received prior intelligence. Mr Ranjani, my last question to which I intend to return tomorrow is —what was the prior intelligence you received and who supplied it?"

The public gallery again descended into a buzz of animated conversation.

The judge thanked Yousop for his question and recessed until ten a.m. the following day.

~~~~~~~~~~

The evening press and television news on 25th May headed their bulletins with the case. The *Straits Times* led with:

### *TISSUE TRAIL MYSTERY DEEPENS*

*The first of the five Tissue Trail defendants appeared at the Central Criminal Court today in a case that has puzzled police from the outset. Investigators privately admit that none of the arrested women were aware they were carrying illegal drugs. The mystery deepened today when Defence Counsel cross-examining arresting customs officer Ranjani pressed him to reveal the source of the prior intelligence, which the defence alleged, must have preceded the arrest. Ranjani denied there had been any such intelligence and that the interception of Catherine Miller had been purely random. The case was adjourned for consideration of legal argument before the cross-examination could be completed. Questioning of customs officer Ranjani will continue tomorrow morning.*

### *Central Criminal Court*
### *26th May 2001, 10:00 a.m.*

At ten o'clock precisely, the three judges entered the courtroom and took their seats on the bench. The clerk called for order. When the court had settled he turned to the lead judge and spoke to him at some length.

The judge addressed the court, "I understand that Mr Ranjani has been unavoidably delayed. We shall have to proceed and return to the defence's questioning of Mr Ranjani later."

Yousop rose, "Sir, do we have any information regarding what has delayed Mr Ranjani?"

"I understand he has been involved in a road traffic accident. His condition is not known. We are waiting for reports," said the judge.

Philip Lee leaned forward and spoke to Yousop, who again addressed the judge.

"If, as we contend, there was prior intelligence in this case it would be known to other members of the customs staff. The defence would like to subpoena Ms Stephanie D'Aunay. Ms D'Aunay was in attendance with Mr Ranjani when the illegal substance was found."

The judge called both counsel to the bench.

"Mr Yousop, we allowed considerable latitude in your questioning yesterday and you have registered your contention that there was prior intelligence and your contention is now a matter of record. But the legal position is as stated by the prosecution yesterday, that how or why customs came to find an illegal substance being imported into Singapore is of no consequence to the case. I must therefore rule that, unless there are questions relating to the fact that the substance was found in the possession of the defendant as opposed to the cause, the court will not sanction the calling of further witnesses from the customs staff."

Yousop asked permission to speak to his team and returned to the bench a few moments later.

"We continue to ask for latitude here, sir, as all parties are having difficulty understanding what lies behind these cases which are the subject of international scrutiny. This hearing provides one of few opportunities to cross-examine, under oath, in a case with serious political implications for Singapore. It is clear that Ranjani at least, knows a lot more than he is saying – or is being allowed to say."

A door to the court opened and an usher entered, came over to the bench and placed a typed note on court-headed paper in front of the judge. The judge read it and frowned.

"Gentlemen, I am afraid Mr Ranjani is not going to be able to assist us any further with our deliberations. He has died of injuries suffered in the road traffic accident earlier this morning."

There was uproar in the public gallery which the judge made no immediate attempt to quell. Lee and Yousop took advantage to exchange reactions. Finally, the judge called for order and Yousop rose, "We ask that our condolences are passed to the family of Mr Ranjani, but in view of this development we ask that your ruling regarding further customs witnesses be reviewed..."

The lead judge conferred briefly with his two assistants on the bench and called both counsel forward. "Gentlemen, we find that we cannot find any legal grounds to change the court's position."

He turned to the clerk, "Please call the defendant."

Catherine Miller was ushered uncertainly to the witness box where she took the oath. She was clearly barely aware of her surroundings or what was happening and the prosecution took her mechanically through the events of the morning of 25th April. She spoke in a low expressionless voice, the judge repeatedly having to ask her to speak up.

The prosecution devoted several questions to the issue of whether or not she recalled any question from any other person relating to her being given the polythene slip to carry, or asked to carry the doll, or any other item she was carrying, or regarding any arrangement to meet with any person after she had entered Singapore. The answer to each and every question had been an unequivocal "no."

When the prosecution had finished Yousop took over for the defence. Yes, Catherine had enjoyed Nepal and yes she had arrived in Singapore in good humour and entered customs still in good humour. When asked if she had been at all nervous she had replied that there was always that slight uncertainty when entering customs after all the films and TV programs about items being planted by traffickers.

Had she been surprised to be singled out from all the various passengers going through customs? Yes she had. And when separated from her friends and taken to a side office? Yes she had. And when the customs officer immediately selected her rucksack to be searched and then from all of the items in the rucksack selected a doll which had been at the bottom of the rucksack? Again she replied "yes," but added that the doll was at the bottom of the rucksack because she was taking it back home as a present and wouldn't need it during the journey.

"Was it not strange to buy the present so early in your trip?" asked Yousop, "and have to carry it for the rest of your trip around the world?"

She became a little more animated with this sympathetic line of questioning and replied, "I did think about that when I bought it – but we so loved Nepal I wanted something to take home from there."

Yousop spent further time establishing her surprise, indeed nauseating shock, when the white powder was found. He went on to re-establish that she did not recall anybody asking to meet her after arriving in Singapore or any other conversation relating to handing over the dolls, or asking to see the doll after arrival in Singapore.

Yousop asked one final question.

"You pleaded 'not guilty' to the charge of carrying a classified substance, namely heroin, into Singapore. Can you please explain?"

"Mr Lee made it clear that the law says I am technically guilty so he recommended that I should plead 'guilty' and ask the court to take into account the fact that I didn't know I was carrying. The alternative was to plead 'not guilty' as I had not knowingly brought heroin into Singapore." Her voice was trembling and she was having difficulty keeping her composure. But she rallied and completed the sentence, "All I know is I did not do anything, either on my own or with anybody else to bring heroin into Singapore, so I have pleaded 'not guilty'!"

The judge asked the prosecution if they wanted to ask the defendant any further questions. They declined.

The judge made notes then looked up.

"This concludes the presentation of evidence in this case. We shall recess to consider our verdict which we will deliver at two p.m. this afternoon."

~~~~~~~~~~

As the minute hand climbed towards the hour of two p.m. the courtroom was quiet and the atmosphere sombre. Even exchanges in the press section were quiet and whispered.

At five minutes to the hour a door opened at the back of the court and Catherine Miller, her shoulders bowed and eyes red-rimmed, was led into the courtroom and to the defendants dock. She was unsteady on her feet and was helped by court ushers as she climbed the two steps.

Philip Lee watched her with a distant helpless disbelief. Yousop was more detached. He had not been so involved. A guilty verdict in a capital case was never a pleasant experience, but he had been there before.

# The Tissue Trail

At precisely two p.m. the three judges entered and the clerk called, "Court rise."

The lead judge took his seat and opened the leather bound file in front of him – court officials and others present resumed their seats. The judge raised his head and looked at Catherine Miller. She was still standing or perhaps cowering was a more apt description. She had the staring eyes of a frightened animal.

The court was hushed. Finally the lead judge spoke.

"In the case of the State of Singapore v. Catherine Marie Miller the court has heard the evidence presented by the prosecution and the questions raised by the defence and has reached its verdict."

"Catherine Marie Miller, you have been accused of carrying diamorphine hydrochloride into Singapore in contravention of the import of Class A Substances regulations. On this count the court finds you guilty. On the matter of weight of substance carried we accept the evidence presented that amount of active ingredient, namely diamorphine hydrochloride was 16.2 grams."

The judge waited while officials took note of the verdicts. He then turned to the defendant, "Do you have anything to say before sentence is passed?"

Catherine Miller glanced at Philip Lee then said, in a clearly rehearsed response, "I do not question the court's findings according to the law in Singapore, but on behalf of myself and the other four young women in the same predicament I ask the State of Singapore if it is content to execute people who no one believes had any knowing involvement with or knowledge of the carrying of heroin?"

The judge paused and wrote down her question then said, "Your comment and question is noted Miss Miller."

He placed his hands flat on the surface in front of him, turned to the clerk and nodded slowly.

The clerk rose and stood alongside the judge holding a black felt four-pointed hat. He raised it and ceremoniously placed the hat carefully and squarely on the judge's head.

The judge looked straight ahead and intoned the sentence.

"Catherine Marie Miller you have been found guilty of bringing into Singapore a Class A substance namely diamorphine hydrochloride and in the weight of active ingredient of 16.2 grams. As proscribed by the

Singapore penal code you have committed a capital offense. The sentence of this court is that you be taken from here to a place where you will be detained until an appointed time when you will be hanged by the neck until you are dead. May God have mercy on your soul."

Catherine Miller's head dropped, her hands gripped the bar of the dock, her arms shook as she sobbed.

There was a gentle murmur as the judge made a note. Then he nodded to the clerk who in turn asked the stewards to help the defendant down from the dock. As the sentence was read Philip Lee sat leaning forward with his head bowed, his hand over his eyes.

The judges rose as one and left the court. Two ushers led the dazed looking figure of Catherine Miller down from the dock and out of the rear of the court. Philip Lee had moved across the court towards the exit where she was being taken and as she reached the exit door he told her, "We shall continue to do all we can."

### *Hospital Canteen*
### *27th May 2001, breakfast time*

Thurston had ordered a collection of newspapers and he and Jaci looked over the reports of the trial over breakfast. It was grim reading. The *British Daily Telegraph* was typical:

## *TISSUE TRAIL WOMAN FOR THE GALLOWS*

*The first of the five woman backpackers in the so called Tissue Trail heroin cases was found guilty at the Central Criminal Court today of importing heroin into Singapore. 24-year-old Catherine Miller of Edinburgh, Scotland was sentenced to death by hanging. The execution is expected to take place at the end of June or the beginning of July. The court was thrown into confusion earlier in the day when it was revealed that a key witness had been killed in a road traffic accident. An attempt by the defence to call a replacement customs witness to pursue their contention that there had been prior intelligence was rejected by the bench. Four more Tissue Trail women face trial. The result of this trial does not auger well for any of them.*

# The Tissue Trail

The *International Herald Tribune* raised the issue of no knowing involvement.

## *"INNOCENT" TREKKER FOUND GUILTY IN CAPITAL CASE*

*24-year-old Scot, Catherine Miller, was today found guilty at the Central Criminal Court Singapore for importing heroin into the Territory in April of this year. She was sentenced to death by hanging and is scheduled to be executed early in July. The case is arousing intense international interest as the Singapore Penal Code is one of few where guilt does not require the defendant to be aware of carrying out the action that constitutes the offense. This is the first of five similar cases to come to trial where the defendant claims to have no knowledge that they were carrying a Class A substance. Nor had they had any contact with any person regarding the carrying of the substance prior to, or after, entering Singapore. Police and drug enforcement agencies are still trying to explain this illogical feature of the case. It is understood that the Foreign Office is preparing a submission to the Singapore Government acknowledging due legal process but indicating that in such a case natural justice should be allowed to prevail.*

*The New York Times* "was hearing" that high level diplomatic protests had been prepared in advance of the trial in expectation of guilty verdicts and were imminent. There was even speculation that the United Nations could become involved.

One report noted that the remaining four cases were scheduled to be heard over the next few days and speculated that the mounting furore of protest would "leave nothing else on the front pages."

Both Thurston and Jaci spent time reading backup articles on the inside pages. Thurston was interested in the effect of the Tissue Trail cases on tourism in Nepal and had read three similar articles when something stopped him and went back over the same articles a second time.

"What have you found?" asked Jaci, getting fed up with him opening and reopening the same papers.

"Something quite interesting," he said, "look at this."

201

# The Tissue Trail

He showed her three articles that told much the same story with the same conclusion – with tourism on its knees as a result of the constant flow of news from the Tissue Trail arrests and court proceedings, the Nepali authorities needed to do something as soon as possible to break the ring and to make it clear to the world audience, particularly in Europe and North America, that it had been broken. But what caught Thurston's eye was the use of three unusual but identical phrases in all three articles in three different newspapers. Jaci was fascinated and carefully re-read all three articles herself and found more evidence of common phraseology and unusual word selection. It looked for all the world as if all three articles had been written by the same author but with sufficient difference for him to present the articles for use as originals by different newspapers. This meant the press was being fed backgrounders from a single source – a common practice in the PR business with which Thurston was familiar in his own sphere of communicating medical research findings. But the important implication was that the press and media were not just reporting, they were being manipulated. It had crossed Thurston's mind more than once that he could not remember a news story which had not only stayed on the front pages for several weeks, but had steadily increased in intensity. If someone had wanted to produce this effect it would normally have been almost impossible – news media just didn't work like that; the standard pattern was for a big initial impact and a rapid fade from view. So had this just happened because of the natural sequence of events in capital cases? Or was there more to it?

Thurston tidied up the papers and sat back. "This is all very well but getting back to basics, what can they do now? The death sentence is mandatory, there is no defence so there is no basis for an appeal!"

"It's a nightmare," said Jaci, turning back to the front page of the paper and contemplating the photograph of Catherine Miller's look of disbelief and horror as the death sentence was pronounced.

As they got up to leave the canteen, Thurston noted, "The rest of the trials are following fairly quickly. In fact, the first of the American trials, Maria Gonzales, started yesterday afternoon."

### 27th May 2001, evening

Lee telephoned Thurston to tell him that although Maria Gonzales' defence had tried to raise the issue of prior intelligence the court had been prepared and had avoided the complication and delay caused by prolonged argument in Catherine Miller's case. Lee thought the trial would conclude the following day.

His prediction proved to be accurate. There were no other complications and after routine submission of evidence that she had carried heroin into Singapore and that the amount exceeded fifteen grams she was pronounced guilty midway through the morning of the second day. Shortly afterwards she was sentenced to death.

The damaging effect on diplomatic relations between Singapore and the governments of the nationals involved in the Tissue Trail cases was clearly demonstrated in a front page article about the Maria Gonzales case in the evening edition of the conservative *Straits Times*:

## TENSIONS RISE AS AMERICAN BACKPACKER SET TO HANG

*Tension between Singapore and the USA over the so-called Tissue Trail heroin cases rose significantly today when Maria Gonzales, 22, of Miami Florida, was found guilty of importing heroin into Singapore and sentenced to death. This is the second of five similar cases to come to trial, the remainder will follow over the next ten days. The Americans are known to have also expressed exasperation with the Nepal Government's lack of progress in identifying the perpetrators of the drug trafficking – leaving visitors including American nationals at risk; but are now expressing serious concern to the Singapore Government over its Penal Code in Class A Drug cases. This requires the death penalty even when the prosecution accepts that the defendants had no knowledge they were carrying the drug, nor made any arrangements to have the substance collected after arrival in Singapore. The Americans are arguing that the case defies any rational explanation–without which no conviction can be regarded as safe. There has been no official comment from the Singapore Government but a source close to the Prosecutor's Office told this newspaper that the rigid provisions in Class A Drug cases were there for a purpose and have served Singapore well. There is no reason to suppose that this case should become the first to see any relaxation. In Maria's home town of Miami where the case had been headlined for ten days in the lead up to the trial, a typical tabloid lead was, "Innocent Maria Heads for Noose in Savage Singapore."*

A broadsheet lead was:

### *STATE DEPARTMENT GEARS UP FOR SINGAPORE BATTLE*

One television station showed shots of Changi women's prison and glimpses of the execution room with four nooses suspended in line over the elongated drop plate. This on its own caused a furore and was picked up by other networks.

And there were three more trials to go.

### *Hospital Canteen*
### *30th May 2001, breakfast time*

Thurston and Jaci spent another breakfast looking over reports of Tissue Trail developments including the *Straits Times* report. "This is getting serious," Thurston observed, "they're now raising the political temperature."

"And alongside that," Jaci added, "Ranjani is the sixth person the operators have murdered because somebody got too close to the truth. In fact nearly seven."

Thurston nodded thoughtfully, "And whoever they are, they've not gone away. We were followed when we went to the flea market."

"Are you sure?" Jaci frowned.

"Not much doubt about it. Not only did I see the same Malay several times only a few yards away, but also when we arrived back at the hotel."

She sat, initially without saying anything, then said, "Was that the same Malay behind us when there was that kerfuffle?"

"Could have been," said Thurston. "In any case I think we need to bring the professor up-to-date and then see who else we need to involve, whether the consulate or the police or, I suppose, the drug intelligence people."

They intended to talk to Aw about it over lunch, but things were rather taken out of their hands. After the routine morning greetings, Aw raised it himself.

"This Tissue Trail business?"

Thurston nodded.

"Somebody close to the case has asked me to have a word with you to see if you would object to spending a bit of time talking to him."

Thurston raised his hands, "Rather depends who we are talking about."

"Philip Lee, one of the defence lawyers, in fact the leading defence lawyer."

"Interesting!"

"One of his junior staff was one of the people who had gone out with Jaci when she first arrived. He was quite taken with her – but even more taken with what her job was with the agency – solving problems which routine methods had failed to solve." Aw paused, "Lee is also aware of the interest the customs and drug people took in you at the airport."

"How did he manage that?"

"I mentioned it," said Aw. "But he already knew. He keeps in close touch with immigration and customs as part of his job. I mentioned it because we need all the help we can get."

"We?" queried Thurston.

"I have every sympathy with Singapore's hard line with Class A drugs, but that stops short of executing innocent women. Now Catherine Miller has been found guilty it rather raises the stakes."

"Well I'm not sure how we can help, but if he thinks we can that's fine with me."

Thurston turned to look at Jaci, "Do you want me to see him first to try to avoid dragging you any further into this?"

"No," she said without expression, "let's do it together."

"Okay. And maybe Lee could help us find out who's following us."

"If anybody can, he can," said Aw, "and he's a partner in a big firm that has good connections with the police and intelligence services. There can hardly be anybody in Singapore who is better placed to help you."

"Let's hope we can help each other then," said Thurston turning to Aw. "When does he want to meet?"

"He was hoping to make it this afternoon."

"Fine with us," said Thurston looking at Jaci.

"Nothing in my diary either," she said.

"Thank you," said Aw. "I'll call him."

It was a brief conversation. Lee said he was delighted that Thurston was happy to talk and it was agreed that Lee would come to the university at four p.m.

Aw replaced the receiver. "Everybody is getting jumpy," he said.

"What do you mean?" asked Jaci.

"He doesn't want to meet in public."

~~~~~~~~~~

Philip Lee arrived punctually at Aw's office at four p.m. In appearance he was pretty much as Thurston had expected for an ethnic Chinese lawyer, small, neat, dapper with black hair creamed to the back. Aw Swee Lim effected the introductions.

"I am not directly involved in this matter," Aw said, "but from what I understand each of you might be able to benefit from getting to know the other a little better. Philip Lee is looking for some new way of tackling the Tissue Trail problem and Edward Thurston with Jacintha Linthorpe would like to know why so many people are taking a serious interest in their activities." He looked from one to the other.

Lee nodded, "And we could be interested in your questioning techniques as ours don't seem to be getting us very far."

"Anything we can do to help," Thurston held his hand out towards Jaci. "This is the lady who keeps producing the magic bullet questions." She gave Thurston a quick smile, but was concentrating on what Lee was leading up to.

"It was my assistant's report about your success in finding minor variations in drug behaviour which led me to ask to meet you," said Lee, "but in fact you were featuring in despatches sometime before that. As a firm we are often involved in drug cases and as a result are in close contact with Customs and Border Control and the name Edward Thurston came up at almost exactly the same time as the Tissue Trail arrests started."

Thurston looked resigned; he had heard it all before.

Lee continued, "It first came up when your consulate picked up a report that your passport had been confiscated in Pokhara."

"Why would the consulate pass such information to you?" asked Thurston.

"Catherine Miller is a British national and when something like this comes up, the various branches of government collaborate and pass on anything they think could be helpful."

Lee continued, "The next mention of Edward Thurston was on the front page of the *Kathmandu Post* as the 'Flying Businessman Rescues Dying Girl.'"

"Yes," said Edward, "but instead of being treated as a hero I was interrogated by Nepali security for three hours."

"So we understand and that's where your name appeared again – we picked up on the reports of your interview with customs and the drug people at immigration coming into Singapore."

"The man-eating Stephanie D'Aunay?" Edward recalled.

"Yes, bit of a hard case," said Lee, "but she does a good job. So what did happen in Nepal, Mr Thurston?"

"Make it Edward," said Thurston.

"If you wish, I'm Philip," said Lee.

Edward repeated his story.

"What seemed to be the problem?" asked Lee.

"Hard to believe, but the conversation, if you can call it that, was with the yak herders."

"Anything in particular?"

Thurston wondered how many more times he was going to have to go over this.

"The unexplained death of the previous leader – and a new vinegary substance they were bringing in, in addition to the salt."

Lee took notes for the first time.

"Death of the previous leader?" Lee queried. "Can you tell me what was said?"

"They put that down to the local Chinese administrators. He had been leading dissent against the longer route needed to bring the new commodity to Lo Manthang and it looked as if he was removed to quell that dissent."

"So the Chinese are implicated?"

"If Tensing's opinion is right then it seems the Chinese were keen to ensure the new chemical did reach Lo Manthang."

"Do you know what the substance was?"

"I didn't at the time – except that it was being used as part of a process involving production of palm oil. But I ran into a Canadian banker – Lauren Chase, who is involved organizing funding for the initiative – and she told me it was acetic anhydride."

"Lauren Chase did you say? Who is she?"

"Yes, you've kept her quiet," Jaci looked surprised.

"Need to know." he said, with an unconvincing attempt at a smile. "She told me the Canadians have a pretty big aid program in Nepal and she was a senior executive with the National Bank of Canada and had been seconded to the Canadian Government to administer it. As a result she was pretty well informed about the palm oil project."

"How did you run into her?" asked Lee.

"She was on the same flight from Kathmandu to Singapore, then I ran into her again at Raffles and we got talking."

"I must check up on her," said Lee.

"Interestingly, she told me about the routine screening processes the drug enforcement agencies undertake including monitoring the movement of acetic anhydride one way and corresponding new cash movements in the other."

"You are becoming well informed," said Lee.

"Too well informed for my own good," said Thurston. "As the aggressive Ms D'Aunay made clear at Changi Airport."

Lee considered this but didn't write anything.

Thurston went on, "And since getting here I've been followed by at least one group of people if not two."

"Two groups?" said Lee. "Are you sure?"

"Well, I'm not in the spook business, but one lot makes themselves pretty obvious, almost as if they want me to know they are there. Then there appears to be a second, less obvious group. The first group will follow me, say, to the hotel in a car driving close enough to be noticed, then get out when I arrive. The others use scooters or rickshaws and slow down when I reach my destination and then drive on. It's only because I've become a bit paranoid and keep my eyes open that I notice the same rickshaw or scooter in the wing mirrors too many times for it to be a coincidence."

Professor Aw laughed, "Perhaps Philip should organize his own team to shadow Edward – there would be so many people chasing him, it'd be like Keystone Cops!"

"As it happens I know something about this," said Philip Lee, "when Edward's name started to come up in despatches from Drug Liaison, the National Criminal Intelligence Service in London telephoned me to suggest that I should take an interest in you and your activities and that they were arranging to have you put under surveillance. That would explain why you've been seeing two lots of followers."

"So my name has been flashing about on the wires has it?" said Thurston, not looking too pleased.

"I think you might have more reason to be grateful than you realize," said Lee, "for instance, in the open air market two nights ago?"

"Now you mention it there was a bit of a commotion behind us," said Thurston, "some chap holding his arm and trying to pick something up then disappearing. Looked as if a woman had struck his arm." Thurston paused, looking at Jaci with concern.

She managed a bit of a grin. "So a knife – a ten ton truck – what difference does it make?"

"Ten ton truck?" Lee queried.

Jaci told him the story. "Two attempts in a week," said Lee, "which backs up the point Warrender wants to emphasize which if it isn't already obvious, is that you and Jaci must remain on red alert."

Lee asked if there was anything else he should know.

Thurston took Lee through the Chaudrai story and the tape being removed.

"If you don't mind I think it would be a good idea if you let me have a copy of this tape. It seems to be the focus of a lot of people's interest."

"I think that would be a good idea," said Thurston. "In fact, Chaudrai's contribution to the conversation is also important. He was born in the Annapurna area and knew the history of the setting up of the palm oil plant the new chemical was being used for, and that the Chinese had originally shown no interest, then changed their minds and finally became so committed that they killed the previous leader to ensure it proceeded."

"So another indicator of Chinese involvement," Lee observed.

"I'd quite like to see it myself," said Jaci pointedly.

"I think we could fit that in one evening." Thurston smiled at her. "In fact, Philip, to get the full picture, you also need to hear Jaci's experiences in Nepal."

Jaci described her involvement in the travel magazine article exercise and the interest of the two Canadians, not just in her and the other women with the cameras, but also the American Foster who had been murdered. She described how Foster's reasons for being on the trek did not make much sense. Why would he be on this low altitude trek when he was claiming to be on his way to the Fishtail base camp for a serious climb? She told Lee how she and Jane had been worried about the Canadians' interest and when finally they had been sure that their rucksacks had been interfered with, they had decided to "escape" by leaving the trek and heading back to Pokhara.

"So you were suspicious of the American, Foster?" asked Lee.

"Yes. He knew far more than had been in the papers – particularly about Edward, and as I've said, his reasons for being alone didn't add up."

"And the Canadians would have picked up on these same suspicions?"

"I'm not sure, but I would have thought so. Why?"

"Just trying to get as much of a picture as possible. It is the fact the drug ring was aware of Foster's involvement which is beginning to make us suspect that this is a more sophisticated operation than was first thought."

"Why is their awareness of Foster's involvement so significant?" asked Thurston.

"Because the involvement of the American DEA was a closely guarded operation and if the Tissue Trail operators found out about it, it means that western drug intelligence must have been penetrated at a high level. Too high a level," Lee added, "for a small scale local drug ring."

There was a moment of reflective silence then Lee added, "So we have established that staying in Singapore puts you two at quite a lot of risk," he paused, "and what I want to move onto next could make it worse."

"Difficult to imagine what could make it worse," said Thurston. "What do you have in mind?"

"You are in the business of unearthing solutions which official channels have been unable to find – as in the medical case which brought you to Singapore?"

Thurston looked at Lee. "Yes ..." he said.

"And they've done it again here," Aw interjected. "The clinical trial was just about to be abandoned because of unexpected side effects when Jaci worked out the cause."

Jaci looked suitably self-conscious. "And it was Jaci's interview with a family doctor which unlocked the Surmil solution in the first place," Thurston added.

Jaci glanced at Edward. "You only find out what somebody really thinks when they are talking about you to somebody else. Thank you," she said with a slight bow and sideways dip of the head, "I think that's the first time you've actually acknowledged it."

"Surely not?" Thurston put on a crocodile frown, then turned back to Lee. "So what do you think we can do?"

"I would have thought it was pretty obvious," Lee said pleasantly. "The traditional enquiry methods by the whole drug intelligence network and the press, not to mention my people cannot work out what the drug ring is doing," Lee explained. "If there is no contact with the women, how are the drug runners planning to courier the substance? Finding out how it was loaded onto the women and how they intended to recover it, is the starting point and we cannot even get to first-base as the American's would call it! If we can answer that question it might be the breakthrough we are looking for."

"But is there any point in trying," asked Jaci, "if there is no hope of overturning the verdict?"

"There is just a chance," said Philip. "If this is not normal trafficking at all, but some kind of conspiracy or as the American's would say, the women have been 'set up,' then it may force even the intransigent Singapore authorities to relent. It is a forlorn hope, but our only hope and this is where you two could come in."

"How do you see us doing that?" Jaci looked puzzled.

"In your business, as I understand it, you find your solutions to problems by talking to the people who take the problem medicine – the patients if you like?" he paused. "The people who are taking the medicine in this case are the arrested women."

He waited for this to sink in. "You want us to interview Catherine Miller and the other women ..." Jaci looked apprehensive, "...would that have to be in prison?"

"There are few safer places," said Lee, who had anticipated this reaction.

"It's not my safety I'm bothered about," she half protested, "it's just the thought of coming into contact with women of my own age in such desperate straits – and who must look pretty awful with the stress and horror of the situation."

Lee stayed quiet, waiting for her to register the point that her involvement could help them out of the desperate straits however unlikely that might be.

Thurston looked at her but addressed Lee and speaking quietly said, "I'm sure I speak for both of us – if there is anything we can do to help I am sure we would give it a go."

Jaci nodded thoughtfully. "That's right," she said softly.

"Thank you," said Lee. "Thank you," he said again, "I know it is a lot to ask." He reached into his briefcase and pulled out three postcard-sized notelets. "In the hope you would agree to help I have prepared a short briefing note or check-list of the factors where it seems to me that interviewing the women might help."

He handed out three copies – including one for Aw. The list was not long and there were no real surprises.

### Factors Relating to Tissue Trail Heroin Arrests:

*Five unconnected arrests of female travellers arriving in Singapore from Nepal.*

*All claim no knowledge of being given the substance or arrangement to collect.*

*Items in which heroin secreted – all local artefacts bought in or near Pokhara in Annapurna region.*

*All five had trekked the Pokhara Poon Hill Trail known as the Tissue Trail.*

*No conversation with anyone about the artefacts other than when purchasing.*

*Suggestion that customs had prior knowledge as to who was carrying.*

*The heroin is an unusually fine powder – suggesting small scale or lab production.*

When they had all read it, Thurston asked Jaci for any immediate reaction.

"Yes, one," said Jaci, "in fact two. The first – all of them travelled directly from Kathmandu to Singapore. Most backpackers travelling in this area take the opportunity to visit Thailand or Burma or Malaysia. Routing direct from Kathmandu to Singapore is unusual."

"Any comment, Philip?" asked Thurston.

Lee thought about it. "I suppose that is just the sort of thing that a lawyer would not be aware of and just the sort of thing we would hope you would be able to add to the mix – but I can't think of any significance of them going directly to Singapore."

"The other thing is that they are all women," Jaci said.

"Oh?" Edward looked at her. "What do you read into that?"

"Nothing more than that, just an observation."

Lee scribbled the two additions to the list. "Anything you want to add Edward?" he asked.

He pursed his lips. "Not on the list," he said, "and not something the women would know anything about but while Philip is here – the cash movement factor. Is anybody looking at that? From what Lauren Chase told me that could produce a link right back to the operators."

"It is normally something which is routine for the drug agencies to track," said Lee, "but I talk to them routinely and nothing has been mentioned."

"And yet Lauren Chase was aware of reports of movement of cash," said Thurston, "and that was some time ago."

"I'd better check," Lee made a note on his pad.

"Anything else?" asked Aw.

Nobody had anything further to add and as the meeting broke up, Aw invited them to his home for a casual evening meal which Thurston and Jaci gratefully accepted.

Lee made his apologies as he had a prior engagement. "As far as looking after you two," he looked at Thurston and Jaci, "it looks as if we need to step up the level of protection. I'll see what we can do – perhaps something similar to a witness protection arrangement. In the meantime, I suggest that you don't take any unnecessary risks and try not to get separated!"

"I think we can handle that!" said Thurston.

"There is another thing," said Lee, "CNN's Victor Najinski would like half an hour with you. He was sent up here by the regional office in Delhi specifically to cover the Tissue Trail case."

"You're beginning to fill my calendar, Philip."

"I've got thirty days to come up with something, Edward. My thought about Najinski is that he is a pretty effective operator but has a different way of thinking – so it's possible you two could spark something! And he has some interesting thoughts on the way the media is behaving."

"Interesting, in what way?"

"As if certain aspects of it are being managed – or perhaps manipulated is a better word."

Thurston and Jaci exchanged glances. "We've got some thoughts of our own in that area," said Thurston. "We've been giving the papers a good going over and found a number of common phrases and unusual word selections. Do you think he would like me to take Jaci along?"

"He would probably want to eat her," Philip allowed himself a rare smile, "but that's up to you!"

### 29th May 2001

Lee called Thurston early the following morning. First, Najinski was suggesting meeting at lunchtime. "I'll be happy to make the introductions – and initially he would prefer just to meet you on your own!"

"OK, can you ask a couple of your people to team up with Jaci for lunch in that case?" Thurston asked. "She'll be alone if I leave her in the hospital."

Lee said he didn't think that would be the slightest problem – there would be no shortage of volunteers. "One other thing," Lee added, "the security people in Singapore have not been picking up anything in the way of cash movement. Lauren Chase must have been referring to something picked up in Nepal – but if the trafficking is into Singapore there should be corresponding movement here, too."

"So if the intelligence agencies have been penetrated, what can you do to check?" Thurston asked.

"I'll have to put my own people onto it," said Philip. "We have a team which specializes in money laundering although that is normally in connection with tax evasion not drug running. But let's see what they can come up with."

# CHAPTER THIRTEEN
## *The Orchestration*

*29 May 2001, lunch time*

Thurston had decided on Raffles as the ideal place to meet Najinski on the basis that it would be better for him not to risk drawing attention to the hospital by meeting the universally recognizable press man there. It would not be unusual for Najinski to be seen at Raffles.

Thurston took Jaci with him – as he had predicted her reaction had been, "If you leave me cooped up in this hospital much longer I'll go crazy." As expected, two of Lee's junior associates had enthusiastically accepted an invitation to have lunch with her as well.

Lee and Najinski had arrived two or three minutes earlier and were seated at the bar when Thurston, Jaci and the two associates walked in. They were ten yards away when Najinski turned to see if there was any sign of his visitor and, as Thurston had not warned him he was bringing three other people, he had no reason to suspect the approaching European was indeed Thurston. The result was that the only person he noticed in the approaching group was Jaci, and that was as far as he got. Admittedly she did look good in a white tailored linen dress which she had added to her wardrobe on her own account since arriving in Singapore. A green sash belt accentuated her figure and her long blonde hair was piled up above large pale green eyes and a full-lipped wide mouth.

Thurston was used to this reaction amongst his clients in the UK despite her efforts to play down her appearance, but it was the first time he had seen her show-stopping effect in Singapore.

Najinski was still looking at her when the group stopped in front of him.

Lee stood to welcome them and introduced Edward Thurston and his assistant Jaci Linthorpe. The tall moustachioed figure with wiry hair standing two inches above his head and the large unmistakable large pink rimmed glasses, stood to return the handshake.

"Jaci and her friends will not be joining us but as they were coming this way we came together."

"Pity," said Najinski, still having difficulty taking his eyes off Jaci.

Jaci and the two boys moved away, "See you later Edward," she said smiling.

"Jeez what a looker she is!" was Najinski's opening shot, the New Zealand bit of his mid-ocean accent came to the fore.

"No. Not too bad is she?" said Thurston following Najinski's gaze. "Got a brain, too."

"I'll bet she has!"

Najinski's openly lascivious reaction to one of his staff, thirty-five years his junior, did not go down too well, and Thurston pointedly moved to the bar and turned his back on the retreating woman. Najinski appeared not to notice. Lee was however aware of the "distinct lack of cordiality" at least on Thurston's part – but there was not much more he could do other than lead them into conversation. "Not good news about Catherine Miller," he said.

"No it isn't," replied Najinski. "Although not exactly a surprise. It will be interesting now to see what reaction we get to the wave of protest that's lining up."

"I don't think I would be too confident of any helpful reaction," Lee said, "on previous form it will only make Singapore more determined to hold the party line."

Najinski turned back to the bar. "What can I get you two to drink? How about a sling, I've quite taken to the local hooch."

"I need to keep a clear head," said Thurston, "so if you don't mind I'll stick to tonic water."

"I'm not staying," said Lee, "I've just dropped by to make the introductions."

Najinski called a waiter, ordered the drinks and a plate of samosas, then turned back. Lee bid his farewells.

"So I see you've been getting into some pretty remote country," said Najinski. "I'd never even heard of Mustang except as a horse."

"I came across it in the *National Geographic* – my sort of territory," replied Thurston.

"Even so, does sound a bit of a stretch flying through that sort of a blow just to take a few shots."

"That does seem to be the conventional wisdom," Thurston replied.

"Mind telling me about it?"

Yet again, Thurston went through his well-practised story of the events leading up to and following his landing at Lo Manthang. "And they think it was the death of the previous leader that's got them excited. Makes you wonder if we're missing something," said Najinski.

Thurston let the question hang for the time being and switched the conversation to Lee's reason for bringing the two of them together.

"I gather you're interested in the way the press is reacting?" said Thurston.

"Not just the press, more the whole media circus!" Najinski leaned down to pick up a leather zipped folder.

"You mean the way the noise level keeps going up instead of fading away!" said Thurston.

"You've picked up on that?" said Najinski, the wind rather taken from his sails. "And when the women are executed it will blow everything off every front page and every newscast across the globe."

"And with protest from every involved government, every last human rights organization and even the United Nations, nothing else will get a look in for a week before the executions," Thurston added, "or for some time afterwards."

"Which in a way should not be a surprise," said Najinski. "The sequence of increasing noise level from arrest, to committal, to trial, then the run up to actual execution is pretty much guaranteed to increase the noise level." Najinski repeated the exact same thought process which Thurston had gone through earlier when going over the morning press with Jaci.

"And in fact, there are signs that there is even more to it than that," Thurston took the wind away again.

Najinski frowned, "What else have you picked up?"

"The full media pack treatment," Thurston explained, "feeding the media background information and pre-written articles and fillers to make it easier to run your story rather than somebody else's. I even came across signs of it in articles on the economic effects." Thurston opened the papers he had brought to show Najinski and had underlined the common phrases and word selections in different papers.

"So you're thinking cross checks with mine?" Najinski looked surprised. "I was expecting a bit of a battle convincing an academic. Do you mind if I add those to my dossier."

"I think we should get copies of both your stuff and mine to Philip Lee," said Thurston, "if what we're seeing here is worldwide, high level, media orchestration then it's a pretty important part of the conspiracy theory he needs to blow the Singapore establishment off its rigid course."

"Conspiracy theory?" queried Najinski.

"Philip thinks the court will need something like proving this is not normal trafficking and the women have been set up in some way if they are to stand a chance."

"Jesus!" Najinski exclaimed. "Well if it's conspiracy you want, this press business goes even further. You can see the evidence of feeder material not only at national and international level, but in the local press in the women's home countries."

He held up a heavy file of newspaper clips from all of the involved countries and indeed others, many of them marked to show unusual common wording. "There are even indications that the local press have been given local sources of additional relevant information."

Najinski showed Thurston a number of examples.

"This is costing somebody a fortune," said Thurston looking over Najinski's notes.

Both had noticed broad editorial differences. "The press in the women's hometowns attack the barbarity of a state which would execute innocent kids. The American national press is particularly critical of the ineffectiveness of drug intelligence functions leaving innocent young travellers at risk. The Singapore, Hong Kong and Chinese press support Singapore's hard line and in Nepal," Najinski noted, "the press is emphasizing the effect of the arrests on tourism. There have been massive cancellations, particularly in the Annapurna Region, which is severely affecting the whole economy."

And still there was more, highly researched statistical analysis of Nepal's tourist trade written in language expected from the *Financial Times* not a local hack; equally detailed analyses and impressively written reports of the influx and distribution of Tibetan refugees in recent years; descriptions and locations of Tibetan refugee camps throughout Nepal; features on Tibetan refugee businesses, from cottage industries in the refugee camps to successful book and map shops and guest house businesses in tourist areas, particularly in the Annapurna Region.

"And this picture of sophistication very much adds to what we're seeing elsewhere," said Thurston.

"What do you have in mind?" asked Najinski.

Thurston told him about the penetration of the top secret American travel article exercise and the resulting deaths of Foster and the two Scandinavian women.

"So it's not just sophistication – they are prepared to take people out."

"So it would seem."

"So why haven't they had a go at you?" Najinski laughed.

"People keep asking me that," Thurston smiled back.

"So there is not much doubt that the media is being orchestrated," Najinski summed up. "But the next question is the big one. Who's doing it?"

"The Chinese," said Thurston bluntly.

"The Chinese?" said Najinski.

"Well what we've gone through in the last half hour tells you it's not a few opportunist Tibetans," said Thurston. "And if you are looking for people able to operate this level of sophisticated media orchestration and penetrate the American DEA at a high level there are not too many candidates there. The Russians barely have that level of capability these days and have no history of involvement in this area. So who does that leave?"

Najinski rocked his head backwards and forwards in thought then shrugged his shoulders, "The Israelis and at a push the French," he said, "and of course the Chinese."

Thurston waited to see if he would take it any further. He was not disappointed.

"Didn't Philip Lee tell me you had taken some video footage that put the Chinese in the frame?"

"Yes, he did, which is why I've got it here," Thurston said patting the side of his briefcase. "If you've got half an hour when we've finished, and a video player at your office, we can run over it."

"What are we waiting for? Let's get a move on," said Najinski finishing his drink and getting up.

"I'll have to wait for Jaci," said Thurston. "As it happens she hasn't seen it yet either."

"No problem," Najinski smiled and sat down.

"Incidentally apart from getting a copy to Philip what are you going to do with the press dossier?" asked Thurston.

"I'll work your stuff into it and send the result to Schultz in Delhi and keep the main file here – and of course, as you say, give Philip a copy."

Thurston called Philip Lee's office to see if he could join in viewing the video, but he was tied up in meetings he couldn't get out of. "I'll make sure he sees it later," said Thurston.

They made their way to the exit and met Jaci returning from her lunch with Lee's boys. They obviously had had a good time.

~~~~~~~~~~

Najinski's office was on the fourth floor of a modern steel and glass structure just off Orchard Street. Najinski had phoned from the taxi to ask for a video projector to be set up and it was ready and waiting when they arrived.

Najinski and Jaci watched the tape starting with the take-off of the nineteen seater Otter from Pokhara turning westwards to fly across the base of the Annapurna massif. They were amazed at the height of the Annapurnas towering over the flight, an impression which became even more dramatic as it turned north into the mouth of the Kali Gandaki Gorge.

"You actually enjoy this sort of thing?" Najinski asked Thurston.

"Actually, yes," Thurston replied, "meat and drink for me."

As the Otter emerged from the gorge, the terrain changed to the rich desert purples, oranges, yellows and greys as they flew out over the Tibetan plain with its snow rimmed horizon.

"Look at that!" Jaci called out involuntarily as the square walled Lo Manthang appeared before them with the string of "ants" coming in from the border. There was more footage of Thurston inside the city walls in the morning and remarkable shots of the yaks of the salt caravan "straggling" their way down from the snow rimmed border in seemingly disorganized twos and threes.

"Yaks are extremely difficult to control," Thurston explained, "but they are so effective at high altitude that the herders put up with their lack of discipline." Jaci smiled as Thurston fast-forwarded to the evening and shots of the campfire.

# The Tissue Trail

"The temperature must have been minus fifteen Celsius," he said, "but the fire and the chang, a sort of alcoholic yogurt, helped!"

He took them through the tortuous conversation with Tensing with Chaudrai interpreting, including Tensing telling them that they suspected the Chinese of killing the previous leader to quell dissent over the longer route. At the end of that conversation Thurston signalled to the technician to stop the projector.

"That was the first suggestion of Chinese involvement," Thurston said, "but what I want you to see and hear word-for-word now are the video sections which follow. First, when I asked about how the palm oil plant project had come about it was too much for Chaudrai to translate, but he was born in the Annapurna Region and knew quite a lot about it himself. This is what he said..."

*The Chinese administrators have controlled quotas for export of commodities such as salt which has been the mainstay of the caravans' survival for centuries. But in recent years they have channelled an increasing amount of salt back to "homeland China" and reduced salt export quotas to a level where the viability of the yak caravans, and the way of life of the semi nomadic Dolpo Pa who operate them, has been threatened. The Annapurna Area Conservation Project, the government agency which promotes tourism in the Annapurnas, hit upon the idea of setting up a palm oil production plant using the caravan to bring in basic commodities used in palm oil manufacturing. This would achieve two objectives: the 1,000 year-old caravan, re-routed into Mustang, would create a major new tourist attraction and at the same time carry new loads to replace the declining salt quotas - helping the caravan to survive.*

*Initially, the Chinese showed no interest in the palm oil plant idea and had refused to cooperate. Then, around the end of 1994, they changed their position completely and became keen supporters of the initiative to the point, as Tensing has described, where it appears they killed the previous leader to quell the resistance to what was a longer route. It took a further four years to change the arrangements and the first of the re-routed caravans came into Mustang in 1999.*

# The Tissue Trail

"We don't yet know if there is any significance in those dates," said Thurston, "but if something happened in the mid- nineties which affected Chinese thinking, it might be important in working out what lies behind all of this."

Jaci had been scribbling notes and took down the dates.

"So whatever this is could have taken five years to put into place," said Najinski. "Which just like the management of the media, it suggests a heavyweight project, not just a local fundraiser."

"Agreed," said Thurston. "Now look at the section I added for the record after Chaudrai himself had been interrogated about the flight by the airline and by the same chap who questioned me – a Major Jha who ran the organization which set up the palm oil plant. I have turned the camera to record myself and, as Jaci takes pleasure in pointing out, taken like that I am not a pretty sight."

*My name is Edward Thurston the photographer who took the video recording of the salt caravan coming into Nepal from Tibet on 21st and 22nd April 2001. I am adding this commentary on 27th April following a telephone call from Captain Chaudrai who piloted the flight and acted as interpreter when I attempted a rudimentary conversation with the leader of the caravan, Harka Tensing.*

*Chaudrai told me that he had been interviewed at length by the airline regarding the flight, which took place in difficult conditions, and the landing on an uncommissioned airstrip. However, the focus of the interview had been by an ACAP administrator regarding the conversation with Tensing – including reference to the death of the previous leader, which Tensing had intimated had been at the hands of the Chinese.*

*The interview had become more aggressive when it became apparent that parts of the conversation had been videotaped. He had left the interview feeling concerned and that there was something seriously wrong. He was passing on that concern.*

*Chaudrai's interrogation adds to my own experience – with my motives for the trip to Lo Manthang being regarded as highly suspicious both in Nepal and even more surprisingly by immigration officers in Singapore. For the record, as a semi-professional photographer, my objective in visiting this area was to try to photograph one of the salt caravans which have only recently become accessible to travellers as a result of a change to their route to Mustang.*

*Whatever it is in this videotape, which has caused concern to some, inexplicably connects to the import not only of salt but also of a common, low cost chemical, brought into Nepal by a difficult route over the high Himalaya. And whatever and whoever else is implicated, it appears that the Chinese were involved in encouraging the establishment of the new route in the mid 1990s and in ensuring that the new route, and commodity, came into Lo Manthang in 2000-2001.*

Thurston thanked the technician who wound the video back and switched off the machine.

Jaci was the first to react.

"When you see it like that," she said, "showing the Chinese initially did not have anything to do with the palm oil plant project, then changed their minds and finally became so committed they killed the previous caravan leader, doesn't leave much doubt does it."

"No it doesn't," said Najinski. "And yet I've been as close to this story as you can get and hadn't even considered the possibility of Chinese involvement. It explains why this video and that conversation is such hot property."

"Right," agreed Thurston. "But all we know after this is that the Chinese seem to be involved because of something which changed in the mid-nineteen nineties and then took something like five years to put in place. It still leaves a string of questions such as why have they taken so much trouble to set this up and why have all the Tissue Trails gone straight to Singapore? And if we find the answers, we will then need some legally water tight way of tying the Chinese into this. What we've got here is purely circumstantial."

"So is anybody doing anything about it?" asked Najinski.

"On the Chinese question Philip is getting his team of money tracers to track the money from the distribution outlets, major cities like Lahore, Karachi, Delhi, Jakarta – and Singapore – back to the source. That nearly always tells you who is pulling the strings."

"And the women coming into Singapore?" asked Najinski.

Thurston paused then said, "Philip has asked us to try our questioning techniques on the women in Changi."

Najinski's first reaction, to give him credit, was to turn to Jaci. "Are you going to do this?" he asked disbelievingly.

She nodded looking back at him, "Yes, I'm going to give it a go."

"Brave woman," he said seriously, nodding in approval, then turned to Thurston. "Jeez, Thurston do you reckon they will let me in on that?"

"A press man on death row?" Thurston smiled at Najinski's optimism. "Not a chance Victor."

# CHAPTER FOURTEEN
## *The Prison*

**7th June 2001**

Thurston had shown Lee the Chaudrai video in the evening after the meeting with Najinski. The next step was to use Thurston's agency questioning techniques on the Tissue Trail women in Changi Prison to see if they could tease anything out of them which Lee's classical cross-examination methods had failed to reveal.

Philip Lee had assembled the arrest reports and statements for Thurston and Jaci to start their examination of the Tissue Trail background information. Over the next day and a half they read the reports and transcripts of post arrest interviews, committal proceedings, and trial transcripts. Lee had arranged the papers in the same order as the arrests had occurred —Maria Gonzales, Karen Leopold, Catherine Miller, Francoise Dumas and Birgit Heller, in case anything occurred as a result of what had gone before.

Nothing of great substance came out of the written material although Thurston raised the point that they were all of different nationalities. "If you stretch a point – Karen Leopold for mainstream US; Maria Gonzales for the Spanish speakers; Francoise Dumas for the French and their connections; and finally Birgit Heller – reported in the press as German but turned out to be a naturalized Australian – so two for the price of one with her."

"I think you might be giving them a bit too much credit," Jaci laughed.

"You should see Victor's analysis of the effort they have put into maximizing local press reaction," said Thurston. "If they can go that far then making sure they've got maximum geographical coverage would be a logical extension."

The Tissue Trail

Nothing of significance emerged from the paper examination. Lee had been expecting something and was disappointed although he thought Najinski would be interested in the "geographical cover" possibility.

"OK," said Lee, "let's concentrate on your interviews tomorrow." He looked at Jaci. "Are you still sure you are happy to face this?"

"Not exactly happy, but if I'm good at something that could help there is no way I'm going to duck out of it."

### Changi Women's Prison
### 11th June 2001

One of Philip Lee's firm's cars, with Lee already aboard, picked up Thurston and Jaci at 8:30 a.m. and took them through the early morning traffic to Changi Women's Prison.

On the way, Edward briefed the other two more fully on his interchange with Najinski regarding the near certainty that the media was being orchestrated.

"It clearly adds another string to the conspiracy theory," said Lee.

Jaci had not shown much interest in this conversation. She was clearly apprehensive; she had never been near a prison never mind inside one. When they reached the high walled prison and got out of the car Thurston took her arm as Lee escorted them to the main entrance of the modern looking brick building. Inside, everything seemed deathly quiet and when something did move it was electronic. She had not expected such a modern building.

They were checked in by prison reception and taken through an electronic security hall to a reception room.

Lee explained that the women would be brought from their cells with a guard and would sit with them with the guard in attendance and be able to speak freely. Jaci had her fingers intertwined as a means of keeping her hands steady.

A door opened and a guard entered followed by a figure in the grey shapeless top and loosely hanging trousers. This first woman was Mexican American, Maria Gonzales. She was small, perhaps 5'3," dark-haired and quiet in a suppressed sort of way —as if the burden of the situation was simply too much for her to carry. She looked to have lost some weight and showed signs of lack of sleep – *but she could have been worse*, thought Jaci.

226

# The Tissue Trail

Lee introduced Thurston and Jaci as "experts in unearthing bits of information which normal processes fail to dig out."

Maria acknowledged them with a quick nervous smile.

Thurston asked Jaci to lead the conversation as she was the same age and had trekked in the same area so she had a lot of common ground and would be able to achieve empathy more easily than he would.

Maria described her first impressions of Nepal and the Tissue Trail itself, then homed in on the shop where she had bought the jacket in which the heroin had been found. They talked around all aspects of the purchase conversation and people they had spoken to in the shop before buying the item. There had been nothing that could have been remotely suggestive of a drug trafficker looking for a carrier or mule. Maria talked about the colorful wool jacket and how it had some similarities to the coloring and patterns of outdoor jackets in Peru and Bolivia and how she had wanted to buy something as a memento of Nepal. They asked if anyone had talked to her about meeting up with them in Singapore. Again, not a glimmer.

The next woman to meet Jaci and Thurston was Karen Leopold – an athletic, fair-haired, well-built woman of around 5'6" who did not look to have lost any weight. In fact, in what many would consider to be typical American, her main emotion seemed to be anger at the ridiculous position of being lined up for execution when she had not had a clue that she was carrying.

Jaci led the conversation again, talking about Nepal, but as Karen did not seem to be suffering mentally as much as Maria, Thurston joined in earlier. The result was the same. She had bought Tibetan mountain walking boots – tough soled but with colourful oiled woolen uppers.

"Where was the heroin in those?" Thurston asked.

"In one of the heels," replied Karen. "God knows why they didn't fill both heels!"

"Were the boots for you or someone else?" Thurston asked for no particular reason.

Karen's brave façade cracked for the first time, tears welled up and ran down her cheeks. "For my boyfriend," she said quietly through the tears.

Lee asked her if she wanted a break but she blew her nose and said she would be alright.

When she had recovered, Thurston led the questioning. This was aimed at finding out if anybody had asked a question of any sort which could have been even remotely related to the process of trafficking – or simply meeting in Singapore. There was nothing and after an hour and five minutes they could go no further.

The French woman, Francoise, was typically emotional and demonstrative almost Italian-esque with her hand and arm movements. She swung between tears and shouting obscenities and periods of quiet. But the result was the same – nothing.

Catherine had asked to be left to the end as she was not feeling well, so Birgit Heller, the German who lived in Australia, came in fourth. She was fair-haired, blonde and blue-eyed. She seemed to be calm, almost as if no one had told her the hopelessness of her position. Jaci and Thurston went through the questioning routine and her demeanor didn't falter. It was almost unnerving. But the answers to their questions were a replay of the others – no mention of any meeting after arrival in Singapore or anywhere else after leaving Nepal. They were missing something.

Over a light lunch, in a surprisingly pleasant visitors dining area, Lee, Thurston and Jaci talked over the questioning –looking for any possible gap.

"When we get a complete blank like this," said Thurston, "not just in medicine but generally, it's because we're making wrong assumptions. So what are we assuming?"

"I suppose the key assumption is that the women are telling the truth," Lee suggested.

"If there was any doubt about that it has been knocked on the head this morning," Jaci said. "There isn't a chance any of them knew."

"So the traffickers would need to have some means of getting at the heroin carrying items after arrival in Singapore, without making any specific arrangement – just follow the women and see where they stay then try to intercept the item?" Jaci suggested without conviction.

"Just about possible," Thurston said, "but it's a pretty risky option. This is supposed to be pretty sophisticated and that would be taking a totally unnecessary risk!"

Jaci bridled at Thurston's rejection of her idea. "You know that and I know that," she objected, "but we have to find a way of breaking out of the box we're in. This isn't getting us anywhere."

Thurston nodded without saying anything.

"When you think about the Surmil case," she calmed down, "it took nearly three weeks to come up with the answer in general practice in the UK and then in hospital here. With the side effects it took what, five days?"

"So what are you saying?"

"I'm saying we have been going half a day here without a glimmer of an answer and we've only one woman to go. It seems hopeless."

"That's not like you," Lee smiled at her, "from what I've seen, you are normally pretty positive. It just needs that chance question or remark, and we can always come back if we think of something later."

Thurston leaned back and looked up at the ceiling. "Whatever we're missing it's got to be something pretty radical – something completely off the wall, like ..." he paused, "like this is not normal trafficking or..." he paused again, "or not just trafficking."

"You mean there is something else to it?" Jaci frowned. "Like what?"

"I don't know," he said, "I'm just working on the principle that the box we seem to be stuck in is the assumption that this is just normal trafficking and that what happens should fit the normal trafficking pattern."

"So you're saying that the normal arrangements to collect the goods after arrival may not apply," Jaci said.

"That's just an example. And talking about arrival," said Thurston looking at Lee, "we still haven't any idea why just Singapore."

Lee raised his hands and shook his head.

"So how do we broaden the questioning?" asked Jaci.

"Let's get Catherine to talk about how she planned her trip as an open question rather than specifically asking about Singapore," Thurston said.

"Worth a go," agreed Jaci, "and I'll see if I can think of anything else."

Nobody was wildly enthusiastic about the idea, but it was something slightly different. At just after two p.m. they returned to the visitors' interview room.

Both Thurston and Jaci felt more apprehension about interviewing Catherine than the others. Thurston, because he had seen the woman at the airport before her arrest looking vibrant and full of fun and he'd heard Lee's descriptions of her physical and mental decline. Jaci, who because of Thurston's closer connection, made her feel more familiar to her. In the last few days, before coming to Changi Prison, Jaci had tried to prepare herself by visualizing Catherine in the worst state she could imagine.

The door from the cells opened and a guard entered the room and turned back to assist the prisoner. Despite all Jaci's efforts, the first sight of

Catherine was horrifying. She was stooping and round shouldered, her cheeks were sunken, her skin grey and lined and her eyes darkened. Thurston could tell Jaci was affected. So was he. To see the effect of what had happened to her in just a few short weeks was hard to believe. If she had been a hardened criminal, used to time in prison, it might have been different but she was barely more than a child – a few months out of university. And to see such a vulnerable harmless woman with her wrists manacled seemed to be the height of human insensitivity.

Lee waited until she had slowly and uncertainly taken a seat and watched her as she looked up, staring first at Thurston then Jaci.

"Catherine, this is Edward Thurston who caught you after you fainted when you were arrested at Changi Airport, and this is Jaci his assistant." Catherine managed a gentle nod of acknowledgement still looking slowly from one to the other. "I have asked them to see you and the other Tissue Trail women because the two of them have an uncanny knack of coming up with explanations when normal processes fail. I have to be honest, their field is medicine, so hoping their methods are going to work here is a little optimistic. But it is the method that is important not the area of expertise. So, as you know, we decided to give them a try."

They had agreed that Jaci would start the process asking gentle questions about the trek in Nepal and how she and her friends had enjoyed it.

"I'm sorry to have to meet you in such awful circumstances," Jaci started uncertainly. "Let's hope we can help."

Catherine managed a faint acknowledgement.

"I hear you really liked Nepal."

"Yes, we did," Catherine replied quietly.

"And friendly helpful people?"

"Yes."

"And you flew to Pokhara from Kathmandu?"

"Yes."

"Was the visibility good when you landed?"

"Yes," Catherine answered. "Why?"

"Because, if it was clear, you would have seen one of the greatest views in the Himalayas."

"You mean Fishtail," Catherine's eyes were becoming a little more active.

# The Tissue Trail

"I mean a 20,000 foot twin peaked ice mountain towering over you the moment you leave the airplane."

Thurston turned to look at Jaci. He had never heard her produce such colourful descriptive language – normally her descriptions were economical in the extreme – a true scientist. He looked back to Catherine to see, what was for her, close to being a remarkable reaction —almost a faint smile.

"Yes, it was clear – you must have been there yourself!"

"Yes, in fact, I was there since you were – I trekked to Ghorapani."

"Ghorapani?" Catherine was now clearly focused on Jaci. "Did you go up Poon Hill?"

"No, I didn't but don't ask – it's a long story."

"You should have – the view of the mountains as the sun came up was beautiful." The transformation in Catherine's demeanour was remarkable as Jaci connected with her through their shared love of the mountains.

Her recall of those last few free days continued – the giant rhododendrons – leeches picked up on bare legs from the long wet glass – seven stone Nepalis carrying sixty pound loads in bare feet and overtaking the trekkers. Thurston stayed quiet, encouraging Jaci to build the interaction. He needed Jaci to get as much memory recall and concentration back into Catherine Miller as possible.

Finally he intervened, "Catherine, it's delightful to hear you got such a lot out of Nepal, but we need to get back to talk about areas of conversation which could help us find out what happened. It won't be as much fun, but could you talk about the day you went to the refugee camp?"

Catherine's reaction to Jaci's mountain conversation had resulted in her sitting forward in her seat, but she sank back when Thurston broke the spell.

"What do you want to know?" she asked, her voice losing something of its animation.

"We want to know what happened at the refugee camp where you bought the doll for your sister," said Jaci leaning towards her.

Catherine described being taken to the Tibetan refugee camp on the edge of Pokhara by the trek leader. She remembered being shown around the whole process of wool making starting with the raw wool being carded and the knots being removed then stretched and spun into a single length. She remembered the loom shed with Tibetan families singing and laughing and being so delighted that she had wanted to buy something to remember the dramatic country and its delightful people. She had bought a doll as a present for her sister.

"Did you remember any conversation with anybody when you were buying the doll?"

Catherine thought about the question, then shook her head, "Only the Tibetan lady who sold me the doll and then only to check which one I wanted and to tell me how much it was."

"Did anyone talk to you about buying the doll before you bought it – to try to get you to buy it for instance?"

"No, I just looked at the various items for sale and chose it myself."

"Did anyone speak to you about the doll after you had bought it?"

Again she thought about it then shook her head, "No, I put it straight into my rucksack. I don't remember anybody mentioning the doll after that."

"Did anybody talk to you at any stage about meeting up once you had arrived in Singapore?"

She thought about it – but it didn't take long, "No. We've gone through this before – there was nothing like that. Nobody mentioned Singapore."

"You see what we're after," said Jaci, "the biggest single puzzle about this whole business is how can anyone organize smuggling if they don't communicate with the person they are expecting to be the carrier? All five women are saying the same thing – none of you knew you were carrying anything and nobody talked to them about taking anything through or picking up anything afterwards."

"Which makes the position we are all in now even more ridiculous," Catherine said, "if it wasn't so serious." She lowered her head and shuddered involuntarily.

Jaci looked at Thurston, signaling she couldn't go any further with this line of questioning and was ready to try to go wider. Thurston looked at Lee who had nothing to add himself and he too nodded.

Jaci switched to the line they had discussed.

"Why did you go direct from Kathmandu to Singapore? Most backpackers going east don't miss Thailand or Burma and most don't miss Malaysia!"

"Simply a lack of time. I was going around the world and only had six months so I couldn't do everything. I wanted to go to Thailand — particularly up to hill tribes in the north. That was one of the things I had to sacrifice."

"Did you know all five of you travelled direct from Kathmandu to Singapore?"

Catherine frowned. "No I didn't. But why would that matter?"

"We don't know. But if all five of you missed out on these same places, it might be significant."

Catherine nodded slowly thinking about it, "I don't remember anybody mentioning going direct to Singapore. The nearest was somebody asking where I was headed after Nepal."

"Oh?" Thurston frowned and sat up in his seat. "Who was that?"

"It was when I was wandering around the refugee camp shop after I had bought the doll. One of the Tibetan boys got into conversation and asked me why I had bought the doll and where I was going after Nepal?"

"How exactly did he put it?" said Thurston.

"He just sounded genuinely interested in my around the world trek."

"And you told him where you were going after Nepal?" asked Jaci.

"Yes – in fact I told him I was going to Singapore then Bali and on to Australia."

"Did he say anything to that?"

"I think he just repeated it?"

"As if he was wanting to check what you'd just said?"

"Not really, more in the sense of wishing he could travel like that himself. Remember, it couldn't have been long since he and his family had escaped from Tibet."

Thurston looked at Jaci – "Any more questions?"

"Yes, just to confirm, he asked both where you were going after Nepal and why you had bought the doll?"

"Yes."

"Anything else, Jaci?"

"I don't think so. I think we need to check with the others – then perhaps come back."

"Have I told you anything useful?" asked Catherine.

"We're not sure," said Thurston, "but we'll be talking to the other four and get back to you."

"Actually there is one question before we go," said Jaci. "I think I know the answer but I'd like to hear it from you. I assume there would be no problem if somebody wanted to get into your rucksack after you had bought the doll."

"No problem at all," Catherine replied. "When you don't need it you just leave it in your sleeping quarters. Why do you ask?"

"We're wondering if the heroin was hidden in the doll after you bought it."

~~~~~~~~~~

Catherine didn't want them to go – they were her contact with the outside world – and her contact with hope.

Jaci looked at the guard as she took a step towards Catherine. He got to his feet but did not prevent Jaci from giving Catherine a long hug.

The guard escorted Catherine from the room and as she reached the door back to her cell she looked back with tears running down her face. Jaci was aware of her own eyes watering and hoped the others hadn't noticed. But Thurston had noticed, and when Catherine had gone Thurston put his arm round Jaci's shoulders to comfort her. "Well done," he said quietly.

Jaci sighed. "Might be nothing at all," she said, "could be just friendly curiosity."

"OK, let's see what the others have to say."

Lee asked the guard if they could see the other four women again. He made a call on an internal line then put the phone down and turned back to them. "If you can do it quickly and finish by five p.m. you can go ahead," he told them, "I'll bring them back in the same order."

While they waited Lee asked, "What are you reading into the direct travel to Singapore?"

"I was hoping you would tell us the answer to that," said Thurston. "What is there about Singapore that is different from other places in the area when it comes to drugs?"

"I'll think about it," Lee said. "Nothing immediately comes to mind."

Maria Gonzales re-entered the visitors meeting room and was escorted by the guard back to her seat.

She looked expectantly from one to the other.

"Thank you for coming back Maria," Thurston smiled. "One of the other women told Jaci something which might just be helpful and we want to check if anything similar happened with you."

Jaci continued, "We were asking you before if anybody had talked to you about meeting up after you arrived in Singapore and you said no. But most backpackers travelling in that area try to go through Thailand to the Golden Triangle or the Hill Tribes or Burma and the Bridge on the River Kwai or Malaysia and Penang. Do you remember any conversation about your travel in general —forgetting any mention of meeting in Singapore or any mention of Singapore at all?"

Maria thought about it. "I can't remember anything," she said, "nobody talked about meeting later —in Singapore or anywhere else."

"No, not meeting," said Jaci gently, "just talking about where you were going after Nepal."

Maria frowned as if trying to recall something then said, "I did talk to a Canadian trekker about why I had bought the jacket – I told him it was just something to take back home to remind me of Nepal. He also asked about my travel plans after Nepal." She hadn't thought anything of it – it just seemed to be general conversation. Jaci told her there had been two Canadians on the trek she had been on and described both Jacques and Pierre.

"The one that chatted to me sounds like the short well-built one – and the second one sounds like the taller fair one. They seemed to be friends."

"So you talked to him and told him where you were going."

"Yes, to Singapore then on to Indonesia and Australia. Is this helpful?" she asked.

Jaci looked at Thurston who answered the question. "We're not sure yet but all five of you travelled directly from Kathmandu to Singapore and that seems to be unusual. If we can find out that all of you had conversations in which you mentioned Singapore then we may have something —if we can find out why going to Singapore is important."

Lee added, "But even if we do find something in this, it may not affect the outcome. We do not want to give you false hope, but anything we can discover might help."

Maria sank back into her chair.

"One more question, Maria," Jaci leaned towards her, "when you were stopped at Changi Airport did it seem to you that you were selected purely by chance?"

Maria didn't take long to answer, "No, it didn't seem to be by chance. The woman just in front of me thought they had selected her – but when she stepped towards them they pushed her aside and made it clear they were after me."

"And when you were searched, did they search everything?"

"No, just my rucksack and went straight to the bottom of it."

"Thank you, Maria. That happened to one of the others. Again we don't know what this all means. But we'll let you know when – if – we work it out."

There were no more questions and they still had three more women to re-interview, so Lee thanked Maria and she reluctantly left them.

While waiting for Karen Leopold, Thurston said, "With the Canadians involved, this is beginning to seem significant."

~~~~~~~~~~

The interview with Karen followed the same pattern and she, too, had been quizzed by a young Canadian after she had made her purchase of the Tibetan mountain boots. His name, she remembered, was Jacques and the description tallied. She also confirmed there had been a second taller Canadian travelling with him. Jacques had discussed with her where she was headed after Nepal and she had told him Singapore and then Australia. She was doing a whistle stop around the world trip.

But Karen volunteered something else, "I am pretty sure that, on the way back from Ghorapani to Pokhara, somebody interfered with my bag. Something had been moved in a way I would not have done myself."

She had also been sure she had been specifically selected at customs– in fact she had seen an immigration officer behind her waving to a colleague ahead, and making it pretty clear he was pointing at her.

Francoise Dumas had been approached by a Tibetan who asked questions about her trek route on a general interest basis and had asked the reason why she had bought the rug. She told him she would put it on a wall as a decoration when she got back home. She had also mentioned she was going to Singapore then east, although she hadn't quite decided which route. She was also pretty certain she had been specifically selected to be searched —not just picked from the passing crowd.

The last of the four to be interviewed a second time was Birgit Heller.

She told them she had been quizzed by a French Canadian guy in his mid-twenties, she thought his name was Pierre and her description again tallied with Jaci's. She had told him she was going via Singapore then to Jakarta. She was interested in volcanoes and wanted to see the location of Krakatoa.

"Did Pierre ask you why you wanted to buy the hat?" asked Jaci.

"Yes, I think he did – I told him I would take it home, something to remember Nepal by – I didn't expect to need it on the rest of the trip as it would be too warm."

Jaci asked her if she had been picked at random to be searched.

"No," said Birgit. "They stopped three of us and stood us in a line – then one of the officers stood in front of us pointing to each one in turn. When he pointed at me, he got the OK from somebody and I was taken into a side office."

Jaci nodded to Lee to indicate no more questions.

"Anything useful in what I told you?" Birgit asked.

Thurston repeated the direct to Singapore reply, "but we have to emphasize that, with Singapore's record, we still have a pretty long shot."

Birgit shook her head, "I was hoping for a bit more than that! I thought you guys were supposed to be magic."

~~~~~~~~~~

"Pity we couldn't tell her more," said Jaci when they were back in the car, "I think that *was* magic."

Lee looked at her. "What do you think was magic?" he asked, seemingly unimpressed. "Not one mention of Singapore by the Tibetans or the Canadians, only when volunteered by the women."

Jaci pulled back and frowned, "but if you wanted to make sure somebody was going to a particular city without putting the words into their mouths isn't that exactly what you would do – just ask where they were going without mentioning names?"

"Probably," replied Lee. "But bear in mind that even if we find the most compelling answer to what is behind this we will still be facing Singapore's determination not to bend in a Class A case."

Thurston shared Jaci's puzzled reaction. "Are you saying you don't accept that they were checking where the women were going after Kathmandu?" Thurston asked.

"No, I am not saying that, but based on what we heard, it would not stand up in court."

"But Singapore was the only place they all mentioned!" Jaci raised her voice in exasperation, "And Singapore was where they all went – and were all arrested."

"I am aware of that," said Lee quietly, "but let's make sure we have things in proportion – and be aware of what we're up against."

"What about the checks that the offending items were bought as presents or mementos?" Jaci's raised voice continued to show her frustration. "Trying to make pretty sure the item would be buried under their day-to-day stuff and not be taken out until they were searched at customs?"

"It fits the picture we want it to fit, but imagine the field day the prosecution would have dreaming up plausible explanations for buying the items," said Lee.

"Fine," continued Jaci, "and what about the involvement of the Canadians who chased me and, it seems, took care of Steve Foster. It all fits like a glove."

"I agree it seems that everything connects, but that is a long way from being a legal case which could shake the Singapore judiciary."

"Surely we aren't trying to produce legal stuff at this stage," Jaci protested. "We're just trying to figure out what the hell is going on in a nonsense situation."

Thurston pursed his lips as he turned his attention to Lee. "I understand your reticence Philip, but as Jaci says, if you take everything together we have to assume that the Singapore theory is right – getting the carriers to Singapore is a key part of this – so the spotlight switches to you. What is it about Singapore that makes it so important?"

Lee shook his head, "I'm afraid nothing comes to mind."

"So we are not really very much further forward," said Thurston. "We may be pretty sure the operators were only interested in women going direct to Singapore, but what was supposed to happen then?"

"We've had a hard day," said Lee. "Let's sleep on it."

# CHAPTER FIFTEEN
## *The Breakthrough*

*11th June 2001*

Thurston and Jaci decided they had earned a comfortable night back at the hotel rather than the hospital. After freshening up they met at the bar to have a drink and to talk over the day. When Jaci appeared she was not looking her normal buoyant self.

"Are you all right?" Thurston asked.

"Seeing those women in Changi has rather got to me," she said, her voice sounded flat and subdued. "And then after it seemed we had really got somewhere this afternoon, now it seems we didn't. Not a good day!"

"OK. Let's think about it over something to eat. We did make progress this afternoon but there's quite a way to go," he said, trying to lift her mood.

She managed a strained smile. "OK, I could eat something."

Jaci ordered a Caesar salad and a glass of white wine. Thurston said he would do the same.

"Why was Philip so negative?" asked Jaci.

"I suppose he thought we were getting a bit carried away with what seemed to us to be quite a breakthrough. He was just trying to keep everybody's feet on the ground."

"Maybe, but his team hadn't made any progress. I would have thought he could have been a bit more appreciative instead of just pouring cold water on everything."

"Let's put it down to professional jealousy. He didn't find the answer. It was your flair for finding the slightly different angle which did it again."

"Thank you," she gently dipped her head in acknowledgement, "I suppose it's the unwarranted assumptions thing again."

"Yep," Thurston agreed. "We had been assuming, without thinking about it, that the operators would have to mention Singapore by name. And it looks as if they deliberately avoided doing that —which left us asking the wrong question."

"Just like Surmil breakthroughs," said Jaci. "Perhaps we should write a paper on assumption testing when we've finished all this?"

"Or perhaps we should just keep it to ourselves and keep making a living out of it," Thurston grinned.

"So what are we assuming or not assuming about the Singapore factor?" Jaci asked.

"Well, the traffickers are wanting the women to get to Singapore with heroin on board so it looks as if there is something different about the way traffickers, or the carriers, are dealt with."

"Dealt with – you mean the way they are screened at customs?" Jaci checked.

"Well now why should we assume that it is at the time when they go through customs?"

"You mean it might be something that happens later – after the arrest?"

"There is one thing I wondered about in the shower," she said, "this business of the women carrying just enough substance to trigger the death penalty and the public analyst saying they could easily have carried a lot more."

"Yes?" Thurston waited for the Jaci follow up.

"Well, does this fifteen gram trigger apply in other countries?"

Thurston looked at her. "I don't know. Why?"

"Well, if it doesn't happen anywhere else, and you've got my nasty mind, you could even think they actually were set up to be caught."

Thurston looked up at the waiter who had arrived with two more glasses of wine. He took a sip and let the wine swirl around in his mouth, a frown gathered as he thought about what she had just said. For a full minute neither said anything, silenced by the thought Jaci had produced almost by accident.

Finally Thurston said, "Let's think about it. How many boxes does that crazy idea tick?"

"You can't be serious, I thought I was joking."

"Well first, we know that all of the women had confirmed Singapore as their next port of call. Secondly, that the items were going to be presents or mementos which meant they would be buried at the bottom of their rucksacks so they could be pretty sure the heroin wouldn't be found before they reached Singapore.

"Third, all five were pretty sure that customs knew who to stop."

Jaci shook her head. "So if you're taking this seriously, somebody was searching for women who bought the sort of thing they would bury in their rucksacks; check where they were going next and if it was Singapore they would find a way, which is not difficult, to load the present or memento with a slip or sachet containing heroin. No arrangements were made to meet in Singapore because it wouldn't have been necessary. Customs had been tipped off to intercept them."

"So, putting it bluntly," said Jaci, "if you accept all that, then you are saying somebody wanted to set these women up to hang."

Both sat silently for a minute, then Thurston said, "That is incredible," and got to his feet.

"Where are you going?"

"To telephone Philip Lee – we need to know if this could be right – and if it is, he needs to be thinking about it as soon as possible."

"So where are you going?" she asked again.

"Somewhere I can't be heard – in any case mobiles are frowned on in the dining room. I'll pop out to the foyer," he told her.

Jaci got up herself, "I want to listen."

Thurston signaled to the waiter they were coming back.

They found a corner where they could not be overheard and Edward dialed Philip Lee's home number. After four rings of the dial tone, Philip Lee answered.

"Sorry to trouble you at home Philip and at this time of night."

Edward put his hand over the receiver and mouthed to Jaci the words, "He's in the middle of his evening meal."

"I only need to ask one question Philip – is the fifteen gram mandatory death penalty something that only applies in Singapore?"

Silence for a few moments.

For Jaci's benefit, Thurston repeated Lee's reply. "Yes, the only other territory with the same low-level mandatory provision is Malaysia. Not India, Pakistan, Thailand, Burma, Indonesia, they all have tough provisions but not so rigid and the courts have discretion."

Philip was not going to put the telephone down now.

"What is behind the question?" he asked.

"Suppose that the reason why they only use carriers who are going to Singapore is that they don't care about the heroin as such, they want them to hang."

Philip was initially silent then asked Thurston if he could call him back.

Edward and Jaci walked back to the table.

"Looks as if we are right again!" she half stated, half asked. In other circumstances her expression would have been justifiably smug but she looked downcast and concerned. "But that is horrific. Somebody deliberately put the women through the whole arrest to trial to execution process. What on earth for?"

As usual Jaci had made the chink in the armour, but it was Thurston who could see where it led. "Because it gives them a means of controlling a worldwide media furore which not only maintains its momentum but actually gathers in intensity. That is almost impossible to achieve."

Jaci nodded slowly, caught half way between being pleased at making the breakthrough, but not wanting to believe it.

"And of course it is perfect for Philip because, if this turns out to be some kind of conspiracy, it could become political not legal. We would be talking serious political embarrassment and dealing with the president's office – not a court room and a judge."

"And that would give the women more hope?"

"Oh, God, yes," said Thurston. "When he talks about wanting something extraordinary and unprecedented he is talking about major political embarrassment!"

"So," said Jaci, "all you want me to do is find out what is important enough to make someone set up something as horrific as this ...and make such an effort to do it?" Her mood had lightened a little.

"I think an early night is called for," he said, "in the true sense of the word."

She looked at him with a thin smile and nodded in agreement. There were three sessions to go in Thurston's Surmil trial but tonight would not be one of them.

"At least you look a bit better than you did an hour ago," he said.

"Well, from the nightmare of this morning, at least we've finished the day with a glimmer of a chance of getting them out of it."

# The Tissue Trail

As they walked across the entrance foyer, Thurston's mobile phone buzzed in his breast pocket. He pulled it out and looked at the screen. It was Philip Lee.

"I think you might be onto something Edward – and it is just the kind of thing which gives us a chance. And Najinski's media orchestration theory could be why they're doing it – it's the almost perfect driver to produce a rising media furore which they can to an extent control."

Lee's same connection with the media management aspect hardened Thurston's confidence in the conclusion.

"So now all we need to know," said Thurston, "is what is so important in July that they need to produce a climax to the symphony then!"

"Exactly!" said Lee. "But tell Miss Linthorpe it has been a good day after all."

"Tell her yourself Philip she's right here," he said handing the phone to her.

When she had finished she told Thurston, "We now need hard evidence, so he will be pushing on with the money tracing. Oh, and he suggests we remind him to buy us a drink sometime."

The smile was back.

# CHAPTER SIXTEEN
## *The Money Trace*

*15th June 2001*

To his surprise Lee had found that the drug intelligence agencies in Singapore were not checking money movements and had immediately put his top man onto it. He made good progress, quickly identifying the new cash movements into Singapore and back to Pokhara and, in fact, on to Lhasa. But on the fifth day he did not arrive in the office and called to say that he couldn't do any further work on the Tissue Trail case. His ten-year-old son had been kidnapped as he was leaving school the previous day, and he had received an anonymous telephone call telling him to cease any further enquiries into the money movements in Singapore. The following morning there had been another phone call telling him they had left the boy at a specified junction close to their residence.

The caller had said, "When you find your boy you will find a minor injury. But understand the message – we know where you are, we know how to get to you and if we need to take action again – the injury will be more significant. This warning applies to all members of your firm." The call had been too short to be traced.

They had found the boy in a terrified state and with a neat incision on the lobe of his right ear. It had been neatly dressed. They were professionals.

The fraud man had documented the progress he had made and told Lee where to find his report. He then asked for a few days off to spend time with his family. Not surprisingly, Lee had agreed.

Lee read over the cash movement report. It confirmed new movement into Nepal with most of it continuing through to Lhasa. It came in, as would be expected in a normal trafficking operation, from major population centres in the region – Delhi, Karachi, Calcutta, Lahore, Dhaka, but the movements were crude. There was the normal re-routing through known offshore banking centres including Bermuda, Panama, the Caymans and the BVI, but it appeared to be half-hearted as if somebody was just going through the motions.

There was one other major oddity – there were signs, which the fraud man hadn't had a chance to follow up, that although the cash was coming in from a variety of population centres, each source was being fed from a single account – the number of which he had logged in the report. Normally each population centre account would be fed by a variety of cash deposits from different dealer sources – never a single feeder account.

He had concluded, "All the indications are that the cash movements are artificial. It would need somebody in the drug intelligence services to be incompetent, or in collusion, for this to go unremarked and unreported through a normal banking system."

"In addition," he had stated, "the movements he had detected were reasonably substantial and trafficking on the scale indicated by the level of cash movement, whether artificial or not, was totally inconsistent with the minute quantities the women were carrying and the alleged laboratory scale production. It must be presumed, therefore, that either the small amount of heroin intercepted so far is just the tip of the iceberg, with the substance getting through by other channels – or this is another element of a totally artificial set up."

Lee telephoned Thurston to tell him what had happened and to go through the report. Lee sounded strangely buoyant. "This is beginning to sound more and more like the sort of thing that could have the desired effect," he told Thurston.

"So this makes it even more important to identify the feeder bank account?" asked Thurston.

"Yes," said Lee, "it most certainly does."

"But who can you ask to follow this up – nobody on your staff obviously?"

"I have two ideas," said Lee. "One is to make a request through the Central Bank here in Singapore."

"But surely the traffickers could reach them in the same way they've reached your people?"

"Agreed," said Lee, "which is why I prefer my second option, which is to use the National Criminal Intelligence Service in London. They have after all been keeping a pretty close eye on things here as Catherine Miller is British."

"You think they'll agree?"

"In these circumstances, yes," said Lee, "and one other action I'm taking is an off the record meeting with Rahman at the prosecutor's office."

"What did you say you wanted to see him about?"

"I kept it vague – 'something unusual about the Miller case' – which could have an impact on the others. Oh, by the way, I dropped in to tell them what they had told us had produced a lead for the first time in the case, and we were following it up with all speed. But I also emphasized that they should not get their hopes up. The legal position hadn't changed."

### Prosecutor's Office
### Central Criminal Court
### 17th June 2001, 11:00 a.m.

After the usual courtesies, Rahman asked Lee what he was finding unusual about the Miller case.

"That there is no evidence of collection or arrangement to collect the substance at this end," said Lee.

"Yes, we are aware of that," said Rahman, "and I have to admit it is also troubling us. But you have more?"

"Yes we do," said Lee. "And I have to warn you that what I am about to tell you is going to sound incredible."

"You have me intrigued..." said Rahman.

Lee took Rahman through Edward Thurston's story, from what he had seen in Mustang to the reactions in Nepal and Singapore which had ensued, the penetration of the drug intelligence services plus the apparent manipulation of the press and media.

"So you are suggesting some high level operation beyond the capability of a few renegade Tibetans?"

"Precisely," said Lee, "but coming back to the absence of any evidence of arrangements to pick up the drug on this side of the border..."

"I've been waiting for you to come back to that."

Lee paused looking at Rahman then said, "Suppose there was never any intention for the substance to be collected?"

Rahman frowned, "What do you mean?"

"We know from talking to the women at Changi that they were all asked where they were going after Nepal and in all five cases it was Singapore. We also know that customs was forewarned as to which woman to search."

"Are you suggesting that they were meant to be caught?"

"Yes, and caught carrying just over fifteen grams. Not the 100 to 200 grams they could easily have carried. All five as you know were carrying between fifteen and twenty grams."

Rahman rubbed his fingers over his forehead. "And only Singapore and Malaysia have the rigid fifteen gram mandatory death penalty," he said quietly, as if to himself. He then addressed Lee, "Not exactly a watertight case Philip, and legally its irrelevant as they are guilty as charged however they came to be carrying."

"I'm aware of that, but if what appears to be emerging is right, then this would not be a matter for the courts – it would be political!"

Rahman considered the point. "In which case I'd better ask you the obvious question, who do you suspect and why would they dream up something as wild as this?"

"I haven't yet got definite answers to either question. Tibet and the Tibetans seem to be involved at every juncture although it's doubtful they could penetrate American intelligence. The Canadians are financially involved in Nepal and in funding the palm oil plant operation and they never seem to be far from any action. But, there is a third possibility..." Lee hesitated, knowing what Rahman's reaction would be to the mention of the Chinese. He wanted to set up this possibility gently, "...the event that started this whole line of enquiry was the medical researcher Edward Thurston taking a video of the caravan leader talking about the unexplained death of the previous caravan leader. He told Thurston that this was to quell dissent about the new longer route needed to bring the intermediate further east. And he made it clear that the Dolpo Pa – the tribal name of the caravan operators..." Lee was still stringing it out... "blamed the Chinese for his presumed murder."

"The Chinese?" Rahman sounded as if he were being strangled. "The Chinese?" he repeated. "You'll need more than this tissue of surmise and innuendo if you're going to suggest the Chinese are anywhere near this!"

"I'm obviously fully aware of that and the whole thing is so preposterous that I have to assume the chances of anything useful emerging from it is remote in the extreme."

"So what exactly is your purpose in coming to see me?"

"Because, ten days ago I put our money laundering people onto looking for the new cash movements which ought to tie-in with the movement of acetic anhydride —i.e., back to Pokhara and, if the Tibetans are involved, back to Lhasa."

"And?"

"After three days the son of the man I had put onto the job was abducted and we were warned off. But more importantly he had made quite a lot of progress and had found movement back to Pokhara and some movement back to Lhasa..."

"So it is the Tibetans..." Rahman stopped, realizing Lee hadn't finished.

"And there was movement coming in from usual commercial centres where the substance would be diluted and sold – but there were signs that this cash was being fed into the system from a single source."

Rahman's puzzled frown had reappeared.

"So are you saying that the cash movement has been set up artificially?"

"That's what it looks like – which strongly supports the overall contention that the women are pawns in a wider conspiracy."

"That is certainly the most compelling piece of argument you've produced so far Philip – potentially."

"And if we can trace the original source of the funds used to set this up then we will have as near proof as we're ever going to get as to who is behind it."

"So where is this account?"

"Geneva."

Rahman shook his head. "And you've got between three and four weeks. Is that going to be long enough to get through the thick walls of secrecy of a Swiss private bank system?"

"This is partly why I have come to see you, Rahman, I can't expect your open support given the legal position, but if I have convinced you that there is something in this – at least I can ask that you do not create the usual legal obstacles. Any delay could be fatal – in all senses of the word."

"I see."

"And of course as you are an integral part of the state judicial machinery, you can make sure that if the need arises for some nimble footwork – you can help ease the process."

"You mean I am well connected, politically as well as legally?"

# The Tissue Trail

Lee didn't need to comment.

"Alright Philip, I will play a straight bat – no unnecessary manoeuvring – but remember, to carry the day with an accusation of state sponsored serial killing you will need proof, not just beyond reasonable doubt but beyond any possible question. And you will need a motive."

"And if I can bring you proof of source of funding?"

"Proof beyond any possible question," repeated Rahman, refusing to commit himself further, "and a motive."

Lee was happy to leave it at that. Rahman would be fully aware of the political implications of Singapore being implicated in a state sponsored execution conspiracy.

## National Criminal Intelligence Service
## Upper Ground
## Blackfriars, London
## 17th June 2001, 7:15 a.m.

Barbara checked the incoming overnight messages; one stood head-and -shoulders above the others. She walked to Warrender's office, knocked on the door and presented it to him.

"Some movement in the Tissue Trail case – a formal letter from Philip Lee asking for assistance."

> J M W Warrender
> National Criminal Intelligence Service
> Upper Ground, Blackfriars, London
>
> Dear Warrender,
> Request for assistance – drug related cash movements.
>
> I refer to the case of State of Singapore v Catherine Miller one of five western women currently being held in Singapore charged with importing a Class A substance, namely heroin. As you will know, Miller has been tried and sentenced to death.
> My firm had set up a local cash trace as we had learned the intelligence agencies were not detecting the movements we would expect in such a case. We are now unable to continue with this

*process and I am approaching you for assistance. I would not trouble you with this if it were not for the fact that locating the origin of the cash which is feeding this trafficking may well be the best chance of identifying the perpetrators.*

*I attach the report produced by the lawyer who was working on the trace until we were obliged for various reasons to stop him. From this you will see the movements he detected are unusual to the point that he suspected they are artificial. This is consistent with increasing indications that the movement of heroin in these cases is also artificial.*

*The Prosecutor's office emphasizes that under the Import of Class A Substances Regulations there is no provision for clemency or pardon, or commuting of sentence, nor for appeal.*

*The only hope is that the explanation for a number of unusual features in this case including and in particular the cash movements I refer to, will prove to be of such a nature as to compel the Administration to review its position.*

*I trust in these circumstances that you will be able and willing to assist. I attach a schedule of the detail we ask you to try to identify and provide.*

*Signed*
*Philip Lee*

"What have we here?" asked Warrender, scanning the transmission. Barbara waited for him to take it in.

"Artificial?" Warrender exclaimed, "if they're right about that then we really do have a conspiracy."

"So we will help?"

"No question," said Warrender, "there's a lot riding on this. Who have we got available?"

"I'll try Nigel?" Barbara raised an eyebrow inviting approval.

"Yes, good man, go ahead. I'll put it in writing later."

"So there is a glimmer of light at the end of the tunnel?"

"Perhaps," said Warrender. "As long as they can work out why. I doubt if the origin of the cash on its own is going to be enough."

## NCIS London
### 19th June 2001, two days later

Warrender had asked Nigel to work quickly and he did. Within thirty-six hours he had picked up the traces identified by Lee's man in Singapore and identified the bank from which the flow of funds was being supplied.

## Philip Lee's offices, Singapore
### 22nd June 2001, 1:00 p.m.

Lee checked with his assistant for significant messages, "Particularly London."

His secretary told him there was a copy of an incoming report from Jonathan Warrender and handed him the typed sheet.

> *National Criminal Intelligence Service*
> *Drugs Division, Upper Ground, London*
> *To Philip Lee, Singapore*
> *22nd June 2001*
> *Drug related Cash Movements*
>
> *Philip,*
>
> *We have taken a significant step in our enquiries. We can confirm that the account receiving cash from the various distribution points previously discussed is, as your man also reported, in Geneva. We can now further confirm that the account is located at the Z. I. R. Bank, Rue Ami de Langemalle.*
>
> *We will now start the process of requesting further information, in particular the origin of the cash coming into that account.*
>
> *We anticipate resistance on client confidentiality grounds.*
>
> *Regards*
>
> *Jonathan Warrender*

## *20th June 2001*

Philip Lee telephoned Thurston and Najinski on a conference line to tell them the receiving bank had been located in Geneva.

"What happens next?" asked Thurston.

"There will now be a formal request from NCIS to the Geneva bank for further details of the account including the source of any incoming funds."

"And then?"

"The bank will resist the application as it is requiring disclosure of privileged information. The two sides will then go into a ritual exchange of correspondence with the bank doing all it can to resist disclosure. NCIS will make the point that the bank is obliged to cooperate if there is clear evidence that the transactions involved are drug related."

"And how long does this ritual take?" Najinski asked.

"It can take weeks as you would expect. Lawyers on both sides will be extremely careful!"

"So it could go beyond the first executions?" asked Najinski.

"It is possible, but the bank will be aware of the time table and it will not be in its interests to be seen dragging its feet with young women being executed at the other end."

"We have until the 6th July – call that the 5th," said Thurston. "We still do not have a motive, no concrete proof it is the Chinese and a Swiss Bank playing silly-buggers. And we have a mere fifteen days."

# CHAPTER SEVENTEEN
## *The Invitation*

**Raffles Hotel**
**21st June 2001, 8:30 a.m.**

Jaci had a sleepless night, still affected by the taxi incident. Thurston breakfasted alone reading over the morning papers, but he found his mental faculties monopolized by the question which had dominated since Jaci's "why Singapore?" breakthrough – assuming it is the Chinese behind the Tissue Trail affair, why had they dreamed up such a macabre conspiracy? But even the ingenious and imaginative Edward Thurston could not invent even the wildest of possible explanations.

He was walking back to his room through the hotel foyer when one of the reception staff intercepted him. Most now recognized him and knew him by name.

"Mr Thurston, someone has called twice this morning trying to reach you." When she told him the name of the caller, Thurston's reaction was to paraphrase Bogart in Casablanca, "Of all the people in all the world the last one he expected to hear from was her."

Thurston raised his eyebrows in surprise and reached out to the receptionist as she handed him a message slip.

*Trying to reach you – will try again at 9:00 a.m. your time. Lauren*

**Raffles Hotel**
**21st June 2001, 9:00 a.m.**

# The Tissue Trail

The call from Lauren came in just before nine a.m. – or nine p.m. the previous evening in Toronto.

"Good morning, Edward," said a smooth educated woman's voice with a gentle North American accent. "Thank you for taking my call."

"Good evening, Lauren," he replied, "no problem taking your call even if it is a bit of a surprise. To what do I owe the unexpected pleasure?"

"Unfortunately it's more business than pleasure, not helped by the Catherine Miller verdict." She sounded quiet even subdued; there was very little sign of the upbeat fun-loving woman he had encountered four weeks earlier.

"Pretty grim business," said Thurston, "and seemingly no way out."

"Are you still being hounded about your exploits in Mustang?"

"I'm pretty sure I'm still being followed but I haven't had any lengthy interrogations recently."

"Good," she said, "I have a proposition to put to you. It's partly professional, partly, I suppose you could call it, humanitarian."

"You have my rapt attention."

"When we met I told you about the extensive Canadian aid program in Nepal and that the salt caravan/palm oil plant exercise was one of the projects we sponsor."

"Yes, I remember."

"That of course puts us close to the Tissue Trail case since it is one of the commodities involved in the palm oil project which is being used to produce the heroin. Needless to say, we are under intense pressure from the governments of the countries whose citizens are involved, in particular our cousins south of the border, to find out what is going on and to put a stop to it. The Americans already have two of their citizens about to be tried and the death sentence in Catherine Miller's case has raised that pressure to screaming pitch.

"There may not be much we can do with respect to the women already arrested, but the pressure is on ourselves and the Nepalis to break the ring and prevent any further risk to innocent travellers. But as I mentioned during our last encounter – the effect of this continuous adverse publicity has decimated their tourist trade and bookings are down seventy percent overall and over eighty percent in the Annapurna Region. And that is having a devastating effect on tens of thousands of the poorest of Nepalis who rely on tourism for their survival."

"Not a good position," Thurston acknowledged. "You are trying to help and the result is young women heading for execution and thousands of Nepalis heading for starvation."

"That sums it up pretty well."

"So what are you suggesting and where do I fit in?"

"First, this is not personal. I'm speaking to you in my capacity as advisor to the Nepal Ministry of Internal Affairs and the proposal or request I want to put to you is in effect from them – or more particularly from ACAP – the tourism and resource management agency in the Annapurnas which I also told you about."

"So I'm back on Major Jha's Christmas card list am I?"

"Whatever his original reservations he can see that you can play a significant role in what we have in mind – so let me get to the point. We intend to televise the breaking of the ring," she replied, "and to break it at the most dramatic and visually impactful point possible. Outside the walls of the medieval city of Lo Manthang."

"Televise? Lo Manthang?" Thurston exclaimed with evident incredulity. "But how are you going to manage that? You're 100 miles from the nearest power source and sixty odd miles from the nearest road."

"We're going to use heavy helicopter transport, one of those ex-Russian numbers they use between Kathmandu to Lukla on the Everest side, and send up a battery powered video satellite rig and crew."

"Jeez! You don't do things by halves do you, Lauren?"

"In a case like this we can't afford to, Edward. We want the media to go into orbit on a worldwide basis to announce the fact that we've broken the ring. That way we deal with the pressure from the Americans for something to be done to stop innocent young women being executed and, just as important in Nepal, to make sure the Europeans and Americans know Nepal is safe again, and get to know with all possible speed."

"So what exactly are you going to televise," he asked, "and where do I come in?"

She hesitated. "We have established that the caravans leaving Lo Manthang to return to the salt lakes at Drabye in Tibet are carrying heroin in exactly the same sort of sachets as the Tissue Trail women were carrying when they were caught entering Singapore. And we have video of the same caravan bringing in the plastic containers of the intermediate acetic anhydride, perfect proof that the caravan is the critical link in the chain we need to break."

"OK," said Thurston, "I think I'm with you so far."

"One of the caravans is due to leave Lo Manthang at the beginning of July to return to its home base. The plan is to televise the Nepali security police finding the sachets of heroin," she paused, "and arresting the leaders."

Thurston narrowed his eyes and whistled and said, "Go on, I'm still with you," an inane remark, but he was trying to give himself time to think. What she was proposing was not going to leave any doubt they were going to blame the Tibetans for the Tissue Trail executions on a worldwide stage, and she was about to ask him to help.

"It is the ideal vehicle," Lauren continued, "we can't do anything about the executions but they will produce a perfect storm of worldwide publicity and just as that happens we can show we've put a stop to it."

"Ingenious," said Thurston, "so how exactly..."

"The Ministry of Internal Affairs is going to offer CNN an exclusive to televise breaking the ring in exchange for ensuring heavy TV coverage in Europe and the Americas where ninety percent of the tourist business comes from – on condition they use the iconic Victor Najinski who is the face of the Tissue Trail affair in South Asia and," she hesitated, "supported by a well known technical expert." She laughed.

"And can I guess who that would be?" Thurston asked, his uncertainty born not of uncertainty as to meaning, but of being unsure quite how he was going to deal with it.

"Oh, just the guy who worked it all out – the guy who came across the intermediate chemical in the high Himalaya and traced it down to Pokhara and then to the palm oil plant. The guy who knows and can explain the chemicals and chemistry involved. And of course, the guy who only a month ago was all over the local press and television as *Flying Businessman Rescues Dying Mountain Girl.*"

"Wow. All guns blazing," Thurston said. "Have you spoken to Najinski and CNN about this?"

"No. Not yet. With Najinski being such a fragile traveller we wanted to know your reaction first. Pretty obviously he is not going to be all that keen but if we can tell him that you're involved we reckon it will help to get him on board." She paused, "So, assuming CNN will cooperate, will you come in on this Edward? You will of course be paid for this and handsomely – it's a professional commission and although the Nepal Government is not rolling in cash we will make sure it is at the market rate."

"I should think the market rate for this would be quite difficult to work out," he said wryly.

"I should think you could name your price," she returned with just perhaps a touch of irritation.

"You misjudge me," he smiled. "I'm not worried about money in a situation like this. I've got a lot out of Nepal over the years so I owe it to them to put a bit back."

"So I'll take that as a yes, shall I?"

"I will need to talk to Philip Lee," he said, "his priority is the women on death row and Najinski and I are working closely with him to try to come up with something which will influence the Singapore administration."

There was a pause before Lauren said, "So when will you be able to let me know." Her tone had gone cold. She was not used to people not agreeing pretty quickly to what she wanted.

"As soon as I can – hopefully later this morning."

Lauren recovered her normal unruffled demeanour. "Oh, and talking about money," she added, "when we last met I mentioned we had picked up traces of cash movement."

"I remember."

"At that time the movement was too thin to be conclusive, but it has built up and is now pretty diagnostic – significant new money flow coming in from major cities and flowing through Pokhara and on to Lhasa."

Again a pause at Thurston's end.

"I'll pass that on to Philip Lee," said Thurston. "And I will get back to you as soon as I can about your Lo Manthang proposition. Incidentally can you tell me a bit more, like how much time do you expect this to take and for that matter when?"

"They're expecting it to take two or three days – including setting up video of the background information, probably in Kathmandu."

"And this will be the end of June?" Thurston asked.

"I think if you blank out the first to the third of July that will cover it."

"Alright," said Thurston. "I'll get back to you as soon as I've checked things out at this end."

There was a pause then Lauren said, "I hope your reply will be positive, Edward."

There was a click on the line and Thurston slowly replaced the receiver. He sat back, hands behind his head. He wasn't sure if there wasn't a hint of a threat in the way she had delivered those last few words. But he decided it was just his overactive imagination.

~~~~~~~~~~

Thurston half-wondered about getting Philip Lee's reaction before telephoning Najinski, but if Najinski wouldn't do it there would be no point. He called Najinski.

"Victor, I think we might be coming to the climax of your media symphony."

"Why, what's happened?"

"I've just had a call from Lauren Chase inviting me to be involved in televising the breaking of the Tissue Trail drug ring."

"So she's popped up again has she? But what's she got to do with it? And why does she want to involve you? You're not a journalist."

"She wants me to help make sure a proper journalist does get involved. She wants me to be your minder," Thurston smiled.

Najinski bellowed with laughter. "How does that work?"

"They want to show that they can stop the supply of one of the essential ingredients in the Tissue Trail ring by showing how the yak caravans currently bring it in and that by putting an end to that it breaks the ring."

"Yaks?" queried Najinski. "Didn't you tell me they don't operate below 13,000 feet?"

"Yes I did," said Thurston. "And as you're a bit of a fragile traveller that is part of the problem. They want to give CNN a live TV exclusive on condition that the iconic Victor Najinski is part of the deal."

"S'truth cobber! You can't be serious."

"I'm afraid I am. They could have broken it at say, the pharmacy in Pokhara, but that doesn't have quite the same television impact as a 1,000-year-old caravan of long haired yaks herded by a tribe of nomadic Tibetans taken against the back drop of the walls of a medieval Himalayan city."

"Nice picture," Najinski groaned. "But can't you go on your own?"

"Oh no," Thurston smiled. "That wouldn't do at all. You're the TV face of the Tissue Trail to millions and would give them the total credibility they need to make this work."

"Are they paying you to lay on this thick layer of smooch?" asked Najinski. "And you are prepared to come along just to be my nursemaid? Why do I find that hard to believe?"

# The Tissue Trail

"Don't worry, there is a bit more to it than that, they want me to be the technical expert," Thurston grinned in anticipation of Najinski's reaction. He wasn't disappointed. Najinski half blew, half spat most of his coffee onto the floor. "This is a laugh a minute," he said wiping his sleeve across his mouth. "So have you said yes?"

"No, not yet. I said I would talk to you first."

"Well I'm buggered if I'm going to freeze my equipment off, turn my pinkies into blackies with frostbite, then die in my own blood and sputum as you put it, just to do a TV slot."

Thurston's voice turned serious. "Bit more than a TV slot," said Thurston. "This looks to be the final payoff. Just before the executions with the world's billions of TV watchers glued to their screens it gives them the perfect platform to deliver their message to the planet."

"And that message is?"

"That message is that the Tissue Trail affair and the five executions is entirely down to Tibet and the Tibetans."

"And you're still going to do it?" Najinski asked incredulously.

"We don't have a choice, Victor. If we're going to have any chance of influencing what they put out or better still to stop it going out altogether we've got to be there. And if CNN doesn't do it they'll get someone else who doesn't know the real story."

"And we do?" Najinski challenged.

"We're a lot closer than most! I'll bet we're the only people on to the Chinese."

"You have a point," said Najinski, "unfortunately!" He paused to clear his throat, "So what happens next?"

"I'll call Lauren Chase back and tell her I'll do it, then I expect you'll get an official invitation from someone in the Nepal Government."

Najinski thought about it still looking for a way out. "I still don't really understand, they must know we don't go along with this Tibetan angle?"

"I suspect they are thinking it will be better to have us with them so they can keep an eye on us than having us running around muddying their waters and accusing the Chinese."

"The problem is," said Najinski, "these people kill to get their way."

"Agreed," said Thurston, "but in this case we have one big advantage, they need us alive to do the broadcast."

Najinski sighed. He was far from being a happy camper. He tried another angle, "Surely it's ten times more important for us to concentrate on trying to get to the motive for all this?"

"I agree nailing the motive is the top priority, Victor. And that is the killer. For my money the best chance we've got of working that out is to be amongst the operators. And if this is the climax it looks to be, anybody that matters is going to be there."

The pause told Thurston he had struck home.

"OK," said Najinski. "Tell your jazzy banker I'll do it and let's see where it takes us."

Thurston put the phone down then called Philip Lee and ran over his conversation with Lauren. Lee found it both remarkable and at the same time disappointing. "So they are closing down the ring but leaving us no nearer solving the key problem?" asked Lee.

"They seem to think there is nothing more to be done to help the five women so they are concentrating on preventing any further arrests and then doing what they can to reverse the effects on the economy of the arrests which have already happened," said Thurston.

"Have you spoken to Victor?" asked Lee.

"Yes. He's not happy, but he agrees we need to be in the middle of this with a chance of influencing things."

"I suppose that makes sense," said Lee not sounding wholly certain. "But what about Jaci?"

"I've been wondering about her," said Thurston. "Bit of a problem. She is not too keen on going back to Nepal for obvious reasons but to stand the best chance of unearthing the motive we need to work together."

"So what are you going to do?"

"Leave it to me," said Thurston.

Lee was about to put down the phone when he stopped, "Where does this leave Lauren Chase? Why did she call you rather than the Nepal Government?"

"The way she put it, she was representing the Nepal Government in her position as an adviser on tourism and financial matters. And I suppose in my case she would not be a cold call."

*Raffles Hotel*
*Thurston's bedroom*
*21st June 2001, 9:50 a.m.*

Thurston called Lauren and confirmed that he was accepting her invitation and that he had spoken to Najinski, who was not deliriously happy, but he thought he would do it.

"Good," she said without emotion. She sounded relieved but not in a pleasurable sense, more in the sense that some heavy pressure had been taken off. "I will ask our people locally to contact you regarding travel details."

He then called Jaci, who by the sound of it was just coming around. He suggested they go down to the Courtyard Bar and he would buy her an orange juice and go over Lauren's call.

### Raffles Hotel
### 21st June 2001, 10:10 a.m.

After he had summarized the conversation with Lauren, Jaci asked him what he made of it.

"Well, first of all she sounded to be under a lot of pressure from different quarters to crack the ring and close it down. I must admit I had not considered the extent of the effect of all this on the Nepali workers – just a pity their broadcast won't do anything to help Catherine Miller and the others."

Jaci was looking a little apprehensive. "I hope you don't want me along with this one, Edward – I don't fancy going back to Nepal after the last time!"

"Hadn't actually thought about it," he lied, "but after all you've done with this it will seem a bit odd if you're not there. But no pressure if you don't think you can face it."

### CNN Offices
### 21st June 2001, 10:30 a.m.

An hour later Victor Najinski was working on the mid-day news bulletin when his telephone rang.

"A call from someone in Nepal, a Major Jha," said the woman on the switchboard, "from the Ministry of Home Affairs in Kathmandu."

"Jha?" said Najinski, mostly to himself, "where have I heard that name?" Then to the switchboard, "Put him through."

# The Tissue Trail

"Good morning, Mr Najinski. My name is Major Jha. I am calling with regard to developments in the Tissue Trail case in the hope you and CNN will help us." Najinski put him in his fifties, mature and well spoken, probably English educated. "I am involved because I'm head of ACAP – the Nepali government agency which manages tourism and resource management in the Annapurna region. That includes responsibility for the palm oil production process which is involved in this Tissue Trail heroin business. I assume you know what I am talking about?"

That's where he had heard the name – it was Jha who had questioned Thurston after his flight into Mustang.

"Yes, I know what you are talking about, Major Jha. Tell me more."

Jha repeated that they intended using a satellite video link to show the ring being broken at a critical point in the supply chain – where the yaks unload their incoming cargo to lower altitude animals. And if CNN would guarantee to use the universally known Victor Najinski as the anchor man, CNN would be granted an exclusive.

"Where exactly will that be?" asked Najinski innocently.

"Lo Manthang on the Nepal and Tibet border. That's where the caravans switch loads. And where the setting is perfect for television."

"Lo Manthang? Isn't that where the business guy rescued the girl with the collapsed lung?"

"You know the story?"

"Not just the story, I know the guy."

"Good. We're hoping he will help."

"But isn't this place at twelve or thirteen thousand feet?"

"That is one reason why we wanted Thurston in on it – he's flown through the gorge, dealt with the altitude, he knows the territory and he's been recommended by somebody involved in funding ACAP."

"OK," said Najinski, "I appreciate you providing me with a minder, but if we're talking that sort of altitude I'm not quite sure it is going to be quite my cup of tea."

"I don't think you need worry," said Jha. "Apart from knowing the territory, Thurston is almost a sort of medic so he will be able to handle any health or physical issues. This is pretty important to Nepal, Mr Najinski."

"I will have to clear the exclusive with my office in Delhi, in case it's cutting across anything else. But I don't expect a problem," he said, hoping that the exact opposite would happen. "OK, Major Jha, assuming an OK from Delhi what exactly is involved?"

"Apart from the live television shots of the interception we need to prepare the background video cuts and interviews so when we make the final interceptions we can just slot the live video segment into the prepared shell. We will need to do the background work in Kathmandu."

"Well, whatever my hang-ups, my employer will be pretty keen for me to do it. When do you have in mind?"

"We expect it will be the first three days in July from Sunday the first through Tuesday the third."

Najinski said he would keep it clear.

### Professor Aw's office
### 21st June 2001. 2:00 p.m.

The professor told Thurston that the word had got out about the success of the trial and there were members of his staff and research students who were keen to take advantage of Thurston's presence to add some further experimental work to the main Surmil protocol. This would of course be at the hospital's expense even though Thurston's name would be the lead on the acknowledgement list of anything published. He couldn't argue with that. In particular, they were interested in looking at and extending Thurston's work on the effect, or lack of it, on rapid eye movement sleep in view of the implication of this to reducing dependence. Thurston was only too delighted to oblige particularly as he wanted to try to do what he could to help in the Tissue Trail affair and was running out of work justification for staying in Singapore. Thurston and Jaci set aside the afternoon to work through the various proposals. The researchers had done rather more work than Thurston had anticipated and at first, the pile of submissions looked pretty daunting but as they worked through it Jaci commented that the level of detail in fact speeded up the process of rationalizing the various proposals and eliminating overlap.

### 21st June 2001

After the day at the hospital Thurston and Jaci took the day's papers and read over them at a bar overlooking Robertson's Quay.

# The Tissue Trail

The trial of Francoise Dumas had started the previous day and the press had enjoyed another high impact visual story, two hundred French students demonstrated outside the Ministry of Internal Affairs at New Phoenix Park, Irrawaddy Road. The Singapore police were normally pretty tight in dealing with any sort of public disorder but with the world's press in legions on the Republic's streets there seemed perhaps to be more than the usual degree of restraint. The students made the most of it, taking things to the point where the police had to move in with a water cannon – more excellent TV. The students had studied the police tactics and any provocative banners would have been removed in seconds. But they waited until the water cannon had opened up on the main concentration of the demonstrators then a small breakaway group unfurled "a beaut" as Najinski described it later:

## *"STOP SINGAPORE SLAYINGS"*

The police removed the banner quickly but the damage had been done. Reuters claimed later that the "Singapore Slayings" message had been noticed and remembered in eighty-four countries and up to 500 million viewers.

Two of the tabloids had photographed the banner and emphasised the play on words by re-casting it as:

## *"STOP SINGAPORE SLayINGS"*

"Quite clever, particularly considering it's the French mucking about with the English language," said Thurston.

"I wonder if this is part of Najinski's media plan or is this just a bit of a bonus?" Jaci asked, spreading the papers across the bar table.

Thurston leaned back, hands behind his head, looking at the ceiling. "What on earth can all this be about, Jaci?"

She looked out over the quay, "I don't know."

"Well you're our only hope, my friend. You cracked Surmil at the last minute in the UK, then saved the Surmil trial with the last patient, then the most difficult of all the 'why Singapore' question."

She turned to look at him, "Are you telling me you want me to go back to Nepal?"

He paused. "I hadn't meant it like that. But since you ask – the answer's yes. I do."

"I suppose I would have two chaps looking after me," she smiled ruefully.

"That didn't take you long to decide," he said.

### Central Criminal Court
### Francoise Dumas Trial Second day
### 22nd June 2001, 10:30 a.m.

The police were out early preventing any more than four or five people gathering in a group. But the students were prepared for this and the TV cameras were left filming empty streets. Until, six of their number dashed out from a small hotel, and knowing where the TV crews were, ran across the bank of cameras unfurling the banner that had played well the previous day plus two more taking a different line:

*"SAVE INNOCENT FRANCOISE DUMAS"*

*and*

*"STOP KILLING INNOCENTS"*

In his evening television report Najinski reported that whereas the protests attracted more worldwide TV cover, they had no effect on the trial except to draw the attention of world TV audiences to the fact that it was taking place.

He went on, "The trial was routine with the exception of the defence trying again to bring out the prior intelligence factor. But the customs officer giving evidence of her search and arrest had denied any prior knowledge and defence counsel had not been able to break his insistence that the French woman had been selected for search at random.

"At four p.m. in the afternoon, the three judges found Françoise Dumas guilty as charged and minutes later the leading judge had the black hat placed on his head and pronounced the death sentence.

"The early evening television bulletins reported that another Tissue Trail backpacker had been found guilty of trafficking heroin and sentenced to death.

"Later editions of both television news and the evening press reported that the French Government was to make a formal appeal to the Singapore administration for a stay of execution, pending reference of the case of Francoise Dumas to the International Court of Justice."

## 22nd June 2001

The French protest led to a new wave of media reaction, the more serious commentators reporting along the lines:

## *"SINGAPORE COULD FACE INTERNATIONAL COURT"*

*and the tabloids*

## *"SINGAPORE DEATH PENALTIES ON TRIAL"*

The Singapore Attorney General's office had issued a terse statement indicating that they would "reply formally as and when a formal approach had been received. It was not the policy of the Singapore Government to respond to newspaper reports."

## 23rd June 2001

The success of the student protests in Francoise Dumas' case led to even wider protest when Birgit Heller's trial started the following day, particularly in Birgit Heller's country of birth, Germany, and adopted home, Australia.

The German Government's reaction was to make it clear that they would be seeking to persuade the European Union to make a submission to the Singapore Administration raising the profile of political protest to a new level.

The trial followed the same pattern and in just under two days, Birgit Heller was found guilty and sentenced to death at four p.m. on 25th June.

The front pages of the western press and TV main story sections carried little else but variations on the trial verdicts, legal and political submissions, and widening student protests.

Meanwhile, the money trace posturing between NCIS and the Z. I. R. Bank was gaining momentum.

# CHAPTER EIGHTEEN
## *The Swiss Bank*

*NCIS London*
*21st June 2001*

Barbara checked the contact details of the president of the Z. I. R. Bank and telephoned his secretary to make sure he was in the country and in a position to receive an urgent communication. She established that he was. His name was Jean Jacob Rousseau.

In the first instance, Warrender e-mailed with a hard copy follow-up:

*Dear M Rousseau,*

*I am approaching you to request information relating to a numbered account held at the Z. I. R. Bank. We have identified several movements of funds into account number 33-ZI-2401 from various points consistent with enquiries into new Class A drug movements in the Far East. Our enquiries relate to a number of movements that are atypical – suggesting that the movement of funds is contrived. In addition, it appears that this seemingly artificial rotation of funds was in turn funded by a single payment into the 33-ZZ-2401 account in 1997. It is the source of this single payment in which we are particularly interested.*

*We look forward to your assistance in this matter.*

*Signed*
*J. M. W. Warrender*

# The Tissue Trail

*National Criminal Intelligence Service*
*Drugs Division*
*Upper Ground*
*Blackfriars,*
*London*

*From J. J. Rousseau Z. I. R. Bank*
*22 June 2001*

*Dear Mr Warrender,*

*Thank you for your e-mail of 23rd June regarding Account Number 33-ZZ-2401 held at this bank. As you will be aware it is not the policy of this bank to respond to requests for details relating to client accounts. I note that your enquiry relates to alleged Class A drug activity. I am aware that special provisions apply with regard to privacy when a recognized enquirer can provide good and clear evidence of drug involvement. However, in this case it appears that you are asking this bank to provide the evidence you need to support your application and, on these grounds, I must decline to provide the assistance you request.*

*Signed*
*J. J. Rousseau*
*President*
*Z. I. R. Bank*
*Rue Ami de Langemalle.*
*Geneva*

"I could have written his letter myself," said Warrender to Barbara. "Right, let's take the next step in the ritual – send him all the details of the transfers and in flows we already have."

Barbara stood and waited. She knew her man after thirty years working with him.

"Oh, and add: 'This enquiry relates to five capital cases in Singapore, which are currently attracting significant media attention. If you are not familiar with the so-called Tissue Trail cases please let me know and we will advise.'"

# The Tissue Trail

Barbara smiled, and returned to her office.

## Z. I. R. Bank, Geneva
## 23rd June 2001, 2:00 p.m.

On receiving Warrender's e-mail, Rousseau called two of his senior directors – Marc Lassale, Chief Accountant, and Claud Reysin to his office.

"Gentlemen, I think you should be aware of this." He passed a copy of each of Warrender's two e-mails to the two Directors.

Reysin, the first to finish said, "Who can fail to be aware of the Tissue Trail cases. There seems to be little else in the news. If we are implicated in that, we would have a problem."

But the older more senior Lassale's reaction was more hesitant, "We need to know just what information NCIS have at their disposal so let's take it slowly and examine the details carefully."

"I agree," said Rousseau, "but at the same time please let me know exactly what we ourselves have on this account. If NCIS is implying an artificial set up of money movement and there are five women waiting to be executed, Reysin is right – this is a pretty sensitive position for us to be in."

*Internal e-mail to Rousseau*
*Monday 23rd June 2001 5:00 p.m.*

*This is to confirm that a large single payment was posted to the account under query in July 1997 from the British Virgin Islands. The sum involved was USD 35 million.*

*From Lassale*
*Chief Accountant*

Rousseau sent out a copy to all board members.

*"From all points of view this further information adds to the sensitivity of the position but we await further contact from NCIS London before considering next steps."*

*To: J. J. Rousseau, Z. I. R. Bank*

# The Tissue Trail

*From: J. R. Warrender, NCIS*
*23rd June 2001 5:45 p.m.*

*Details of fund flows are being prepared with the intention of having these with you by close of play on Wednesday 27th June. In view of the urgency in this matter may I presume to ask that you will have the information we have requested to hand in the expectation that the information we are providing will be satisfactory?*

*Warrender*

*E-mail from Rousseau to Warrender:*
*24ʰ June 2001 8:45 a.m.*
*We await your further information with interest.*

"That is about as non-committal as you can get don't you think?" asked Warrender.
"I'm afraid so," said Barbara.

*E-mail from Warrender to Rousseau:*
*Z. I. R. Bank*
*25th June 2001 5:45 p.m.*

*Please find attached full details of transfers and movements referred to in earlier correspondence. Please also note details of corresponding movement of acetic anhydride —a key intermediate in the manufacture of diamorphine (heroin). The combination of these movements is a standard indicator of new heroin activity. I also attach a summary of evidence prepared by the defence indicating that the whole Tissue Trail affair is a highly sophisticated operation with further indication of Chinese involvement.*

*We trust this information is sufficient to justify your cooperation in this matter.*

**Z. I. R. Bank**
**25th June 2001, 8:30 a.m.**

# The Tissue Trail

Rousseau had circulated the information and correspondence provided by Warrender to all board members, eight of whom were present at the meeting called for Friday morning.

"A week today the first of the so called Tissue Trail defendants is due to be executed," Rousseau said, setting the tone for the meeting. "And if the information being requested by NCIS is going to be of any use to the defence they must have it by, I suggest, midday Wednesday 4th July. That means we have three working days to reach a decision and if we so decide, to release the information requested.

"And then only if we have established the final link in the chain – at the moment we are showing British Virgin Islands as the starting point, but that is clearly a staging point, and we need to know the original source of the cash deposit."

"And it is now clear," said Lassale, "with the possibility of Chinese involvement, why this information is so important to them."

A predictably animated debate proceeded between the "preserve privacy at all costs" school and the opposition pointing out the damage that would be done to business if any of the women were executed and it was subsequently found that information held back by Z. I. R. might have saved them. It was a fairly even battle with perhaps a slight advantage to the "release the information lobby" until Chief Accountant Lassale introduced a new point.

"As we know the defendants were carrying only fifteen to twenty grams of heroin each. For five of them that is less than one hundred grams in total. The cash movements we are looking at are hundreds of thousands of dollars. Even at maximum dilution there is no correlation between money levels and the level of substance being trafficked."

This stopped the debate in its tracks. "So how do you suggest taking it from there?" asked Rousseau.

"I say we do not give way on our privacy position on the basis of figures which do not bear scrutiny."

There was general muttering of approval around the table.

"And the deposit of thirty-five million US Dollars in 1997 equally does not connect," said one of the younger board members.

"I suggest," said Rousseau, "that we put these points to NCIS and ask for clarification."

# The Tissue Trail

The door opened and Rousseau's PA entered, "Sorry to interrupt Sir, but I think you would want to see this..."

It was a faxed copy of a letter from the Swiss Federal Department of Finance to the Directors of Z. I. R. Bank Geneva. Rousseau scanned it then read it out:

> *"Gentlemen, We have today received a request from the US Treasury asking the Swiss Government to emphasize that the normal provisions for bank privacy are required to be relaxed when good and clear evidence of connection to illicit drug activity is provided.*
>
> *We have copies of correspondence in this matter.*
>
> *We assume you will take due note of the US Treasury representations with which we concur."*
>
> *Minister of Finance."*

There was, in effect, a communal sigh around the table at political interference typified by Reysin's remark, "Do they not believe we can manage these matters for ourselves?"

Rousseau called for calm. "Please remember gentlemen, there are five young women awaiting execution none of whom had any idea they were carrying heroin. Please imagine what our government would do in similar circumstances. I suggest that we agree with the Chief Accountants proposal and meet again next Tuesday to make a final decision. In the meantime we should ask NCIS to clarify, indeed reconcile, the figures we have been given. Are there any other matters?"

"Yes," said Marc Lassale. "Assuming that Warrender is right and we do find a single source of the funds it will result in the Tissue Trail women defence team accusing whoever it is of premeditated murder. And if it is the Chinese, can you imagine the reaction of the Singapore establishment to that?"

"I am not sure if that is any of our concern," said Rousseau. "All we are being asked to do is provide accounting information in a Class A drug case."

"No," Lassale argued. "What we are being asked to do is to destroy our reputation for confidentiality on a worldwide stage in a high profile case on the basis of an empty threat. The legal position is crystal clear. The women are guilty under Singapore law with no appeal so it would require a political decision by Singapore to sanction clemency or a pardon. My view is that without the most compelling of motives for this alleged action by the Chinese – or anyone else – the Singaporeans will simply not relent whatever we do or whatever information we supply."

"So you are arguing that Warrender and the defence team need to establish a motive which in our view will create a reasonable probability that Singapore would be forced to relent."

"I think that sums up my position perfectly," said Lassale.

There was general assent and Rousseau closed the meeting.

### *National Criminal Intelligence Service*
### *26th June 2001 12:00 p.m.*

Barbara brought in the cable from Rousseau. Warrender read it twice.

*Dear Warrender*

*I regret we cannot give you a final answer. There is a major inconsistency in the figures we are examining. The large single payment you have detected in 1997 at $35M, is so far in excess of the value of the small amounts of substance being moved as to be irreconcilable.*

*The standard required by the code on drug cooperation is "good and clear" evidence. I trust you appreciate our dilemma.*

*There is a further issue with which you may be able to assist. We take the view that Singapore would not relent without both a clear connection back to the Chinese —which you are hoping we will provide —but also a clear motive without which the whole conspiracy defence lacks credibility.*

*We have called for a full board meeting on Tuesday 3rd July. Please be assured that the information you seek will be on hand and ready for transmission as and when a decision to cooperate is made.*

*For your information, we have traced a sequence of cash movements back to the British Virgin Islands but there appears to be one more, possibly two, which we have so far not identified.*

*Please provide your best advice regarding the cash inconsistency and the underlying motive.*

*Rousseau*

Warrender leaned back in his chair and looked at the ceiling. Warrender rarely showed any sign of emotion, but on this occasion he did.

"Bloody hell, what are they playing at?" He swore. "Have they not read the file? The whole thing is artificial – totally contrived – so there should not be any expectation of normal correlation!"

"But what about the question of motive?" Barbara asked.

"That is a more serious problem," said Warrender. "And he has a point. We will have to keep close to Philip Lee on that, as he presumably will have the same problem with the Singapore authorities."

*From: J. M. W. Warrender*
*To: Philip Lee*

*Heavy going with Z. I. R. Bank. They are querying the inconsistencies between cash and amounts of drug despite advice that the exercise is contrived. We are also advised that we will not be able to close the loop with Z. I. R. unless we can identify a clear and credible motive for the alleged Chinese action.*

*Your comments or advice would be appreciated.*

*Warrender*

## Philip Lee's Office, Singapore
## 26th June 2001

At Lee's request Thurston, Jaci and Najinski came to his offices to review the position before three of "the team" disappeared into the high Himalaya. Lee had arranged the meeting in the boardroom; impressive with dark panelled oak walls and oil paintings of notables both from the firm and from the Singapore administration. Pride of place was given to the politician who had taken the swamp, which had been Singapore Island and turned it into the financial and political powerhouse it was today – Lee Kuan Yew.

Lee updated them on the latest from Warrender which was that Z. I. R. were still dragging their feet, but they were balking at the lack of motive a position with which he had sympathy.

On the question of inconsistency of cash and amount of substance, Najinski shared Warrender's frustration, "They are not taking on board that this is totally artificial. The $35 million will be the slush fund to get this whole charade in place —somebody pretty influential running the whole thing, plus presumably people like Jha on the ground in Nepal, plus most of the Canadian ex-pat community in Nepal and somebody organizing the Singapore end."

"That's right," Thurston agreed, "tell them to stop looking at this as if it were a normal drug ring – nothing could be further from the truth."

"Don't worry about that," said Lee. "But the major and potentially fatal stumbling block still remaining is the motive. But on the positive side at least we are down to two clear final steps."

"I suppose the money trace is largely out of our hands now," said Thurston. "It's down to Warrender and the Z. I. R. Bank." (*He could not know how wrong that assessment was going to turn out to be.*) "It's the motive that we seem to be as far away from as ever – and no way we can see getting a line on it."

"So does it make sense for three out of 'the team' to go haring off to the Lo Manthang?" Jaci asked, perhaps still hopeful of not having to go back.

"Well unless Najinski wants CNN to give him the boot, he's got to go," said Thurston.

"And Thurston and Jaci are more likely to solve the motive problem working together," said Lee. "So the question is where do they need to be?"

"Arguably it's not where we need to be but with whom," said Thurston repeating the arguments he had gone over earlier with Najinski. "Who is going to know the true motive? We all have our suspicions. Jaci would put her money on Lauren Chase but she's in Canada, there have to be some suspicions about Stephanie D'Aunay but of the players we know, Jha must be the prime target."

"Can't see him running the show," said Najinski. "But he is just about senior enough to be in on it."

"So we carry on as we are," said Lee. "I will hold the fort here with the drug liaison team and work with Warrender on the money trace."

"And we three head for the lions' den in Nepal," said Najinski, "targeting Jha and anybody else he seems to be palling up with."

"And another point we need to discuss," said Jaci, "we can see that they have Tibet and the Tibetans in their sights but quite how it's going to finish up we don't know. Jha could edit it to say anything he wants once they've got what they want from you two."

"She's right, easiest thing in the world," said Najinski.

"OK, try this," said Thurston, "suppose we put together our own version of a broadcast using extracts from my Mustang tape. We can do a detailed version providing a record of all the evidence and a headline version for your boss Barry Schultz to use as the basis for a news report implicating the Chinese."

"Now that is good," said Najinski. "Why didn't I think of it? How about we both produce a draft then you bring your footage down to the office, we'll stitch something together."

"No problem," Thurston replied. "We haven't got much time, can we do it tonight?"

"Suits me," said Najinski. "If we both sketch out drafts we can agree to text and edit tonight."

"One other thing," Jaci chipped in. "Suppose our friend Major Jha springs some nasty surprise when we're up rubbing noses with the yaks, and assuming no phone coverage, would we have any way of communicating any new development to Delhi?"

"Good question," said Najinski thinking about it, "there is one possibility although it's a bit limited, for each new position we transmit from we normally do a quick test transmission – we could use one or two of those to send the odd few words – if they're not watching us too closely."

"You'd have to be pretty careful," Jaci said. "Whatever this is about, it's pretty important to somebody."

Nobody argued.

### CNN Offices
### 27th June 2001, early evening

Thurston had drafted two text and video sequences – one virtually a full "witness statement" from the first videotape of the Harka Tensing conversation through to Chaudrai's palm oil plant history, to Najinski's media orchestration thesis and Jaci's brilliant questioning of the women at Changi. This would provide a full evidential background for both Philip Lee in dealing with D. C. Rahman and Barry Schultz at CNN.

But it was the shorter news headline version, which would play the more critical role – particularly if events went down to the wire. The two news headline versions were remarkably similar. "You should have been a hack," Najinski said. It did not take long to pull it together into an agreed script.

# The Tissue Trail

*Thurston/Najinski headline news sequence -*

*Najinski: "I am reporting exclusively from the lost city of Lo Manthang (walled city in background) at 13,000 feet on the Nepal Tibet border where the Nepali Security Police are about to arrest the leaders of the Tibetan salt caravan you see behind me. They are charged with supplying a key chemical used in production of the heroin at the centre of the Tissue Trail affair.*

*But although this suggests that Tibet, or at least Tibetans are the key protagonists let me hand over to medical researcher Edward Thurston who first uncovered evidence of heavy involvement of the Chinese."*

*(Thurston takes up the commentary)*

*"Earlier this year I met the leaders of the salt caravan who told me they had been forced to take a new longer route to bring a new chemical into this part of Nepal."*

*(A static visual of the modern plastic container with Chinese script taken from Thurston's video appears on the screen.)*

*"When I asked what he meant by 'being forced' he told me that their previous leader had died mysteriously after leading a revolt by his yak herders complaining that the new route added six weeks to a journey which already took five months of the year. Soon afterwards he had been found dead with no obvious sign of injury although he had been perfectly fit and healthy. When I asked who they suspected he had replied, 'The people who wanted the new chemical brought in – the Chinese.'*

*"The revolt collapsed. The new chemical was intended for use in a palm oil manufacturing plant near Pokhara but it was subsequently found that part of the shipment was being diverted to produce diamorphine hydrochloride – or pure heroin. Backpackers trekking the Tissue Trail near Pokhara were then unwittingly used to carry the heroin on to Singapore, a state with a mandatory death penalty. We still do not know the whole story but evidence is mounting that far from being a small scale exercise operated by a few Tibetans, the Tissue Trail affair is a highly organized, sophisticated and indeed international, operation."*

*(Najinski takes up commentary):*

# The Tissue Trail

*"The defence lawyers need two more links in the chain of evidence to complete a watertight case that the women are the victims of a political conspiracy involving the Chinese – and if they succeed in finding these two links they believe that the Singapore Administration would be forced to relent. The Singapore authorities have a copy of this report and a fully detailed dossier of the supporting evidence. Victor Najinski for CNN Far East, at 13,000 feet in the lost Kingdom of Mustang on the border with Tibet."*

~~~~~~~~~~

Najinski nodded with satisfaction, "That should stop the Delhi office from rushing into accepting Jha's version of things." Lee had asked them to let him have a copy when it was finished. "Why don't you drop in after you have finished tonight?"

## Central Criminal Court
## D. C. Rahman's office
## 27th June 2001, 9:30 p.m.

Prosecutor Rahman had agreed to meet Lee at his office late that same evening. He was fully aware of the time factor. Rahman's department had set up the video projector and screen and while the tape was being inserted Lee told him that it revealed the Singapore Government would be fully aware of the evidence that the Tissue Trail heroin imports were totally fabricated and not trafficking in the normal sense of the word.

Rahman's reaction was predictable, "Philip, as you are fully aware, whether fabricated or not, it doesn't affect the legal position."

It took twenty minutes to go through both tapes, rewinding occasionally if Rahman asked a question. When it had finished Lee waited for Rahman to react. "I agree this would be pretty embarrassing," said Rahman, "but this is still a Class A drug case and that will be the prime consideration."

"Might I suggest that if five western women, including two Americans, hang and the government is shown to have been privy to this information," Thurston tapped the side of the projector, "this would be more than embarrassing."

278

Rahman picked up a type copy of the script.
"I assume you brought this copy for me?"
"Yes D. C., I did."

### NCIS London
### 27th June 2001, earlier the same day, 8:00 a.m.

An overnight message from Philip Lee told Warrender he was sending
two videotapes via express courier service. "The contents of the videos are
important and I urge you to view them at your earliest opportunity,
particularly if you are making slow progress with the Z. I. R. Bank."

"God, Barbara, how soon can we get our hands on them?"

She checked her watch and the international time zone clocks on the
wall. Late on Thursday 29th or early on Friday 30th. "You hadn't got
anything lined up for the weekend had you?" he half smiled at her.

### 28th June 2001

Thurston and Jaci looked at the morning papers over their usual orange
juice and coffee. The front pages were dominated by photographs of Karen
Leopold, the last of the five Tissue Trail defendants to be tried and the most
glamorous.

"Assuming we are right and this is a set-up," Thurston said, "getting a
blue-eyed blonde all-American woman as the last of the five to be tried is
another master stroke."

~~~~~~~~~~

The TV stations were concentrating on both the blonde American and
the inventiveness of the students in getting their banners in front of the
cameras. Student protests were still in evidence but it was the US State
Department's accusation, which raised the diplomatic tension further:

### "STATE DEPARTMENT ACCUSES SINGAPORE
### OF OPERATING BARBARIC LEGAL CODE"

"The gloves are off," said Najinski. "The press have been making that sort of accusation for some days but this is the first time we've seen it at government level. And they're backing it up by calling for a meeting of the UN Security Council."

"Not much chance of them getting anything clear-cut out of that, with China and Russia involved," Thurston suggested.

"Agreed," said Najinski, "but it could give Singapore an honourable way out if they wanted one."

But Singapore showed no sign of wanting a way out and just after four p.m. on the 27th June, after a textbook trial, blonde, blue-eyed Karen Leopold was found guilty and sentenced to death.

### *Singapore*
### *27th June 2001, evening*

The evening and overnight press and TV had picked up a rumour that at least three of the Tissue Trail women were going to be executed together. As every network had the same story Najinski and Thurston concluded that the Tissue Trail spin doctors had been hard at work again – particularly as there was widespread distribution of photographs of the elongated drop plate and four suspended nooses. One publication of course had heard the four were going to be hanged together. The surmise was that Singapore wanted them out of the way as soon as possible as the worldwide protests were causing serious embarrassment.

"They have squeezed everything off the first three pages for days and yet they still find a way to up the temperature," said Najinski, who shook his head in admiration.

### *NCIS London*
### *28th June 2001, 5:15 p.m.*

The videotapes had been delayed and didn't reach NCIS offices until just after four p.m. Warrender, Barbara, cash trace "Nigel," and two departmental lawyers watched both versions twice.

"We have to get these to Geneva at the earliest," said Warrender.

"Well unless you can get them to work over the weekend," said Barbara, "Monday morning is the earliest they are going to see anything."

"What on earth can this be about?" asked Warrender. "All this effort must be for something pretty significant."

# The Tissue Trail

One of the lawyers commented that he thought both Singapore and Z. I. R. Bank would dig their heels in "unless we can establish a rock solid motive."

Warrender was standing looking down, holding his chin in his hand deep in thought. "I would think CNN would want to have a quiet word with the State Department before accusing the Chinese of deliberately arranging the execution of five young women. That could delay things a bit. Anyway we've all seen the evidence. Let's get these tapes off to Switzerland and think about it over the weekend."

~~~~~~~~~~

Back at the Raffles hotel there was a message at reception telling Thurston that Lauren Chase had phoned and wanted him to call her back. Thurston asked Jaci to listen in while he made the call.

"She keeps popping up just when I least expect her," Thurston said.

He dialed what looked like a direct line number. It was picked up almost immediately.

"Chase," said a woman's voice in clipped tones.

"Thurston."

"Edward," the voice immediately softened and sounded genuinely warm and welcoming. "Thanks for calling back so quickly. Look I won't keep you long, but two questions. First, are you bringing your assistant up to Kathmandu? Jaci, wasn't it?"

"We haven't decided yet. After her experiences last time she is not too keen. But why do you ask?"

"Well there are still some aspects of this whole thing we haven't got to the bottom of yet, from what you tell me she is pretty bright and the two of you have a reputation for fathoming the unfathomable!" She laughed down the phone. "So she would be welcome if you can persuade her to come." Thurston turned to Jaci with a part smile and part raised eyebrows.

"I'll talk to her."

"And as to her previous unhappy experiences, I think we can assure her of a pretty secure berth."

"Thank you, Lauren. I'll be..."

"There is one other thing Edward, the video you took on your first trip to Lo Manthang, the one that caused all the excitement?" her voice rose, confirming the question.

"Yes Lauren, I haven't forgotten. Not likely to."

"Well it occurs to me that there could be parts of that which could be helpful in the CNN report. Would it be a problem if I asked you to bring a copy with you?"

Thurston hesitated briefly, "I can't see that being a problem."

"Good," she said, "I'll let Major Jha know. Thank you for your help, Edward."

"My pleasure," he said, replacing the receiver and turning to Jaci. "So you have a new fan."

"Yes, it looks as if I do," said Jaci. "And Major Jha finally gets to see your incriminating video."

"Yes," said Thurston thoughtfully. "That could put a couple of cats amongst the pigeons."

"Yes it could couldn't it," she said looking concerned. "Isn't it going to be difficult to go along with their Tibetan angle once they've seen that?"

"Good question," said Thurston, "but what do you suggest? That we back out and leave the women to their fate?"

Jaci let out a long sigh, "No, we can't do that, but this ACAP news thing seems to be getting more and more threatening."

"No, it's not looking like a barrel of laughs is it? But Professor Aw's dinner might be good."

"At least we can look forward to that," said Jaci wistfully.

With the clinical trial finally complete, documentation was being finalized prior to signing off by Aw Swee Lim for the medical school and Thurston as the contractor. It would then need Vilnius Villiumy to sign off for Imperial Pharmaceuticals. The additional research items were still under way and would be dealt with separately and published when complete.

The dinner Thurston had referred to had been arranged by Aw Swee Lim to celebrate the trial's success and invited everybody who had worked on it including his own staff – in total there were twenty-two of them. As a Malay himself, Aw had chosen the atmospheric "Tepak Sireh" close to the former Sultan's Palace in Kampong and booked a private room.

Towards the end he made a handsome speech complimenting Thurston and Jaci on their scientific inventiveness – in the face of considerable difficulty. Whether he meant the antics of Imperial's Villiumy or the Tissue Trail case he left open.

Jaci spoke to thank them for making her feel at home. She hoped she would have an excuse to return to Singapore.

Thurston also thanked the team for their professionalism and, if the effects of the trial on Surmil were as Professor Aw expected, he would make it an annual pilgrimage to return to Singapore to celebrate.

As they shook hands at the end of the dinner, Thurston and Jaci told the Professor they were leaving the following morning for Kathmandu and to participate in the Nepali newscast of the closing of the drug ring. Aw looked surprised, "In view of all you have told me isn't that taking a bit of a risk?" he asked.

"It is," said Thurston. "But we have talked it through and agreed that the best chance of finding the reason for all this is to be where the action is and the same argument applies to being in the right place to influence the final version of the broadcast."

"Rather you than me," said Aw turning to Jaci and offering her his hand. "So not quite sure whether we are going to meet again on this trip, Jaci. So all the best of luck, I have enjoyed working with you." She took his hand, but pulled him towards her planting a light kiss on his cheek.

"I've enjoyed working with you too, Professor," she smiled.

Aw and Thurston shook hands warmly. "Look after yourself," Aw said, "and look after this delightful young lady."

Thurston nodded and thanked the professor, but this was not a situation he liked at all. He could not always expect to be in total control of events but it was rare for him to be in a position where he had no control or influence over events at all – almost a feeling of helplessness. The only certainties in the situation were that Jha's people were going to blame the Tibetans for the Tissue Trail affair and they were going to do it on a worldwide platform. Alongside that at least, he and Jaci were going to be in a position to work their magic if something came up on which they could work. But it was the uncertainty as to exactly what Jha was up to and why, which caused the real problem. Until he knew that it was like trying to plot a path through a dense fog.

With tension in the air, Thurston and Jaci made no attempt to make any further progress with their private trial. In fact, both spent rather restless nights.

# CHAPTER NINETEEN
## *The Yak and Yeti*

*1st July 2001*

Jha had arranged for travel documents to be delivered to Raffles for Thurston and Jaci and to CNN's office for Najinski. Najinski travelled to Raffles by taxi and the three of them carried on to the airport together. The mood was subdued. All felt much the same way, nobody knew quite what to expect; backing out was not an option and all were unable to shake a sense of foreboding.

The taxi made its way down the four-lane road towards the airport. Thurston recalled the last time he and Jaci had taken this route – albeit in the opposite direction, when she had arrived from Dhaka and, despite being almost unconscious with fatigue, she had looked like a million dollars. Even in jeans and an open denim shirt she still looked good.

At the airport they checked in and went to the lounge to wait for the flight.

"I'm getting used to this," said Jaci. "Before this trip I was always with the cattle."

But despite the attempts to make light conversation, Jaci's anxiety wasn't too far below the surface. Not too surprising, he thought, the last time she had been in Nepal she had been chased across the base of the Annapurnas for nearly three days by two Canadians who were subsequently reported to have killed the American DEA agent and possibly the two other camera women. And that was followed by the high tension of her makeover disguise and overnight escape from Nepal via Dhaka.

Thurston put his hand on her arm. "You can still change your mind."

"How can I?" she asked, "I keep telling you, you're useless at cracking these problems without me, so I've got to come if we're going to crack this one and give the women a chance."

"I'm not going to argue with you," he looked at her. "At least not now. And I keep telling you they will have to look after us if they're going to get what they want out of the broadcast."

"You are always an optimist, Edward."

Thurston turned to Najinski. "No hope for you, Victor. You're on the hook."

"Thanks, Thurston, you're a real pal."

Najinski had two sets of travel documents, the first sent by Jha for the Kathmandu flight, but Jaci spotted a second package in his briefcase. In the lounge he opened both envelopes and pulled the contents. Jaci caught sight of the masthead of one of the sheets from the second envelope. It was an ornately designed card with a neckband. The masthead looked like the five rings of the Olympic movement.

"That looks interesting, Victor," she nodded at the package.

"It's media accreditation for something I've got to cover in a couple of weeks time," he replied without elaborating.

~~~~~~~~~~

The flight to Kathmandu was uneventful although Thurston tried to keep Jaci's mind occupied by pointing out the key points on the way north which she had missed with her night-time makeover diversion. The touch down at Kathmandu was just after three p.m. local time in good weather but in a gathering afternoon cloud. As guests of the government, Jha had promised they would be treated accordingly and they were ushered off the flight and chauffeured to the C Gate at the terminal reserved for private flights. Thurston recalled Lauren Chase being accorded similar treatment.

Just inside the terminal entrance a beaming Major Jha, unmistakeable in his heavy dark rimmed glasses, met them surrounded by some dozen or so men including five armed security police. One of them Thurston recognized as Inspector Pandeh who had been the security man on the Lo Manthang flight.

Jha addressed Thurston first, perhaps expecting a mixed reception. "I am pleased to meet you again, Mr Thurston," he said shaking his hand. "I regret that on the last occasion we found ourselves in less...er – relaxed circumstances."

Thurston smiled pleasantly, "Perhaps you could explain that to me sometime, Major?"

Jha then shook Najinski's hand, "Thank you for agreeing to help us with this, Mr Najinski."

"I hope I'm not going to live to regret it," Najinski said lightly. "I gather things can get pretty rough up there."

"I am sure there will be no problem," said Jha. "We are using a heavy freight helicopter built to deal with these conditions." He turned to greet Jaci, and in the process to close down Najinski's line of conversation. "And this is the delightful Miss Linthorpe I've heard so much about?"

"All good I hope," said Jaci with a polite smile.

He introduced the three of them to members of his team, which included three ACAP executives, plus the manager of the facility where they would be recording the background video sections. He was introduced as Gil Desai, a slim, medium height Indian looking man in his mid-forties wearing a pale brown almost sandy coloured suit with an open necked white shirt.

Jha told them he had booked the traditional Yak and Yeti Hotel because, "I gather Mr Thurston and Miss Linthorpe are already familiar with it and from my point of view it is convenient for the recording facility. May I suggest that after you have settled into your quarters that we meet to discuss the structure and content of what we are planning to do. I've booked a private room for the purpose and laid on a light supper." Thurston noted his very British terminology.

The whole group, including the security personnel, were transported into the city in a convoy of three Japanese four-by-fours. Major Jha and, to Thurston's surprise, Inspector Pandeh rather than Gil Desai, accompanied the three Westerners in the largest of the three vehicles. Thurston attempted to converse with Pandeh, but he did not seem comfortable and most of the conversation was based on Jha giving them a rundown on points of interest. The short convoy finally drove down Kathmandu's four-lane Main Street, Durbar Marg, towards the Royal Palace before turning right into the courtyard of the Yak and Yeti.

Jha had organized prior check-in – the desk only needed to check their passports which they asked to retain.

"As guests of the government you are each assigned your own security officer while you are in Nepal," said Jha. "Inspector Pandeh will accompany you to your rooms with your assigned officer. I will see you a little later."

Led by porters carrying their baggage and followed by Inspector Pandeh and three security policemen, Thurston, Najinski and Jaci made their way to their rooms. Najinski as the representative of the contracting organization CNN had been allocated a suite on the top floor. Thurston and Jaci had been assigned less exotic, but superior rooms on the first floor.

"So you finally get to stay here," said Thurston to Jaci.

"Yes," she said, "but interesting that Major Jha knew I had been here before. How would he know that?"

"I suppose you were booked in even if you didn't stay."

"Even so," she said sounding unconvinced. "But it's a nice place." She looked around at the classical Nepali décor in dark wood and white almost cream walls. "I didn't have much time to notice last time."

Her voice was dull and lacked its usual sense of fun.

Thurston checked that Pandeh was out of hearing and asked her if something new was troubling her. "Yes," she replied, "they're being polite and friendly but there's an undercurrent – like these security guys who Jha says are for protection – but make me feel more like keeping us under guard."

Thurston nodded slowly. The same thought had occurred to him.

"I think if you don't mind Edward, I would prefer not to be in my own room – even if the atmosphere isn't quite up to any more fun sessions for the time being," she managed a smile.

"Oh, I don't know," he grinned, "it would add another parameter to the list of ambient conditions – raw fear."

"How will you explain it to Jha or Pandeh?"

"Well if I need to explain I'll tell the truth – that after what happened last time you are nervous about being left alone."

"OK," she said, "let's see what we can get out of Major Jha and his merry men and find out what is really behind all this."

"It's a bit different this time isn't it?" Najinski said. "I assume the people you talk to in your medical sphere are normally being cooperative. If you start querying Jha or his people, they're more likely to clam up."

"Or turn nasty," said Jaci.

"So bearing in mind we're not dealing with a sympathetic audience," said Thurston. "We will have to tread carefully."

# The Tissue Trail

"Or you could take the opposite view," said Najinski, "try to ruffle their feathers and try to shake something out of the trees."

Jaci laughed at his mixed metaphor welcoming an opportunity to break the tension. "What kind of trees have feathers, Victor?"

~~~~~~~~~~

Rather than prolong things, Jaci checked into her own room but Thurston took her bag into his. Half an hour later they emerged to find their respective security men standing at ease outside each door.

"The only time I've seen this before," said Thurston, "was in a top notch west end hotel which had a Middle Eastern potentate in residence."

"Yep, pretty common for royalty or the filthy rich," said Najinski. "Not so common for ordinary mortals."

~~~~~~~~~~

Jha had laid on western style sandwiches and Nepali samosas with beer and soft drinks so they could get straight down to work. There were nine in the meeting, Thurston's three, Jha, Desai, the three ACAP men plus, again, Inspector Pandeh.

"I don't plan to keep you long," said Jha. "All I need to do is hand out this list of video segments we want to prepare prior to the arrest itself from which we can assemble the final broadcast. Speaking of which Mr Thurston, I gather you agreed to bring a copy of your Lo Manthang tape. We are most interested to have a look at it to see if you have any footage which could help – in fact we are rather assuming there will be."

Thurston opened his briefcase and pulled out a video-cassette. It was one of the copies which did not include the addition he had recorded after Chaudrai's phone call. He handed it to Jha who thanked him and passed it to a technician telling him he would come through in two minutes. Jha turned back as Desai handed out two sheets of printed script.

"As you will see the first page is a draft of headline broadcasts. The second is a list of points which can be added in for longer news broadcasts. I think for tonight, if I can just ask you to check for understanding and any important questions, then we can meet in the morning to start work

288

finalizing the scripts and start shooting. Please help yourselves," he said, indicating the various plates of food.

~~~~~~~~~~

Jha's guests started to look over the two page summaries while Jha disappeared, presumably to have a look at Thurston's tape.

### *CARAVAN ARREST HEADLINES – FIRST DRAFT*

**Opening shot**– *Live backdrop: the walled city of Lo Manthang. Loaded yaks ready to set off over the border and back to their home base in Tibet.*

**Najinski, CNN**: *I am reporting for CNN from the Nepal - Tibet border where Nepali security police are about to break the drug ring behind the Tissue Trail heroin affair. Behind me this high altitude yak caravan was about to leave on the final leg of its six-month return trek to its home base in Lake Drabye, Tibet. But instead, the caravan leaders are being arrested accused of bringing in a key intermediate chemical used in the manufacture of heroin. These sachets (Najinski shows the camera four polythene sachets each containing a fine white crystalline powder) are being used to carry heroin back to the home base of the caravan for their own use but are identical to those found hidden in the baggage of the Tissue Trail women in Singapore. This is final proof, say Nepali Security, that the caravan is the centre of the ring and if it is stopped the ring will be broken. I have with me research chemist and professional photographer Edward Thurston who will explain the background.*

**Thurston**: *Historically the caravan brought salt over the Himalaya from Tibet to trade for cereal from the Indian plains. But with declining salt export quotas the caravan has started to carry other commodities including, this year, acetic anhydride intended to be used in the manufacture of palm oil [still shot of palm oil plant near Naudhara in Nepal and shot of the manager]. However, the same chemical is also a key intermediate in the manufacture of heroin. After interviewing the leader of the caravan myself in April I followed the movement of the chemical to the palm oil plant near Pokhara and then discovered part of it was being channeled to the dispensary at the Pokhara International Clinic. [still shot* *showing chemist in white coat at the dispensing bench]. It subsequently transpired that the Tissue Trail heroin was being manufactured at the clinic and was then secreted in dolls, rugs, boots, and other artefacts made in Tibetan refugee camps [stock shot of refugee camp manufacturing line] then sold in the camp shops.*

*[Stock shot of typical Tibetan refugee shop with range of artefacts for sale]. The items carrying the drug were bought by backpackers who carried them on to distribution points including Singapore.*

**Commentary over to Major Jha.**

**Jha:** *CNN is here today at the invitation of the Annapurna Conservation Area Project because the Tissue Trail arrests have brought Nepali tourism to its knees and left thousands of Nepalis destitute, not to mention five female tourists to death row in Singapore. What we are seeing here is the end of the Tissue Trail heroin ring. From today there need be no further fear of Tissue Trail heroin trafficking in Nepal and travellers can return to enjoy the magnificent Himalayan scenery and friendly warmth of its people.*

*[Section – to be added. Major Jha/Edward Thurston cash movements.]*

**Najinski:** *This is Victor Najinski CNN – at 13,000 feet in the Kingdom of Mustang on the border of Nepal and Tibet signing off from the closure of the Tissue Trail heroin trafficking ring.*

They moved on to the second page after Desai had told them that he had prepared the list of additional information assuming that a number of the sections would be available from Edward Thurston's video footage. He based this on the report Major Jha had written after his interrogation of Thurston at the Pokhara security office. He nodded towards Thurston in acknowledgement.

## CARAVAN ARREST – ADDITIONAL INFORMATION SECTIONS

**Description of the salt caravan coming in from the border.**
**Source:** *Extracts from Thurston's video of caravan – explaining origin and route from Lake Drabye in Tibet.*

**Description of route from Mustang to Pokhara via Kali Gandaki Gorge.**
**Source:** *Extracts from Thurston video recording of flight through Kali*

*Gandaki Gorge to show the dramatic terrain through which the chemical was transported to the palm oil plant.*

**Palm oil plant.**

**Source:** *Thurston's video shows acetic anhydride containers at the palm oil plant including shot of the manager.*

**Pokhara Clinic:** *Point of heroin manufacture.*

*Shows diverted acetic anhydride containers on dispensing bench. Shots of pharmacy technician.*

**Source:** *Nepal Television News, voiceover by Thurston.*

*Tibetan Refugee camp near Pokhara: showing cottage industries - manufacture of dolls, rugs, etc.*

**Source:** *Nepal Television News voiceover by Thurston.*

**Refugee camp shops:** *Showing artefacts (dolls, rugs, boots) for sale.*

**Source:** *Thurston video*

**Singapore Changi Airport Customs:** *Polythene packets of heroin found in Tibetan artefacts taken from the Tissue Trail women coming in from Nepal.*

**Source:** *Live Singapore Customs video recording arrest of Catherine Miller voiceover Thurston.*

**Description of elements of trafficking:** *Couriers, mules, cash tracing, after entry pick up.*

**Source:** *Thurston voiceover new recording.*

**Comment from Major Jha / Edward Thurston:** *Cash tracing to be added in final stages.*


Thurston sat back and pushed both sheets away from him.

"It looks as if somebody knows his way around the television business," he said.

Gil Desai explained that he had spent five years in the news department at Doordashan, the Indian State Television channel.

"That seems a bit of a come down, Main Street Delhi to backstreet Kathmandu."

"I'm only here for three months to the end of July – I'm on special assignment."

"That sounds interesting," Thurston said inviting him to explain further.

"I'm working under the auspices of Nepal Television but the contract is with ACAP. They wanted somebody with experience of international transmissions."

"I'm sorry, Mr Desai, it sounds as if I'm cross-examining you – it's just natural curiosity."

At this point the door opened and Major Jha reappeared. "Who is cross-examining whom?" he asked.

"I was giving Gil Desai the third degree about his background at Doordashan," said Thurston. "ACAP has obviously done all it can to make a good job of this."

Jaci caught Thurston's eye and she mouthed the word "creep." Thurston gently shook his head with a faint smile then turned to Jha.

"I see you have me down as an authority not only on the chemical processes but the caravan itself —not to mention the arrest at Changi Airport!"

"Indeed," replied Jha, "that is why we went to the trouble – and indeed the expense of involving you."

"I thought Edward's main role was to be my minder," said Najinski, managing a bit of a grin.

"Bit of an all around hero," Jaci said drily.

"Very interesting content by the way, Mr Thurston, if you don't mind there are quite a few sections we would like to use," said Jha.

Clearly he wasn't going to comment on the Tensing section, at least not yet. Thurston exchanged glances with Jaci.

"That is a spare copy," Thurston said, "I'm glad you think it might be useful."

"What do you think of the drafts we have prepared?" Jha asked.

"It's complete and professional," said Thurston. "But we had rather hoped there might have been something which could help with the Singapore situation – and at first reading there isn't."

"I understand," said Jha. "I am sorry that what we are doing does not help in that direction."

"Yes. It's a pity," said Thurston, "seeing it all strung together like this makes you realize how much has gone into this; re-routing the caravan, setting up the palm oil manufacture, then heroin production at the clinic, then organizing the distribution through the refugee camps."

Jha seemed to be ready for this. "I don't think it was that much trouble, Mr Thurston. ACAP were already in the process of setting up the palm oil plant and the import of the intermediate including setting up quality control at the clinic. All the traffickers had to do was piggyback onto what ACAP was doing anyway. So I would take the opposite view –they had to make very little effort on top of what was already there."

"Even so, this looks to be a bit beyond the capability of a semi-nomadic tribe and a few refugees," Najinski commented.

To Najinski's surprise, Jha almost smiled. "I agree, they must have had assistance and that is something we will address at the same time as the arrests, or shortly afterwards. But I would prefer not to say any more for the time being."

"Major, I see you have included shots of the palm oil plant and the dispensary – do you mind if I see them?" Thurston asked.

Jha looked a little hesitant but nodded to Desai who opened a well organized file and produced two photographic prints. The shot of the palm oil plant was as Thurston remembered it; set in a small clearing surrounded by thick large leafed foliage, giant rhododendron bushes and some slender trunked trees, which he could not identify. The photograph did not show the Nepali worker he had met initially but the more senior man who had asked Thurston to leave. He had not noticed at the time, but the man was clearly Tibetan or of Tibetan origin with darker skin, high mongoloid cheek bones and narrow oriental eyes. The shot of the dispensary held a similar surprise. The chemist or dispenser in the white coat standing by the bench and holding a plastic container of acetic anhydride was also of Tibetan origin.

Thurston pushed the prints along the table to Najinski and Jaci. Najinski looked thoughtful but said nothing. Jaci made no attempt to hide her reaction – a clear frown.

"You look concerned Miss Linthorpe." Jha said.

"It's nothing," she said. "Don't mind me."

To her surprise, Thurston did not comment on the Tibetans in the photographs – at least not directly. "Looking at this in general terms Major, are you satisfied that this Tissue Trail trafficking is just about making a few dollars?"

"As I told you before Mr Thurston, all the hard work was done for them so I have no problem seeing this as simply trying to make a few dollars as you put it." Jha's agitation level was rising but Thurston pursued the question.

"Are you aware that the defence teams in Singapore believe there is rather more to it?"

It was the turn of the ACAP team to look at each other. There was a heavy silence before Jha replied.

"Yes, we have followed the trial reports," he spoke with a quiet intensity, "and we regret what is happening in Singapore, but we can do nothing to influence it. What we can and must do and I apologize for repeating myself, is to put an end to the damage being done to thousands of our poorest countrymen by a few renegade tribesmen and refugees."

Again a pause. In that unguarded sentence Jha had removed any doubt on two matters – first that they were targeting the Tibetans and secondly, that nothing was going to get in his way.

Thurston had to make a choice. Despite his attempt to probe gently to create more latitude for his questions it wasn't working and Jha was losing his cool. So should he back off – or continue raising the temperature? His decision wasn't difficult. There were less than ninety-six hours to the first execution. This was no time to back off.

"I'm sorry I have to ask this Major, but your script portrays the 'renegade tribesmen and refugees' as you call them, as willing participants, yet as you have seen from my video recording the tribesmen operating the caravan were very much against it until the previous leader died in mysterious circumstances."

Jha now looked like thunder and he leaned forward pressing his hands face down onto the table in front of him and in a raised voice said, "We are aware that not all questions in this matter have been answered but now we have proof that the caravan is a critical part of the ring, there is no reason to delay closing it."

Thurston had raised the stakes and seemed intent on provoking Jha further so Jaci joined in, "Even if that means finishing up blaming the wrong people."

Jha turned to face her. "You are aware, are you not," he said, addressing all three of them in little more than a low hiss, "that heroin in the same polythene sachets as the women carried into Singapore, are known to be hidden in the cereal sacks which the caravan are taking back to its home base at Lake Drabye?"

None of the three replied immediately. "Well are you?" Jha asked, his voice rising further.

"Yes we are," said Thurston, "But..."

"But nothing!" interrupted Jha, now virtually shouting and looking specifically at Jaci. "If they are bringing in the intermediate and taking out finished product how can they be the wrong people?"

Thurston responded to Jha's rising volume by speaking quietly. "What we are suggesting is that it might be in the interests of all parties to allow a few more days in the hope that on-going enquiries will reveal the whole story."

Jha clenched his fists and leant forward speaking as if he had a tight band around his chest, "You do not appear to be listening, lady and gentlemen. We have large numbers of Nepali working people on the verge of starvation; we have final proof that we can break the ring – which cannot survive without the intermediate, and you are asking us to delay?"

When she thought about it afterwards, Jaci was aware that the next question would have seemed inspired but the truth of the matter was it just came out – "Major, what is causing the time pressure for you in getting this broadcast out?"

Jha raised his fists and brought them down with full force onto the table and almost out of control shouted, "I have been working on this since 1995, first without the Chinese cooperation, then with resistance from the caravan people we were trying to help. Then the people we were trying to help turn it into a drug ring and now I'm told my job's on the line if I don't produce this media furore before..." He stopped himself. He had said more than he had intended.

Jaci turned on her full man-eating smile. "I'm sorry if I've upset you, Major, but what is happening in the next few days which makes getting this newscast out so important?" Jha had calmed down and he raised his hands with his palms facing outwards at the same time shaking his head, indicating he would go no further. He stayed quiet while he fully regained his composure; then ignoring Jaci's question, he turned to Najinski. "Mr Najinski, these questions have no bearing on the project in hand. We have a contract with CNN to televise and broadcast the breaking of the drug ring. Can you please confirm that you intend to proceed?" Jha's voice was now calm but cold.

Najinski looked at Thurston, who gave the faintest of nods.

"Yes, Major Jha, we will."

"Then I suggest we meet again at eight in the morning to finalize the texts and to start work on the voiceovers," Jha gathered up his papers and stood up. "Inspector Pandeh and his team will escort you to your rooms. Are there any more questions about your accommodation arrangements?" he asked, clearly signaling that he would not accept any more questions related to the broadcast content. He looked at the three of them in turn. "Good," he said collecting his papers and briefcase, "then I will bid you good evening and see you first thing in the morning."

Jha was followed by Desai and the three ACAP executives. Inspector Pandeh waited with the rest of the security men until Thurston, Najinski and Jaci stood up to leave, then followed with his team in close attendance.

Thurston looked at the other two. "I think we could do with a nightcap. Can I suggest Victor, that we use your handsome suite."

"More than welcome," said Najinski. He would normally have accompanied the welcome with an extravagant "come this way" gesture. But Najinski was not in the mood.

Thurston told Pandeh what they had in mind. He responded by telling Thurston the security officers would wait outside Mr Najinski's room until Mr Thurston and Miss Linthorpe were ready to return to their own rooms. Despite his apparent acquiescence, Thurston thought Pandeh still looked a little uncertain. But when he made no further comment Thurston turned and lead the other two towards the elevator.

# CHAPTER TWENTY
## *The Motive*

Thurston had seen Najinski's suite before. In fact he had slept in it – or rather spent the night in it – with the elegant and enigmatic Lauren Chase. It was itself elegant and spacious and divided into sitting and dining areas. He remembered the rosewood dining table and handsome carved dining chairs of the same wood and the matching serving sideboard. In the lounge area there was a three-piece suite with three equal length deep-seated sections in a rich medium brown and burgundy semi-floral pattern in a silk fabric. They were arranged around a square dark wood table with inlaid marquetry of a magnificent tiger. Tall silver candelabras and other polished silver ornaments added to the sumptuous impression and the whole effect was set off by oil paintings of major Himalayan peaks behind villages, or Hindu chortens with prayer flags blowing in the wind.

"Not bad," he said looking around.

Jaci watched him. "You don't normally take so much notice," she said, "it is almost as if it's familiar."

Her powers of observation and perception, wholly welcome in her capacity as a clinical investigator, took on a different hue when she directed them at people "with whom she had a personal connection."

"You could be right," he said.

Najinski broke into the awkward moment, "So as a result of you two practicing your interrogation skills we know that Desai is here to work on whatever is happening in July and Jha's job is on the line if he doesn't deliver his broadcast by some date in July. So all we have to do to complete the whole Tissue Trail jigsaw puzzle is to work out what the hell it is. Anybody have any new ideas?" As he spoke he opened his mini bar – or rather a handsome well stocked full size drink cabinet. "I think I need something to help engage the brain – what can I get you?"

Thurston and Jaci accepted soft drinks rather to Najinski's disappointment. "I think we need to keep a clear head," said Thurston. "But don't let us stop you."

"You won't," he said, emptying two small bottles of brandy into a balloon glass and taking a good first swig.

Jaci had opened up a complimentary copy of the *Kathmandu Post* which the hotel had left on the dining table and was idly moving it backwards and forwards on the polished surface, "I think it is interesting that Major Jha is clearly under heavy pressure from somewhere or somebody way above him. He didn't just look worried about his job, I'd say he was genuinely scared."

"Not too surprising I suppose," said Thurston. "Whoever is behind this hasn't shown much regard for human life – what is the death count so far – six?"

They were now sitting around the table sipping their drinks. Jaci had stopped pushing the newspaper around and left it opened up with the full front page facing upwards. Thurston scanned it for a few seconds then said, "Look at that – five items on the front page and every one is Tissue Trail related."

The main headline above a large photograph of Changi Women's Prison was:

## *UN SECURITY COUNCIL FAILS TO AGREE ON TISSUE TRAIL RESOLUTION*

### *New York, Saturday:*

*Russia and China both refused to support a draft Security Council resolution urging the Singapore Government to stay executions in the so called Tissue Trail heroin cases pending further review of the five cases. Both took the familiar line of objecting to interference in the internal affairs of member states.*

*A spokesman for the US, UN delegation was quoted as saying that, despite the failure to agree a resolution, his government hoped that even at this late stage the fact international concern had reached a level where the Security Council had become involved, would persuade the Singapore judiciary to reconsider their position. He added that if two "innocent" Americans were to die in these circumstances, relations between the two nations would be seriously damaged.*

The second feature was headed:

## FOUR TISSUE TRAIL WOMEN COULD HANG SIMULTANEOUSLY ON FRIDAY

The item confirmed the previous rumour that at least three of the Tissue Trail women would hang simultaneously on Friday 6th July– the two Americans, Karen Leopold and Maria Gonzales, together with Catherine Miller. The US and British Governments were planning last minute appeals as was the European Union foreign affairs office in Brussels. Diplomatic efforts to save the women would carry on until the last minute.

Yet another article reported that substantial numbers of students were entering Singapore with the intention of setting up mass demonstrations on the date of the executions. The Singapore authorities were trying to find ways of refusing entry to as many as possible but many had transit visas which could not be legally resisted.

A third item headline was:

## SECURITY POLICE CLOSE IN ON TISSUE TRAIL OPERATORS

*Major Jha, head of ACAP, told this newspaper today that he believes Nepal police are close to identifying the operators of the Tissue Trail drug ring and were hopeful of breaking it in the next few days. Asked if he could give any indication as to who the perpetrators were, Major Jha said there was little doubt that Tibetans were involved but refused to be drawn further. A spokesman for the Ministry of Internal Affairs said, "It would be a matter of great relief to Nepal to see the ring broken and the economy restored to normal levels."*

Thurston was about to turn the page when Jaci noticed a one-inch column filler at the foot of the page.

# The Tissue Trail

## *NEPAL OLYMPIC DELEGATE CHANGE*

*Nepal's delegate to the Moscow IOC Meeting 13-16 July, Indira Patel has been taken ill and will be replaced by Mrs Aisha I Ratna.*

Jaci frowned, "IOC? Isn't that what your media pass was for Victor?"

"Actually yes," he said.

"Well let's have a look then!" She spoke as if she were a child to an errant parent.

Najinski opened his briefcase and pulled out the envelope with the five rings of the Olympic movement across the top. He pulled out the contents and placed the media pass and letter on the table. The cover letter was from the International Olympic Committee, Chateau de Vidy, Lausanne. Jaci picked up the stiff ornate card to which the letter referred.

*International Olympic Committee*
*Media Accreditation*
*Victor Joseph Najinski Cable News Network*
*112th International Olympic Committee Session*
*World Trade Centre —Mezhdunamarodnaya Hotel, Moscow*
*13-16 July 2001*

"I hope you don't have to ask for that hotel by name," she joked, then picked up the card as if to make sure she wasn't misreading something. The smile disappeared.

"Look at the date," she said, now frowning and looking at Thurston. "How much closer can you get to the middle of July than that!"

Thurston was also now looking puzzled. Jaci continued with her train of thought, "If the Chinese are behind this then the timing certainly fits, their change of mind in the mid-nineties, missing the 1997 vote for the 2004 Games then getting everything set up for the 2001 vote for 2008 fits like a glove." She was still looking uncertain, as was Thurston whose reaction was rather different. "But we're talking about a string of killings, penetration of US drug intelligence, high level press manipulation, a Swiss Bank manoeuvring cash..."

Najinski had stayed silent, his gaze riveted on the invitation but then spoke quietly. For Najinski, to speak quietly had as much impact as delivering an aria from a rooftop. "Jaci is right," he said without drama, "this is the answer, this is the motive that everybody is screaming for and I've been sitting on it for months. I should have seen it before but if you will bear with me I think it will become clear why I didn't."

Najinski pulled his briefcase towards him and extracted two files.

"When I first joined CNN in 1993 they told me that what finally got me the job was my report for the BBC on the last day of the Monaco IOC meeting and in particular the announcement of the result of the Millennium Games hosting vote. In fact, more particularly, the reaction of the Chinese delegation to the announcement of the result. It was for me the most gut rending transformation from delirious delight to utter desolation I have ever seen – and my crew managed to capture it on camera. I'll show you the transcript to set the scene but it is the second part, the political reaction, that matters.

"I had been a correspondent for the BBC in the Far East for twenty years prior to joining CNN and had built up a pretty good network of political contacts in Beijing. When they offered me the job the first thing they asked me to do was a full report on the Chinese reaction to losing the vote. They had already had reports that the reaction had been pretty severe. My report confirmed what they had heard but went a lot further. To understand what is happening now and what is behind the Tissue Trail affair you will need to read both sections." He pushed the two file copies towards them and laid them open on the table in front of them. "I think if you start there," he said placing his forefinger a third of the way down the page, "you will get all you need."

The President read out the result in reverse order, so what he actually said was:

*"The votes cast in the final round were, first, Beijing..."*
*...at which point the Chinese reacting to the translation of the word "first" leapt into the air and started celebrating, jumping around hugging each other believing that they had won. Then – the slow realization that the President had not finished – and delight turning to doubt as they slowly turned around and retook their seats – and then waited for him to complete the sentence "...* ***first Beijing...43 votes.*** *" There was a slow agonized realization*

*that 43 votes were not enough. To see people who had been jumping and hugging in ecstasy slowly crumble into shoulder heaving sobbing and tears of distress, made ten times worse because seconds earlier they thought they had won, made it one of the most heart rending bits of human television even an old hack like me has ever seen.*

Najinski removed the first file and pushed the two copies of the second file in front of them. "There may have been real human distress in Monaco but there was heavy-duty political humiliation in Beijing. This was my report to Schultz."

### Report to Head of CNN Far East, New Delhi 15 November 1993

### Beijing Reaction after Loss of Millennium Games Hosting Vote 1993

*The Chinese took the loss of the Millennium Games badly. They had seen the accolade of hosting the first Games of the 21st Century as a right and proper acknowledgement of their presumption that they would become **the** superpower of the 21st Century. Some hardliners had argued that a decision of such political significance should not have been left to an open or democratic vote; to lose to "insignificant Sydney" was an unnecessary and intolerable loss of face. In the days following the vote, heads rolled at all levels of the Chinese Sports Federation and even in government.*

*There were even those who favoured abandoning the Olympic movement as a "western celebration." The argument to remain in the movement was won comfortably enough but the fact that it had been raised was a clear indication of the seriousness of China's reaction.*

*And what no one in Beijing seemed to doubt was that the main reason for their failure at Monaco was western rejection of Chinese treatment of dissent in general, and in Tibet in particular. So the problem was clear enough but given that Beijing would not remotely contemplate any change in its attitudes, policies or practices, what should their reaction be?*

*One respected political analyst known for accurately reflecting*

# The Tissue Trail

*Beijing's thinking wrote:*

*"The loss of the Millennium Games to Sydney, initially just a blow to Chinese pride has proved to have a more deep rooted significance. China is a 'sub-continent' with a massively disparate population of 1.5 billion, Muslims to the west, Hindus to the south, Mongols to the north and the main body of ethnic Chinese in the centre and to the east. With such a conglomerate of populations and beliefs and traditions preserving law and order and a structured society and still observe the West's vague concepts of democracy, human rights and unspecified aspirations to freedom is not a realistic proposition. One only has to remember the effect of dismantling the political structures of the Balkans and the USSR in the interests of democracy and independence. Order and organization was replaced by chaos, mass killing and universal corruption. China is not going to abandon the good order of the last fifty years simply to acquiesce to Western ideals. Rather it will be a matter of educating the West to recognize political realities."*

*This was the sort of thinking which it is believed influenced Chinese response to the Millennium Games loss. Reaction could have been contained simply by managing reaction to the loss of face and then by making sure that their next application would be better prepared, their lobbying better organized and they would drop the damaging assumption that their political power and influence would be sufficient to carry the day. But recognition of the deeper implications led to a subtle but significant shift of ground. Beijing decided that their determination to maintain good order, at almost whatever the cost in human rights terms would remain undiluted but in addition they would actively seek every opportunity a) to demonstrate the damaging effects of abandoning policies designed to preserve good order and b) to discredit those factions whose attitudes and actions threatened good order.*

*The loss of the Millennium Games and the perceived role played by Tibet and their fellow travellers was seen as one of the first opportunities to implement this more aggressive strategy although at the time of writing this report there is no clear plan as to how this might be done.*

# The Tissue Trail

*The final step in Beijing's thinking given the wider agenda was that the next application to host an Olympic Games would be overseen at government level and not by the "amateurs" of the Olympic administration within the Sports Federation. The Beijing Olympic Venue Committee still served as a convenient and politically acceptable front but with its brief coverage any opportunity to "educate the West" it would be dealt with at the highest levels and chaired by a ranking minister who I understand had an intelligence background.*

*Victor Najinski November 1993*

There were two handwritten side notes both of which were to prove highly significant. The first was:

*In a case such as Tibet any action taken must implicate Tibet as a nation - not just a few renegade extremists.*

The second:

*In private exchanges sentiments of revenge against Tibet and their fellow travellers have been noted but for obvious reasons have not been committed to the record.*

Thurston blew out a long release of breath. "I see Victor, so losing the Millennium Games did in fact strike rather deeper than simply losing the right to hosting."

"Yes, without question."

"You're expecting to be asked this so I'll ask it," Jaci said. "Why didn't you see the connection earlier?"

He had time to think about it while the two of them had been reading his report to Schultz.

"It's because I saw this taking shape in Beijing's corridors of power and that didn't connect with long haired yaks, medieval Himalayan cities, and nomadic Tibetan tribes. The two worlds simply didn't come together. But the connection is the deliberately generated media furore and seeing that invitation threw the switch."

Jaci and Thurston thoughtfully absorbed what he had said, but Najinski had made his "Damascene moment" crystal clear and it removed the need for any further debate.

"OK, so there isn't any doubt that this is the answer," said Thurston. "But this is still going to be difficult to sell in a court of law. You were pretty close to the action but legally it is still hearsay."

"You are beginning to sound like Philip Lee," said Najinski.

"Oh, and one other thing, while we're picking the bones out of this," Thurston pursed his lips. "You must have had some remarkably good contacts Victor – that reference to revenge is pretty sensitive stuff. If that had got out ..."

"I did have, shall we say 'close contacts,'" said Najinski, "that didn't come from official sources."

Both Jaci and Thurston looked at him but he didn't expand beyond saying, "Just trust me."

Jaci and Thurston exchanged glances but left it. But "it" would become significant later.

Najinski changed the subject, "You have to hand it to whoever conceived this. They've got the media, politicians and diplomats all screaming to know who is behind the executions – and in the white heat they have expertly built up to a climax, the Lo Manthang broadcast blows the lid off it – blazing the blame on the Tibetans to every corner of the earth. So one effect of this will be to virtually remove any Tibet sympathy votes against the Chinese next week."

"And, if as you hinted Victor," said Jaci, "revenge against the West is part of it, they manage that with five Western women going to the gallows."

"But the main effect and what they're really after is that sympathy for the Tibetans will go out of the window for years and justification for China's hard line will be reinforced for years. For them it is a perfect result."

"I think we are all now singing from the same hymn sheet," said Najinski starting to pull Jha's broadcast texts back together. As he did so he spotted the two incomplete sections at the end of both the headline and the added detail sections. Both dealt with cash tracing. There was silence as the three of them pondered the point. It was Jaci who broke it.

"I wonder why they needed to go to the trouble of setting up the false cash movement at all?" said Jaci. "You would think Tibetan involvement at all other points would be more than enough?"

"And yet it must be important," said Thurston. "Lauren Chase made quite an issue of it when she gave me the run down on what was going on in the first place..."

"In this very room wasn't it, Edward?" Jaci looked hard at her boss – and clinical investigation partner – and sexual performance guinea pig – in fact somebody who was becoming a bit of a player in her life.

He couldn't help smiling. "It seems, my friend, that I only get to sleep with beautiful women these days if it's in the line of professional duty."

Jaci maintained her hard look ignoring the implied compliment but with the merest hint of embarrassment. "That's an interesting comment, Edward" she said, "are you suggesting your exotic banker only slept with you to see what she could get out of you?"

"Or suggest to you?" Najinski joined in the fun.

Thurston looked serious, "Now that is an interesting thought. What I was just about to say, when my sex life was dragged kicking and screaming into centre stage, was that she also made quite a thing of the cash movements when she rang me to suggest this little caper."

"Wouldn't surprise me if she turns out to be running the whole thing," said Jaci. "She's got a tray full of silver spoons in her mouth, she probably owns the bank rather than works for it. She has whole populations falling over themselves to treat her like a queen and men falling into bed with her at the crook of her little finger – it would take something like this to give her a bit of excitement."

Najinski smiled, "Jaci, your jealous streak is showing!"

Jaci calmed down, tossed her long blonde hair and edged her way back to the subject. "So what you're saying, Victor, is she makes it clear that the cash movement is a big deal and yet for some reason Jha is leaving the full detail to the end." Thurston reached forward pulling Najinski's Beijing reaction report towards him in order to read part of it again. He slowly followed what he was reading with his forefinger and stopped half way down the second page, his brow lightly creased in thought.

"I wonder if that's it?"

"What?" asked Jaci, trying to see where his finger had stopped. It was over one of the two handwritten notes.

"If you forget the cash trace, the rest of the Tibetan connections covers the nomads, the palm oil plant manager, the pharmacy technicians, the artisans making dolls and other artefacts in the Tibetan refugee camps, and then the traders. They are all Tibetan but at the middle and lower levels of society. But read this note in Victor's Beijing briefing:

*'In a case such as Tibet any action taken must implicate Tibet as a nation – not just a few renegade extremists.'*

"That's why it's important," Thurston's voice was rising. "The cash goes back to the source of the operation. And Lauren made it clear it was going back right through to the banking system in the capital Lhasa."

Najinski nodded, "You mean right back into the heart of the Tibetan establishment. That completes the 'whole country' bit."

"I think I'll change my mind about that drink if you don't mind, Victor. I think we've earned it," Thurston suggested.

"Me too," said Jaci, smile in evidence.

Najinski poured a scotch, a G&T ...and another brandy for himself.

When Najinski had finished dispensing, Thurston raised his glass. "To the team," he toasted. "But with more work to be done. It looks as if we have a serious motive, but do we really think we can get something as incredible as this past a Singapore court?"

"Well it's exactly what Philip said he would need," Jaci remarked, "something incredible and unprecedented. That way it gives Singapore a way out without creating a precedent. Nothing like this would ever come up again."

"I momentarily forgot Philip," said Thurston, "but he's the one who's going to have to get it past the judge."

"Or even the president," said Najinski. "At least he's Chinese. He'll have a pretty good feel for it."

"Well if Lee can confirm that the source of the cash feed is Beijing," said Thurston, "he will have as much proof as he could possibly wish for that the Chinese are behind this."

"I wonder if Atlanta will want to check this with the State Department," Najinski said. "Accusing a major power of serial killing normally results in some sort of exchange with the Hill."

"Jeez! How long would that take?" Thurston frowned.

"Don't worry!" Najinski assured him, "your Tensing video will have been in Atlanta forty-eight hours ago and when something like this happens there is no such thing as a weekend. If Atlanta wants the State Department, the phones would have been hot within minutes. And with two American citizens due to die on Friday, there will be no hanging about – oh dear – sorry," Najinski grimaced.

"OK," said Thurston. "The next priority is to get all this to Philip."

Thurston opened the door to tell Pandeh they needed a few more minutes to make a call.

Pandeh responded by telling him he thought "the telephone lines were not working."

Victor tried to get an outside line but reception confirmed the lines were down. Pandeh was right. All three of them then tried their mobiles – only to find no cover.

"I think they've cut us off," said Najinski. "This is starting to look unpleasant."

"It also changes things," said Thurston turning to look at Jaci. "I think we are going to have to get you back to Singapore – first thing tomorrow morning."

Her initial reaction was to wrinkle her forehead in objection. She did not want to be left out of the final action. But on second thought, she was apprehensive as to exactly what Jha and his people had in mind.

"Now we've cracked the motive there is nothing more important than getting this to Philip," Thurston said quietly.

"No, I suppose not," she agreed.

"So I'll tell Pandeh that is what we intend so he can brief Jha and I'll come with you to the airport."

Thurston looked at his watch – "In another few hours the bank in Geneva should be examining the Tensing video – that should make their eyes water!"

"It is all coming together," said Najinski. "As long as Jha can keep his trigger finger under control for long enough."

"And we can get the motive back to Philip," said Thurston.

Pandeh and two of his men escorted Thurston and Jaci to Thurston's room.

Jaci was surprisingly down.

"What's the matter?"

"Aah, nothing," she said, "except I'm out of the plot and the excitement after tonight."

"At least you'll be safe."

"S'pose so. But doesn't seem like much of a consolation."

They were sitting on the bed side by side.

"Do you fancy another nightcap?" he asked.

She stood up in front of him, pushed him back on the bed and jumped on him.

"Not the drink sort of nightcap," she said sitting astride him and starting to pull his tie off.

He looked up at her, "I wouldn't have thought you'd be in the mood," he said.

"I don't have to be in the mood," she said, starting to work on his shirt, "it's purely in the line of business."

Even so, Thurston noticed she took no notes and the stopwatch stayed in its box.

## 2nd July 2001

The next morning he asked her how he had done. "Almost average," she said seriously, "but I was fantastic!" She grinned.

"Not too much detail in the report though."

"There'll be enough," she said.

"How many left to complete the full schedule."

"One," she laughed. She was no longer feeling too down about leaving Nepal.

They tried the room phones and mobiles again. There was no change.

Thurston was keen to get Jaci to the airport so they had ordered room service for 6:30 a.m. and were on the way to Tribhuvan Airport accompanied by Pandeh and one of his guards at 7:00 a.m. Thurston left a note for Najinski at reception.

It was a quiet morning and it was not difficult changing Jaci's return flight. Thurston tried his mobile without success and yet there were plenty of passengers wandering about with mobiles to their ears.

Frowning he said, "Somehow they've managed to get at our phones. I think it's just as well you're getting out of here."

Thurston guided her gently with his hand lightly on her lower back. When they reached the departure gate he turned her gently and pulled her towards him.

"Make sure you get to Philip as soon as you reach Singapore."

"Don't worry, I will."

He was still holding her gently and looking down at her.

"What?" she asked, feigning puzzlement with an exaggerated raising of the eyebrows.

"See you soon."

"I hope so," she said, "I didn't have a good feeling about this trip to start with and it hasn't got any better."

He drew her firmly to him and kissed her.

When she had checked her boarding pass and passport at the departure gate she turned and with a wave and exaggerated sad face with the corners of her mouth turned down, she disappeared.

"Right Inspector Pandeh, let's get back to the studio."

Five minutes later he tried to call Jaci on his mobile phone but it was still dead.

On the way to the studio Inspector Pandeh made no attempt at conversation.

At the studio, Desai was at the entrance to meet them. He managed a bit of a smile but Thurston thought he seemed to be ill at ease.

Inside it was reasonably well lit and well appointed and the studio recording room was a hive of activity with a variety of recording sets and scenes including, he noted, a prepared backdrop of Lo Manthang with the horizon of snow covered Himalaya behind it. He also noted that there were three sets where the backdrops were still covered.

Najinski was already recording. He looked to be in reasonable humour so he hadn't been asked to do or say anything yet which troubled him.

Desai handed Thurston three scripts to look over and asked him to study them and then rehearse before recording. Desai would listen and if necessary direct. There was no sign of Jha. After a quick skim Thurston could see these were introductory pieces with nothing he could object to or disagree with. He was keen to speak to Najinski but he would have to bide his time.

He worked through the first three scripts without difficulty and within forty minutes they were "in the can." Najinski came to a break point at about the same time and Thurston told Desai he needed a quick break. Desai pointedly looked at his watch and asked if he could keep it to five minutes as they had a lot to get through.

Najinski was still in reasonable humour.

"Have you asked Desai about the two missing Jha sections?" asked Thurston.

"Yes, and Desai says Major Jha is working on them and they will be ready later this afternoon."

"Did you ask Desai what the general content was?"

"Yes, and he was reluctant to say – but I pointed out that this was going out under CNN's name and I had the responsibility for editorial content – so I needed to know. And finally he admitted that the centre piece of both Jha sections was the cash movement going back to Lhasa."

"Any particular reason why these two sections were being held back?"

"Only because Major Jha wanted to be right up-to-date with the latest information. I responded to that with what you Brits called 'an old fashioned look.'"

"So that is the final nail in the coffin for the case against the Tibetans?"

"I guess so."

"And our cell phones don't work."

"No, they've taken mine to have it looked at by their technicians – if you give them yours they'll do the same for you. In fact, this young chap hovering here is waiting for yours. I'd forgotten."

Thurston handed his cell phone to the young Nepali who then moved off quickly.

The two men returned to their respective section recordings which followed the running orders they had seen the previous night – with no surprises. They ate a light lunch on the hoof and kept working.

At three p.m. Major Jha appeared. He was in full uniform for the cameras and not showing any of the warmth he had managed to raise on the previous evening.

"I'm sorry about your mobile phones, gentlemen," was his opening gambit. "Our technical boys are having a look. It appears your SIM cards have been cleaned out by some sort of radiation but from what source we do not know."

"Well we won't need them in Upper Mustang over the next couple of days," said Thurston. "But it would be good to get them back tonight."

"We are doing what we can," said Jha without enthusiasm.

"In the meantime I hope you won't mind if your office staff let us use your land lines?" asked Najinski.

Jha nodded without saying anything. Najinski moved on to the missing sections.

"Yes, I gather you are interested in those," said Jha. "I will have them finished in half an hour but I can tell you I am summarizing the cash movement position which I believe you know shows cash from sale of the Tissue Trail heroin working its way back to Lhasa."

There was no point in challenging Jha over this. It was a fact that money was going back to Lhasa even if artificial. What was more important was Lee proving that the whole ring of cash movement was being fed from a single source rather than a number of large population centres as was normal – and hopefully that that single source was Beijing – and better still from a government department in Beijing.

"It would be helpful to see these sections," said Najinski, "so that my sign off is in line with what you're saying and also tie in with Mr Thurston's explanations of how drug rings operate."

"As I have already told you, you will be able to see these elements at about half past three. So if you will excuse me I will complete the texts and then do the test recordings." Jha turned and headed towards one of the recording studios accompanied by a small entourage.

### Geneva Switzerland
### 2nd July 2001, 8:00 a.m.

Rousseau welcomed the board members to "this serious meeting."

"I think you know why we are here. There can have been few meetings of greater significance in the long history of this firm."

A video projector had been set up to show the Thurston/Najinski version of the intended broadcast.

"I am sure you will be keen to see the intended newscast," said Rousseau. "But first I want you to see the response from Warrender at NCIS regarding the alleged inconsistencies between cash and substance levels — raised at the last meeting by Claud Lassale."

From Warrender NCIS
To Rousseau Z. I. R.
Sunday 1st July 2001

*I have noted your question relating to the apparent discrepancy between the small amount of substance involved in these so called Tissue Trail cases and the substantial levels of cash involved as reported by your bank and have referred this question to Philip Lee the defence lawyer. He has replied as follows:*

*"The import of heroin into Singapore in the case of Catherine Miller and others in the so called Tissue Trail affair is not*

*trafficking in the normal sense. There was no contact between the defendants and any third party, either regarding carrying the substance into Singapore nor arrangement to collect after entry.*

*All indications are that the so-called trafficking has been set up artificially for what seem to be politically motivated purposes.*

*The basis of this conclusion is summarized in the draft newscast prepared by CNN's Victor Najinski and the medical researcher Edward Thurston, a copy of which has been couriered to you.*

*Philip Lee's response to your query is unequivocal. He accepts that the market value of the drug substance involved is negligible but it is the cost of setting up the artificial trafficking— involving people operating at senior levels in both Nepal and Singapore — which has required funding at the substantial levels we have observed.*

*I trust that this explanation, together with the CNN newscast, will enable your board to agree to release the identity of the origin of the funds used in this exercise.*

*On the question of motive we await further advice.*

*Warrender*

Rousseau turned to Lassale. "Do you have an immediate reaction, Claud?"

Lassale replied, "My only concern is the best long-term interests of the bank, as indeed, I am sure is the case for all of us. If we can be satisfied that this whole incredible exercise is artificial then Warrender's explanation for the apparent inconsistencies is logical."

"Reysin?" Rousseau turned to the younger member who had shared Lassale's view at the last meeting.

"I agree with that. Perhaps we should see if the CNN newscast convinces us that it is indeed artificial."

"Unless there are any other comments..." said Rousseau. Lassale immediately interrupted, "I'm afraid I do have a further comment. The last sentence admits they still do not have a motive and without that their threat to make this accusation against the Chinese, in my opinion, is an empty one."

"I note your position Claud, perhaps we can come back to it after we've seen what the intended broadcast has to say." A few seconds later the Thurston/Najinski video played to the riveted bankers.

At the conclusion of the projection Rousseau said, "Gentlemen, you have now seen the situation we face. I think the action we have to take is becoming clear."

He looked at Lassale for a first response.

"Who do we consider to be our client in this matter?" asked Lassale.

"I think the best way to answer that is to read the statement I have prepared in the expectation of this outcome," said Rousseau, distributing copies of the document.

*To whom it may concern:*

*Z. I. R. Bank has been acting as a clearing and distribution bank for movement of funds at the request of the Whickham Cay Bank of the British Virgin Islands. We have not provided any banking services other than the transfers of funds as requested.*

*At the BVI Bank request we have set up an account at Z. I. R. to transmit and receive funds to and from specified accounts in Lhasa, Dhaka, Delhi, Karachi, Lahore, and other major population centres. The highest number of transactions, though not the highest volume of cash, has been to Lhasa in Tibet.*

*In addition to the movements listed above, payments have been made to individuals in Nepal and Singapore and Canada.*

*Following a formal request to the Whickham Cay Bank they have advised that the funds which serviced these movements were received as a single deposit of USD 35M from the Development Bank of China, Yuetan, Beijing in November 1996.*

Rousseau waited for them all to finish reading and then said, "The Development Bank of China exists almost entirely to supply and manage funds for Chinese public sector projects."

At this point the internal phone on Rousseau's desk buzzed. He frowned and picked up the receiver, clearly not pleased, and listened for a few moments. "You had better bring it in, Helene."

The door opened and Helene, Rousseau's PA, brought in a single sheet which he read then addressed the meeting:

## The Tissue Trail

"It is an e-mail from Warrender at NCIS London but originating from Philip Lee – the Tissue Trail women defence lawyer in Singapore:

*Please be advised that the date of the executions of Catherine Miller and others has been brought forward from six a.m. local time on Friday 6th July to six p.m. on Thursday 5th July.*

*There has been no public announcement and none is expected. It is believed that the move has been made to forestall, or at least minimize, the effect of the expected mass student demonstrations, which are known to be planned to coincide with the original timing of the executions on Friday morning.*

Rousseau didn't wait for any comment before saying, "Gentlemen, I think the position is clear as also is the action we have to take and take now."

"I am sorry," said Claud Lassale, "but nothing I have heard changes the position I stated earlier – I do not believe CNN will make such an accusation against the Chinese in an open broadcast without a clear and compelling motive. For our part breaking the confidentiality code, on which our competitiveness and therefore our survival depends, is as serious a decision as we would ever be asked to make. I am afraid therefore that unless I am satisfied that a clear and compelling motive has been established that I cannot vote in favour of this information being released."

"You would prefer to risk being pilloried for withholding information which could save the lives of five innocent young women?" said Rousseau barely able to hide his anger at this open challenge to his authority.

"I think you could turn that argument on its head," said Lassale. "There would be adverse publicity in the short term but what the business community will remember in the end is that even faced with this degree of pressure the Z. I. R. Bank did not cave in."

Rousseau was aware of several signs of acceptance of that point around the table.

"As you all know, a decision on breaking confidentiality has to be unanimous. Claud has made his position clear. In the circumstances I will have to inform Warrender that we will need good evidence as to why the Chinese have taken this action – if indeed they have."

Lassale proposed that an off the record vote be taken but not minuted. Rousseau agreed.

There were five votes in favour of revealing the account information without delay and three in support of Lassale's position. A long way from 100%. The meeting was closed.

Ten minutes later Rousseau sent a modified e-mail to Jonathan Warrender at NCIS in London.

### NCIS Blackfriars, London
### 3rd July 2001, 8:26 a.m.

Rousseau's e-mail was timed at 9:25 p.m. European Summer time, 8:25 p.m. British Summer Time – and 4:25 p.m. in Singapore. This was Tuesday 3rd July – just over forty-eight hours before the brought forward execution time of Catherine Miller and the others.

Warrender received the e-mail statement from the Z. I. R. Bank at 8:26 a.m. and was reading it when Barbara stuck her head round the door to ask, "Have you got it?"

"Yes, I have. They are taking a hard line."

"You are sending it straight off to Philip?"

"Yes..." said Warrender.

"You seem a little hesitant."

"I am a little hesitant," he said, "but it's only that I rather share their view. And it means that unless sometime in the next forty-eight hours somebody comes up with an answer which will convince the Singapore establishment, I think we are going to be disappointed. But let's send this first and I'll ask Philip what is happening on the motive front."

Five minutes later he had a reply from Philip Lee:

*Thank you for the e-mail regarding the outcome of the Z. I. R. Bank source enquiry. That response is perhaps what we had expected here. And I have heard nothing from Thurston, Najinski or Jaci Linthorpe for over 24 hours. There have been reports of telephone line problems in Kathmandu but that would not explain why there has been no mobile phone contact.*

*I am a little concerned but will keep you informed.*

*I will advise Barry Schultz at the CNN office in Delhi and ask him to keep Atlanta informed.*

*Philip Lee*

"Oh, dear," said Barbara, "it looks as if we are going to be disappointed after all."

"It does not look good," said Warrender.

### Central Criminal Court, Singapore
### 3rd July 2001, 5:30 p.m.

Philip Lee telephoned D. C. Rahman with the disappointing news of Z. I. R.'s position.

"I am afraid without either the account source or motive you are not giving me much of a chance," said Rahman, "...in fact it's a sine qua non. Do you have any idea, however far-fetched, what the motive could be?"

"No I don't," Lee replied.

"So what is happening on the motive front?" asked Rahman.

"The medical researcher Thurston, and his assistant, who have unravelled most of this so far, are still together and are with Najinski in Nepal, so let's hope they can make one last breakthrough."

"And what's the latest regarding CNN's broadcast casting us as the villains of the piece?"

"I wish I knew, all three of them are incommunicado. What you can be sure of is that they will be doing everything they can to work it out and get it out."

Rahman paused before saying, "Philip I don't normally wish the defence well but this case is different. Good luck – and I mean it!"

Philip Lee's next phone call was to Barry Schultz at CNN in Delhi to bring him up-to-date with the Z. I. R. response.

"The other reason I'm calling is that I've lost touch with Najinski and Thurston and his assistant and it is on them we are relying for the final piece in the jigsaw – the motive. I have an unfortunate feeling that this loss of contact is not accidental."

"That could be a problem. Without a motive the US State Department is indicating they will lean very heavily on us to avoid openly accusing China of serial killing."

"My contacts in Singapore are saying the same thing – and if anything, with China being our regional economic superpower, we have even more reason not to want to upset them."

"So," said Schultz, "with the US dragging their feet not wanting to get into a diplomatic incident with China and Singapore dragging their feet trying to preserve one of their most sacred cows, what odds would you give us?"

"I think I would leave the bookmakers out of it and start praying," said Lee.

# CHAPTER TWENTY-ONE
## *The Kidnapping*

*Nepal TV Studio Pokhara*
*3rd July 2001, 5:45 p.m.*

Thurston was fuming with frustration. The technicians were still "having problems" with their mobile phones, the land lines were still down and Jha and his team had still not completed the missing cash movement sections. Thurston and Najinski had finished their own sessions, subject to any fine-tuning needed if there were any surprises in the missing sections.

Jaci should have arrived in Singapore two or three hours before and he was concerned, not just for her personally, but to know that she had managed to get to Philip Lee with the final link.

However, frustration was about to give way to something rather worse.

Just after ten to six the door into the studio opened and Major Jha appeared carrying a folder of papers. He marched straight up to Najinski and Thurston.

"First the texts for my two remaining sections," he said, handing both one of the single sheets. "But you may find the second item to be of greater significance," he added, handing over the envelopes. "These letters have come by courier from a part of the city where the telephone lines are not affected. I am afraid that neither is the bearer of good news."

Thurston's immediate apprehension was that this had something to do with Jaci. He was right.

*To Edward Thurston:*

# The Tissue Trail

*It is a matter of serious concern that you are disputing certain aspects of the caravan arrest report. This report is important to us and to ensure your complete compliance and cooperation, both Sheila Najinski and Jacintha Linthorpe have been taken into our care.*

*If you wish to see these ladies again unmarked, and we have in mind rather more than incisions to ear lobes to which Philip Lee's money tracer was subjected, you will follow instructions to the letter and not make any attempt to contact anyone outside the newscast working group.*

*It has proved helpful to us that Miss Linthorpe survived the recent taxi incident in Singapore.*

There was no name or signature but the reference to the two earlier incidents left no need for further identification.

Thurston glanced across to Najinski who was looking white faced; the letter in his hand shook.

"They've got Sheila," Najinski said quietly, his voice also shook.

Thurston turned to Jha who was standing watching them impassively.

"I suppose you're going to tell us you know nothing about this."

"I am just the platoon commander," said Jha. "I just do as I'm told. But I have explained ad nauseam why this is so important to Nepal…"

"Bullshit!" Thurston exploded. "This has nothing to do with the Nepal Government."

Jha smirked at Thurston's outburst and was about to reply when the door to the studio opened again and he stopped immediately, the smirk disappearing. An athletically attractive blonde woman came into the room with two well-built Nepalis in attendance. She was wearing black close fitting expensive looking jeans and a fashionable shining black leather anorak. Her hair was swept up into a ponytail. She wore little make-up and the stark white light of the studio emphasized her strong, almost angular, jaw line.

"So we meet again, Mr Thurston." she said with an amused smile.

"So it would seem," said Thurston turning to address Victor. "I think you may recall me mentioning Ms Stephanie D'Aunay?" Thurston said by way of introduction, emphasizing the "Ms"

"So this is the charismatic Victor Najinski," she acknowledged, turning briefly to look at him before turning back to ask Jha how things were going. Jha deferentially moved so that she turned away from Thurston and Najinski and spoke quietly to her.

She turned back, standing with her legs slightly apart, "So even after what you have just been told you are still feeling rebellious, Thurston?"

"If looking for accuracy in what we are reporting is rebellious, then yes," he replied.

D'Aunay stepped forward, swung her right arm back and brought it back with a wide arc and struck him hard across the face. Two of Pandeh's guards moved closer to his side, hands on their weaponry.

Thurston passed his hand over his smarting cheek. "You may have the upper hand," he said, "but there is no need to treat us like idiots."

"I think we are in a position to treat you in any way we wish, Mr Thurston – but our only concern is to ensure that you and Victor Najinski here transmit the newscast as per script."

"Even though you've kidnapped my wife?" Najinski asked icily.

"Don't be naive Najinski; all you need to worry about is getting the job done according to contract. Although on second thought you may wish to worry about the fact that from here I am in charge of the caravan arrest and the newscast. Your instructions for the immediate future are that you may move about within the confines of the hotel or the studio as long as you are accompanied by Inspector Pandeh's security men."

"But without telephone, Internet or cell phone contact," said Thurston.

"Correct."

"So we are in effect captive and incommunicado?"

"I don't necessarily agree with your choice of words, Thurston," she said, "but you seem to have a good understanding of your position."

Jha was standing next to her – "Gentlemen, we will arrange something for you to eat either here or in your rooms at the hotel, whichever you prefer."

"Do you have any objection to us eating together?" asked Thurston sarcastically.

Stephanie D'Aunay stepped in front of him and grabbed his face with her right hand, with just enough force to enable her nails to make an indentation in his skin. Looking into his eyes she said, "Perhaps in the next few hours, Mr Thurston, we will have an opportunity to see just how brave you really are?" She slowly released her grip continuing to look into his eyes then turned and spoke briefly to Jha before walking towards the door.

"I'll see you in the morning, gentlemen," she called back as one of Jha's men opened the door for her.

Thurston recalled her demeanour in Changi Airport Customs enjoying her moment of control. But this was at a whole different level and once they were up in the high Himalaya she would have no constraints over how she chose to enjoy her power. As he and Najinski walked out of the studio, Najinski said, "That woman is a nasty piece of work, not a good idea to get on the wrong side of her."

"Might be a bit late for that," said Thurston rubbing his face. "What was it Jaci had said? *I didn't have a good feeling about this trip from the start and it hasn't got any better.*"

The two of them were escorted under Pandeh's guard from the studio back to the hotel and to Najinski's suite, choosing not to converse until they were alone or at least out of earshot.

Thurston's thoughts were fragmented. Thinking of Jaci he knew that throughout the last three to four months a "connection" had grown between them that was beyond the close chemistry that can develop between professionals. He thought of Emily and how he had learnt from her death what it was like not to appreciate how valuable something was until it had been lost. Now, he thought, it might happen to him twice in a year. He berated himself for not reading the situation for what it was and allowing Jaci to be alone in Nepal, even as it had seemed at the time, for just a few minutes.

His second concern was for Victor who he reckoned was not as mentally strong as his flamboyant demeanour suggested, and who would not be at his best in the extreme weather conditions they would face at and on the way to Lo Manthang.

His third concern was how on earth they were going to get their conclusion regarding the "the motive" to Philip Lee or to Barry Schultz at CNN now Jaci had been intercepted, and they had no phone or Internet connection. And now they were about to disappear into a remote part of the Himalaya where it would not matter whether their mobiles were operational or not. The one remaining channel of communication was the video satellite equipment and the test transmission.

With Pandeh in attendance there was little opportunity to talk, although Thurston did ask Najinski what was happening regarding his satellite video equipment and the team operating it. Najinski told him his team were due in first thing on Wednesday morning, intending to unload at Pokhara Airport and to transfer the equipment to the heavy duty helicopter ready for the flight to Lo Manthang. Thurston asked if that wasn't cutting it a bit fine to which Najinski replied this kind of last minute movement was par for the course in the news business. Talking business, he was still able to converse normally. But back at the hotel, Najinski was still in a state of shock. He had been in enough tight scrapes reporting from the world's hot spots but this was different, with Sheila in the hands of this group. Whoever they were they had shown that human life was of little consequence. It was not a situation Thurston had experienced before either but somehow his mentality was more pragmatic – finding it natural to take the view that unless he got on with trying to make things happen he had no chance of finding a way out.

Thurston and Najinski were served supper in Najinski's suite not that either had much of an appetite. Two of Pandeh's men were stationed at the door. Thurston had checked the windows out onto the balcony and found them firmly locked. Then he searched to see if he could find any sign of microphones although not being in the business he wasn't sure what to look for. But for what it was worth, he could not see anything obvious. Najinski managed a thin smile at Thurston's spy antics. At least it helped take his mind off Sheila.

Over a spicy soup, Thurston asked Najinski what he made of Jha's now completed broadcast sections. "Pretty much what we expected – full on focus on the money flow into Tibet. If that hits the wires the Tibetan goose will be well and truly cooked."

"Which puts even more pressure on us getting the Olympic Games motive out to CNN."

"Well I hope you have one or two bright ideas," Najinski said. "I'm a complete blank."

He was, however, beginning to get used to the idea that Thurston would have some sort of suggestion whatever the situation, although in this case he wondered if even Thurston might find ideas hard to come by.

"Well all we've got at the moment is the test transmission – just a few seconds and Jha watching us like a hawk. In the spy movies they would come up with some kind of prearranged code or signal so the first question is, do you press boys have any kind of universal procedure in place to tell the other end you are in trouble?"

Najinski considered the question. "No, I've been in enough scrapes to have come across anything like that if it existed. All you can do is improvise on the spot using words you would never use or wear a hat you would never wear and hope they notice. Why, has something occurred to you?"

"There is something. Although I can't see it being quite enough."

"Well let's hear it."

"If a pilot loses normal voice communications with air traffic control he can enter a number into a thing called a transponder which shows up on the ATC radar screen to identify his flight and his position."

"Great help!"

Thurston ignored him. "Normally ATC tells the pilot to 'squawk' the number he wants him to use as his ID. But there are three numbers the pilot can enter of his own volition to indicate trouble – 7700, which indicates an emergency and 7500 – hijack is in progress – 7600 is wireless buggered."

"So all we need is an airplane and get it hijacked?" asked Najinski unimpressed but still with his sense of humour in place.

"Patience, Victor. Suppose we tell our hosts that for a satellite test transmission we have to start the test message with a recognized CNN code to prove the message is kosher."

"Go on."

"And the code we use is say 'squawk 7700 7500,' i.e. emergency – hijack in progress.

He waited for Najinski to register what he was saying then went on, "Even if there isn't a flier watching the transmission they'll know there's something wrong if the message starts with a bunch of hieroglyphics they've never seen before. And if nobody recognizes what it is, the next step is to Google it and they'll get an idea in a few seconds just from the word 'squawk.'"

"OK. So that tells them we've got a problem – then what – please tell me there's more?"

"There is and it's pure genius," said Thurston, his imagination on full burn now he was into flying. And trying to take his mind off their predicament.

"Airports have short ID codes as in LHR is Heathrow, JFK is New York."

"OK," said Najinski, "I think I can get my head around that."

As a private pilot Thurston always carried his flying license, logbook and IATA handbook in case an opportunity came up to fly. He already had the handbook open in front of him.

"If I tell you the Beijing code is PEK and Moscow is SVO what do you make of this?" Thurston laid out a clean sheet of paper and wrote:

*PEK motive SVO 7/16*

Najinski looked at it for a few seconds and became almost animated. Pulling out a felt tip he wrote on the next line:

*So the whole message is...*

*Squawk Emergency Hijack in progress*

*BEIJING motive MOSCOW 16 JULY*

"You're catching on. We could even bring LXA for Lhasa into it and really start to get adventurous," said Thurston.

"Let's not get carried away here. I'm more worried about them not realizing these are airport codes."

"God, you're hard work, Najinski. By starting with the squawk emergency numbers they know we're into flying language so it shouldn't take a bunch of bright world travelling hacks long to see it."

"OK," said Najinski. "And I don't suppose a team at CNN would take long to get to the Moscow IOC Meeting from that. Yeah, could work, but how do we get that into the test text?"

Thurston thought about it. "How about a second page in the test transmission – we make sure the first code page gets out in a few seconds then hope we can get away with a second page without being spotted – some kind of bullshit story like testing for focus with large and small print. We could even try a short message."

"Worth a try," said Najinski. "Not more than one hundred words though and preferably half that."

"But the other problem we've got is that it is going to look as if the Olympic Games hosting is the motive and we have to find a way of telling them it goes much deeper than that. So if the CNN team is going to get to this cold they are going to have a bit of a problem, so I think they are going to need a bit of help."

"Like what?"

"Not sure."

Having come up with something constructive the gloom lifted a little and the two men spent another couple of hours playing with different ideas.

Thurston said he was sorry Najinski had gotten involved in the caravan arrest resulting in Sheila being kidnapped. "You obviously have a close relationship."

"You're right," said Najinski. "It works pretty well. We get on even though we spend a lot of time apart with my travelling. Sheila occupies herself with an antiques business she runs on a small scale on the net. So the time when we get back together is special, a kind of recurring novelty if you like. And what about you – you seem to be getting on pretty well with Jaci?"

"Yes, can't deny that and obviously our hosts think so, too, or they wouldn't have bothered to intercept her – although who it is that has been close enough to draw that conclusion is a good question."

Najinski puckered his brow, "That is a good question."

Thurston started to collect his case and papers to take his leave. As he did so he said, "Talking of relationships between professionals, Victor, you mentioned being closely connected in Beijing. Is that a good story?"

"You've been around long enough to know how things can get pretty close between people you are thrown together with in business – it doesn't have to undermine a relationship like Sheila's and mine. In fact, if your main relationship is strong enough it can add to it. In this case the person I was close to in Beijing added some pretty significant colour to the overall picture."

"Like the suggestion of revenge?" Thurston smiled. "Have a good sleep, Victor. See you tomorrow."

"I don't think I'll be sleeping much tonight," said Najinski. "I'll play around a bit more with your message ideas."

At the door Najinski stopped.

"What is it?" asked Thurston.

"My close contact in 1993," Najinski was looking thoughtful.

"Yes?"

"She was a junior member of the Beijing Government in 1993, I mean really junior, a second secretary or something similar but close enough to the action to know what was going on. But she has continued to make progress and the last I heard of her, she was head of the Commercial Section in the Chinese Embassy in Washington."

"How long ago was that?" asked Thurston.

"Actually only about three months ago."

"So you've kept in touch with her?"

"Couple of times a year."

"You think she could help us?"

"I don't know, but I thought I would mention it. Coming up with ideas is your department."

"Do you remember her name, Victor?"

"Oh, yes," said Najinski. "Chen Lanju."

~~~~~~~~~~

Back in his room, Thurston tuned to the local news station on his bedside radio to try to pick up the latest headlines. The station was focussing on the imminent breaking of the Tissue Trail ring and the hope for rapid recovery of the economy as a result. There had been no new development with the women on death row in Changi, although press and media worldwide were reporting last minute efforts to stop the hangings.

The newsreader also reported that the Security Police were expecting to make another significant arrest in the Tissue Trail case in the next twenty-four hours. Thurston wondered who else would be in the firing line.

### Yak and Yeti Hotel
### 4th July 2001, 5:30 a.m.

Najinski and Thurston ate an early breakfast in Najinski's suite as Jha had told them they intended to take-off early to beat the wind in the gorge. As predicted, Najinski had not slept well, if at all, and instead had been working on the one hundred word summary both for the second test transmission page and a script for a hurried last minute transmission to CNN in Delhi.

He had in fact got a pretty good summary down to around forty words in a mixture of old telegram and text message abbreviations.

Thurston skimmed it then read it again slowly. "Pretty crisp, Victor. Good thinking, but one good idea deserves another. Isn't there somebody who was even closer to the action? Your Chen Lanju lady?"

Najinski hesitated.

"What's the matter, Victor, worried about skeletons getting out?" Thurston allowed himself a light smile.

"No you Pom! Just thinking that is one of your better ideas, she was in the front row in 1993 and is now a respected operator in Washington. Not far off being brilliant!"

Thurston was still in what he liked to call his "Einstein mode." "The difficulty is how to frame a question to her. She is not going to want to incriminate her employers."

"There's not much we can do about that from up here," said Najinski, "let's hope US diplomacy can handle it. Whatever, I'll add her name to Philip Lee's and I'll get the boys to set the kit up with these two pages already built in to the test transmission." He stopped and frowned. "I suppose you realize that this could just be signing Sheila's death warrant? Not to mention Jaci's."

Thurston had been waiting for him to bring this up and was ready to try to reassure him. "Look, if we pull this off, the people holding Sheila and Jaci will see it on TV and head for the hills like rats from a fire. They won't have time for anything else."

"You are an incredible optimist, Thurston."

"Only because I don't much care for the alternative."

Najinski printed a page bearing both sets of text with the instruction across the top:

*TEST TRANSMISSION*

He printed four copies and gave two to Thurston.

"You're becoming quite a good bullshitter, Victor."

"No worries, Edward. In my business I've had plenty of practice."

"A few lives depend on this particular bullshit," said Thurston quietly.

The two men stood hesitantly facing each other then let it go and hugged, each wishing the other good luck.

~~~~~~~~~~

In the lobby, Stephanie D'Aunay and Major Jha waited for them, together with Inspector Pandeh and six security men. Thurston and Najinski had dressed in heavy outdoor gear with wind, rain and cold protection, plus dark glasses and goggles. They almost looked like Himalayan climbers!

"Good morning, gentlemen," said the blonde. "I trust you have slept well but whether you have or not we must move. The forecast for the gorge is for wind at 10:30 a.m. – a little earlier than usual."

"Any sign of our mobile phones?" asked Thurston.

"I'm afraid not," said Jha. "The technicians think they have found a solution and hope to fix them today but they would not be of any use anyway. Once we take-off there is no signal."

"Why am I not surprised?" Thurston said under his breath.

"I will need to check with the camera team," said Najinski.

"They are already waiting at the airport," said Jha. "You will be able to check with them then."

### *Kathmandu, 6:45 a.m.*

The two men were escorted to the four-by-fours and driven to the freight section of Tribhuvan Airport. Jha sat in the front with the driver, the glass partition closed. They swept like royalty up to the ex-Russian Mi-17 which was surrounded by Nepali Security Police, the CNN camera crew, and airport staff in a melee of activity. The huge squat helicopter with a low rounded body and five drooping rotors created the impression of a giant mechanical spider. In fact, an ugly giant mechanical spider.

Thurston had flown in one of these before, flying to Lukkla on the Everest side. "You pile your rucksacks and travel gear into the centre, rope it down, then the punters sit on the floor around the edges leaning on the side walls."

"Good start," said Najinski. "I'm expecting to die on this flight anyway – the least you could have done is arrange a bit of comfort."

"Tough," said Thurston. "Blame the Russians."

At Najinski's request, he and Thurston were escorted to the area where the camera team was checking their equipment. Najinski spoke at some length to the senior man. Initially, Inspector Pandeh stood in close attendance and listened to the conversation but once satisfied that it was simply about equipment and technicalities, he moved out of earshot but left two of his men on guard. As soon as Pandeh was out of range, and taking the risk that the two less senior men would not be too hot on English, Najinski told his technician, David Sterling, that what he was about to say was going to sound pretty irregular. For reasons that would become apparent, he was to continue to act as if the conversation was normal and to avoid looking surprised.

"Things are not as we would like with this broadcast and we strongly disagree with what we are being forced to transmit."

"I thought these security guys were looking a bit heavy," said Sterling.

"So we have come up with two ways of getting our own message out. One is typed onto two pages which have been folded neatly to fit into the palm of my hand and I will pass them to you when we shake hands at the end of this chat. We'll be telling our hosts that we need to send a test transmission with pre-planned codes so that Delhi can check that we are who we say we are. We need you to get these messages into the unit somehow – so the text is included in the test transmission."

"Shouldn't be a problem," said Sterling. "What's the second idea?"

"If that doesn't work we want to have a fall back. The idea is to get one of us to be able to transmit for thirty seconds and repeat the second test sheet words. The question is, can the kit be left on and ready to go – so that if an opportunity comes up we can react instantly?"

Sterling thought about it, "I think you could do it, Victor, you are familiar with the equipment – it would be more difficult with someone who hasn't used it before."

"I would prefer it to be Thurston, he seems to be happier with this cloak and dagger stuff."

Thurston was standing a little distance away looking at the equipment. Najinski and Sterling joined him. "We need you to know how to operate this," said Najinski. "And now is as good a time as any."

Sterling started to show him the ropes. Stephanie D'Aunay immediately walked up to them.

"What's the delay? We need to move."

"We're just checking we know how this works in case Sterling here gets mountain sickness or any other problem."

"Do it on the flight," she ordered. "We need to go."

She looked at Thurston with a sort of malevolent anticipation.

### Flight to Lo Manthang, 9:00 a.m.

As Thurston had predicted, they sat on the floor leaning against the sides of the helicopter.

Sterling had arranged for the equipment to be laid in front of them secured to the deck but open so the controls could be seen. They went over the procedure repeatedly until both Thurston and Najinski could repeat it back to him without the slightest hesitation. Sterling had been in the Signals

Corps and it showed. During the conversation Najinski managed to transfer the folded sheets of paper without being seen.

The helicopter laboured into the air with its heavy load and headed west towards Pokhara and the Annapurnas. The weather was overcast and there was no sight of the southern wall of the Himalaya, instead the main impact on the senses was the roar of the engines and the rattle of metal on metal as the heavy vibration shook the old machine. There was little opportunity for conversation.

Sterling appeared to be checking his technical manuals but Thurston could see he was reading and, it seemed, marking the test sheets. Thurston then saw him insert the test sheets into something at the back of the manual as if he was updating the text with a new bulletin. Jha and D'Aunay were watching but didn't seem to think he was doing anything suspicious.

He then pulled a video camera and extension towards him and asked one of his men to hold the manual up so he could take footage of some of the pages. It was difficult to do this with the heavy vibration and gusts of wind making it difficult to hold the camera steady. Finally Sterling was satisfied. "Test transmission texts in place," he told Thurston and Najinski openly.

Najinski was not terribly interested. The roar and vibration of the engines plus the increasing gusts of wind were about as much as he could handle. Stephanie D'Aunay had become more closely interested when Sterling started taking video shots and was clearly indicating to Jha that she was not happy. Jha passed a roughly scrawled message to Najinski:

*We need to see what has just been recorded.*

"I think I can hide it," said Sterling in a low voice to Thurston. "We have a backup recording cylinder so we can store footage we want to hold back and send later ..."

Thurston nodded, hoping his attempt to look unconcerned was more convincing than it felt.

### *Overhead Pokhara, 10:00 a.m.*

It took an hour from take-off from Kathmandu to reach Pokhara where they had originally intended to land but with the anxiety to beat the wind they kept going. Sterling kept working with equipment recording and videoing both voice and pages from the manual. From time to time,

Thurston stood up to look out of the window and check their position and after passing Pokhara and Lake Phewa he stayed upright as they passed over Ghorapani and Poon Hill; then they started to turn slowly north into the gorge.

"This is where it could start to get choppy," Thurston told Najinski.

"Thanks," said Najinski still sitting on the floor. "I thought it already was."

Two minutes later Thurston added, "Victor, even sitting down there if you look up and out of the window you will be able to see the peaks of the Annapurnas. We are flying at about 12,000 feet. Those peaks you can see are Nilgiriand Annapurna South both 12,000 feet above us."

"Am I supposed to be impressed?"

"Yes, you are supposed to be absolutely bloody amazed!" said Thurston.

They were now well into the gorge and though the wind was giving the helicopter a bit of a pounding, it was not going to be a major problem.

Stephanie D'Aunay was spending her time on some sort of military telephone, presumably keeping track of happenings on the ground at Lo Manthang.

"Hopefully the good lady will share the news with us at some point," said Najinski.

Thurston stood watching progress as they climbed out of the top of the gorge and over the village of Kagbeni and onto the Tibetan plateau, then over the fortified villages at the end of vertically sided ridges. But his mind was elsewhere, wondering where Jaci was and feeling totally helpless. He had given Najinski the most optimistic outlook but in Jaci's case as opposed to Sheila, they would know that she had been close to the action throughout and even if their plan succeeded she could still be a threat to them. The outlook for her was not good. And of course the same applied to him. This took his memory back to Stephanie D'Aunay's projected test of his bravery.

The "lady" finished her latest telephone call and came over to them with Jha close behind her. "Just to update you gentlemen," she shouted over the noise, "everything is going to plan. The return loads have been transferred from the low-level animals to the yaks ready for the return trip to Lake Drabye. Nepal Security have confirmed their intelligence that heroin is being carried in small sachets in the return loads of cereal. When we land and are in position with your cameras ready to go Najinski, we will first record the security men locating the heroin sachets. That will be followed by

Inspector Pandeh describing to the leaders what they have found and that will be followed by the arrest of the four leaders who will be handcuffed and led back to the helicopter."

Najinski had called Sterling over to listen to the briefing. It was Sterling who told D'Aunay the first thing his team needed to do was to send a thirty second test transmission to Delhi and wait for their confirmation they were receiving and it was at the right strength and quality.

"What does the test consist of?" she asked.

"We take live footage of the location then check text focus from medium and short ranges."

"What were the papers you were discussing on the ground at Kathmandu?" she asked.

Sterling didn't bat an eyelid. "Mr Najinski keeps the identification codes secure until the last minute as part of our security procedure, so that if the equipment is intercepted by unauthorized operators and they try to transmit without the security codes, head office will know straight away."

"So what did Najinski write Sterling?"

"Three airport codes and two squawk codes."

"Squawk codes?" she queried. "Perhaps you had better show me the paper?"

Thurston's spine shivered. He hoped it didn't show as much as Najinski's suddenly white complexion. He looked at Sterling wondering how he managed to look so calm but thinking, *How the hell are you going to get out of this?*

Sterling put his hand in his inside pocket and pulled out a sheet of A4 and spread it out on his knee.

There were three codes and two numbers written in heavy fibre pen:

**SQUAWK KAT POK LMTG 5000 6000**

In the process of setting up the test transmission, Sterling had the foresight to produce another page.

D'Aunay turned to the anchorman. "And what do these codes mean, Mr Najinski?" Thurston held his breath acknowledging that the lady was in fact pretty bright.

"They are air traffic control codes for the airports involved in this transmission – Kathmandu, Pokhara and one we've made up as it doesn't have a code yet – Lo Manthang.

"And the numbers?"

"Random, no significance."

She turned to Jha, "Show this to our pilots when we land, Major."

"And I think we had better inspect your test transmission before you send it, Mr Sterling."

"Of course," he replied.

When she had returned to her position, Thurston spoke under his breath to Sterling, "Smart, now how do we get out of showing her the test?"

"Working on it," replied Sterling, looking straight ahead.

*11:30 a.m.*

Thurston watched as the helicopter slowly approached the walled city. He could see the yak caravan some three to four hundred yards further towards the snow covered horizon denoting the border of Tibet. The helicopter approached slowly, trying to avoid causing panic amongst the animals. It landed some quarter of a mile short of the city walls about 800 yards from the caravan. Despite the distance, some of the yaks unused to any mechanical noise had become agitated, some had started heading away from irritation towards the border.

The landing was gentle and the machine sank slowly onto its suspension cylinders. The pilots quickly switched off the engines and less than a minute after touching down, the doors were opened. The first to alight were the six officers who would carry out the arrest, their immediate role to ensure the caravan and its leaders did not become too dispersed. Inspector Pandeh sent the squad off towards the caravan simply to take up position. The remaining security officers formed a guard for the six strong CNN party including Najinski and Thurston.

Jha had brought a small four-by-four jeep looking vehicle for his own and Stephanie D'Aunay's transport, which was being eased down a ramp. It had a rack of electronic equipment mounted at the rear.

"We will help you carry your video satellite equipment to the transmission point," said Jha.

"Very kind," said Sterling, "but it's pretty portable and we're used to moving it into new positions at short notice."

"As you wish," said Jha. "But you have come up to 13,000 feet pretty quickly without acclimatization and we don't want you or any of your team to be affected by AMS."

Sterling looked blank.

"Acute mountain sickness," Thurston explained. "Remember I briefed you to be alert for headache or heavy persistent coughing?"

Sterling nodded in acknowledgement adding, "What I would like to do is finish the assembly now, then we can carry it ready to go." Sterling looked meaningfully at Thurston, which Thurston took to mean they might be able to record during the half-mile trek to the caravan.

Pandeh came over and handed the A4 sheet to D'Aunay, "The pilot confirms that these are the IATA codes for Kathmandu and Pokhara and that the numbers are random."

She handed the sheet back to Najinski. "So far so good," she said. "But we will need to see your test transmission. We had better see that before we start moving, we can pick it up on our monitor." She pointed at the rear of the jeep.

### 12:15 p.m.

Sterling set up the video camera and it started running.

After a few seconds of indeterminate flashing images, the screen steadied and showed the code he had shown D'Aunay and Jha on the flight – LAT POK LMTG 5000 6000. This image clicked off and switched to live shots of the immediate surroundings, the dry desert terrain, the grey brown lower hills, the snow ring at the horizon and, as he turned to his left, the walls of Lo Manthang. He lifted the angle of the camera to take the brilliant blue sky —"as a test of maximum light intake," he explained, "we then take shots of pages of the operating manual to check that we can transmit copies of documents." He held the manual open while a cameraman took video of the pages and showed how they came up on the screen.

"So we could include the arrest warrant?" D'Aunay asked.

"No problem."

"Then all I think I need to do now is to examine your manual?" she asked with a smile of self-congratulation.

Thurston was already thinking he hoped that the stand by recording would work as their airport and squawk code effort was about to be discovered. He exchanged glances with Najinski —still looking as pale as a sheet – although that could have been down to any of a dozen reasons.

Sterling handed over the manual, seemingly without concern. D'Aunay started to turn the pages slowly and deliberately. Thurston waited for the outburst or the acid remark. After thirty seconds, she reached the final page. There was no reaction. Thurston looked at Najinski hoping he did not look surprised.

D'Aunay looked a little disappointed and handed the manual to Jha. "Please make sure I haven't missed anything, Major."

Jha also examined the manual carefully. His reaction was the same. There was nothing untoward.

"I'm a little disappointed, Thurston," she said, still looking attractive in her close fitting black jeans, heavy duty black outer zipped jacket which came almost up to her nose and a black long peaked hat. "I had expected you to be a bit more resourceful. In fact, I was looking forward to a bit more of a challenge."

"I am sorry to have disappointed you," he said without expression. She took a step toward him but whatever she had in mind she stopped herself muttering, "patience Stephanie" under her breath.

"Let's go," she said and climbed into the jeep which drove just ahead of them.

Thurston walked alongside Sterling who was carrying part of the satellite equipment.

"How did you do that?"

"Got the paper into blank compartment in the cover of the manual. It was only two sheets, remember? And the content of your test sheets I recorded while messing with the kit on the flight but recorded it on the reserve can."

"So when do you suggest getting that sent off?"

"I was going to suggest now, on the way to the caravan, but as they've got a monitor they would pick it up. So we'll have to wait until we've finished the main transmission and try then perhaps, when we're packing up."

"OK," said Thurston. He moved away from Sterling and towards Najinski who was definitely not his normal ebullient self.

"You don't look your normal self, Victor."

"I don't feel my normal self, in fact, I've got a bit of a headache."

"How bad?"

"Just a headache so far. Nothing dramatic."

"OK, but let's not take any risks. Take a couple of these." He had a pack of Diamox in his waist bag, "You shouldn't be getting this, Victor, it normally picks on fit young men!"

Najinski managed a pale smile.

"One thing I'm not looking forward to," said Thurston, "is the look on Tensing's face."

"Yeah, he's not going to be too impressed is he?"

"No he's not and that's after they've found heroin sachets he won't know anything about."

They walked slowly and in silence towards the caravan, the weather calm, the sky clear blue, the temperature -15 degrees Celsius. A fading moon hung over the snow-ringed horizon.

Pandeh's arrest party had fanned out and taken positions beyond the caravan to prevent making a break towards the border. They would not try to break back towards the gorge as the lower altitude would not suit the yaks.

Tensing knew Jha after several meetings while ACAP was setting up the new load and provided the extra funding to pay for its transport – although this took the form of additional cereal and other supplies as coin money had not penetrated the remote high Himalaya of the semi-nomads' homelands. Seeing the armed agents approaching had puzzled Tensing more than alarmed him and then, seeing Jha and Thurston approaching, he had actually broken into a smile.

Jha had picked up a bit of the Tibetan dialect in the course of the earlier meetings, but he had a fluent Tibetan speaker with him.

Sterling and his camera team took up positions close to where the leaders were gathered around what had been an overnight camp fire and started taking live shots which showed up on the monitor the jeep was carrying. Tensing and his men had seen themselves on screen before – on Thurston's video camera screen three months earlier. But this was bigger and even more dramatic and the excitement was palpable.

Tensing welcomed Thurston and Jha warmly. So far he had no reason to do otherwise although it would not take long before he started to ask what was going on and the reason for the presence of Jha and the armed men.

Once the excitement had died down, D'Aunay instructed Najinski to take an introductory shot of herself as a member of the International Drug Liaison organization and Jha as head of ACAP and to "make the on-screen introductions."

"Now let's go through the actions and record the scripts, again," D'Aunay instructed.

With Sterling operating the video camera, Jha led Tensing and the other three leaders to one of the yaks and opened one of the phadsee (salt sacks) finding several white sachets in the neck. Jha opened a sachet and invited Tensing, now looking concerned and apprehensive, to first smell then taste the white powder. Tensing frowned, not understanding what was happening or what the white powder was until the interpreter told him. He said something to his co-leaders, each looking from Jha to Thurston to the camera, confused and terrified.

Jha opened two more of the salt sacks with the same result. The contaminated sacks had obviously been marked.

Jha nodded to Pandeh who called his men in – one to stand closely by the side of the four leaders. D'Aunay was watching the monitor on the back of the jeep with a look of satisfaction. Pandeh was handed a document which he proceeded to read in English first and the interpreter repeated in the dialect. Sterling was shown the document and told to video record it.

Pandeh proceeded, "Harka Tensing, we are arresting you and the leaders of this caravan. You are charged with involvement in the production of heroin namely the supply of a key intermediate used in its production and secondly taking heroin back to Tibet for distribution. Anything you say will be taken down and used in evidence. You will be taken into custody in Pokhara pending further proceedings."

The interpreter looked at Jha, unsure how to translate the last phrase.

"Just say pending trial."

The four men, two in tears, were handcuffed and stood under guard a few yards from the rest. Their wives gathered in panic around Major Jha clamouring in fear and panic trying to understand why their men were being taken. Pandeh's men moved them back none too gently. Tensing had looked questioningly at Thurston who could do nothing except offer a barely perceptible shake of the head. Tensing was looking back helplessly and bewildered, his wrists tied behind him.

The video shots were as dramatic as Najinski had predicted with a perfectly deep azure sky, the desert foreground, the snow fringed horizon, the ancient walled city, and the yak caravan.

Against this background, Thurston and Najinski, with Pandeh's men in close attendance but off camera, completed their sections as per script.

D'Aunay told Najinski to repeat two of his sections as his voice was so low and lacking in energy that as D'Aunay put it, it was "like listening to a corpse."

"I take it we can edit out the 'dead sections,'" she laughed, "and replace them?"

"Yes, we can do that," said Sterling flatly.

Jha completed his cash tracing section with obvious enjoyment and he announced that the raw material was "in the can."

"Except for one final section," said Stephanie D'Aunay, her tone somewhere between menacing and anticipatory.

"We do not believe the caravan operators could have played their part without expert assistance. We are satisfied that we know where that assistance came from. Mr Sterling, please make sure you are continuing to record."

She turned to Edward Thurston and waved Inspector Pandeh forward.

### 2:45 p.m.

Pandeh stood in front of Thurston.

"Edward Thurston, you are under arrest, charged with aiding and abetting the process of diverting part of the load of acetic anhydride from the caravan operators to manufacture diamorphine hydrochloride or heroin at the dispensary in the International Clinic at Pokhara. On a second count you are charged with aiding and abetting the organization of transportation of heroin to Singapore by at least one of the five accused. Anything you say will be taken down and may be used in evidence. You will be taken into custody in Pokhara pending further processing." Two of Pandeh's men had moved to either side of him, hands on their weapons.

Najinski came to life and stood looking wildly around him.

"What on earth are you doing...?" he didn't complete the sentence. One of Pandeh's men punched Najinski in the stomach, stopping him instantly. Another stood in front of the camera. Jha told Sterling to switch it off.

"We will add the final section and edit the tape when Mr Najinski has quietened down."

D'Aunay walked up to Thurston pushing her face close to his, "You may remember in Singapore I told you I had enough to hold you – and since then things have only got worse from your point of view. As it is I think we will need a further chat when we get back to Pokhara. I shall look forward to it." She turned to Pandeh, "Please handcuff Mr Thurston."

Najinski recovered but no longer inclined to argue. Stephanie D'Aunay smiled at him, clearly enjoying herself.

"Imagine the hero turns villain headlines now, Mr Reporter –the hacks will have a field day. And the unkindest cut of all," she continued, "the man who had the brains to work out what was behind the Tissue Trail affair – well nearly – finds his brains turned against him helping us strengthen the one weak part of the plot – the ability of the Tibetans to produce the heroin using the intermediate from the caravan. The one thing you didn't spot was the small poppy field at Naudhara, just behind the palm oil plant, where the Tibetans had grown the heroin poppies. One of the beauties of Nepal is that with the variation in altitude, temperature, and climate, some part of it will be suitable for growing a heroin poppy crop and of course they did not need very much of a crop to produce one hundred grams of substance."

Thurston's mind was a kaleidoscope of realizations and self-recriminations and remaining questions starting with Jaci's bad feeling that this was not a good situation and was going to get worse; Lauren Chase had suggested that Jaci should come up to Kathmandu for the preparation of the video to make it easier to intercept her; that it was Lauren Chase who had personally persuaded him to participate in the CNN newscast as the technical expert. And that had resulted in his contribution, virtually serving as his "confession"; it was Lauren Chase who, within ninety-six hours of him making contact with the caravan in the first place, had picked him up at the hotel, set up the case against the Tibetans and even suggested that he was a "news magnet" who could become useful in dissemination of the message when the time came. Could she have envisaged all that from her very first contact? Did it matter that Lauren Chase was Canadian, even French Canadian and so were Stephanie D'Aunay, Pierre and Jacques? It was after all Canada which poured millions into Nepal in aid including the whole caravan intermediate/palm oil plant initiative; what was the Canadian role, if any?

And the thought which was the granddaddy of them all – the real sickener – that this would explain why he had survived when so many others close to the Tissue Trail affair had been removed even though they had admitted trying to take out Jaci. He had been the perfect fall guy from not long after his first interview with Jha, and probably from his "interview" with Lauren Chase.

# The Tissue Trail

His overarching emotion was anger at his own ineptitude in not giving more thought to the nonsense of his survival. And that, despite his success in working out what lay behind the Tissue Trail conspiracy, had failed to work out, despite all the signs, that he himself had been a significant element in their plot from the beginning.

And now he had to endure the final step in the process. "Mr Najinski, we can now complete the final missing section," Stephanie D'Aunay said, handing him and David Sterling a sheet of text. "This will be inserted after Thurston's arrest."

Sterling recorded Najinski narrating the text from autocue:

*"I had not been made aware of Edward Thurston's role in this affair until the last few moments. This is an unexpected and surprising development. But when I think back the evidence is formidable.*

*Edward Thurston is a chemist and an expert in drug manufacture and earlier this year he chartered a 19-seater aircraft to get through the Kali Gandaki Gorge to reach Lo Manthang where he was in talks with the caravan leaders. This raised the suspicions of Nepali's Security forces in the first place and led to them to observe his contact with the operators of the palm oil plant from where the intermediate was diverted and with the dispensary at the Pokhara Clinic where the heroin was manufactured. But he was involved, not just in the production of the Tissue Trail heroin but, it seems, with the women carrying it to Singapore. He travelled with Catherine Miller, the British woman due to hang in less than twelve hours from now, first from Pokhara to Kathmandu and then with her onward flight from Kathmandu to Singapore. He was so close to her that he caught her when she fainted outside the office where she was arrested. It is standard practice for traffickers to travel with their mules or carriers.*

*There are in fact strong indications of Thurston's wider involvement in drug trafficking. Nepal's enquiries into his activities through the international drug liaison network reveal that he has travelled extensively in drug production areas including recently both the Thailand and Afghanistan heroin poppy growing regions and that as a result has led to the British tax authorities investigation of his rapidly rising income.*

*A few weeks ago, Edward Thurston was a local hero after rescuing a dying mountain girl, but today he is being taken away in shame. And so with the arrest of the one time hero it appears that the final link in the Tissue Trail drug ring has been identified and closed. And Nepal and its tourist industry can breathe easily again."*

Sterling held the shot for a few seconds, then D'Aunay ordered him to stop the recording. She turned to Thurston, legs slightly apart as if she was going to have another go at removing his head, but if that was in her mind she restrained herself.

"How do you like that, Mr Thurston?" she gloated. "Not quite as clever as we thought we were eh?" She pinched the flesh of his neck and twisted it making little effort to hide her enjoyment in inflicting pain. The shock of it brought him to his senses and he told himself to stop wasting time looking backwards – there would be plenty of time for that. He started to try to work out where things would go from here. His first thought was that David Sterling was intelligent and resourceful and would now understand how the land lay. But getting the "motive messages" back to CNN was now going to be largely out of Thurston's hands.

D'Aunay instructed Najinski and Sterling to go back over the arrest recording with Major Jha adding in Najinski's introduction to Thurston's arrest then editing into the clean final form.

In fact, after inserting Thurston's arrest, deleting Najinski's dead sections and removing the remarkably well-recorded section of Najinski being winded, nothing else was needed. D'Aunay was happy with the section introducing herself and Najinski at the opening and told Sterling to start transmitting from that point. The two treatments – the introductory headline version and the longer explanatory versions in all took eleven minutes to transmit. The transmission was completed at 3:32 p.m. Nepal time, which was a quaint quarter of an hour ahead of Delhi and ten hours forty-five minutes ahead of Atlanta where it was 4:17 a.m. on Wednesday 4th July. The overnight shift of the international news department was monitoring news screens from around the world.

Thurston was led away to join the other prisoners, thinking that it wouldn't take seconds for anyone with the remotest knowledge of the true sequence of events to realize that what Najinski had just recorded was impossible. His charter of the Otter was supposed to be his first contact with the Dolpo Pa but this was only a few days before the first arrest of women carrying heroin into Singapore. Of course there had been no reference to time-line in the script Najinski had been forced to read. And the Tissue Trail operators only needed the value of Thurston's involvement and arrest for the duration of the transmission. By the time his involvement was found to be as artificial as the rest of it there would be far bigger fish for the press to fry. "What a disaster," he thought.

Najinski and Sterling walked back towards the helicopter. Najinski was looking pretty down; Sterling was still carrying the action part of the video satellite camera.

"It may not be as bad as you think," said Sterling under his breath. "Using the reserve cylinder I think I've managed to send everything – including your sucker punch."

"You know David, it's pretty sobering, but there was not one statement in that piece on Thurston's arrest that was actually a direct lie. Just omission and innuendo – producing a result that was a total travesty."

"I know – we carry a pretty heavy responsibility. One word out of place can alter the sense of almost anything."

# CHAPTER TWENTY-TWO
## *The Reaction*

### *CNN Offices New Delhi*
### *4th July 2001, 1:30 p.m.*

Barry Schultz had issued instructions that any communication connected to the Tissue Trail affair should be alerted to him immediately whatever he was doing.

As a result he was watching the first ACAP satellite transmission from Lo Manthang as it came in at 3:15 p.m. local time. It led with the astonishing arrest of Edward Thurston with, at first hearing, a good case against him. But his second reaction was, if this is all he was going to get, it was of no use to the women in Singapore. Even so, he immediately transmitted it onwards to Atlanta and told his own team to stand by. "We can only hope that there will be something else from Najinski."

### *CNN Head Office, Atlanta, Georgia*
### *4th July 2001, 4:30 a.m.*

Barry Schultz's transmission from Delhi was on the screen being watched by the CNN Atlanta night duty staff one of whom, Ron Stein, was fully briefed on the Tissue Trail affair.

Stein watched it with the identical reaction to Schultz —amazement at the arrest of Thurston who he had been told was responsible for unravelling the conspiracy, and secondly that there was nothing here to help the Tissue Trail women; not even anything to justify getting the CEO out of bed and definitely nothing to justify getting the Secretary of State out of bed.

He had also been told that without a viable motive the Swiss bank would not budge on the final source. They would be laughed out of court. In fact, they wouldn't even get to court.

An hour later, one of the night shift team was monitoring the CNN news screens from around the world. From Honolulu to Helsinki and London to Las Vegas every screen was covering manoeuvres by courts, media empires, governments and still the UN, pressuring Singapore to relent. Then suddenly one of the screens changed. It was Kuala Lumpur, significant because it was next door to Singapore. A new headline appeared:

### *TISSUE TRAIL EXECUTIONS BROUGHT FORWARD*

The rest of the screens followed like a collapsing line of dominoes, all with the same basic report – a clear indication of an organized leak:

> *Rumours are circulating in Singapore that the first four Tissue Trail executions are being brought forward from six a.m. on Friday 6th July to six p.m. on the evening of Thursday 5th July in an attempt to take the steam out of protests scheduled for dawn on Friday.*

### *CNN Offices New Delhi*
### *4th July 2001, 4:10 p.m.*

Nearly an hour after the first video transmission, the satellite receiver started to come to life again.

The monitoring team watched as a brief fifteen second transmission came through from the Lo Manthang crew:

*TEST TRANSMISSION*
*Squawk 7700*
*Jaci Sheila N 7500*
*PEK motive SVO July 16th*
*Verify Lee, Chen Lanju*
*Chinese Embassy DC*

Ron Stein looked at it with his mouth open and brow furrowed.

"What on earth is this gibberish? Can someone call Barry!"

Barry Schultz was there in seconds but ten others had beaten him to it. All looked at the screen in bewilderment. Nobody knew what the code was.

"What's this about Jaci and Sheila? Is that Najinski's wife?"

"Looks like it with 'N' behind it."

"Who the hell is Chen Lanju?"

"What's PEK?"

"Let's start at the beginning," Schultz interjected, trying to establish some sort of order, "Can somebody Google 'squawk'?"

Several pairs of hands attacked several keyboards.

"What's the old name for Beijing?" somebody said while fingers continued to tap.

"Peking," about six voices said at once.

A few seconds later, "PEK is the International Airline code for Beijing airport."

"So we're in airline speak?" asked a voice.

"That's right," said another voice. "I've got 'squawk' on Google. It's the term air traffic control uses to tell pilots what ID code to use so they can track them on the screen."

"So what about 7700 and 7500?"

More finger work.

A female voice scored the next point. "I've got it. Squawk 7700 is emergency, 7600 radio failure, 7500 is hi-jack in progress. They are predetermined codes pilots can use to send messages to ATC."

"So Jaci and Sheila Najinski hijacked?" queried Schultz.

"Kidnapped?" said a voice.

"That's got to be it," said Schultz, "7700 means emergency or something's wrong. If Thurston's been arrested and the two women arrested you're damned right something's wrong. And that means what they're sending is under duress. What about the rest of it?"

"It looks like they're using PEK to mean Beijing, what about SVO?"

The woman was winning with the airline codes. "That's the old code for Sheremetyevo airport, that's Moscow."

"So Beijing's motive is connected to something in Moscow on 16th July? Talk to me people," Schultz demanded.

A short pause then the woman again, this time quietly, "Only the IOC meeting in Moscow."

"Great," said another reflecting the deflation felt around the table.

"So if it is the IOC meeting, what's on the agenda there?"

"Voting for the 2008 venue?"

"Olympic Games hosting. Surely that's not enough?"

There must be something else.

Schultz studied the short message, "It looks as if they are expecting to have a problem with this – that's why they're suggesting another source, and a Chinese source at that. I'll get onto Atlanta. If she's in Washington they ought to be able to track her down."

"They'll have to move fast. We've got less than twenty-four hours."

Schultz went back to his office and telephoned the overnight crew in Atlanta.

"We've got something through from Nepal but so far it doesn't seem to help much."

He described what they had seen.

"Better get it over here anyway; even if Olympic Games hosting doesn't sound as if it's going to cut the mustard."

The satellite receiver in Delhi came to life again thirty minutes after the first message. Another single page only a third used:

*4:15 p.m.*

> *Urgent Schultz CNN*
> *Caravan arrest final step. Chinese media plot to blame Tibet just b4 executions and IOC2008 vote 16 July. To verify see VN BBC 1993 report VN media orchestration study and Z I R cash reports. To verify check Chen Lanju VN Govt contact Beijing 1993 Now Embassy DC.*

### Delhi
### 4 July 2001, 4:18 p.m.

Schultz asked his PA to get Philip Lee on the phone, "Wherever he is and whatever his is doing." And also asked her to dig out the report Najinski had done just after joining in 1993. He remembered the report clearly but he had never dreamt that the Chinese reaction would have gone this far.

# The Tissue Trail

*Delhi, 4:23 p.m.*
*Singapore, 6:53 p.m.*

By the time his call had got through to Philip Lee, Schultz had almost finished reading Najinski's 1993 BBC report. When his desk phone rang he grabbed the receiver. "Thank God I've got you! We have contact with the Lo Manthang crew but no good news I'm afraid. The Nepalis have arrested Thurston on a charge of aiding and abetting and Sheila, Najinski's wife, and Jaci Linthorpe have been kidnapped. So whatever they transmit is coming under duress."

"Why on earth have they arrested Thurston? That doesn't make any sense," said Lee.

"It wouldn't stand up in court but they managed to make it sound good rolling out everything from his flight to Lo Manthang through to catching Catherine Miller at Changi. And of course it adds a shipload of credibility to their overall anti-Tibet story."

"So that's Thurston and Jaci out of the action and we still haven't got a clue as to the motive?" asked Lee, not even trying to hide his exasperation.

"Not quite true," said Schultz. "They have sent a short piece with the test transmission stating that this effort to blame the Tibetans for the Tissue Trail executions is linked to the Chinese reaction to losing the Millennium Games in 1993."

"I don't follow," said Lee.

"The Chinese blame the Tibetans and their western sympathizers for their loss of the Millennium Games which was seen as a political disaster in China. To prevent it happening again they have manufactured this worldwide furore over the western women lining up to hang and blaming the Tibetans with this broadcast just before the 2001 vote for 2008 games."

There was a pause, then Lee said, "Which would remove or reduce anti-Chinese western sympathy votes."

"Exactly."

Another pause.

"And kill sympathy for Tibet not just now but for years," said Lee thinking out loud.

"So you think this could be right?" asked Schultz, his voice conveying considerable surprise.

"I do not agree with what they have done, in fact I violently disagree

**348**

with what they have done, but politically it is ingenious."

"It's almost as if you've seen the report Victor Najinski wrote for CNN when he first joined?"

"Well I haven't. Why do you say that?"

"Because this is exactly what his analysis suggested after talking to his Beijing contacts —taking a firm line on maintaining law and order and at the same time looking for opportunities to show what happens when good order is sacrificed for other considerations. In this case, tying it in with an Olympic Games vote provides a perfect media focus and an opportunity to gain a degree of revenge for the 1993 debacle."

Another pause before Lee said, "As a broad general principle I agree with their approach. For a multi-ethnic continent like China you either make good order your priority or you allow the country to descend into destructive ethnic chaos. However in this case, leading five young women to execution as a means of generating then controlling a media storm cannot be remotely justified. But that is not the issue here."

"What is then, Philip?"

"That none of these young women knew they were carrying heroin but under Singapore law they must hang. The only possible escape is to prove that this Tissue Trail affair is politically motivated and for the Singapore authorities to be persuaded ... or forced to accept that no crime in the true sense of the word was committed."

"So where are we now in establishing your proof?" asked Schultz.

"The combination of the Thurston/Najinski broadcast tape, Najinski's media orchestration evidence and what we have seen today leaves no doubt that it is the Chinese who are the architects. But proof beyond doubt, which the prosecutors are looking for relies on evidence from the Z. I. R. Bank that China funded the operation. And Z. I. R. are holding out on client confidentiality grounds until they are satisfied that there is a clear and present motive. With regard to the motive, Najinski's BBC report you tell me is pretty compelling, but I would be happier if there is some more direct evidence, somebody who was actually there."

"There may be a chance there," Schultz told Lee. "One snippet of information they managed to transmit is that a close government contact of Najinski's in 1993 is still active and is on the staff of the Commercial Department at the Chinese Embassy in DC."

"Why on earth did he not tell us about this guy before?"

"The guy is actually a girl, but I don't think that is relevant. I don't know the answer to that but something in the circumstances in which Thurston and Najinski found themselves in the last two days has unearthed this Chen Lanju. We've got Atlanta trying to track her down. Let's hope she's in town. How are we doing for time?" asked Schultz.

"It is 6:15 a.m. in Singapore, just under twelve hours to execution," said Lee. "And I'm due at the prison to update the women with the latest situation."

### Atlanta
### Eleven hours to execution
### 4th July 2001, 6:00 p.m., (local)
### 5th July 2001, 7:00 a.m., (Singapore)

CNN Chief Executive Alistair Shawshank had been alerted and joined the team.

Stein carefully briefed him with everything that had come through.

"Bloody European bankers, if they would get off their fat arses it would be a no brainer."

Neither Stein nor Schultz in Delhi commented.

Shawshank carried on, "I reckon this Chen Lanju woman is going to be important. I think in view of the time I'd better try and shortcut this and get in at the top. I'll have a word with my man on the Hill."

While he was waiting for the call to go through he asked Schultz if he had given any thought to who should speak to Chen Lanju assuming "she was on the planet."

"I'd assumed you would have to go through channels and it would be somebody at the State Department," said Schultz.

"Trying to brief somebody new with this can of worms would take a week," Shawshank responded. "So it needs somebody who is already up to his eyes in the detail. And as seventy-five percent of those who fit that bill have gotten themselves arrested or kidnapped, our choices are a bit thin."

"If you're really pushed," said Schultz, "I could give it a crack."

"I've got a better idea," said Shawshank, "Chinese to Chinese – Philip Lee."

*That's why he's CEO,* thought Schultz.

"Now that I can handle," said Schultz. "Do you want me to call him?"

# The Tissue Trail

"No Barry, you've done a great job, but I'll take over from here. But stay on the line and listen to this."

Shawshank's phone was buzzing. It was his "man on the Hill."

Schultz was on a conference line to Atlanta so couldn't hear the "man on the Hill" responses, but he didn't need to.

"Now hang on to your hat for the next bit. We've had a load of traffic via satellite in the last couple of hours and everybody from Singapore to Sing Sing is totally convinced that these crazy sons of bitches have set up this Tissue Trail business as a political manoeuvre to reduce sympathy for Tibet. It's both a general long-term objective but in the short term it reduces Tibetan sympathy votes going against China in the 2008 Games vote next week. I'll go through the logic with you but the killer for me is that Philip Lee, the defence attorney and Chinese himself, is totally sold."

Schultz liked the way his boss had twisted it around so that the hard to sell Olympic aspect became a subsidiary to the more easily understood long-term objective.

"In Chinese terms it's only five lives, Alistair – being brutal about it. For them it's a small price to pay —but bottom line there is nearly enough here for me to run with it. But there is something we need your help with. The Chinese Embassy have a woman on their staff who was a junior in the Beijing Government in 1993. Apparently Najinski knew her when he was with the BBC. In fact it's Najinski who has managed to let us know about this woman by satellite from 13,000 feet up in the Himalayas."

"No there is nothing about this case which isn't screwball. He is probably dying of mountain sickness as we speak. But the important thing is he reckons this woman will backup Lee if we can ask the right questions. And she was right in the middle of it."

"Where is she? She's in DC?"

"I'm suggesting that once we, or rather you've made official contact, we get Philip Lee to talk to her. He's Chinese and he knows the case inside out."

"OK, Alistair. Get back to me as soon as you can when you've located her. We need to speak to her tonight. Hope you hadn't got anything lined up for 4th July!"

Shawshank laughed, "He just said we already get two bites at the British cherry. Thanksgiving to welcome them in and July 4th for kicking them out – so this year we'll have to make do with just one of them. At least Lanju won't be too fussed about 4th July."

351

Shawshank looked at his watch. It was 6:20 p.m. Wednesday 4th July in Atlanta, 7:20 a.m. Thursday 5th July in Singapore. Ten hours forty minutes to execution.

Schultz called Philip Lee partly to tell him Shawshank would be taking over for CNN, then to ask if he would be prepared to talk to Chen Lanju, if they could find her. Lee confirmed that he would be delighted to talk to Chen Lanju.

### Atlanta
### 4th July 2001, 6:25 p.m., (local)
### 5th July 2001, 7:25 a.m., (Singapore)

Alistair Shawshank phoned to say they had located Chen Lanju – she was on a flight back from Denver and not due to land at Dulles International until just before midnight.

"We have told the Chinese we have an urgent matter to discuss and they will make sure she is informed as soon as contact can be made to call into her office."

"Midnight, that's one p.m. in Singapore – just five hours to go. This is getting very tight."

Shawshank maintained close contact with Philip Lee who in turn kept Warrender informed. And Warrender maintained the all-important contact with Z. I. R.

### Lo Manthang
### 4th July 2001, 6:00 p.m.

Stephanie D'Aunay and her growing entourage returned to the helicopter and took shelter from the falling temperature and, unusually, the rising evening wind. She had spent thirty-five minutes with the pilot talking to Air Traffic Control at Jomsom just north of the gorge. She finally announced that the wind was too strong to fly back tonight and that they would have to spend the night as best they could in the helicopter and leave hopefully at first light in the morning.

Major Jha told them there were emergency rations for just an eventuality.

As people were trying their best to find places to lie down there was a moment when Thurston made eye contact with Harka Tensing who lifted his handcuffed wrists showing his curiosity as to why Thurston was in a similar predicament. All Thurston could do was offer a faint smile and a slow shake of the head.

### Lo Manthang
### 5th July 2001, 5:30 a.m., (local)
### 5th July 2001, 8:15 a.m., (Singapore)

It was not a comfortable night although Thurston, used to rough travelling, managed a few hours sleep facing towards the centre of the chopper and rested his head on his overnight bag. But looking at Najinski's drawn face and haggard expression, Thurston could tell he had little, if any, sleep.

### Pokhara
### 7:00 a.m. (local)
### 9:45 a.m. (Singapore)

The weather was calm and the helicopter took off just after first light. They landed at Pokhara where both Thurston and the CNN crew including Najinski were taken to staff quarters at the airport. Inspector Pandeh's men were, as usual, in close attendance. The caravan leaders were seen being taken from the flight but were not seen at the airport accommodation.

Thurston was taken to a separate single room. He was anchored to the bed by one end of the handcuffs.

Two sandwiches and a glass of water had been left within reach and he proceeded to despatch them as a survival breakfast.

At 7:30 a.m. Stephanie D'Aunay came into the room, still looking smart but not looking pleased.

"I am concerned that CNN has not, so far, broadcast the arrest." She pushed him back on the bed and sat astride him. The last time this had happened it had been Jaci and the hour that had followed had been intensely pleasurable. The omens for a repeat performance were not good.

She leaned forward repeating her predilection for gripping his face with her curled fingers and thumb but this time there was no holding back and she drew blood before lowering her hand and repeating the grip, but this time with his windpipe. With her weight on his chest and her left knee pinning his free arm he could not breathe and was unable to do anything about it. Surely she wasn't going to finish him off now he thought – if there was something wrong she would need to know what he knew about it.

He felt her fingers relax her grip on his throat and the weight of her knee lift from his free arm. He opened his eyes to see the expression he was becoming too familiar with – the mixture of malevolence and enjoyment.

"Not yet Thurston," she said, "but if this is not resolved in the next two or three hours we will have to go a little further."

She slapped him hard across the face in both directions then got off him and left the room.

### Dulles International Airport
### 4 July 2001, 11:00 p.m., (local)
### 5 July 2001, 12:00 p.m., (Singapore)

The flight crew had told Chen Lanju that her embassy would like to speak to her when she landed and they had arranged for her to be taken to the business section of the first class lounge. They had not given anymore detail except that a lawyer would like to speak to her from Singapore.

She was smoothly whisked away from the flight as soon as it had docked and taken by electric trolley to the lounge.

There was no one else in the lounge except for a stewardess who made sure she was comfortable and brought her a cup of a China tea. She rang the embassy and was told that the lawyer who would like to speak to her was Philip Lee, a defence lawyer in the Tissue Trail case. That is all they knew, but if she needed any help or advice the ambassador was standing by.

"I see," she said, "the ambassador up at this time of night. This is heavy duty."

She dialed the number. After two rings, Philip Lee answered.

"I am sorry to inconvenience you at this time of night..." Philip Lee started but she immediately interrupted him and in Mandarin asked him a number of questions to confirm his identity. He confirmed that he was calling about the Tissue Trail affair.

"I cannot begin to imagine how I can be of assistance, Mr Lee, but please proceed and may I first ask, or perhaps I should say confirm, that this conversation is being recorded?"

# The Tissue Trail

"It will not be recorded until we reach a point where you agree to it being recorded."

"Then do go on."

He went through the preliminaries to confirm that she was aware of the Tissue Trail cases and that the first executions were imminent. "It is from this point I would like to record the conversation," he told her.

"I understand, but for reasons I am sure you will appreciate, I need to be circumspect in what I say and to re-record if on reflection I am not happy with my initial answer."

"Agreed."

"In the course of my work on the defence I have been involved with a man called Victor Najinski —who I believe you know or have known?"

"Let me listen to your questions, Mr Lee, and if I have a comment I will say so. If I do not comment you may take it I am not objecting to your statement. Yes, I do know Victor Najinski."

"I believe you were both in Beijing in 1993?"

Silence at the other end.

"And you were in government at the time of the loss of the Millennium Games to Sydney in 1993?"

"I was what the British call an assistant private secretary."

"Najinski reported to CNN when he left the BBC that Beijing had reacted badly to the loss of the Millennium Games hosting and to what he reported as the catastrophic loss of face."

Silence.

"There were serious repercussions, with sackings and resignations and responsibility for the next application to host the Olympic Games was removed from the Sports Federation and given to a specially constituted Policy and Operations Group. That is to say they were not just to draw up plans but also to implement them?"

"That is a matter of record."

"Let us call it the POG to save time." He sensed her smile.

"Can you describe the brief the POG was given?"

"I would prefer to answer specific questions."

"But you know what the brief was?"

"I know what I was told at the time but I do not know if anything changed after my involvement ended. Mr Lee, can you tell me where this is going?"

"We are in a position, where if we can provide an informed and respected opinion on certain questions, it might still be possible to achieve a stay of execution for the condemned women."

"I understand."

"Is it your opinion that the Beijing Government in 1993, put part of the blame for the failure to secure the 2000 Games on the loss of votes due to western sympathy for Tibet?"

Silence.

"Did the POG brief include taking action to reduce sympathy for Tibet as Victor Najinski reported?"

Silence.

"CNN is planning to make a worldwide broadcast in the next few hours which will clearly indicate that Tibet and the Tibetans have organized the Tissue Trail trafficking. Do you have any comment?"

"Please wait a moment," she said, considering her reply. After a few moments she said, "No, I do not have any comment."

"It is being suggested that this broadcast will have the effect of reducing sympathy for Tibet and prevent China losing sympathy or protest votes —as occurred in 1993."

Silence.

"From what you know of the brief, would the effects of the CNN broadcast as I have just described them, achieve the objectives set out in that brief?"

"A moment please." After a few seconds she said, "Yes, the effects you describe are consistent with the objectives set out in the brief."

"Thank you. This brings me to my final two questions. From what you know of the Tissue Trail affair and in particular what I have just told you, is there anything which is inconsistent with the brief to the POG?"

Silence.

"And finally, if Beijing had been involved in this is there anything which Beijing would not have sanctioned?"

"Wait a moment please." After a few moments she replied, "I am not privy to government policy on what would or would not have been sanctioned. I think you will have to weigh the effects as you have described them, against the actions taken and draw your own conclusions."

Lee considered her answer then said, "I do not think I can ask you to go further than that. I am very grateful for your help."

# The Tissue Trail

"There is one additional observation," Chen Lanju said, "The POG was asked to produce a plan which would achieve long term as well as short term political objectives."

Lee considered the point. "Thank you again. I think I understand the significance of that last remark."

"To the extent that I may have helped, what do you intend to do with this information?"

"In the first instance we will be passing it to the Board of a Swiss Bank."

"You must explain that to me sometime."

"Perhaps you might prefer it if I ask Victor Najinski to explain?"

Silence.

And then she said, "Good luck."

He put down the phone.

To his assistant he said, "I think if she had added 'think of Tiananmen Square' to her 'draw your own conclusions' sentence, her feelings on this could not have been clearer. As it is I think her carefully worded addition regarding achieving long term political objectives was as far as she could go to tell us that our conclusions are right – and that she is not over the moon with what has been set up in the name of law and order. Let's hope our Swiss Banker friends are bright enough to see it and let's hope we still have time!"

He read through the transcript once more then scanned it, then e-mailed to Schultz, Shawshank, and Warrender.

He closed with the sentence:

*I am Chinese as is Chen Lanju and we are satisfied that the Tissue Trail affair is a conspiracy wholly consistent with the intentions of the Chinese after the events of 1993. The evidence compiled by CNN strongly supports this conclusion.*

To D. C. Rahman, Lee added:

*We therefore ask the Government of Singapore to stay the executions of Catherine Miller, Francois Dumas, Birgit Heller, Maria Gonzales, and Karen Leopold, pending a review of the political position which these circumstances create, irrespective of the strict legal provision.*

He scan faxed the document to CNN Atlanta, CNN Delhi, NCIS London, and to D. C. Rahman.

The time was 11:45 a.m. in Atlanta, 1:45 p.m. in Singapore. Four hours fifteen minutes to execution.

*Offices of Z. I. R. Bank*
*Geneva, Switzerland*
**5th July 2001, 5:45 a.m., (local)**
**5th July 2001, 1:45 p.m., (Singapore)**

Rousseau and Lassale were also taking advantage of staff sleeping accommodation with a junior on duty to alert them to any incoming phone calls or e-mail relating to the Tissue Trail case.

At 5:47 a.m. the e-mail from Lee copied to Warrender with both his own reaction and that of Chen Lanju, pinged onto the monitor. The junior alerted both men. A strong coffee awaited them when they appeared a few minutes later. The printed off reports lay on the desk.

When they had finished reading the reports it was Lassale who spoke first.

"I think the wider political perspective set out both by Lee and Chen adds credence and I think the way she answers Lee's last two questions confirming Chinese involvement without incriminating herself, is brilliant."

"But?"

"It's a finely balanced judgement but I must stick to my position. Breaking confidentiality in my opinion could be the death knell for the bank whereas even if the executions proceed any reference to the bank will be limited to a few seconds in the backup detail of CNN's broadcast from the wilds of Nepal, and will be buried in the furore surrounding the executions."

Rousseau looked angry, "And that is your final position?"

"It is, but I repeat it is a fine balance. If we became part of the headline news as opposed to a footnote, I think the balance of judgement would change."

"Then there is nothing more to say for the moment," said Rousseau. "We will have to wait and see what CNN will do. I had better let Lee and Warrender know."

The rest of the board had all signed statements each giving Rousseau and Lassale authority to make the final decision. They could not take the risk of communications breaking down trying to reach all eight members.

Rousseau's e-mail to Warrender was timed at 6:50 a.m. in Geneva, 2:50 p.m. in Singapore; three hours ten minutes to go.

~~~~~~~~~~

On receipt of his copy of the Chen Lanju interview and Lee's own statement, Barry Schultz took two actions.

First, he personally went live onto the Far Eastern CNN Networks under a "BREAKING NEWS" banner and took an action, which had nothing to do with saving Catherine Miller or the other women. Using the video opening of the Lo Manthang transmission showing Stephanie D'Aunay and Major Jha, together with photographs of Sheila Najinski with her husband from file and of Jaci with Edward Thurston taken during the video assembly at CNN's offices in Singapore, he produced the following News Flash:

> "Stephanie D'Aunay of International Drug Liaison and Major Jha, a Nepali civil servant, shown in this caption, are being sought by Security Police and Drug Enforcement Agencies on suspicion of kidnapping the wife of CNN's reporter Victor Najinski and the beautiful young assistant of Edward Thurston —recently in the news for saving the life of a mountain girl in Nepal. Both women are believed to be in danger. Anyone with any information regarding the whereabouts of Jha or D'Aunay please call urgently on either of the two numbers given below."

His purpose was simple if crude – to try to cause panic amongst those working for D'Aunay or Jha.

Schultz knew he was putting his job on the line but he was determined to do what he could to help Najinski and his wife.

The first of his News Flashes went out at 3:45 p.m. in Singapore, 1:00 p.m. in Pokhara.

Secondly, he checked with Shawshank who immediately approved. It was a second "Breaking News" Flash designed to pile the pressure on the Z. I. R. Bank and the Singapore administration:

# The Tissue Trail

"We are hearing strong rumours that there are significant developments in the Tissue Trail case in Singapore with only hours to go to the first executions. We understand that the defence team is close to convincing the Singapore authorities that the Tissue Trail affair is a politically motivated conspiracy in which the five condemned women were not involved other than having heroin secreted in their baggage without their knowledge.

It is being reported that Singapore has been waiting for two final pieces of evidence before finally reviewing the position and that the first of these was provided by a government official of a major power earlier this afternoon. The defence team is confident it can close the final link in the chain and hopeful that this can be achieved before the execution deadline of 6:00 p.m."

### Pokhara Airport
### 3:38 p.m., (local)
### 5:53 p.m., (Singapore)

Stephanie D'Aunay crashed through the door into Thurston's room followed by Pandeh and two of his men who proceeded to tie him firmly to the chair, D'Aunay in the meantime was standing over him, her hands on his shoulders shouting into his face.

"Desai has just noticed you have added ninety seconds to the time we needed for our transmission, what did you transmit you bastard?" She administered a double backhanded lash to his face, which drew blood from both corners of his mouth.

Thurston, still not speaking, wondered what methods of persuasion she would employ when she had finished bludgeoning his face to a pulp. He did not have to wait long. A third man was carrying a highly polished small wooden cabinet, which he placed on a table close to Thurston's chair.

D'Aunay sat astride his bound thighs looking down at him. The look in her eyes was not a pretty sight. "I can promise you, Thurston, you will regret not answering my questions more promptly." She gestured impatiently to the security man carrying the box with a motion telling him to open the lid. It contained about twenty small brown glass phials in three horizontal rows. "It is no good resisting," she said, "nobody can withstand the effects of this little box. I am told the agony is exquisite."

# The Tissue Trail

He did not respond and she removed the first phial from the centre of the central row. As she inserted the syringe into the inverted phial she told him that as a pharmacologist he would appreciate the pharmacology of the mixture of strychnine and adrenaline based injections – even without the chemicals, the sub-periostial injection was extreme in its effect. The varied dose levels, she explained, enabled her to balance the effect of the injection to match the individual's tolerance level. This way she could achieve maximum degree of pain while at the same time maintaining consciousness.

"Am I supposed to be impressed?" he asked, to quote Najinski.

She didn't even bother to slap his face again. Instead she ignored his bravado and, drawing the first dose into the syringe she explained.

"The real beauty of the technique is that injecting one side of the body creates an exquisite level of agony with the other side initially free of pain which accentuates the effect. Very clever, the Chinese—almost like a simulated heart attack."

She made the injection into the muscle of the upper arm and leaned forward, "I like to watch the eyes." The effect was everything she had promised. The penetration of the tip of the syringe into the sheath of membranous tissue lining the bone and the massive agonizing muscle spasm, first in the upper arm spreading across the right hand side of his body, caused him to try to arch his back and momentarily black out. The effect lasted about ten to fifteen seconds before slowly fading. He was trembling with pain and saliva dripped from the corner of his bloody mouth.

"It doesn't take long," she said smiling down at him, "if I don't want it to." She re-loaded her syringe. "This time the effect will last a little longer – and we can keep extending it. Not many people get past forty-five seconds before they are foaming at the mouth and screaming like a baby. Unfortunately, I haven't got time for some real fun —I need to know what exactly you have done to cause CNN to delay and what was in that transmission. Too much has gone into this to take any risks at this stage." She settled herself and re-injected.

He knew he could not withstand more of this and decided to try to speak while he could still control his jaw movements. She showed some disappointment that he had not put up more of a fight.

He told her that they had run into resistance with the credibility of their theory that the Chinese were behind the trafficking – as he had discovered on his first contact with Harka Tensing. The extra footage they had transmitted was to suggest they try to locate an old Chinese contact of Najinski's who had been in government in Beijing at the time of the 1993 vote.

"And why would that delay the transmission we sent out yesterday afternoon?"

"I presume the politicians are trying to work out who is telling the truth."

She started to draw a third injection. "If you have ruined this Thurston, I promise you a slow and agonising death."

The door crashed open for a second time and Major Jha burst in. "Stephanie, you need to see this."

She swore, "And just as I am starting to enjoy myself. Just a second, Major," she said as the point of the syringe touched his upper arm.

"This can't wait," she looked back at Jha, the expression on his face didn't leave any doubt.

She laid the syringe down on the table and climbed off Thurston but this time she didn't try and knock his head off— she administered a karate chop to his damaged upper arm muscle. He passed out.

When he came round, his arm still shuddering with pain, D'Aunay had not returned and through the open door he could hear the sounds of feverish activity including the sound of a television with its volume not far from maximum.

Pandeh's men had disappeared and he was in the room on his own. Seconds later, Stephanie D'Aunay appeared at the door with some sort of handgun. She raised her arm and fired shouting, "You bastard, Thurston!" then turned hurriedly and disappeared. The shot hit him in the shoulder muscle of the other arm. He was conscious of some pain although not as severe as he had just experienced – and a lot of blood.

For a few moments nothing happened until Gil Desai appeared and started loosening Thurston's bonds.

"What on earth's happening?" asked Thurston.

"CNN is running flashes of Stephanie D'Aunay and Jha and appealing to anybody who knows their whereabouts to contact them as they are wanted in connection with the kidnapping of Victor Najinski's wife and," he smiled, "your beautiful assistant."

"So what are they doing?"

# The Tissue Trail

"I think they realize that this broadcast isn't going to happen and that the whole Tissue Trail thing has collapsed. I think they are making a run for it. They got half their money up front so I suspect they are heading for the border with at least part of their spoils now their faces are plastered all over every TV screen. I've just seen them leaving at speed in one of the four-by-fours."

Gil Desai was clearly not part of this, other than as a professional television man. If there was any doubt his next comment confirmed it.

"Your Jaci Linthorpe is being held at the Pokhara clinic. As far as I am aware no harm has come to her – she has just been kept under sedation. I had better take you there to re-unite you and at the same time have that wound looked at." He had now finished freeing Thurston who immediately tried to stand up but needed Desai's help. He had very little use of either arm.

Desai looked at him as they walked as quickly as Thurston could with his useless arms and cramped legs. "You probably don't know but they've brought the executions forward twelve hours."

"What!" yelled Thurston, "what's the time now?"

"Half past one," said Desai.

"Good God, that's quarter past four in Singapore – only an hour and three quarters to go. Have you got a mobile phone I can borrow – and can we take one of your crew with us – I can't even press the buttons?"

"Let me do it," said a voice with an antipodean accent. "Jeez you look a mess, Thurston!" Najinski and David Sterling had come up behind him.

"I thought you might want to get together," said Desai handing Najinski his phone, "and Pandeh's men have lost interest with Jha disappearing."

"Good to see you alive and well, Victor. Any news of Sheila?"

"Not yet."

"Gil Desai has offered to take me to the clinic where Jaci is being held. Would you come with us – I'd like you two with me when I talk to Philip."

Najinski nodded. Thurston knew Lee's number by heart and Najinski dialed as Thurston dictated. Desai helped Thurston into the second of the two remaining four-by-fours.

"You know the executions have been brought forward, Victor?"

"Just heard."

"Can you hold the phone? I can't lift my arms."

"I'll put it on open line," said Najinski, just as Philip Lee picked up in Singapore.

"It's Edward, Philip, but no time for pleasantries. What's going on?"

Lee responded, "They located Chen Lanju and she produced a compelling insight which to me confirmed the Chinese role. The transcript of that is with CNN and D. C. Rahman and also NCIS so we therefore presume, Z. I. R. CNN is running news flashes – one saying there are major developments but without detail. Rahman's offices are saying they won't do anything without the details of the Chinese account confirming the link, and Z. I. R. is still refusing to reveal the details."

"What more could they possibly need?"

"Warrender says, reading between the lines, it looks as if they think they can ride out the storm and prove their resilience on the confidentiality front."

"So the lives of these three women..." Thurston started.

"Five women," said Lee, "I've just been told they are going to hang all five today. Four together, then one with another batch."

"Jeez, and Z. I. R. knows this?"

"They will shortly."

"What exactly does CNN's 'new development' flash say?"

"Not much more than that."

"So is there anything that would make Z. I. R. move?" asked Najinski.

They were now drawing into the entrance to the clinic, "Let's keep talking. Philip, we think Jaci is in the Pokhara clinic and we've just arrived there. But we'll keep the line open."

"Do you know if she is alright?" asked Lee.

"I think so," said Desai. "Jha has just kept her sedated."

"Why don't you go and check on her and call me back?" said Lee.

"OK," said Thurston, "and we'll see if we can come up with something to put a bomb under Z. I. R."

Desai went into reception telling them he was one of Major Jha's staff and that he wanted to see Jaci Linthorpe. The receptionist gave him the room number and told him the security man who had been outside her room had disappeared after seeing the major and Ms D'Aunay on the television. She asked a nurse to go with them adding that Miss Linthorpe had been very heavily sedated and may well not be conscious.

Gil Desai said he would wait for them.

The nurse opened the door to Jaci's room and went in, returning immediately. "She is actually awake. I told her she has visitors."

Thurston stuck his head around the door. Jaci's pale face looked toward him from the white pillow and after a moment checking she wasn't hallucinating said, "You've taken your time Edward," followed by, "and you look a real mess." Tears started to roll down her face.

He sat on the bed and she flung her arms round his neck impacting on both shoulders. He winced. "What's the matter?" she asked, pulling back.

"Long story – but right now I can't do much with my arms. But even more important we've only got just over an hour to come up with something to stop the executions in Singapore."

He called to Najinski to join them and quickly summarized the position.

When he had finished, Jaci said, "Seems to me the Swiss are banking on the probability that they will not actually figure much in the news. All the press will be bothered about is the women being executed."

Thurston and Najinski looked at each other and Thurston said, "While awaiting Ms D'Aunay's pleasure this morning I was playing around with an idea to put pressure on Singapore and Z. I. R. There is a sheet of paper in my breast pocket if you can fish it out, Jaci.

"The idea," said Thurston, "is to put down what the press would write after the executions when the blame game starts, and to send the draft to Z. I. R. and Singapore legals before the executions –the effect is quite dramatic."

## *CHINA, SINGAPORE AND SWISS BANK ACCUSED, AS WESTERN GIRLS HANG*

*The failure of a Swiss bank to reveal the source of funding for the Tissue Trail conspiracy resulted in five innocent women being executed in Singapore today. The Singapore Government was known to be demanding two final pieces of evidence to justify intervening in a Class A Drug case for the first time in its history. The first was revealed earlier today when evidence was produced virtually proving that the Tissue Trail affair was a politically inspired conspiracy. The second, and crucial piece of evidence required by Singapore, was held by the Geneva Bank Z. I. R. but the bank refused to disclose it under its private client confidentiality undertakings.*

*The Singapore Government was fully aware of the evidence*

*pointing to the existence of a Chinese conspiracy and that the women played no active part in the movement of heroin and could not possibly have known they were carrying heroin. They still proceeded with the executions.*

*The effects of this case on Swiss Bank confidentiality and Singapore's mandatory death penalty remain to be seen. The backlash in international relations will be more immediate.*

*END*

Desai had been typing it into his computer as soon as he had seen Thurston's copy. It was ready to send.

"To Warrender first," said Thurston, "then Lee and CNN. Let it go."

Thurston then tried to call Lee on his mobile.

Lee was on his way to Changi and had to take the call re-directed to his mobile. He told Thurston he would put him back to his office and ask them to take down the transcript and send it off to D. C. Rahman. Desai had already sent his copy to NCIS and CNN both in Delhi and Atlanta.

At 5:20 p.m. Singapore time the CNN post-execution article had been double e-mailed to Z. I. R., D. C. Rahman, Warrender at NCIS, and both Schultz and Shawshank at CNN.

### Z. I. R. Bank
### Geneva, Switzerland

The e-mail pinged onto the screen at 5:22 p.m. Singapore time. Rousseau and Lassale had finished reading it at 5:24 p.m.

Rousseau and Lassale looked at each other. Neither said a word. For the first time in many years, the two bankers broke into a run and arrived at Rousseau's PA's desk, breathless.

"Helene," said Rousseau, "please send the account declaration by e-mail to Philip Lee's office and send three times. Once you have done that please send to CNN and NCIS. Lassale is getting Philip Lee on the phone."

The account declaration statement from Z. I. R. pinged onto the screen at Philip Lee's office at 5:28 p.m. It read:

*Z. I. R. Bank confirms that it has been acting as a clearing and distribution bank for movement of funds at the request of the*

*Whickham Cay Bank of British Virgin Islands. We have not provided any banking services other than transfers of funds as requested.*

*At the Whickham Bank request Z. I. R. set up an account to transmit and receive funds to and from specified accounts in Lhasa, Dacca, Delhi, Karachi, Lahore, and other major population centres. The highest number of transactions, though not the highest volume of cash, has been to Lhasa in Tibet.*

*In addition to the movements listed above, payments have been made to individuals in Nepal and Singapore and Canada.*

*Following a formal request by ourselves to the Whickham Cay Bank they have advised that the funds which serviced these movements were received as a single deposit of $35M from the Development Bank of China, Yuetan, Beijing, in November 1996.*

Lee forwarded his copies to D. C. Rahman who passed on his recommendation to the Attorney General and President's offices. Lee estimated that all recommendations and supporting documentation were in the hands of the intended recipients by 5:44 p.m.

### *Changi Women's Prison, Singapore*
### *5th July 2001, 5:25 p.m., twenty minutes earlier*

Shortly after taking Thurston's call, Philip Lee made his way back to Changi Women's Prison. There was nothing more he could do, but he could be reached via his mobile or by the prison office. Philip's PA had standing instructions to call him if anything came in relating to the Tissue Trail affair which she did immediately— but he was already with Catherine Miller and reception was bad.

Z. I. R.'s e-mail was received by D. C. Rahman at 5:47 p.m.

Rahman immediately forwarded it to the president's office and telephoned to alert them that it had been sent. The time was ten minutes to six.

CNN received their copy at nine minutes to six and Shawshank instantly issued an order to freeze any further news on the Tissue Trail without his personally signed authority.

The president's office had the stay of execution drafted and ready for signature, but under established rules an execution could not be stayed without a signed hard copy. A signed fax was deemed to qualify. An e-mail attachment did not.

The president signed the order and issued instructions for it to be faxed to the Governor of Changi Women's Prison with an e-mail copy and telephone call to alert them to its imminent arrival.

The signed fax was sent at four minutes to six.

The telephoned alert and copy e-mail was received at three minutes to six.

The execution room was put on standby to receive the incoming signed fax direct to its own extension.

At two minutes to six the fax receiver rang and seconds later the printer started to print.

Fortunately, the president's office had the foresight to send the normal first page of disclaimers and caveats after the signed order page and this was later judged to have saved fourteen seconds.

### Changi Women's Prison, Singapore
### 5th July 2001, 5:55 p.m.

Catherine was manoeuvred into position under a noose at the left hand end of the drop plate and she heard the quiet whirr of the electric motor as the final, fine adjustments were made to the length of the noose. She started to struggle, tears rolling down her face. The executioner gently but firmly restrained her, then stood in front of her looking into her eyes and lowered the black felt hood over her head. She tried to scream but nothing happened. The noose was lowered into position and she felt the executioner's fingers gently press it evenly into position.

She thought she heard a heavy door open and more people enter the room. And she was sure that there was movement on the drop plate; she could feel the vibration. Then she remembered Lee saying something about two or three others being executed at the same time. She thought she heard crying but such awareness as she was capable of was concentrated on her own predicament and any external sounds were largely drowned by the heavy felt hood.

There was now perfect quietness as the executioner waited for the prison clock to chime at 6:00 p.m. Catherine was close to vomiting and was conscious of wetness running down her legs.

## The Tissue Trail

The completed signed order from the president's office was received by the Execution Chamber printer with the second-hand showing fifty seconds to go until six o'clock. The officer in charge grabbed the order, checked it with a quick glance then dashed the five yards to the door into the chamber – and without waiting to turn the door handle crashed through it and yelled, "STAY EXECUTION!"

Catherine did not hear the clock strike six, but jumped involuntarily at the sound of a violent crash.

Then... nothing. She waited, sure she had not moved. There was no pain in her neck and the drop plate still seemed to be supporting her feet.

She was sure she had heard the expected violent crash but instead of the reverberating echo she had heard so many times before, she was aware of the sound of agitated human voices, then hands grabbing her shoulders, strong arms around her lifting her —and the noose being loosened then removed. The hood was pulled up and over her head. The first thing she saw was Philip Lee openly weeping.

He managed to say, "I think we've done it!"

She fainted into his arms.

# CHAPTER TWENTY-THREE
## *The Aftermath*

No attempt was made to restrain the hugs, kisses, tears, and laughter. Catherine Miller was helped to a cubicle where she changed her underclothes.

Each was offered water or a fruit juice and sweet biscuits.

Philip Lee emotionally held Catherine in his arms for a full minute and then said, "There are one or two people who we need to inform." He sent a four-word e-mail, with text message copy from his mobile phone to D. C. Rahman, Edward Thurston, Victor Najinski, Jaci Linthorpe, Barry Schultz, Brian Shawshank, and Chen Lanju.

### TISSUE TRAIL EXECUTIONS STAYED

That message became the headline on almost every television news summary and almost every newspaper front page across the globe over the next twenty-four hours.

One paper printed:

### TISSUE TRAIL EXECUTIONS SLAYED!

Thurston and Najinski were still sitting in Jaci's bedroom at the clinic waiting for six o'clock. They were not aware that they were in an area with no mobile phone signal. At four minutes past six the telephone rang. Jaci picked it up and listened then handed the receiver to Najinski, "It's for you – from CNN in Delhi."

Barry Schultz said, "Two bits of good news, Victor. First, Sheila has just walked into a police station near the Red Fort unharmed." Victor Najinski momentarily stayed still and silent looking dead.

"She's safe!" he shouted.

Barry was still on the line but Victor was no longer in a state to listen and Jaci took the receiver back from him.

"Barry, this is Jaci. Victor's a bit excited."

"Nice to meet you," said Schultz. "And the other bit of news, if you don't already know, is the executions have been stayed!"

Now Jaci stopped dead, her lower lip started to quiver. She lowered the receiver. "The women are still alive," she told the others quietly holding her head in her hands, "they've stayed the executions." Her shoulders were heaving.

At almost the same moment Gil Desai yelled from reception, where he had only just succeeded in turning the television to CNN, "they've done it. They've stopped the executions."

"Whose side are you on?" Najinski yelled back.

"Once I heard both sides of the story it wasn't rocket science. I'm just the producer."

"I would like to hug somebody," said Thurston, "but I can't lift my arms."

Jaci's sobbing gave way to tearful laughter. It was an emotional few minutes. Then Thurston remembered Tensing. "Gil, can you take me back to the airport, I need to see what's happening to Tensing and his men – they will still be terrified and nobody will have told them what's going on. And I'd better find out if I'm still under arrest."

Jaci was already out of bed, a bit unsteady but pulling on her jeans, T-shirt, and sweater. "I'm coming too."

"Are you up to it?" asked Thurston.

"You are asking *me*?" her tear-stained face now laughing. "You look as if you've gone fifteen rounds with a couple of yetis."

"Let's all go," said Najinski, "we might even find a serious drink."

"Can you speak any Tibetan?" Thurston asked Desai.

"Not a lot, but a few words."

"You've got the job!"

Tensing and his three co-leaders had been held in an area normally reserved as a passenger waiting room. When the door opened and Tensing recognized Thurston and Najinski, his face lit up. Desai's vocabulary turned out to be inadequate for any meaningful communication but he managed to locate a member of the airport staff whose command of Tibetan was more helpful. Thurston told Tensing that he would try to sort things out in the morning and now that D'Aunay and Jha had left the scene he hoped that they would be able to return to Lo Manthang.

They returned to the arrivals hall where Desai went in search of someone in authority and returned with a middle-aged Nepali civilian, with two other men in suits flanking him.

Desai smiled, "This is the Deputy Mayor. We know each other and I've given him a quick rundown on what is going on."

He spoke in a local language and the council officer seemed to quickly grasp the situation. The Deputy Mayor then spoke in English telling them he would arrange for them to return to the clinic as guests of the town.

Najinski checked to see if there were any flights due out of Pokhara as he wanted to get back to Delhi to see Sheila as soon as possible, but he was told there were none until the morning. The Deputy Mayor started to organize a taxi but Desai said he would transport them back to the clinic. Thurston asked if he was still technically under arrest. The Deputy Mayor smiled and said he would sort that out in the morning.

### Pokhara International Clinic
### 6th July 2001, 7:00 a.m.

Desai had managed to set up a portable television away from the melee of officials and press men who had gathered in and around the clinic when the word had spread that the three people who were the centre of every news channel were there.

Thurston was anxious to see how the television news was dealing with the affair, but his first priority was to speak to Philip Lee. Overnight Desai had located the confiscated mobile phones, which were now receiving signals and were fully charged.

Philip Lee told Thurston that the executions had been stopped with nine seconds to go. Thurston whistled. He confirmed Z. I. R. had reacted to the accusation piece. "Did I recognize your hand in that, Edward?"

"Bit of a joint effort," he replied.

Lee asked Thurston what had happened to him and he quickly summarized.

# The Tissue Trail

"I'll watch the news in a minute," said Thurston. "But how are the press dealing with it?"

"Last minute change of heart," said Lee. "No mention of China or ACAP or Z. I. R. but they are talking about some medical researcher. Watch it, particularly CNN. By the way are you coming back to Singapore? I think D. C. Rahman would like to meet you and Jaci."

"I hadn't thought about it but yes, it would make sense. What will happen now, with the women?"

"I think they will make a point of not reversing the guilty verdict but go down the route of granting a pardon."

"When they haven't done anything a pardon is never quite satisfactory is it?" asked Thurston.

"I doubt if the women will be quibbling," said Lee. "Edward, I'm sure you've got people crawling all over you up there. Let me know when you are coming and say hello to that young lady of yours for me."

"I've been listening quietly," said Jaci. "Good morning, Philip. Well done. Brilliant effort."

They turned to watch the television Desai had rigged up. They were in the middle of a local channel being quoted by CNN:

*"...the medical researcher who was recently feted in Nepal for rescuing a dying mountain girl from the remote city of Lo Manthang, is believed to have played a major part in ending the Tissue Trail drug ring. A technical expert in drug manufacture, he had advised the Nepal authorities on how to ensure breaking of the ring by cutting off the supply of essential chemicals and destroying the production sources near Pokhara in the Annapurnas."*

The screen showed a number of shots of Thurston, including the nineteen-seater Otter which had flown the dying mountain girl out.

"I suppose that's better than nothing," Thurston shrugged with good humour.

"Which is more or less what I've got," said Jaci smiling.

The report switched back to the international coverage:

*The Nepali authorities will now go on an all out offensive to bring the tourists back to the Himalaya and bring the economy back to life.*

*And today's major news again. In a last minute change of*

*heart, the executions of all five of the Tissue Trail women at Changi Women's Prison in Singapore were stayed with seconds to go. The defence team have hinted that a review of the evidence had cast doubt on the calculation of the amount of heroin the women were carrying and as they were carrying marginally over the death sentence limit it was ruled that the verdicts were unsafe.*

*Reports are emerging that a medical researcher who had been working with the Nepalis to dismantle the drug ring has been instrumental in having the calculation reassessed.*

"So we are now into cover-up mode," said Thurston. "Nobody wants any political embarrassment."

Photographs of the five women followed and scenes of celebrations in their various hometowns filled the screens.

Against a shot of the forbidding walls of Changi Women's Prison the reporter said, "There is speculation that although the women will remain technically guilty the president will grant pardons."

"So the Chinese get away with this scot free," Jaci frowned.

### 6th July 2001

The Deputy Mayor could find no record or paper work justifying the arrest of Tensing and both Stephanie D'Aunay and Major Jha were nowhere to be seen. So he took the matter into his own hands and arranged for Tensing and his co- leaders to be flown back to Lo Manthang later in the day.

Najinski had said his good-byes and flown out to Kathmandu en route to Delhi to be re-united with Sheila. "I will be in touch," he said, embracing Jaci and clapping Thurston gently on the back, "but I'm not sure if I want to work with you again," he laughed.

Thurston spent most of the rest of the morning with the medics checking over his shoulder wounds. The flesh wound from the pistol shot was improving. The muscles damaged by Stephanie D'Aunay's injections were not doing so well.

Jaci was still suffering from the effects of prolonged sedation and was being monitored in her own room.

# The Tissue Trail

## 8th July 2001

Two days later, Thurston and Jaci returned to Singapore to meet Philip Lee and Aw Swee Lim. Villiumy had flown out from London to sign off the trial. Villiumy's only reference to the Tissue Trail affair was to remark that Thurston seemed to have been a little distracted by local events.

In a strained atmosphere, Villiumy signed the trial results and wasted little time on pleasantries before collecting his papers, closing his briefcase, and getting up to leave.

Aw could not resist a parting shot. "You do realize Dr Villiumy, that if you had not proceeded with the trial we would have done so on our own volition?" Villiumy turned purple, but held his counsel.

Imperial's drug went on to be a major success, making millions of dollars in the process and leaving the UK Inland Revenue keeping a close eye on the returns of a certain Edward Thurston.

~~~~~~~~~~

A week later, Philip Lee delivered a dossier on the whole affair to the president's office —a copy of which was delivered formally to the Chinese Embassy. It included a report from Z. I. R. Bank listing payments made. These included $3 million to a Major Jha, a number of smaller payments to a variety of individuals and officials in both Nepal and Singapore. Philip Lee was surprised to see that beneficiaries had included officials at the Central Criminal Court in Singapore. When asked about this later, Lee's reply was, "I suppose they had to make sure that the trials were expedited rapidly and in any event in time to ensure that the executions were carried out before the Moscow IOC vote."

But the eyebrow raising entry was $20 million to a certain L. C. Chase.

Details of these payments were never made public.

Without this evidence there was nothing to link Lauren Chase to the Tissue Trail affair. But five months later she quietly left her job as Vice President at the National Bank of Canada.

Over a beer sometime later, in fact over several beers sometime later, Najinski and Thurston, meeting in London, discussed what would make a woman who had everything allow anyone to persuade her to direct an operation —the success of which depended on the death of innocent young women.

"Tough one," said Najinski, "but I think Jaci got somewhere near it. Do you remember that conversation where you were suggesting you only got to sleep with beautiful women these days in the line of duty?"

Thurston nodded, "Along those lines."

"In the middle of that she said something like '...wouldn't surprise me if she turns out to be running the whole thing; she's got a tray full of silver spoons in her mouth, probably owns the bank rather than works for it, has whole populations falling over themselves to treat her like a queen and men falling into bed with her at the flicker of her little finger – it would take something like this to give her a bit of excitement.'"

Thurston took a swig of his beer, "That could make sense," he said, "I often wonder why Bernie Madoff made more money than he knew what to do with and became Chairman of NASDAQ then threw it all away with his ponzi scheme."

"And going back a few years, do you remember Patti Hearst, newspaper heiress, being caught 'looking excited' toting a gun as a member of a hold up gang?" Najinski asked. "I think Jaci's got it right again, Edward, in Lauren's case, but in some ways perhaps your solution is even better, getting your excitement at the same time as making a few dollars."

"You might be right, Victor, but I reckon I've overdone it with this one!"

The two of them kept in fairly regular touch and followed through what happened to the rest of the players.

Major Jha was arrested as he tried to cross the border into India and was detained by Nepali security charged with kidnapping and conspiracy. As detailed evidence of his role emerged, the charges hardened and he was ultimately tried on Class A drug trafficking offenses. In the less rigorous penal regime in Nepal, and taking account of his long and unblemished public service contribution as head of ACAP before being blown off course by riches he could never have dreamed of, he was given a twelve-year prison sentence. He was also charged in connection with the death of Captain Chaudrai, but these charges were dropped on lack of evidence linking him directly to his death.

~~~~~~~~~~

Stephanie D'Aunay was arrested as she arrived in Toronto. She had evaded police and security in Nepal by wearing a dark wig and dark glasses, which she had removed just before going through customs to prevent queries over passport appearance.

She was detained under a general charge of conspiracy in connection with drug trafficking at the request of both Nepal and Singapore Governments, the latter following up with applications to extradite her to Singapore. A long legal battle ensued with her lawyers successfully arguing that such charges in Singapore could lead to the death penalty. On this basis extradition was denied but after two years in custody, while the decision was reached, she served a further ten-year prison sentence in Canada. Thurston did not press charges with regard to her little box of pain tricks.

~~~~~~~~~~

Brothers Jacques and Pierre Menton, Canadians from Quebec, were questioned on the basis of Jaci's report of friction between the two Canadians and the American Steve Foster, but no evidence was found connecting them to Foster's death. A link was established between them and the two Swedish women who had joined Jaci in the travel magazine spying exercise and were found murdered in a refugee camp in Pokhara. They had died of injected morphine overdose and the syringes used had been found under sacks of raw wool in the refugee camp where they had died. DNA traces and fingerprints had identified the killers. Nepal went through the formalities of applying for extradition but withdrew without an extended legal battle on condition the two brothers were tried in Canada. With clear evidence of premeditated murder, both were sentenced to sixteen-years in prison.

### 20th July 2001

Two weeks after the stay of execution and at Jonathan Warrender's request, Edward Thurston and Jaci Linthorpe were entertained at a restaurant not far from the National Criminal Intelligence Service offices in Blackfriars. Warrender brought his assistant Barbara Murdoch to join the party.

"We just wanted to meet the two of you. We see quite a lot of action in this job but this must be the most colourful we've ever been involved with – and nine seconds is about as close to the wire as we've ever been. After seeing your ingeniously contrived post-event accusation go through, we just sat there waiting to hear if the executions had been carried out. We didn't get a message from the embassy until ten past six."

They discussed the case for three hours, Warrender concluding that it was now almost as if nothing had happened. Neither version of the caravan arrest had been broadcast, so China's role had not been exposed. The cases against Major Jha and Stephanie D'Aunay did not hit the headlines outside their home countries.

Thurston did comment that he still had a couple of sore shoulders to show for it all.

~~~~~~~~~~

To his great surprise when he got back to the office there was an e-mail from an L. C. Chase.

*Congratulations, Edward. I admire your powers of deduction and delegation but not perhaps your choice of people to trust!*

She had added a rather plaintiff second line:

*Bit of a shame.*
*P.S. There was no Canadian connection beyond government funding.*

~~~~~~~~~~

Three weeks later, Thurston took Jaci to Edinburgh for a lunch with a Mr and Mrs Miller and Catherine. Catherine had recovered well, although she still looked thin and drawn. Thurston's injured shoulder was still a bit stiff but Jaci was back to normal.

During lunch, Catherine had asked Thurston, "It was you that helped me when I fainted after being arrested wasn't it?"

"Yes it was," he replied, "but it was pure coincidence."

"And the two of you came to see me in Changi and asked me about going directly to Singapore?"

"Yes," Jaci replied.

# The Tissue Trail

"So what's all this about you just being an expert in drug calculations, Mr Thurston?"

"There was a little bit more to it than that," said Thurston. "The questioning session we had with you in Changi was the killer. It was Jaci noticing that the Canadians and the Tibetans asked where you were going after Nepal rather than specifically asking if you were going to Singapore which led to us unravelling the mystery."

~~~~~~~~~~~

Thurston had arranged for them to return to London overnight. After an excellent meal they returned to their sleeper.

"Isn't there one more session to finish the protocol?" he smiled. She held up her right hand. It was holding the stopwatch.

In the morning she finished her last report.

"How did I do?" he asked with a straight face.

"Just about up to scratch," she said, unable to avoid a grin.

Over a champagne breakfast, Jaci looked at Thurston, her expression just a little forlorn, "I suppose now we're going to have to go back to being professional?"

He smiled at her. "Yes. But I'll drink to that," he said, clinking glasses.

~~~~~~~~~~~

## *Post Script*

At the Moscow IOC Meeting in July 2001, Beijing won the vote to host the 2008 Olympic Games. Even though the Tissue Trail plot had failed, they had in general, laid the ground well. They went on to organize one of the most spectacular Games ever staged.

Printed in Great Britain
by Amazon.co.uk, Ltd.,
Marston Gate.